PRAISE FOR
RIO YOUERS

"*Point Hollow* proves Rio Youers to be the real thing. His prose flows without a ripple and his conflicted, multidimensional characters— even the villain—demand you care. The edge-of-the-seat finale is as relentless as it is terrifying."

—**F. Paul Wilson**, author of the Repairman Jack series

"Rio Youers is one of the most promising new writers to come along in ages. *Point Hollow* is a dark and twisted thriller full of small-town secrets, horrific murders, and the way evil takes root if we're not careful. Read it!"

—**Christopher Golden**, author of *Snowblind*

"Rio Youers has written an incredible story with all the right ingredients to keep a reader turning the pages quickly—and staying awake in the dark! Marvellous and creepy!"

—**Heather Graham**, author of *Waking the Dead*

"Rio Youers's storytelling is so charming, so affable, so apparently effortless, that you're still grinning like an idiot when the sheer horror of his imagination leaps up and suckerpunches you in the gut."

—**Robert Shearman**, author of *They Do the Same Things Different There*

RIO YOUERS

POINT HOLLOW

A NOVEL

Distributed in Canada by
Publishers Group Canada
76 Stafford Street, Unit 300
Toronto, Ontario
M6J 2S1 Canada
Toll Free: 800-747-8147
e-mail: info@pgcbooks.ca

Distributed in the U.S. by
Diamond Comic Distributors, Inc.
10150 York Road, Suite 300
Hunt Valley, MD 21030
Phone: (443) 318-8500
e-mail: books@diamondbookdistributors.com

Library and Archives Canada Cataloguing in Publication

Youers, Rio, 1971-, author
    Point hollow / Rio Youers.

Issued in print and electronic formats.

ISBN 978-1-77148-330-8 (pbk.). ISBN 978-1-77148-331-5 (ebook).

   I. Title.

PS8647.O58P63 2015   C813'.6   C2015-900094-7
                        C2015-900095-5

Edited by Samantha Beiko
Proofread by Michael Matheson

A **free** eBook edition is available
with the purchase of this print book.

CHIZINE PUBLICATIONS
Toronto, Canada
www.chizinepub.com
info@chizinepub.com

CLEARLY PRINT YOUR NAME ABOVE IN UPPER CASE

Instructions to claim your free eBook edition:
1. Download the BitLit app for Android or iOS
2. Write your name in **UPPER CASE** on the line
3. Use the BitLit app to submit a photo
4. Download your eBook to any device

Canada Council   Conseil des Arts
for the Arts   du Canada

We acknowledge the support of the Canada Council for the Arts which last year invested $20.1 million in writing and publishing throughout Canada.

ONTARIO ARTS COUNCIL
CONSEIL DES ARTS DE L'ONTARIO
50 YEARS OF ONTARIO GOVERNMENT SUPPORT OF THE ARTS
50 ANS DE SOUTIEN DU GOUVERNEMENT DE L'ONTARIO AUX ARTS

Published with the generous assistance of the Ontario Arts Council.

Printed in Canada

For my mother, Lorraine May,
who knows all about mountains, and how to conquer them.

POINT HOLLOW

A NOVEL

CHAPTER
ONE
1984/2010

The mountain spoke to him.
    Oliver looked east, where the ragged peaks scraped the sky's pale belly. The sound had traversed the miles and echoed in his mind. Not words, but a command. It was followed by a stillness that made him wonder if the world had stopped breathing.

    "Did you hear that?" Oliver asked his mother.

    She was watering her plants, her thumb capped over the end of the hose to create a spray. Rainbows sparkled in the mist. "Hear what?"

    "It sounded like thunder."

    She looked at the sky, a deep and characterless blue, as if it had been painted by an artist with no talent for texture. "I expect it was Mr. Sawyer's truck backfiring again. He should drive that old shitbanger directly to the junkyard."

    "Yeah, maybe," Oliver said, but he knew it wasn't Mr. Sawyer's truck, because he only ever drove it to and from town, which was to the south, and this sound had reverberated from the east. From the mountain.

"*And you didn't hear anything?*" Oliver asked.

"*No, but I'm in a world of my own here.*" She directed the spray at the marigolds. *Her face was bleak despite the sunshine. Broken, almost.*

But it was so loud, *Oliver thought. He looked east again. The mountain shimmered in the heat. At thirty-four hundred feet, it was the tallest of the peaks surrounding the town of Point Hollow. To the outside world it was called Old Bear Mountain, but everyone in town called it Abraham's Faith.*

Oliver strolled to the eastern edge of his garden. Fourteen years old, with wide blue eyes and a wave of black hair. Sweat glistened on the bridge of his nose. His young heart thumped eagerly.

"*What do you want?*" *he whispered, and Abraham's Faith replied with its mighty voice. Oliver thought the sky would crack like ice and fall in jagged blue pieces. He turned to his mother—she must have heard that—but she carried on spraying the flowers, deaf to everything.*

Again, not words, but a command. It rippled through the ground and into his soul. A feeling. A certainty. It was like seeing shapes in the clouds, or hearing music in the rain. And Oliver was less frightened by the fact that the mountain had spoken to him, than he was by what it would do if he didn't obey.

As if to emphasize, the mountain boomed again. Its edges trembled.

"*Yes,*" *Oliver whispered. A tear slipped from his eye.*

He knew what he had to do.

———

Seven-year-old Ethan Mitchell had been missing for three days. He was last seen playing in the front garden of his home in Lafayette, New Jersey. "I was watching him from the living room window," Ethan's mother told police. "The phone rang and I answered it—five seconds, maybe—and by the time I moved back to the window, he was gone." Police worked around the clock, following leads, exhausting resources. They assured Ethan's mother, and the media, that no stone would be left unturned, although everyone knew that—without positive development—hope was growing frail.

Oliver knew the numbers: approximately eight hundred thousand children reported missing in the United States every year. An average of two thousand per day. A huge majority returned home safely—children that had been lost or injured, family abductees, or runaways. Nonfamily abductees made up a smaller percentage, of which a fractional subset could be classed as stereotypical kidnappings. New Jersey police did not have sufficient information to determine that Ethan Mitchell fit this latter subset, but Oliver knew that he did . . . because Oliver had taken him.

When the mountain called, he answered. He *served*.

Always.

And now, only three days after taking Ethan Mitchell, he was serving it again.

"Oh . . . could you grab that for me, please?"

The little girl had hair the colour of fall leaves and a delightful splash of freckles across her cheeks. She was wearing a Justin Bieber T-shirt, blue jeans, and Crocs. Ten years old. Maybe eleven. Oliver processed this information in less than a second. The news reports and "missing" posters would obviously feature her description, and her red hair and T-shirt were details that people would remember. He had second thoughts, but these, too, lasted less than a second; Oriole Avenue was otherwise deserted, an empty baseball park on one side, and a withered patch of grass on the other. Nobody there now. The situation was perfect.

He was carrying an empty box, with a rolled-up newspaper tucked under one arm and a knapsack slung over one shoulder. He needed to give the impression that his hands were full, and he acted as if the box were the heaviest thing in the world. On top of it he had placed a Transformers toy, still in its colourful packaging. As the little girl walked toward him, he tilted the box so that the toy slipped off and fell to the ground at her feet.

"Megatron," she said, and he asked if she could grab it for him. She picked it up, looked at it for a second, and then stood on her tiptoes and tried to slide it back on top of the box. Oliver puffed and lowered the box an inch, no more, his arms trembling. He dropped his shoulder so that the knapsack slipped into the crook of his elbow.

"I need another pair of hands," he said with a smile.

"I can't reach," the little girl said.

"My car is right there." He nodded toward a silver Chevy Impala—nondescript in every way—parked on the road less than ten yards away. "You wouldn't just throw it on the back seat, would you? I'd really appreciate it."

She didn't hesitate. She turned, her bright hair flicking over one shoulder, and skipped toward the parked car.

"Is it unlocked?"

"Sure is."

She opened the door and tossed the toy onto the back seat, but then paused, as he knew she would, looking at the bright gift bag, festooned with bows and ribbons, that he had placed on the seat—just out of reach.

He came up behind her.

"What's that?" she asked.

"My daughter's birthday present," he replied. He opened the passenger side door, threw the newspaper and knapsack into the footwell, and placed the empty box on the passenger seat. He also opened the glovebox, where he kept the duct tape. "It's a Zhu Zhu Pet. I'm not sure if I got the right one. She wanted Mr. Squiggles."

"Mr. Squiggles is *brown*," she said, as if everybody knew this. "And it should say right on the box."

Oliver smiled and gave her a dumb-adult shrug. "Take a look, if you like."

Again, no hesitation. She kneeled on the back seat and leaned toward the bag. Oliver acted quickly. He grabbed the duct tape, closed the passenger door, then pushed the little girl onto the back seat and climbed in behind her. In less than a minute she was bound, gagged, and thrown into the gap behind the driver and passenger seats. Oliver stepped out of the car, walked calmly around to the driver's side, got behind the wheel, and drove away. The entire grab—from the moment he dropped the toy to the moment he pulled away—took less than two minutes.

He drove to his home in Point Hollow, with music softly playing, the sun falling to the west, and the little girl crying and squirming in the gap behind his seat.

———

Oliver's fear had turned to exhilaration—a from-the-gut feeling of being moved by a higher power, something beyond his comprehension. It was like the moon's tidal pull. His heart drummed so hard that it hurt.

"Mom, I'm going out."

He knew she wouldn't ask where he was going. She never did.

"Dinner at five," she said. "Make sure you're back."

"Sure."

"It's spaghetti and meatballs."

"Sure."

Oliver reeled from his house and started down Cold Creek Road. The knapsack on his back was packed with only two items: a flashlight, and his father's hunting knife. He had no idea how long he would be gone, but would eat blueberries and dandelion leaves if he got hungry, and drink from the spring to quench his thirst.

Abraham's Faith would look after him.

It rumbled in the east, drawing him on.

Late afternoon heat bleached the air, making everything too white, even the roads, gleaming like burnt chrome. Sprinklers whirled and air conditioners hummed. People languished on their porches, barely dressed, fanning themselves and drinking lemonade. An ice cream truck weaved a tempting melody through a dozen neighbourhoods, and Oliver imagined children tagging along behind like a school of minnows. He passed Blueberry Bush Park, where teenagers played baseball, bare-chested, while their girlfriends watched from the bleachers. A radio beside them played the new song by Duran Duran.

He walked on. The town would soon give way to natural beauty. The roads would end. There would be no buildings or streetlights, only the world, wild and raw. Numerous trails snaked through the forests, followed rivers, and scaled several peaks, although no trail came close to Abraham's Faith.

It boomed at him, and coupled with the exhilaration was a sense of worth—of having been chosen. Of all the people in Point Hollow, the mountain had selected him. Being wanted, and having value, was something Oliver could get used to. And so he fairly skimmed along the sidewalk, fully prepared to do what was asked of him. He had a flashlight. He had a knife. He needed only one more thing.

Matthew Bridge was ten years old. Loose brown curls and a smile that seemed always mischievous, but rarely was. He was in his front garden, giggling wildly, trying to avoid the sprinkler spray as it oscillated toward him. His small body glistened, coloured by the sun. Water trickled from his curls. He leapt. The sprinkler caught him and he laughed, and then stopped, noticing Oliver watching from the sidewalk.

Matthew wiped his eyes. "Hey."

"Hey."

"You're Oliver, right?" Point Hollow was a small town. There were no strangers.

"Yeah."

Matthew looked at the knapsack on Oliver's back. "Where are you going?"

Oliver managed a dry smile. He felt Abraham's Faith looming behind him: a shadowy puppeteer, working the strings.

"Treasure hunting," he said.

Matthew frowned and stepped closer. "What kind of treasure?"

"I'm not sure. I found a map buried in our garden. An old map, so it might be gold."

"No way," Matthew said.

"Uh-huh." Oliver nodded. "It's got to be worth looking, right?"

The sprinkler shimmied around and sprayed Matthew again. He squealed delightedly and stepped out of its range, closer to Oliver. Water sparkled on his shoulders.

"Do you want to come?" Oliver asked.

"Where's your shovel?" Matthew asked. "You can't dig up treasure without a shovel. Everybody knows that."

"The map said it was buried under some rocks. I don't need a shovel, but I could really use some help moving the rocks."

"Yeah?" Matthew frowned again. "How far is it?"

"A mile," Oliver said. "Maybe two. It's just off the orange trail. Close to Rainy Creek."

"I don't know." Matthew shrugged, then turned and looked at his house. "My mom said I have to tidy my room this afternoon. I'll catch hell if I don't do it."

"Okay, that's cool," Oliver said. "You're probably not strong enough to lift the rocks anyway."

"I am, too."

Oliver started to walk away.

"Wait!" Matthew said. He grabbed his T-shirt and sneakers from the porch, jumped the fence at the bottom of his garden, and ran after Oliver. His small shadow flickered on the sidewalk. "Wait up! I'm coming with you."

The mountain flexed its grey muscle and shook its forested shoulders.

"Let's go," Oliver said.

———

The little girl was sleeping by the time he arrived home. She had exhausted herself, crying and squirming. Strands of red hair clung to her face. He lifted her from the gap between the seats, cradled in his arms, and carried her into his secluded house. She woke when he placed her on the sofa. He saw realization, and then terror, bloom in her eyes. Her frail body tensed. More tears.

Oliver walked away from her—couldn't stand to look into those fearful eyes. He crossed the living room and stepped onto the rear deck. The midafternoon sun blazed. Small birds sprayed the sky, and far below, Point Hollow lay nestled among waves of green. A toy village, like something a collector would arrange around a train set.

Let this be the last time, he thought, and looked east. Abraham's Faith claimed the sky. It swallowed his soul. He heard it—felt it. The children, too. Their bodies were piled high. A mountain inside a mountain. I can't do this anymore. Let me go.

His world was a long, bright scream. It was a highway of broken glass. He stood on the rear deck and beseeched the sky's emptiness, wanting to fly, to be drawn into that belly of endless silence, where he would float, untroubled, until he turned to ash and rained into the ocean.

———

Oliver ran through the high grass and Matthew followed, laughing, wanting to show the older boy that he could run just as fast. A spring glittered ahead of them. Oliver reached it first, scooped chilled water into his palms, and splashed it over his face. An osprey took wing from a nearby tree, swooped close to the water, and then, with a cry, arced into the deep sky. Oliver watched it until Matthew drew alongside him.

"I can run fast, too," Matthew said. His face shimmered like the water.

"I wasn't racing," Oliver said.

Matthew smiled and looked around, hands on his hips. Only ten years old, yet Oliver thought he looked unusually adult, like a man who has found his place in the world.

"Is this a river?"

"It's a spring," Oliver said. "It comes from the mountain. It's cold, even though it's shallow. Try it."

"Drink it?"

"If you like. Or splash it on your face."

Matthew's small hands slipped among the pebbles and emerged cupped, the water trickling through the cracks of his fingers. "So cold," he said, and gingerly dipped his face into his palms. Gooseflesh rippled across his forearms. He shivered.

"Good?"

The younger boy grinned and nodded, then reached into the spring and splashed Oliver. A child again.

There was a forest on the other side of the water. Mostly spruce and fir. Beyond this, the ground became ragged and grey. The grass faded. Flowers lowered their heads. A mile of dark landscape that sloped into the foothills of Abraham's Faith, where it became darker still—trees hooked out of shape, fractured rocks, bunched like knuckles. The mountain gathered against the sky, like a storm cloud that never moved.

Oliver took off his sneakers, rolled up his jeans, and started to cross the spring.

"Where are you going?" Matthew asked.

"To get the treasure," Oliver said, carefully planting his feet between the slippery rocks and pebbles. The icy water lapped around his shins.

"But you said it was near Rainy Creek," Matthew said. He pointed north, where the long grass danced. "It's that way."

"No, it's on the other side of that forest. Come on."

Matthew sighed and looked back toward Point Hollow. He could see the top of the water tower and the clock on the town hall. He thought of his mother. She'd be worried, probably looking for him. He took a step backward.

Oliver had reached the other side. "Are you coming?"

"I'm not sure."

"But we're nearly there . . . just through those trees."

"I don't know, Oliver."

"It'll be like Indiana Jones. And if we find gold, we'll be rich." Oliver rolled down his jean cuffs and slipped on his sneakers. "You can buy whatever you want. Shit, if we find gold, you could buy the school and fire Miss Bramble. Nobody likes that bitch. You'd be a hero, Matthew."

This made him smile, but for only a moment; he knew what was on the other side of the forest. "But the mountain is that way."

Like all of Point Hollow's children, Matthew had been taught to keep to the trails and stay away from Abraham's Faith, the same way he'd been taught to not talk to strangers or go swimming in Wiley's Crook, where the current was so strong it would pull you under in a heartbeat. Matthew's father told him that giant rattlesnakes lived on the mountain, and his best friend, Bobby Alexander, told him that trolls lived there. Matthew, of course, believed both were true.

"We're not going that far," Oliver said. "And I'll be with you. I'll look after you."

Matthew hesitated. Sweat dripped down his back. The trees behind Oliver looked so dark—so dead. The idea of buried treasure proved too persuasive, however. He kicked off his sneakers and started to cross the spring. The water came up to his knees.

"Cold!" he cried.

"Keep going," Oliver said.

Matthew stumbled and splashed and made his way to the other side. He held out his hand and Oliver took it, like a friend.

"I'm going to fire Mr. Nordhagen, too," Matthew said with a grin.

They walked through the forest, having to twist their bodies among the tightly grown trees. Strips of sunlight slanted through the canopy, but it wasn't enough, and Matthew's heart jumped in his chest. He stayed close to Oliver, flinching at every sound—chipmunks scrambling through the branches, or cones clattering to the forest floor, all too loud in the stillness.

"Are you scared?" Oliver asked.

"No," Matthew said. "Well, maybe a little."

"It's okay. I'm with you."

"I know. I'm glad."

They emerged—after too long—into daylight that felt as refreshing as the spring water. With the forest at their backs, Matthew felt separated from everything he knew. He had never veered from the trails before, and even though the sunshine felt good on his face, his heart still pounded hard.

"We're close now," Oliver said.

But they weren't close; they walked for another forty minutes, toward the mountain, clambering up rocks and over fallen trees. Matthew's heart ached and his legs trembled. He thought about his parents, how worried they would be, and how much trouble he was in for not telling them where he was going. He'd be grounded for the rest of the summer. No doubt about it. He'd probably get a spanking, too.

They climbed higher. The sun worked on them, wearing them down.

"So tired," Matthew said.

"Not far now."

Higher still. The green of the Catskill counties spread out below them. Grey roads, as thin as pencil lines, weaved through the scenery, and the lakes and rivers flashed like ice. Point Hollow looked so small from this distance, no bigger than Matthew's thumb. The only thing keeping him from going back was the fear of being alone, of having to stumble along the lower mountainside. What if he fell? Nobody would know. Nobody would find him. And he certainly didn't want to walk through that endless forest on his own.

"How much farther?" he groaned. His small chest hitched and he really had to work at keeping back the tears. He wished more than anything that he'd stayed home. He would have cleaned his room by now, and his mom would have taken him to Fiddle's Dari-King for—

"We're here," Oliver said, and pointed.

Matthew stopped. "I don't see anything."

"There . . . look."

It took him a moment to see what Oliver was pointing at: what looked like a shadow in the rock face, but was actually a fissure—a narrow opening—disguised by the deliberate placement of rocks.

"What is that?" Matthew asked.

"A cave," Oliver replied. He scrambled up the incline beside the opening and started to heave some of the smaller rocks aside. They tumbled noisily and Matthew had to step out of the way as they rolled toward him.

"Is the treasure in there?" he asked.

"Help me out." Oliver had quickly uncovered the upper portion of the opening, but the rocks were larger lower down and he couldn't shift them on his own. He tried, though—pushing against them, his face burning.

"I'm not sure we—"

"Just help me out!" Spittle flew from Oliver's lips. His eyes were diamonds. Matthew nodded and swallowed hard, then scrabbled up beside him, and together—using their arms and legs—they were able to dislodge three heavy rocks.

The opening gaped, a jagged triangle, wide enough for them to slither through.

Oliver's grin was jagged, too. He slipped off his knapsack, unzipped it, and reached inside.

"Are you going in?" Dust clung to the sweat and tears on Matthew's face.

"Fuck, yeah. We both are."

"Not me." Matthew shook his head. "No way."

"Fine. Stay out here. It'll be dark soon." Oliver pulled a flashlight from his knapsack, flicked it on, and directed the beam into Matthew's eyes. "Or you can come with me. And the light. Your choice."

Oliver snaked into the mountain and Matthew followed.

———

He had built a house off the beaten track, as close to Abraham's Faith as he could get. It was accessible by a road that he had carved, and one you wouldn't find on any GPS device. The garage had three vehicles inside: the nondescript Impala, an '07 Corvette, and a one-ton Silverado, fitted with a plow for the winter months. The house was filled with luxury items: leather furniture, computers, flat screen TVs, a hot tub on the rear deck (overlooking Point Hollow, two miles away). Oliver often hosted parties, and all the town notaries would be there: the sheriff (who had the easiest job in America), the mayor (second-easiest), along with various members of the town council, all of whom looked up to Oliver. He was success personified. Point Hollow's favourite son.

For his continued service, the mountain had looked after him.

But oh, he was weary.

He carried the little girl down the steps of his rear deck and into the wild country surrounding his land. She was still bound, still gagged, too tired to struggle, which made carrying her easier. Her bright hair swayed and her eyes shot terrified glances between him and the sky. He felt her heartbeat fluttering through her body.

He moved east—*pulled* east. A route he knew well and had made many times since that summer's day in 1984. He splashed across the shallow spring and through the dense acreage of spruce and fir. Bluebirds cried at him, bristling their delicate feathers. The trees groaned, branches twisted, as if turning away. He passed through and tramped along the discoloured landscape, wending a route into the mountain's foothills. It roared hungrily and urged him on. And maybe the little girl heard it, too, because she moaned and fresh tears spilled from her eyes. They fell on the dark rock and dried instantly in the sun.

This was the longest and most dangerous part of the journey, not only because the terrain was treacherous, but because he was exposed. No one ever came out here, though. The trails and hunting zones were miles away, and there were countless signs warning of the danger (no detail on the signs—only that single word, red on a yellow background: DANGER). But if some adventurous hiker decided to stray from the trails or disregard the signs, and if they chose to cross acres of unmarked land and brave tangles of dark forest . . . then yes, there was a possibility he would be seen. Highly unlikely, of course. In fact, Oliver believed that if every DANGER sign were disposed of, and every gnarled and twisted tree burned to the ground, people would still stay away, because the mountain would *keep* them away. It was Point Hollow's haunted house, and it was evil.

How much farther? A little boy's voice in his mind. He heard it every time. *Matthew,* Oliver thought. *His name was Matthew.*

He reached the cave just as the sky in the west started to run red. It was going to be a beautiful sunset, and all Oliver wanted was to watch it in silence. Ninety-four miles away, at her home in Deer Grove, PA, the little girl's parents—so distraught, barely able to form sentences—gave information to the police. Friends, neighbours, and townspeople were questioned. Abandoned buildings were searched. Dumpsters, trashcans, the trunks of parked cars . . . all searched. Certain information was released to the media, while investigators cross-referenced details with the disappearances of children in nearby locales.

Her name was Courtney Bryce. Eleven years old. He would read all about her in tomorrow's newspaper. She was always the first to help, apparently. The first to laugh. But none of that mattered now. She could be a bag of straw or a faded photograph. Her strong heart and bright smile would mean nothing in the mountain.

Oliver set her down while he dislodged the rocks from the cave's zigzag mouth. More rocks than he used to have to move, but he was stronger now. Everything equal. Perhaps sensing the mountain's hunger, Courtney moaned louder, cried harder, and tried to shuffle away. But she couldn't get far. Oliver set aside the last rock, picked her up, and carried her into the darkness.

———

Matthew clutched the waistband of Oliver's jeans as they weaved through a tunnel that ran deep into the mountain. The flashlight's beam floated across uneven sediment, slick with moisture. Matthew thought of bats and spiders. Worse: trolls and giant rattlesnakes. His skin crawled and he felt his heart shuddering, even in the tips of his fingers. He didn't want to be in here. Not at all.

The ground was as uneven as the walls on either side, and slippery, too. Several times they stumbled and needed each other for support. Matthew fell hard on one occasion, grazing both knees. He lost his grip on Oliver's waistband and for one second was horribly alone. He cried out and the flashlight's beam jerked toward him. The older boy grasped his forearm and lifted him to his feet.

"I grazed my knees," Matthew groaned.

"Don't be such a baby."

They walked on, following the hollow vein as it meandered through the mountain. Before long, the walls opened and the craggy roof drifted higher, until even the flashlight's beam couldn't pick it out. The floor crumbled away and they clutched each other, choosing their steps carefully, and even though it was too dark to see, Matthew knew they had emerged into some sort of cavern. The air felt different, and he heard water dripping distantly. It echoed, reminding Matthew of the sound his daddy's stomach made when he nuzzled in for a goodnight hug. Up high—way up—he saw chinks of daylight where the sun found frailties in the mountain. He felt like an insect in a Mason jar, holes punched in the lid.

"This is it," Oliver said. He seemed to have a thousand voices.

"I want to go home," Matthew said. His tears shimmered in the flashlight's glare. "I'm scared."

Oliver tried to step away from him, but Matthew held on to his waistband.

"Let's just go. Please."

"Not yet," Oliver said. He jerked his hips and Matthew's grasp fell away. The flashlight's beam stretched into the darkness. It fell on a twisted, glimmering shape less than ten feet away. Oliver walked toward it, his breath catching in his throat. Matthew whimpered like a hurt animal and followed close behind. He didn't want to see whatever the flashlight had picked out. Nothing in this place could be good.

Realization came in increments. To begin with, Matthew thought the shape was an empty sack, and that the objects jutting through the dusty material were rocks. Only they were too smooth to be rocks. They actually looked like . . .

"Bones," Oliver said.

Not just any bones. Not a bear's skeleton, or a coyote's. Matthew's young mind clicked and processed, referencing school work and comic books and movies. Can't be, he thought, but as they stepped closer and the flashlight revealed more, he realized he was looking at human bones . . . a human skeleton.

All the breath jumped from his lungs and his legs sagged. He uttered another hurt sound and grasped Oliver's arm. Oliver shook him off. He rolled his wrist slowly, allowing the light to play over the skeleton, head to toe and back again, as if he were caressing it.

"Jesus," he said.

Matthew couldn't say a thing.

It was propped against the cave wall, legs splayed and skull turned sideways, covered with a wrap of leathery skin from which a few strands of hair floated like cobwebs. Its eye sockets were empty holes and its grin was overly long, as if it had too many teeth. Its clothes were crumbling rags, and the fingers of one hand were curled inward, as if he or she had died with a clenched fist. And were it not for the boys' raptness, they would have noticed an obvious, and terrible, fact much sooner: the skeleton, from head to toe, measured less than four feet in length.

"It was a child," Oliver said.

Matthew, still, said nothing. His heart roared. He thought he should hear it echoing in the cave, making the walls tremble and dust sift from the cracked and rugged roof. How cruel that the only light shone on something so terrible.

It was just the beginning.

Oliver moved the flashlight to the left, following the wall, and there, less than two feet from the first, was a second skeleton, curled into a fetal position, draped in dust and rags. Small bones and wisps of blonde hair. Another child. A little girl.

Beside her, another child's skeleton . . . and then another.

"What is this place?" Oliver asked.

Matthew grabbed Oliver's arm again. Shallow breaths were kicked from his lungs by the force of his heartbeat. So many thoughts and emotions typhooned through his mind that he thought they might whip him upward, twirling, like a helicopter. It hurt to think that he had been in his garden less than three hours ago, playing in the sprinkler spray, with everything he loved so very close.

"Want . . . go home," he managed, squeezing Oliver's arm.

"You're not going anywhere," Oliver said.

In a matter of moments, the flashlight revealed more skeletons, all children—ten, fifteen, forty—huddled in groups of three or four. Brothers and sisters, perhaps. Matthew closed his eyes and dropped to the damp ground. He drew his arms in, not wanting to touch anything, feeling like he was adrift in a sea of bones. When he opened his eyes, he saw Oliver standing a short distance away, shining the light on a boy-sized skeleton, dressed in blue jeans and Converse All Stars. He moved on, then stooped to pick something up, and as he lifted it into the light, Matthew saw that it was a skull, no bigger than a softball.

"A baby," Oliver said, letting it fall through his fingers. It hit the cave floor and broke like glass.

And yet more . . . everywhere the light shone. Drifts of bones. Hollow skulls, glimmering softly, smooth as pebbles. Here: a scatter of pieces, like a box of dropped matches. There: a framework of bodies that had fallen against one another, melded by dripping water, looking like the skeleton of some undiscovered creature. Everywhere: a holocaust; a nightmare; fairy tales with unhappy endings.

"There must be a hundred bodies in here," Oliver said. There was disconcerting awe to his tone, as if he really had found treasure. "Maybe two hundred."

Matthew blinked huge tears from his eyes. The sobs rolled through his chest, crashing against his ribcage like boulders. He looked at the seams of light above—as bright, yet distant, as the stars.

"What could have done this?" Oliver asked.

"The mountain," Matthew said, and knew this for certain. It wasn't trolls or giant rattlesnakes. It was Abraham's Faith. Swollen and evil. "The mountain . . . it eats children."

"Yes," Oliver agreed. He unzipped his knapsack and reached inside. The hunting knife looked too big in his hand. The blade gleamed. "And now it's going to eat one more."

Matthew's body turned numb. His mind, too. A white tundra where no thought or feeling existed. When thought came, it came with claws: I'm going to die. *Oliver stepped toward him, crunching on bones. The knife caught the flashlight's glare, the same shape, and almost as bright, as a flame.*

"The mountain spoke to me," Oliver said.

I'm going to die.

"It told me to bring you here."

I'm going to die.

"It wants you, Matthew."

I'm going to—

He saw his mother's face, and with such clarity that he thought she was beside him. His body flushed with life and he reached for her—suffered a moment's disorientation when she wasn't there.

Oliver closed the distance. Bones crunched. The blade flared.

Reality dawned.

I'm going to die.

Matthew clawed at the ground and grabbed the first thing his hand fell upon—didn't know if it was a rock or a bone, only that it was solid—and threw it toward the light. A perfect shot, mostly luck, but it surprised Oliver. He stumbled and the flashlight spilled from his hand. It clattered to the floor and for a moment the light blinked, and then it went out.

Darkness.

"Son of a bitch," Oliver snarled.

Matthew pushed himself to his feet and flailed blindly. He managed several uncertain steps before tripping, falling to his hands and knees. Dust flowered, stinging his eyes, coating his lips. He coughed and spat, picked himself up, teetered, then slammed into a wall. He dragged his hands along it—

Please God, oh please . . .

—and his fingers moved from rock to bone. He pulled back, but not before feeling the empty eye sockets and nose cavity. Gossamer hair brushed the back of one hand. The skeleton toppled sideways and broke into loose pieces.

"I can hear you," Oliver said.

Matthew heard him, too—scratching like an animal as he searched for the flashlight. He swayed breathlessly in the opposite direction. Again, four or five weak steps before falling to his knees. He cried out and clawed at the ground. Another skeleton—there were so many. Matthew felt fragile bones beneath damp fabric, and something else: a shoe. A sneaker, to be exact. Canvas, with a distinct rubber toe cap. He remembered Oliver shining the flashlight on the boy-skeleton dressed in blue jeans and Converse All Stars, and it was like a flare went off in his head. The position of the skeleton helped orient him. His head snapped right. *That way,* he thought. He picked himself up and flew through the darkness.

Oliver found the flashlight and hissed with delight. Matthew heard him flick the switch—nothing—then slap the barrel into his palm. The flashlight blinked with each solid slap, showing Oliver in cold bursts. He had the knife between his teeth.

Please oh please . . .

The cave floor rose and Matthew took it in keen strides. He came to a wall and ran his hands along it. Five steps, six . . . and all of a sudden the wall sloped inward—disappeared. *The tunnel,* he thought, stumbling into it with overwhelming hope. Another glance over his shoulder at Oliver, who fluttered in the gloom. He gave the flashlight another firm whack and it flared into life. Matthew stretched his arms to either side and felt the slick wall to his right. He used it to guide him, staggering through the fissure. It kinked and twisted and ascended all too gradually. He put his head down and threw one foot in front of the other.

Light filled the narrow space behind him.

Oliver was coming.

"You can't get away, Matthew."

The tunnel veered right . . . left . . . on and on. Matthew pushed forward with everything he had. He felt the light behind him, snaking through the twists and turns. He heard Oliver's sandpaper breaths.

"I'm coming for you."

Matthew ducked left and stumbled right. His throat rasped. His body trembled. Another right turn and there it was: a pale whisper of daylight. *The relief was flood water. It pulled him under. Drowned him.*

"The mountain always gets what it wants."

Matthew drew his arms to his sides and ran hard for the exit. One more *turn and he saw the opening to the cave—that jagged triangle they had squeezed through. He lunged for it, reaching with his entire body. The sky looked impossibly blue.*

And then he slipped and fell—hit the ground hard. He tried to get up but slipped again.

The light extended into the tunnel behind him. Matthew dared another look and there was Oliver. His eyes were small and hard. The knife trembled in his hand.

Matthew got to his knees, half-crawling, trying to get up.

Oliver growled like a dog. He was so close.

Only fear. That was all Matthew knew. It consumed him. He screamed and grappled the cave wall with both hands, digging in with his small fingers, pulling himself to his feet. He stumbled toward the mouth of the cave. Daylight drenched his face and he inhaled it, as if resurfacing from deep water, but he wasn't out yet. The opening was up high. He leapt for it, grabbed the top rock, and pulled with everything he had. He used the gaps between the lower rocks like rungs, jamming his sneakers in, climbing from one to the other.

He was almost out—sliding his hurt, dirt-streaked body through the opening—when he felt Oliver's hand curl around his ankle.

"Get back here, you little bastard."

Matthew grabbed a rock and held on. Blood oozed from his fingertips. Oliver pulled harder, but he was only using one hand and Matthew was able to twist his ankle free. He kicked out with both feet, and felt contact— the sole of his right sneaker slamming into Oliver's face. It was enough. Oliver stumbled backward and slipped, and Matthew scrambled through the opening. He jumped to his feet, crying wildly, and zigzagged down the mountain.

His mind burned and smoked. He ran into the woods, directionless, and didn't stop until it was too dark to see.

―――――

Oliver emerged, alone, into the bruised light of evening.

Abraham's Faith had fallen silent.

For now.

Hopefully forever, he thought. He held out his arms and breathed deeply of the freedom. Hope coloured the edges of his mind, like the sun on the horizon.

She had cried. So many tears.

"Let that be the last time."

I can't do this anymore.

He concealed the opening with the rocks he had earlier displaced. Each one slotted into an exact position, as precise as a jigsaw puzzle. They blended with the sloping mountainside. Became a shadow. An unknowing eye wouldn't look twice.

Sunset, but it felt like a new day. Oliver absorbed the stillness, and then—with the little girl's tears drying on his T-shirt—he stepped carefully down the mountain and walked home.

From Oliver Wray's Journal (1)

Point Hollow, NY.
June 7, 1997.

Genesis 22:2: *He said, "Take your son, your only son Isaac, whom you love, and go to the land of Moriah, and offer him there as a burnt offering on one of the mountains of which I shall tell you."*

Well, *something* happened, that's for sure.

It has started again—that quaking, furious voice. There is no reprieve, and I have tried various methods of silencing it: drugs (legal and otherwise); alcohol; running away; therapy (which, to be fair, may have worked if telling the truth had been an option). They have offered temporary alleviation, at best—masked the problem, but not remedied it. The mountain speaks to me, and I need to know why. It may be the only way to silence it for good.

Where did the children come from?

What happened to them?

Boom and thunder. It keeps me awake. I pace the rooms of my home with my hands tied in my hair, my body aching. I beg the mountain, but it won't stop until it gets what it wants.

After the incident in 1984—when little Matthew scrambled from my grasp—I descended into what my parents called my "challenging period." I became solemn and introverted. My father reasoned that this was natural behaviour for a boy going through adolescence. The teachers concurred, and I was left to grow out of it. What they didn't know was that my quietness and reserve was down to an inexplicable fear of the mountain's certain repercussions. It had wanted a child, and I had failed it. Perhaps it would draw me into its darkness once again, knife in hand, and make me push it into my own heart. Perhaps it would unleash the spirits of the children—howling and vengeful—and they would come to me in the small hours, tapping on my bedroom window until I went insane.

Years passed, I heard nothing, and emerged timidly from my "challenging period." I convinced myself that the incident was partly imagined. It was preposterous to suggest that the mountain had spoken to me. I started to smile again, and relax. Abraham's Faith splashed its shadow on the town, but I wasn't as intimidated as I used to be.

The day after my twenty-second birthday, in July of 1992, it spoke to me again. I was eating breakfast at Sally's Country Kitchen when the voice thundered across the miles. I dropped my knife and fork and clutched my head. The waitress came immediately to my table and asked if I was okay.

"Did you hear that?" It was the same question I had asked my mother eight years before.

"Hear what, sugar?" And almost the same reply, except my mother would never have called me sugar, or anything sweet.

I blinked hard and looked at the windows, amazed that they hadn't blown inward, shards of glass hanging from splintered lathes. The sound echoed inside me. It felt like ash on my soul.

"Nothing," I said, retrieving my knife and fork with trembling hands. "I get migraines. Terrible . . . they . . ." Speaking was useless. I shut up.

"You need anything? Glass of water?"

I felt its voice, almost *saw* it—like black fire in my mind, flickering and man-shaped. Its burning hands reached for me.

"Hungry," I said.

"You still got a plateful of eggs, sweetheart."

"Not me." I looked at the waitress. I imagined blood trickling from the corners of my eyes—my brain hemorrhaging under the load. "The cheque, please."

Conflicting feelings. Again, an undeniable sense of pride, having been chosen—the warmth and assurance of being *wanted*. And fear, of course, that I would fail it again, or that the mountain wasn't booming at all and I was losing my mind. This was a terrible time for me. Three or four weeks of heavy drinking, losing sleep, missing work. I became a shadow, and Abraham's Faith did not let up. It coerced and commanded. At last I went to it, my soul stripped and pure. I lay among the rocks and wept, looking for peace. The mountain wrapped its arms around me and I felt its austere love.

Danielle Dewberry. Eight years old. I drove all the way to North Carolina, believing it prudent to make the grab as far from my front door as possible. Five hundred and seventy miles, and Abraham's Faith was with me for every one of them. She got into my car easily enough, but struggled all the way home, never tiring. Ten hours of kicking and twisting. I avoided tolls and drove the speed limit; the last thing I needed was to see blue lights flashing in the rearview. I parked on a deserted side road just outside Point Hollow and walked from there to the mountain, carrying the little girl on my shoulder, needing to stop and rest frequently. I uncovered the opening to the cave—just as I had in 1984—and gave the mountain what it had been crying for.

Or so I thought.

Roar and bang—those burning, black-fire hands again.

The therapist's name was Dr. Wendi Kim. She had the kindest eyes and a manner that set me immediately at ease. She invited me to "release" and I wanted to, I really *did*. There was a copy of the *New York Times* in her waiting room, and I had just finished reading about the disappearance of Danielle Dewberry, eight years old, from Louisburg, NC. I elected to *not* "release," and instead offered a string of lies. Dr. Kim listened and underlined our first session with a prescription for trazodone, which I duly took, and which gave me an erection that lasted twelve hours, but didn't stop the mountain.

Ryan Lloyd-Lewis, five years old, from Montrose, PA. A classic mall snatch, and a little closer to home, too. I couldn't bear the idea of another ten hours in a car with a struggling child. Not only that, but a long journey presented more chance of something going wrong. You learn by your mistakes, I guess.

I gave him to the mountain.

Rumble and boom.

I drove to Stewart Airport and hopped on a flight to Chicago. I still heard Abraham's Faith, more furious than ever, so caught another flight, this time to Seattle. Twenty-five hundred miles away now, looking at a different ocean, yet I still heard the mountain. It was a part of me. *Inside* me. I couldn't run away.

Walter Hillier. Eight years old. Stowe, VT.

"Let that be the last time. Please. I can't do this anymore."

Silence.

It was like tripping the exosphere—not at the point where sound can't travel, but at a level so far removed from *everything* that you cannot hear *anything*. I drifted there for days before touching down and, with trepidation, resuming normal life. The children I had taken became three more names on a list that expands by the hour. The investigations faltered. Their faces faded from milk cartons and the backs of envelopes.

Small-town life happened. I fell in and out of love, like a song on the radio, or a chick flick. I switched between jobs and earned a little extra on the side designing leaflets for local businesses. I fell in and out of love again: the chick flick sequel. My mother died of cancer in 1995 and I was happy for her. She'd had a miserable life—had never stood up for herself, or me, during my father's episodes of tyranny.

Life. Goes. On.

Nothing from Abraham's Faith. Not a squeak. I cast it from my mind—didn't need to think about the terrible things I had done to stay its voice, its hunger.

It was over.

Until six days ago, driving home from work—a bone-shaking explosion that nearly flipped me off the road. Five years had passed since I'd last heard it. Since I'd felt those black-fire hands clutch my soul.

I pulled over, rested my head against the steering wheel, and wept.

June 9, 1997.

I've been trying to ignore the mountain for eight days now. I am paralyzed with exhaustion. Haven't slept and can hardly eat. I'm growing weak. Mentally . . . physically.

I need to find out what happened up there. I need to stop this.

June 14, 1997.

Went pure, looking for guidance, for tranquility. The wilderness is my church. It's where I worship. The trees understand me like no person ever has. The animals and birds, too. I go among them, naked, and suffer no judgment. There is no need for mask or pretense. I am one of them. I am pure.

Four days and nights, eating the fruits of the earth, my body smeared with ochre and charcoal. I had hoped this deference would appease the mountain. But no, it still demands of me.

It is a wicked god.

June 18, 1997.

My brain is like a time bomb. *Tick-tock-BOOM!*

Don't make me do this.

June 22, 1997.

3 weks of hell and earth . . . pray for me might kill myslef cant think adn im sooooo weak I cant do anythign. Please dog please help a brothr out.

June 24, 1997.

Victoria Guy. Six years old. Deep River, CT.

I can't lie, I feel a little better. Not ready for jumping jacks, but there's light at the end of the (*CAVE*) tunnel.

Still . . . he rumbles. He burns.

June 26, 1997.

Connor Wright. Seven years old. Flemington, NJ. He thought I was his Uncle Tookie. He came easily enough, for sure—didn't start crying until we crossed the New York State line, and then he cried all the way to the mountain.

His eyes were the same as mine. The same shape. The same colour.

I can't do this anymore.

June 27, 1997.

Silence.

And I trip . . .

July 9, 1997.

Point Hollow is a largely unremarkable—yet undeniably picturesque—spit of civilization nestled in the Catskills. Its single claim to fame is that Washington Irving once rested here, and remarked: "Point Hollow is a wonderfully useless little town. I shall not hasten my return."

It has grown to be less useless in recent years. There are several quality stores and restaurants, a used car lot, and a sizable lumber mill that employs more than two hundred people. The flea market on Main Street (we called it the Scratch; locals have a nickname for everything, including that damn mountain) was recently razed to the ground, and a shiny new Super 8 will be erected in its stead. The verdant acreage surrounding Point Hollow has long-appealed to outdoor enthusiasts, and soon they'll have a place to kick off their hiking boots. I'm sure it's just a matter of time before Dunkin' Donuts and the Golden Arches muscle their way onto Main Street.

All that aside, this is home. I have lived here all of my life, and despite aforementioned difficulties, I wouldn't want to be anywhere else.

I am stained, it's true. But so is the town.

The whole goddamn town.

Maybe it's Abraham's Faith, casting its broad shadow, making everything dark. Or maybe it's the fact that Point Hollow is surrounded by ridges and peaks, offering it an isolated quality. Locals often call the town "God's Footprint." Another nickname, and perhaps an attempt to imbue a measure of divinity. It fails; regardless of natural beauty, there is nothing godly about Point Hollow. It is like a mad man's beautiful eye.

There is an eggshell veneer over just about everything, and you sense it will crack under the merest pressure. I am not the only one who feels it. This is apparent in the expressions of the townspeople. Their smiles are too wide, maintaining appropriate tension lest the weaknesses appear. Everybody is affable, but there is something under the surface. Something unspoken. I am no exception; I offer pleasantries like they are going out of fashion, but beneath my eggshell veneer lurks a monster that listens to mountains.

It is in the trees—the way they chatter and whoosh. It is in the buildings, too. There is menace in their structure and placement, and the bricks are subtly dissymmetric, so that, when walking, you experience a mild discomposure. The windows have no life. I never feel, looking at them, that there is anything happening on the other side. They are a façade, one of many, disguising the truth.

The wind blows differently in Point Hollow—and yes, almost certainly because the town is in a bowl. It doesn't shriek or howl. It doesn't huff or puff. It chills me to the core when it blows, because it sounds, for all the world, like a sobbing child.

I'm not suggesting that Point Hollow is a bad place, only that it *senses* badness, and covers it. I would liken it to an ornate stone on an evildoer's grave. And the evil is obvious.

Abraham's Faith.

What happened up there all those years ago?

The truth is buried somewhere in this town, and I'm going to find it.

July 27, 1997.

Kip Sawyer is the oldest man in Point Hollow. His exact age isn't known, but his older brother (not *much* older, it has to be said—maybe six years) was killed in the Second Battle of the Marne. That was World War I, summer of 1918, so it would be fair to assume that Kip is in his early- to mid-nineties. He walks slowly, carefully, with the aid of two sticks, can't see worth a damn, but there's nothing wrong with his thinker. He was on the town council until three years ago, and you'll often find him at Blueberry Bush Park, or sitting in Cuppa Joe's, magnifier in hand, zipping through the *New York Times* crossword.

I've known him, obviously, all my life. He's always been around, like Abraham's Faith, or the red mulberry—fantastic for climbing—on the corner of Burgess and Willow. I often wonder how I appear to him. Kip Sawyer was old when I was born, twenty-seven years ago. I must be like a housefly, bopping senselessly against a window.

"Good afternoon, Mr. Sawyer."

He glanced up from his crossword, his washed eyes squinted behind his glasses, identifying me by voice and outline. He wore a floppy hat, and I saw streaks of sunscreen on the backs of his hands. Blueberry Bush Park was as busy as it ever gets: a few kids playing ball, Frisbee . . . couples sprawled in the sun, catching rays, making out. Lazy Sunday afternoon. Kip Sawyer was in his preferred place: a bench beneath the generous shade of a sugar maple. He would remain there until the sun found a way through the branches.

"Young Oliver Wray," he said with a smile. "Temporary town during the depression. Eleven letters."

I shrugged and shook my head.

"The fourth letter is a V."

I have always been too scared to talk about the mountain. It knows my name, after all, and where to find me. I certainly never discussed what Matthew and I discovered in that deep place during the summer of 1984, and Matthew held his silence, too—terrified, probably, although I heard he'd been lost in the woods for three days, and was found trembling and delirious, so I'm not sure how much of the incident he recalled.

So how could I find out what happened up there—who the children were, and how they met their fate—without revealing what I know, or unmasking, and showing the town my darkness?

"Hooverville," Kip said.

"I'm sorry?"

He scratched the letters into the empty boxes and moved his magnifier to the next clue. I sat on the ground in front of him, partly in the shade. Sunlight tattooed my right side. I could see the edge of the mountain from my position and considered the myriad skeletons trapped in the gloom. Kip adjusted the newspaper and the movement caught my eye. There was a picture of Connor Wright on one of the pages. Missing for over a month now. His eyes were like mine.

Where are we going, Uncle Tookie?

Kip folded the newspaper and he disappeared.

"How can I help you, Oliver?" he asked.

"I'm curious," I said.

"Join the club," Kip said, and winked at me. "That doesn't go away as you get older. You get wiser, sure, but that only makes you *more* curious. It's life's way of jerking you off, but never quite finishing the job."

"Sounds like my ex-girlfriend," I said.

"Life is the most beautiful woman you'll ever sleep with," the old man said. "But she'll kick your keister if you don't treat her right."

"I guess."

"Bronze man function. Seven letters."

"I have no idea."

"That's because you haven't thought about it. Most things can be solved with a little thought, Oliver."

I nodded, but groaned inside. I didn't want this conversation to turn into the maxims of Kipling Sawyer, nonagenarian and crossword enthusiast. I had to draw rein—get to the point.

"What's wrong with this town?" I asked.

He looked at me, frowning, but there was a mirthful tilt to his lips. He nodded once, set the magnifier and pen down, and then gazed at the children playing ball behind me. His rheumy eyes widened. I wondered how much he could see—if the children were more like shadows. Or ghosts.

"Why would you ask such a thing?" His gaze fell on me. It was surprisingly heavy, considering the way his lips tilted, but I took comfort knowing I was a blur to him. A housefly.

"I think you know," I replied firmly. "Everything is so goddamn pristine—so Norman Rockwell. The little pink houses, the white picket fences. I'm just suspicious, I guess. It's like the husband who cheats on his wife and brings her flowers. I think this idyllic exterior is covering something more sinister."

"Is that so?" Kip uttered a dry laugh that turned into a cough. He fished a Kleenex from his shirt pocket and covered his mouth. It took him a few moments to catch his breath. The birds whistled and the sobbing wind rolled through the branches.

"Something feels . . . *off*," I said.

He wheezed, blinked hard, and dabbed silver flecks of spittle from his lips. "Do you think the town is full of Nazi war criminals? Something like that?"

"No." I smiled, trying to curb the intensity. I was aware of the edge applied to my tone, but it's hard to fish when you don't have any bait. "I just have trouble believing that something so perfect can be genuine."

"Why don't you just accept it, Oliver?" he said. "Stop worrying about it."

If only, I thought.

"This isn't a problem unless you make it a problem."

"You've lived here all your life," I said, and that edge was back. "You know this town. You *breathe* it, and know its history better than anyone. I just want to know if anything ever happened here. Anything . . . untoward."

"There's a well-stocked library on Main Street," Kip said.

"Yes, there is, and you'd think I'd be able to find *something* about Point Hollow's history, wouldn't you? There are books about the Catskills, and Point Hollow is mentioned, but it's cursory, at best— the triviality we learned in grade school: the first settlers arrived at the end of the revolution, and Point Hollow was established as a town in 1810. Other than that . . ."

I held out my hands: empty.

Kip nodded, and he still had that strange smile on his face. He knew something, I was certain of it. *This isn't a problem unless you make it a problem,* he'd said, which was another way of saying, *Let sleeping dogs lie.* He took off his hat and ran a hand over his hairless head. His eyes closed for a moment and I imagined him listening to the children playing, drifting momentarily from my company to a place of ignorance, filled with spurious smiles and deeply dreaming dogs.

"There's nothing wrong with this town," he said. He opened his eyes and absorbed my outline. I saw his pupils contract behind the cataracts, like twin faces drawing away from twin windows. "The people here are happy. They live in nice homes and breathe fresh air. There are no slums, virtually no crime, and the streets are clean. The schools are excellent, and Cuppa Joe's serves arguably the best coffee north of Guatemala. Whatever suspicions you have can safely be laid to rest, Oliver. Point Hollow is a wonderful place."

And what about the dead children in the mountain? I almost asked, but zipped my lip.

Kip went back to his crossword, which was his way of dismissing me, but I wasn't quite done. I allowed a minute or two to pass, regaining composure, somewhat unsettled by his reticence. A plane roared overhead, vapour trails scoring the sky. I listened to the children play. Kip's pen moved as if it were dancing with his hand. I took a deep breath and said:

"What about Abraham's Faith?"

It was as close as I dared to get. I felt my heart drumming in my chest and prayed my expression would not betray me. I looked squarely at Kip. His eyes flashed with uncertainty and for a second— no more—his mirthfully slanted lips disappeared into the lines of his face.

"What about it?" he asked. Was his voice trembling?

"Look on any map and it's called Old Bear Mountain." I linked my fingers to keep my hands from shaking, and noticed that the old man had done the same. "Yet we call it Abraham's Faith. Why the nickname?"

He shrugged. "One of those small-town affectations, I suppose."

"Does it have anything to do with the Bible story?" I pushed. "Abraham taking his son to the mountain, to sacrifice him at God's command?"

Kip sighed. The pen rolled from his lap and dropped between the slats of the bench's seat. A flicker of agitation touched his brow. "You're asking a lot of questions, Oliver. Don't you have anything better to do on a Sunday afternoon?"

I reached beneath the bench and retrieved his pen. "What can I say? I'm a troubled man."

"I'd say you are."

I held out the pen. He reached for it and yes, his hand was shaking quite badly.

What do you know?

His fingers closed around it and I held on for a moment before letting go.

"This is a God-fearing town, Oliver," he said. "The church is an important part of who we are. This was truer in the past, before the many distractions of modern life. There was a time when the church was all we had. And so yes, I'm sure the mountain's sobriquet is derived from the Old Testament, but for no other reason than that we had—and still have—absolute faith in our creator. And why wouldn't we, when living in such a beautiful part of the world?"

I smiled and nodded. "God's Footprint."

"Indeed."

I got to my feet and my smile widened, as false as everything else in this town. Kip Sawyer knew more than he was letting on, but he wasn't about to share it with me.

"One more question," I said.

That mirthful tilt of the lips again. "But of course."

"Do you believe that an inanimate object, or place, can be spiritually possessed? That evil can exist in something non-living?"

"We're veering into the paranormal now," Kip said. "Quite a departure from the Bible."

"Not really," I said. "The Book of Revelation 18:2: '*And he cried with a mighty voice saying, Fallen, fallen is Babylon the great, and is become the habitation of demons, and a hold of every unclean spirit, and a hold of every unclean and hateful bird.*'"

He regarded me thoughtfully for a long time. I saw a small muscle in his jaw working. Eventually he replied, "Yes, Oliver, I suppose I do believe that evil can reside in just about anything."

I nodded and looked at the mountain. "But something would have to *make* it evil, do you agree?"

"I do," he said. "Something . . . or somebody."

October 14, 1997.

Today I went to Abraham's Faith and searched the skeletons (looking for clues, information—anything), but found nothing that helped. A few trinkets. A small wooden toy. I looked at the boy-skeleton dressed in blue jeans and Converse All Stars, and noticed the initials J.C. stitched into the collar of his T-shirt. Jacques Cousteau? Jesus Christ? Johnny Carson? The initials were interesting, but useless. This was, however, the only child dressed in jeans and sneakers. The others wore simpler clothes, most of them rotted to rags, clearly from a different time. Easy to deduce that J.C. had been brought here much later. Or perhaps, like me, he had been *called* here, and had given his own life.

That's one way of attaining silence.

March 20, 1998.

Almost nine months and nothing from the mountain. It hangs in my life like a picture. Silent. Unmoving. But how long before it booms again, ravenous?

One year? Ten?

Or maybe it's over.

How can I pursue a normal life, walking this tightrope, never knowing?

For my part in this, I feel I am owed the truth. You can forget

Dr. Kim and trazodone. Ditto grade-A drugs and sunset on the Pacific. The truth is the only thing that can help, and it may forever elude me. But know this: until my dying day I will endeavor to find out what happened on that mountain.

And what it really wants from me.

It had been a long time since Matthew had woken up screaming—more than twenty years, and back then his parents had been there to comfort him, and assure him he was safe. He never remembered the dreams he'd pulled himself from, only that they were dark and damp. He assumed that someone, or something, pursued him through the darkness, but this aspect of the nightmare was blessedly vague.

The screaming stopped, but the nightmares followed him into adulthood. Once, sometimes twice, a week. They stemmed, almost certainly, from a childhood incident of which he had no memory: ten years old, lost for three days in the Catskill Mountains. He was eventually found, shivering like a new fawn, nine miles from home. But how he came to be there . . .

No recollection. Zero.

Kirsty had shown concern during the blossoming phase of their relationship, but it was a fallacious thing, and had worn thin quickly. They had been married for six years, but emotionally divorced for the last two. On the occasions he awoke, bathed in perspiration, the bed sheets so damp you could wring drips from them, Kirsty's response was invariably disdain, as if it were a childish habit he had never grown out of. She would often remove to the couch, uttering imprecations. Her caged-cat temperament had twice impelled her to strike him as he blinked the nightmare from his eyes.

But for more than twenty years he hadn't screamed. He'd trapped it in his throat and eased it out in a succession of shallow breaths. Until two nights ago. The nightmare had dragged him deep and he'd burst from it howling. Kirsty had ripped from her side of the bed as if something had crawled under the sheets and bitten her ass. She'd thrown a glass of water at him and slapped his face. Matthew cried into the early hours, confused and ashamed. Kirsty didn't come home from work the following day. She called him at nine P.M. and told him she needed time to think—not to mention a good night's sleep.

"You need help, Matthew."

"I see Dr. Meeker every Thursday. A hundred and twenty dollars an hour. How much help do I need?"

The screaming episode had been the catalyst, preceded by two years of discontent and falsehood. Silence. Lies. Verbal and physical abuse. Adultery. And that was just Kirsty. Matthew, for his part, played the victim. His submissiveness was Kirsty's fuel.

"This isn't working," She sat at the kitchen table, looking at its scuffed wooden surface, massaging her temples with her forefingers, avoiding eye contact. Matthew didn't know why she couldn't look him in the eye, given everything they had shared during their six years of marriage. He had seen her pee and shower (and pee *in* the shower, on one occasion). He had lifted the hair from her face while she vomited. He had peeled open her labia and gazed wondrously and wonderingly inside her, like an astrologer gazing at the surface of some newly discovered planet. He had made love to her—been inside her, as deep and close as it was possible for anybody to get. They talked, shared secrets, laughed with and at each other. They used to hold hands in the movie theatre, like teenagers. They had sworn their vows before family, friends, and before God. They were *togetherness*. No longer individuals.

But she couldn't look him in the eye. Matthew believed this was their most intimate moment of all: the beginning of heartbreak; something that would scar them both. And she couldn't face it.

"What do you mean?" he asked. It was a knucklehead question—of *course* he knew what she meant. But he wanted to make her work at breaking his heart.

She sighed and glanced up, but not at Matthew. Her blue eyes skimmed toward the window, where the blush of sunset pressed against the blinds. She kept massaging her temples, as if ending their marriage was giving her a headache. Just another inconvenience, like their rowdy neighbours.

"Look at me," he said.

She looked at the table.

"Look at me, Kirsty. At *me*."

"I don't want to look at you, Matt. I'm so tired of looking at you."

Matthew's shoulders slumped. He leaned against the sink, shuffled his feet, and let silence happen. He had always thought of it as a Mexican Silence—both engaged in the other's downfall, with no good coming from it. Moments like this could only be resolved with conversation, but stubbornly they resisted. Which meant, of course, that Kirsty was right; it wasn't working. Matthew had known it for a long time, but held on because he loved her. He hadn't forgotten the rare glimmer in her eyes as she walked down the aisle. He wasn't ready to let go.

He took a seat at the table beside her, touched her upper arm. She didn't pull away from him, but he felt her stiffen, as if it were the first time he had touched her. A stranger becoming overly familiar. Her muscle flexed as she went on massaging her temples. Infinitesimal beats, like her small heart.

"We should talk about this," he said, breaking the silence, standing down. He had dropped his weapon and spread his arms. Kirsty unloaded on him, bullets tearing into his flesh. No mercy.

"There's nothing to talk about. I don't feel anything for you. No love. No emotion. You're like that plant: dried-up and wilted. You don't excite me anymore."

She trailed off, making disinterested gestures at the peace lily on the shelf, its flowers brown and drained. Matthew had always liked that plant. It used to bring colour into the kitchen, but neither of them had watered it for a long time. He imagined the wretched thing sucking moisture from the air, straining its green lungs. He felt a sudden impulse to throw a mug of water into its soil, but Kirsty had reloaded and was rattling rounds into him again.

"This isn't a marriage, Matt, it's a prison sentence. I can barely stand the sight of you, and I hate when you touch me."

He removed his hand from her arm.

"We're in a loveless, empty relationship, and I don't want it anymore. I will not settle for anything less than happiness, and you haven't made me happy for a long time."

His riddled corpse slouched off the seat and settled, bleeding and useless, on the floor beneath the table. Tears tracked soulfully from his eyes. The kitchen window was a burning orange rectangle.

And still she didn't look at him.

She went to bed early. "Sleep on the couch," she said. "I don't want you near me." Her feet thundered up the stairs and across the floorboards. He heard the shower sprinkle into life and the pipes sang behind the walls. Matthew imagined her soaping her small breasts beneath the hot spray, her mouth open, her long hair clumped over one shoulder. The suds would be running down to the thick nest of hair between her legs. Auburn pubic hair, turned dark by the water. He imagined her fingering herself, thinking about one of her lovers, venting frustration through orgasm. He imagined snagging the shower curtain to one side and beating her with a hammer, over and over, until her skull cracked and little pieces of her brain clogged the plughole.

The shower stopped. Her feet thumped across the floorboards. The bedsprings made a bouncy, laughter-like sound as she slumped onto the mattress. Matthew turned on the TV and watched ESPN until his eyes ached, then flipped over to the Sci-Fi channel. *Alien* was on, but it was near the end. Sigourney Weaver was running around the Nostromo in her underwear. He masturbated, then flicked off the TV and went to sleep.

———

"Okay," Matthew said.

"Okay?"

"I concede that it's not working."

She rolled her eyes. "Fucking Sherlock Holmes," she said, and he winced. Of all the bullets she had fired at him, this hurt the most. The other stuff, as hard as it was to hear—how she didn't feel anything for him anymore, how she couldn't stand the sight of him—was brutal honesty, and he couldn't hold it against her. But rolling her eyes and saying, "Fucking Sherlock Holmes" was just plain spiteful.

"Do you have to be so nasty?" he asked.

She looked at him for the first time in . . . how long? Matthew frowned; he couldn't remember the last time she had looked at him. He'd hoped to see a warmer emotion in her eyes, something approachable and encouraging, but there was only ice. When she looked away, after only a second, he felt a fat bird of relief take wing from his shoulder.

They were in the kitchen. Again. It was their favourite venue for altercations, although they liked to spread them around the house. They had made love in two rooms: the bedroom, and the living room. They had argued in every one, including the downstairs powder room. *Rule of thumb,* Matthew thought. *If you argue in more rooms than you fuck in, you should take it as a sign that something is wrong.*

Kirsty slurped coffee from a huge mug she had stolen from Starbucks. She'd crammed it into her purse after she finished drinking and strolled out, leaving Matthew to follow guiltily behind. He hated that mug. He hated the way it made her hands look small, and the way she'd fill it to the brim and slurp.

"Did you want to say something?" she asked. The window blinds divided her into concertinaed strips, like a portrait on a Chinese fan.

"Well, I . . ."

"Spit it out, for Christ's sake."

"I think we should separate," Matthew said.

She nodded. She slurped.

"A trial separation," he continued.

"A *trial?*" Her eyes flicked his way with a sound like katanas being drawn from their scabbards.

"Yes," he said, and his voice sounded surprisingly firm. "It's for the best. A few weeks away from each other—"

"I'm not moving out. *You* can move out." Her face disappeared behind the full moon of the mug's base. *Sluuuuurrrpp.*

"That's fine, I'll . . ." He sighed at the thought of having to move into his parents' home in Brooklyn. Thirty-six years old and back with Mom and Dad. He didn't want to do it, but it was either that or a flea-pit room in the Bronx. "I'll sort something out."

"You'll move in with your parents, you mean."

"Probably, yes."

"You won't be able to bring girlfriends home." She grinned wickedly.

"I have no intention of bringing girlfriends home." Matthew showed her his ring finger. "I'm married. To you. This is a trial separation, not the end. We'll get together in a few weeks, maybe a month, and see where we stand. I'm doing this because I love you. Because I want to save our marriage."

"Jesus Christ couldn't save our marriage."

"But we have to try."

"I don't love you anymore."

"I know." He bled before her, downcast, his head hanging. "But maybe the time apart will help you find what you're looking for."

She finished her coffee with a terrific, rattling sound, and left the mug on the countertop. Matthew would normally clean up after her—put her cereal bowl and giant mug in the dishwasher, wipe the counters, clean the coffeemaker—but not this morning. He would be gone by the time she got back from work, and she could clean up her own shit.

"We're just putting off the inevitable." She walked from the kitchen, into the hallway, pulled her jacket from the hook and slipped it on. "It's a fate thing, baby."

Matthew rolled his eyes. This was her favourite saying, picked up from one of her favourite crappy reality TV shows. He imagined screaming it into her face—*It's a FATE thing, baby*—while he used a pizza cutter to divide her heart into eight equal pieces.

"Will you be here when I get home?" she asked.

He stepped into the hallway behind her. His bare feet left ghostly prints on the laminate flooring. Fake wood. Just like everything else.

"No," he said.

She picked up her purse, glanced at him again, and unlocked the front door. He stepped toward her and held out his arms, throwing himself onto the firing line.

"Hug?" He gave her half a smile. He thought she would bang rounds into him again, or sneer at him and leave, but she surprised him. It wasn't a hug, exactly; she merely leaned into him and pressed one hand between his shoulder blades. The sort of hug you might give an annoying relative. But Matthew made up for that. He curled his arms around her body and pulled her close, wanting her to feel his savage heartbeat.

"Matthew," she wheezed. "You're hurting me."

Good, he thought. *Now you know how I feel.*

She pulled away from him, lowered her eyes, opened the door.

"I'll call you," he said.

She nodded, then left. He staggered—pierced with bullets holes, shrapnel, mortar rounds—into the kitchen and dropped lifelessly into a seat at the table. He started to cry. A thousand well-earned tears. They made an impressive puddle on the table's surface, as if he had knocked over a small glass of water.

He looked at her huge mug on the kitchen countertop. Brilliant rage swept through him and he lunged, grabbed it, cocked his arm to throw it at the wall. But he couldn't do it. She loved it in a way she didn't love him, and he couldn't hurt her like that. Matthew's arm trembled. More tears ran down his face. He placed the mug on the countertop and bled all over the floor.

CHAPTER
THREE

Dr. Meeker's office was on Lexington at 33rd. Matthew took the R train to Union Square, then hopped on the 6—a much busier train—where he was pushed into a corner between the doors and a heavyset man with a face-tattoo like Mike Tyson's. Minding his own business, not wishing to talk to anyone, Matthew folded his newspaper into the smallest possible rectangle and started to read.

"Three hours," the heavyset man said to him.

"I'm sorry?" Matthew looked at him and frowned.

"Three hours," the man said again, and pointed at Matthew's newspaper. He had folded it to the story on Ethan Mitchell and Courtney Bryce—two children, from the neighbouring states of New Jersey and Pennsylvania, who had gone missing within the last week. Their smiles were painfully bright, even in black and white.

"I don't understand what you—"

"Missing children that are killed . . . usually dead within the first three hours," the man explained. He shrugged. His dark eyes were red-rimmed, as if he hadn't slept. "How long have they been missing?"

Matthew read the caption beneath the photographs. "The girl . . . four days. The boy . . . seven. A week today."

"They're dead."

Matthew rolled his eyes. The train jerked and shuddered and he used his core muscles to keep from pressing against the man. "Maybe, but they haven't found the bodies yet, so there's still hope."

The man grunted and started to read over Matthew's shoulder, mumbling, lips moving. Matthew ignored him and focused on the story. New Jersey and Pennsylvania police had started to explore the possibility of a connection in the disappearance of the two children. They had very little to work with, however. No witnesses. No physical evidence. The files were paper-thin and growing colder every day. Even the media coverage had cooled down, but had been rekindled when Ethan's father was arrested for physically assaulting one of the investigating officers, claiming the police were not doing enough to find his son. This rash action called his character into question, and added another leaf to the file.

"I would have done the same thing," the man with the Mike Tyson tattoo said.

The train approached 33rd, squealing like a broken toy. Matthew waited for the doors to open, then slapped the newspaper into the heavyset man's hand and stepped onto the platform. He was barged and bumped and swept toward the exit, and for half a second he wished he was back in the town he had grown up in—Point Hollow—where crowds didn't exist, and where space and time were beyond measure.

———

Silence again, but not of the Mexican variety. This was an abstract silence; Dr. Meeker's method, always, was to let the patient talk first. Never a "hello" or a "how are you?" He maintained that the opening words were the most important, and set the tone for the session. He would sit and wait for however long it took. Matthew tested him once—sat in silence for forty-five minutes before thinking, *If I wanted the silent treatment I could have stayed at home with Kirsty.* Then he opened his mouth and told Dr. Meeker exactly this, and Dr. Meeker had nodded, half-smiled, and asked Matthew if he had used the forty-five minutes of silence in a productive and meditative fashion.

Dr. Meeker had an unorthodox, yet effective, way of encouraging conversation.

"Remind me to give you my new home telephone number," Matthew said as he took a seat opposite the doctor. He slumped into his favourite position. He knew the seat—had sat in it once a week for the last five years. It was a second armchair to him.

"Oh?" Dr. Meeker said. He didn't even raise his eyebrows.

He knows, Matthew thought. *I've been telling him about my marital problems for the last two years. You don't need to be a goddamn shrink to realize why I have a new telephone number.*

"I don't need to tell you why," Matthew said. "You already know."

"I suppose I do," Dr. Meeker said. "But I want you to tell me anyway."

Matthew took a deep breath and let it out slowly. "I'm currently residing with my parents in Bay Ridge; Kirsty and I have separated." That word—*separated*—was too jarring, too irrevocable. He amended, but with noted uncertainty, "A trial separation."

"I see. A mutual understanding?"

"I suppose, although *tactical* is a more fitting word."

Dr. Meeker nodded. He was a handsome man approaching retirement age, although you would think him ten years younger, with dark mottled skin and hands so precise and still they appeared to be carved of wood. The wrinkles around his eyes made them look brighter, somehow, shooting outward, the way a child will draw the sun's rays. He rarely moved during their sessions—sat with his legs crossed and his careful hands linked. He spoke only when he needed to, and his words had the effect of pulling the loose end of a ribbon, then leaving it for you to fully unwrap.

His office, like ninety percent of real estate in Manhattan, was compact yet efficient. It supported his counsel of orderliness and utilization. There were no distractions, only essentials: two comfortable chairs, the obligatory couch, a coat stand, and a desk upon which few items resided. He was not a man of simple means, but rather one who emphasized the fundamentals.

"Only generals and chess players speak in terms of tactical manoeuvres," he said. His bright eyes were as comfortable and familiar as the chair. "Care to elaborate?"

"I took the initiative," Matthew said. "I suggested a trial separation because I wanted Kirsty to see that I am both strong and open to compromise—two qualities that she forever tells me I lack. This way, when we reconcile, I'll have a firmer platform from which to move forward."

Dr. Meeker didn't move, didn't speak. He sat in his chair with his legs crossed and his fingers linked, like the subject of a painting in a scholar's den. They were on the twenty-fourth floor. This high up, the sounds of the city were muted, like something trapped in a bottle.

"If I may," he said finally, and actually moved, unlinking his fingers, opening his hands. "You suggested a trial separation not to benefit your marriage, but to underscore your character?"

"Both," Matthew said. "I hope."

"Okay, but a compromise would suggest that she is giving something, too."

"I guess," Matthew said.

"You guess." Dr. Meeker tugged the ribbon.

Matthew considered this for a moment, stroking his beard, as Dr. Meeker resumed his static pose. Kirsty wanted the separation. She didn't ask for it, but she *wanted* it. She had the house, the car—everything. But what was she giving him? In what way was she showing a compromise, a willingness to make it work?

Simple answer: she wasn't.

Matthew unwrapped: "I actually undermined my character, didn't I?"

"I don't know the parameters of your agreement."

"I gave her what she wanted. I thought she'd see strength in my understanding, but all she'll see is weakness in my surrender."

"That depends on Kirsty's character," Dr. Meeker said.

"I can't do anything right."

"And that depends on *your* character."

They were silent for a moment. Matthew could hear the doctor's watch ticking. He closed his eyes and flew away, working his wings with every emphatic second.

"Let's not question your motive for suggesting the separation," Dr. Meeker continued. "You need to think about how you're going to use this time away from Kirsty. There's no benefit in simply separating—relying on the adage 'Absence makes the heart grow fonder'—only to reconcile with the same broken pieces. You need to repair the weaknesses. If you're truly strong, then Kirsty will see it. And if she doesn't, you'll be strong enough to deal with it. Do you understand what I'm telling you, Matthew?"

Matthew opened his eyes. "I think so."

"What I'm saying," Dr. Meeker said, "is that for the next three, four weeks—the duration of this trial separation, however long—you need to accept that Kirsty is not a priority. You need to nuke this perception of the man she wants you to be, and discover the man *you* want to be."

"Sounds great," Matthew said, one eyebrow cocked. "Where do I begin?"

"By dropping the pessimism and the sarcasm."

He lowered his eyebrow.

"You're an intelligent man, Matthew," Dr. Meeker said. "Vulnerability is not an excuse for obtuseness. You don't need me to tell you what to do."

"I know," Matthew whispered.

"Yes." With one word, he tugged the ribbon.

Matthew remembered being barged and pushed on the train platform, and how the open green of Point Hollow had called to him, if only for one second.

He unwrapped.

His childhood memories were haphazard, at best, like a comic book with most of the panels blacked out—an aversion to recall no doubt drawn from the time he had been lost in the woods. They'd left Point Hollow shortly afterward, in the fall of 1984. His father landed a job at an accounting firm in Midtown, and they loaded up and never looked back. The relief was like a kite catching the wind. Matthew's father, originally from Utica, had never taken to Point Hollow. He once described it as a beautiful reflection in a broken mirror.

Some things were clear in his mind: how the trees behind his old house looked like they were ablaze when the sun went down; how the Stars and Stripes flying outside his school would snap rhythmically, angrily, when the wind eddied within Point Hollow's bowl; and how the whole town had looked small and fractured, like something dropped from a great height, the day they left.

This tortoise is bound for the Big Apple, he remembered his father saying, strapping cases to the roof of their station wagon. His little sister had laughed and clapped her hands, and his mother started singing "New York, New York." A small group of friends had gathered on the corner of Maple Road to wave them off. His father gave the horn a couple of happy toots, and Matthew had looked past his sister and seen a few of his buddies: Yo-yo Jones (bouncing his Yo-yo), Tim Lutz (Lutz the Klutz), and Bobby Alexander—his best friend—with his Mets cap turned backward and his round belly sagging over the front of his jeans. Matthew had waved until they had turned the corner and were out of sight.

The station wagon rumbled down Main Street with its rear axle sagging, past the town hall and the Scratch and Buzzcut Billy's. *It all looks so small,* Matthew had thought. *So dark.* But when they crossed the town line, it was like a light had been flicked on and he could suddenly see—as though he had been gripped in the world's tightest bear-hug, and could suddenly breathe.

They never returned. They hardly even thought about it.

"I think I need to get away," Matthew said. "Get out of the city for a few days. Get my head together."

"That sounds like a fine idea." Only Dr. Meeker's lips moved.

"I've been thinking about Point Hollow."

No reaction.

"That's the town I grew up in."

"I know."

"I haven't been there since the day we left. Twenty-six years ago."

"I know that, too."

"Do you think it's a good idea to revisit my past?"

Dr. Meeker considered this in his silent, stationary way. "Your priority, Matthew, is to be true to yourself. This means soul searching, and asking yourself what you still hope to achieve in life. If a trip to your hometown complicates this process, then no, it's not a good idea. But if you feel it will be a benefit, then you have my full endorsement."

Matthew nodded. "I told you about my recurring nightmares, right?"

"Unresolved anxiety . . . repressed memories."

"From the time I was lost in the woods."

A near imperceptible nod from the Doctor.

"There's so much . . ." Matthew searched for the right word. "So much darkness in my head. I can *feel* it. It's like a cloud, constantly raining. And despite our talk-therapy sessions, Dr. Meeker, I think it's getting worse. *Stormier.*"

"What makes you say that?"

"I woke up screaming the other night, for the first time since I was . . . Jesus, maybe thirteen, fourteen years old. Not only that, but I've been having strange thoughts lately. Terrible, violent thoughts."

Dr. Meeker tilted his left eyebrow a fraction. "Such as?"

Matthew chewed his lip and looked at the backs of his hands.

Dr. Meeker waited.

"I would never hurt Kirsty," Matthew said. He used the thumb and middle finger of his right hand to twirl his wedding ring. "I couldn't hurt anybody. You know that about me."

An immaculately dressed statue.

"But I've been having these . . . *reveries,* I guess the word is, where I *am* hurting her. Not just hurting her." He took a deep breath. His wedding ring gleamed. "Killing her. Violently. With a hammer. A hatchet. A power drill."

Nothing from the doctor.

"It's a bloodbath in my head sometimes."

Not a flicker.

"And I'm thinking that—like the nightmares—they could be linked to my repressed memories."

"They're a pressure release," Dr. Meeker said. "Thoughts of spousal homicide are not uncommon during periods of duress."

"But so violent?"

"Often, yes."

"And if I'm waking up screaming, my nightmares must be more intense."

"You've been under a great deal of stress."

Matthew sighed and studied the backs of his hands again. "Yes, I have."

"Do you believe a trip to Point Hollow will help?"

"It might shake loose a few memories—shine a light on the darkness. That has to be a step in the right direction. And at the very least, I'll get out of the city for a while."

Dr. Meeker nodded. "I applaud your assertiveness, but suggest you apply an element of caution; memories can often be overwhelming."

"I know," Matthew said, and closed his eyes for a moment. He flew, his precious wings extended, over mountains and lakes and forests. "But I hope they can be healing, too."

They said nothing for the next few moments. Matthew was a bird. Dr. Meeker was a statue. His watch marked time with a sound like falling years.

———

He woke that night with a heavy sob. It trembled in his throat and would have developed into a scream had he not clapped one hand over his mouth. The nightmare broke apart in his mind, as weak and dark as charred paper. *Running,* he thought. *Enclosed . . . trapped.* He fumbled for the lamp on the nightstand and flicked it on. The light was like warm water.

He shrank among the bed sheets, his heart thudding, trying to cling to the sounds of the house—the sounds of outside: distant traffic and trains. Anything to move him farther from the dream. He blinked his tear-filled eyes.

What do I have to do? he thought. He sensed that something was trying to reach him, or break him. Amid the darkness he held inside, something was calling his name.

Matthew got out of bed and walked to the window, feeling like he was ten years old and expecting, when he looked out, to see Point Hollow. But it was Bay Ridge, of course, his parents' neighbourhood, with Manhattan's glow painting the darkness to the north.

His reflection in the glass was small and pale.

"What do I have to do?"

He answered his own question, looking beyond the city's lights where, across the miles, Point Hollow was waiting.

———

"Hi there, you've reached Kirsty. I'm not available to take your call at the moment, but you know what to do after the beep."

She'd taken his name off the voicemail. *The bitch*, he thought. It used to say, *"Hello, you've reached Kirsty and Matt . . ."* (even though *"Matt and Kirsty"* rolled off the tongue better). He'd been erased. He wondered what else she'd done. Repainted the walls? Bought a new bedroom set? Anger bubbled over inside him.

The *bitch*.

BEEP!

He couldn't speak. He cut the call and hissed, *"Ffffffffuuuuuccckkk yooooooooou"* across a dead line. He counted to ten and called again.

"Hi, Kirsty." His voice was smooth and even. It was *chilled*—the voice of Bootsy Collins, if he ever had to make such a call. "Yeah, it's Matt. Listen, I'm not going to be around for a few days. I'm actually blowing town, you dig? Maybe we can hook up when I get back. I guess we should talk. Anyway, take care of yourself. Keep it real."

You dig? Keep it real? Hmm, maybe a little heavy on the Bootsy, but no matter. The call was made, his bag was packed. It was time to light the darkness.

Time to go home.

Chapter
Four

He showed his bluff: jack high.

"I can't work out," Sheriff Tansy said, "if you're lucky or stupid."

They were in the Rack, the only bar in Point Hollow, a small yet colourful establishment on Main Street. There were no surprises in the Rack—a horseshoe bar, several TVs flashing CNN or the ball game, a scuffed pool table, and a jukebox that played only country and light rock. The walls were decorated with sports memorabilia and portraits of the town and its surrounding beauty. Neon signs buzzed in the windows.

Thursday night was Poker Night. The table was lined with the same old faces: Sheriff Edgar Tansy, who in twenty years had never had to break a sweat (just as well, considering his high cholesterol and the fact that he was forty pounds overweight); Tommy Whipple, who owned Sure as Shot Sporting Goods and, with Point Hollow's booming popularity among hunters and hikers, had gone from driving a Chevy Malibu to a Cadillac CTS; Dr. Lionel Ruzicka, Point Hollow's long-serving physician, who knew the town's secrets as if they were his own (but not *all* its secrets, Oliver thought); Rupert Grayson (just Gray, if you were smart), foreman at the lumber mill, as tough as a tree and apt to break your arm if you called him by his Christian name; and, of course, Oliver Wray, self-made millionaire and Point Hollow's favourite son.

"I'm not lucky or stupid, Sheriff," Oliver said. "I just know how to win."

"I guess you do," the sheriff said, and pushed the cards across the table. "Your turn to deal, hotshot. Be good to me. You know I'm good to you."

Oliver nodded, shuffled.

Did he like these people? He searched their eyes as he flipped the cards between his fingers, showing them a smile that was in every way false. No, he didn't like them at all. He didn't like anybody, really. *Be good to me,* Sheriff Tansy had said, and Oliver could smile and pretend until the stars fell from the sky. He mirrored the town in this regard: pretty to look at, but with a darkness too deep to shine a light on.

He placed the cards facedown on the table and invited Gray, to his left, to cut the pack.

"Shit on that," Gray said, waving his meaty hand over the top of them. "It's time to change my luck."

"Let me know how that works out for you," Oliver said, starting to deal.

He was owned—body and soul—by Abraham's Faith, although his many years of servitude could not diminish his love for Point Hollow. It was a stale place, yes, but it was home. Every trail. Every flower. Every tree. The rivers were his arteries. The mountains were his bones. His graphic design business was successful enough that he could live anywhere in the world, but being bound to Abraham's Faith wasn't the only reason he stayed. Even if it released him (and surely it would; he'd paid his dues), he would stay. He *knew* Point Hollow—everything about it. *Broaden your horizons,* someone once said to him. Some motherfucking prick. And Oliver had asked him if he would move to a shack in Tibet, or adopt an Ashanti family, or choose a new wife, in order to *broaden his horizons.*

Fucker.

Point Hollow would always be home. He didn't want subways and skyscrapers and streets choked with people that couldn't speak English; he wanted little pink houses and deer in the back garden and breathtaking starlight. He felt as if the rivers and lakes and trees were his family. An embodiment of his inner-being. If you could dig out his soul and plant it, mountains would grow, rivers would ripple, flowers would bloom. He knew every blade of grass, every branch and pebble, for miles around.

He would, on occasion, live in the wild. He'd venture beyond the trails and hunting zones, wearing not a stitch, and forage for food just like any other animal. For days on end, in a world where *nothing* was man-made. No noise pollution or human voices. The only smells were pine and spruce and moonlight. He slept on the forest floor or curled among the rocks. He tapped into his animal-and-bird-self and purified his body. It was euphoric.

"A pile of horseshit," Gray said, tossing his cards into the middle of the table.

Oliver had the nine of diamonds and the three of spades. You fold that hand ninety-nine times out of a hundred. The bet came to him and he raised.

"Son of a whore," Tommy Whipple said.

"Where are your balls, Tommy?" Oliver asked.

"Don't you worry about my balls," Tommy said, throwing his chips in the pot. Dr. Ruzicka and the sheriff were right behind him. Oliver dealt the flop: Queen of hearts. Ten of hearts. Two of spades. Everybody checked, except for Oliver, who had nothing, but raised anyway, forcing Tommy from the hand. It was so easy to fool these people. He'd been doing it for years.

"What have you got, Doc?"

"Shit," Dr. Ruzicka said, meeting the raise. "It's only money."

"And you, Sheriff?"

"I'm in, goddamnmit." Sheriff Tansy laid his money down. His left eyebrow twitched

The turn revealed the three of diamonds. He shouldn't be able to win this hand on a pair of threes, but he was going to.

The doctor checked. Sheriff Tansy checked. Oliver raised.

"Not this time, Oliver," Sheriff Tansy said.

Oliver smiled.

Dr. Ruzicka folded.

"Just me and you, Sheriff," Oliver said. "Again."

Dr. Hook came on the jukebox singing "When You're In Love With a Beautiful Woman," and the game was momentarily disrupted when Drunken Debbie Kendrick—the Rack's favourite barfly—pulled Tommy from his seat and demanded a dance. Tommy acquiesced, humouring the guys, and the clientele applauded as the couple stepped and staggered. Oliver smiled and clapped his hands, his mask slipping—only for a second—when he noticed Bobby Alexander shooting daggers at him from across the bar. Oliver grinned and Bobby turned away. *He sees through me,* Oliver thought. *God only served him a half-scoop of brains, but he's the only one who doesn't trust my smile.* The song ended. Tommy kissed Drunken Debbie's hand, dropped into his seat, and the sheriff looked at Oliver and said:

"Game on, hotshot. Let's see the river."

Oliver burned and turned. The three of clubs.

Trip-threes, Oliver thought. *God loves me.*

"You got nothing," the sheriff said.

"I got everything," Oliver said.

Which was true. The mountain had taken care of him, but the things he had achieved—the success of his business, the townspeople that loved him, the children he had snatched without trace or repercussion—could also be attributed to guile. He was a fox. A smokescreen. A walking illusion. These people watched the news and read the papers. They knew about the missing children, and had not the first clue that he was responsible. Veneers and façades. They shook his hand and called him a friend.

Right on cue, as if he were aligned with the cosmos, the TVs tuned to CNN flashed photographs of Ethan Mitchell and Courtney Bryce. All smiles and big eyes. The happiest kids in the land when those photos were taken, but deep inside the mountain now, and never to smile again. The TVs were muted, but Oliver didn't need sound to know what the report was about. New Jersey and Pennsylvania cops had compared what scant notes they had to see if there was any correlation in the children's disappearance. They had nothing, though. Oliver had covered his tracks and nobody could touch him. Even Sheriff Tansy, sitting directly to his right, looked at the screen, then dropped his ignorant gaze to Oliver and nodded.

"Think you're one step ahead, don't you?"

"Always," Oliver said.

"I wouldn't be so sure."

The report ended. Replaced by a commercial for United Airlines.

"All-in," Oliver said.

"Son of a bitch." The sheriff looked at him closely, trying to peek beneath the mask. "Think you can scare me?"

He had learned to smile when he realized that he was alone. His childhood was cold water: an ocean in which he was adrift, occasionally riding crests, more often being pulled under. Mom and Dad were distant islands, always out of reach, no matter how hard he swam. His mother's island was full of withered plants. His father's was a wedge of grey rocks, hammered constantly with rain. Oliver was dragged and swept between the two, and eventually learned to look not east or west, but *up*. The sun burned and shimmered. He smiled and found his own atoll. White sand and glimmering coral. He pulled himself ashore and grew.

His mother took ill when he was twenty-four. Terminal cancer. Her island crumbled and within a matter of weeks was swept away by the ocean. Oliver thought the old man would follow soon after. Not from a broken heart—Jesus, no—but because he smoked sixty cigarettes a day and often coughed yellow and black wads of phlegm into his fist. He was known to imbibe, too, and recklessly. Still, the old man's island was as tough as it appeared, and he was still alive to this day. Oliver gave the impression of caring very much for him, but this was purely to bolster his impeccable image. Heaven forbid the town should think him uncaring. He visited often. An hour of acrimony, three times a week.

You're going straight to hell, the old man had said to him recently. Sixty-seven years old. A Vietnam vet who'd lost his right eye in the Battle of Khe Sanh, and his sensibility and hope in everything that came afterward. *You can't pull the wool over the devil's eyes. He's going to ride you like a goddamn surfboard.*

And you'll be right beside me, Oliver had said.

Alone in his ocean. A smile-shaped atoll. No friends, only certain individuals he could abide more than others, like Sheriff Tansy (always good to have the law in your corner) and the rest of the guys he played poker with on Thursday nights. Then there was Tina Quinn, who hated everyone (just like him), but still had certain urges (just like him). She was as dirty as a barn floor, too—would have him shoot his spooge on Oreos and gobble them down like the Cookie Monster.

He smiled endlessly, beautifully. He supported local businesses and gave generously to charity. People stopped in the street to talk to him. Old ladies hugged him. He had a plaque on a bench in Blueberry Bush Park. In 2006, Mayor Woolens awarded him the Key to Point Hollow after his handsome donation helped keep the doors of Rising Pine Elementary open.

Everybody loved him.

Oliver looked up from his cards and caught Bobby Alexander's gaze.

Well, *almost* everybody.

"Okay," Sheriff Tansy said. His eyes flicked from his cards to his chips. He licked his lips and nodded. "All-in. Do or die."

"Do or die," Oliver said, and showed his cards. "Trip-threes."

"Son of a buck," the sheriff groaned, setting down two pairs— queens and tens. He pushed the remainder of his chips toward Oliver, shaking his head, half smiling. The other guys hooted, guzzling beer, smearing drips from their chins. Oliver nodded and grinned and hated them all.

"Nice knowing you, Sheriff," he said.

Sheriff Tansy shrugged. "The devil's children have the devil's luck."

Oliver made horns of his forefingers and held them to his head, then flipped the cards and the dealer button to Gray, and displayed his perfect smile.

Fleetwood Mac on the jukebox, and Drunken Debbie danced alone. It was after midnight and the guys had gone home (the sheriff weaving drunkenly away in his cruiser). The Rack was almost empty—just a few midnight cowboys, those without families to return to, or jobs to wake up for. They slouched at the bar staring into their drinks. The TVs had been switched off. The neon beer signs in the windows were cold and dark.

One for the road.

"Jack Daniel's," Oliver said. "Drop of water, a little ice."

Bobby Alexander sat on the other side of the horseshoe. Normally, Oliver would ignore him, but he'd had a few drinks and his restraint had slipped a gear. He looked up and their eyes clashed.

"You don't like me much, do you?"

Bobby's brow furrowed beneath the peak of his Mets cap. He sighed, chest trembling, opened his mouth, but said nothing.

"I see you around town," Oliver pressed. "Big old Bobby Bear, so friendly with everybody else—stopping to say hello, helping the old folks with their groceries. Makes me wonder why I'm so different . . . what it is about me that you don't like."

Bobby sipped his Pepsi-Cola. He was a big guy—six-four with a copper brush cut and a belly that sagged between his open legs. His hands were scuffed and scarred; he used to work at the mill until a heart attack—last summer, and only thirty-five years old—slowed him down. Now he sorted mail at the post office.

"Maybe it's because our personalities rub," he said, shrugging his heavy shoulders. "Or maybe it's because you're . . . well, *distant*."

"Distant?"

Bobby nodded.

"I think most people would disagree with you," Oliver said. "I think they would argue that my integrity, and my constant giving-back to the community, are not the actions of a distant man."

"And don't forget the fact that you built your house two miles away." Bobby took another sip of Pepsi. His gaze met Oliver's, then flicked away. "On a hill. So that you can look down on us?"

"Is that what you think?"

"Yeah, that's what I think."

The jukebox fell silent but Drunken Debbie kept dancing. Her fly was unbuttoned. She had red wine stains on her blouse. She mumbled something, staggered, and jigged to the melody in her head. Oliver gave Jesse, the bartender, a twenty and told him to make sure Debbie made it home okay. "Call a cab or drive her yourself."

"You've got a heart of gold, Mr. Wray."

Oliver winked and finished his drink.

Bobby stared at him.

"You really are a bitter man," Oliver said.

"Maybe I'm just a curious man."

"Surely curiosity requires a modicum of intelligence?"

Bobby offered a dry smile. "You shouldn't underestimate me."

"You give me no reason to do otherwise."

"So you're not looking down on us?"

"It's not in my nature," Oliver said. "You heard Jesse—I've got a heart of gold."

"Then what *are* you doing up there?" Bobby looked at him squarely, his small eyes almost lost in the folds of his face. "What's so special— so *secret*—that you couldn't have built your ivory tower a little closer? On that scratch of land at the north end of Jefferson Avenue, maybe, among the people you love so much."

"I'm closer to nature up there," Oliver said. "It helps keep me pure."

"I'm not buying it."

"Good, because you probably couldn't afford it." Oliver slipped off the barstool and stepped around the horseshoe. He leaned close to Bobby, and whispered so that no one else heard. "Look at you: fat as fuck and one heart attack closer to the grave. You won't live to be fifty, I bet, and you'll never have a penny to scratch your fat ass with. The only reason you don't like me is because I've got everything and you've got nothing. You're just an overweight prick seething with envy."

Bobby's lips trembled. "Looks like I touched a nerve."

"You'll never touch anything of mine." Oliver said. He imagined the mountain's darkness and threw it all on top of Bobby Alexander. "You'll never come close."

He turned around and left the Rack before anybody saw the smile crash from his face. The night air was warm and still, thick with the scent of trees. He stepped out of the streetlight and crossed the road to his car. Gunned the engine and screeched down Main—ran the red light at the Grace Road intersection and didn't even notice. He made it home in under three minutes, furious at himself for letting Bobby get under his skin. To make matters worse, he'd lost his cool, lowered his mask. So *foolish*. The kind of reaction that could raise suspicion and get him caught.

Oliver killed the ignition and stepped out of his car. Just being here—home, among the trees, where he belonged—filled him with calm. Several deep breaths and Bobby faded from his mind. Several more and he was smiling again.

———————

Two o'clock in the morning. Oliver sat on the rear deck and revelled in the silence. He let it drape over him like the perfect woman, who could touch him in every place he needed to be touched, and draw from him the seed of his nature, and make it flower. Was this the beginning of a new life, in the shadow of Abraham's Faith, but not in its service?

He could only hope.

It hulked in the east, satiated, its belly filled with children. He had failed it only once, but he had been young then. Unready. When the mountain called again he had answered, albeit reluctantly. It had rewarded him with a long period of silence, and he had flourished.

He looked at the stars. Billions strong. A porous night. It was just as silent down here. The town, two miles distant, was a splash of light, as if some of the stars had fallen. Nothing stirred, not even the trees. Oliver clutched his chest and felt his heart vibrate through the small bones in his hand.

Such moments needed to be embraced. So many people took this peace and stillness for granted, but it was during these periods that he learned his world and developed his public image. He moved in and out of love, first with a sensuous, green-eyed beauty from Rochester—a photographer named Amber Beale who captured his heart in flashes. She had spooned with his soul and, with her touch and her pictures, shown him a universe beyond God's Footprint. His second love was an older woman—married—who, with her authority, had found his weakness for being used. She had left upon his body the belt marks of her passion, and the pain was like a flame in the night. He had cried like a dog when they parted, but the mountain had scooped him into one stony fist and used him like no woman ever could.

His business, Manta-Wray Design, started out small, but boomed as the world moved into the computer age. He learned every program on the market, and soon had the credentials—and the guile—to approach affluent companies in the northeast states. His client base expanded. He rented office space in New York City and employed a small team of graphic designers. The next stop was the west coast, and then the world. Manta-Wray Design currently employed one hundred and fifteen people, and had offices in North America and Europe.

Oliver looked toward the mountain, feeling its dark pressure. He hated it. Loved it. A strict yet giving father.

He yawned and slipped into light sleep, only for an hour or so, but he woke with a skin of sweat on his forehead and a blunt pain in his lower back. He stood up and stretched. The world remained deep and silent, only the sound of his body creaking. Wiping his eyes, he stepped inside, flicking off lights on his way to bed. He had built this house six years ago, secluded among the trees. It was open plan, ultramodern, lots of glass. There were no pictures on the walls. No plants or pets. Some would consider it sterile. A few of his guests had commented—tactfully, to their credit—on the absence of life, to which Oliver always replied: *Look out the window, and you'll see all the life you can handle*. He walked down the hallway, stopping briefly in his study to write in his journal: *July 29, 2010: Four days of silence, and I am elated*. He turned off his computer and reached to flick off the lamp on his desk, but his hand diverted to a folder sitting atop a pile of invoices. He flipped it open. There was an old black and white photograph inside. A reprint. He took it out and stared at it.

"Man of the mountain," he said. "Original me." He brushed one finger over the man in the photograph. "Who are you?"

The mountain had been silenced. Perhaps forever. . mystery continued to elude him, but he felt he was g The people of Point Hollow couldn't (or wouldn't) hel libraries offered scant, irrelevant information. But the Int impossible to censor. He found out a little more about Point Hu past. A church fire in 1923 that killed eighteen people. A shoo in 1953—six dead. A mass suicide in 1971, and Point Hollow population was thirteen souls smaller. Old Kip Sawyer hadn't mentioned any of this when Oliver had asked him what was wrong with the town. *Nobody* had mentioned it. Even Sheriff Tansy—who was supposed to be his friend—had glossed over it all, suggesting that selective disclosure was one of the benefits of life in a small town. In other words, there were no records of these incidents. They had been covered up.

But why?

Despite the hours he had spent surfing, he found only one small thing he could link to the children in the mountain: this photograph. He had pulled it from a website that chronicled the history of the Catskill Mountains. It was not particularly remarkable, but it had snatched Oliver's attention immediately.

The man in the photograph looked to be in his mid- to late-thirties, but it was difficult to tell with such an old print; he could easily have been in his early twenties. He wore charcoal clothes and had a mess of dark hair. His face was a pale smudge, his eyes a cluster of characterless pixels. Only his mouth indicated emotion: a thin, hooked smile. No, it was a *leer*. Too creepy to be a smile. He had three children with him, aged somewhere between four and eight years old. The caption that accompanied the photograph read: *Family fun in the Catskills. Date/photographer unknown.* However, the children's expressions challenged the notion of "family fun." Even though the quality was not good, Oliver could see that they were terrified . . . crying.

But the thing that caught Oliver's attention was behind the man and the children: sloping, jagged rock face divided by a zigzag opening. Oliver recognized it in a heartbeat. It was *his* opening. *His* mountain.

Oliver imagined the photograph being taken (he'd had it dated to the early twentieth century, judging from the garments and hairstyles, although it was impossible to be specific) just moments before the leering, smudge-faced man led the terrified children into the mountain, where they would remain forever, turning slowly to bones.

"Who are you?" Oliver asked again. He touched his leering mouth, trailing his finger down to the children's frightened faces. "What did you do?"

Silence.

Still.

Original me, Oliver thought. He slipped the photograph back into the folder, placed it on his desk, and flicked off the lamp. He walked, in darkness, to the hallway, and then to his bedroom, where he stripped naked and swayed between the covers like air. He fell asleep in moments and dreamed about the horizon.

CHAPTER
FIVE

Point Hollow was one hundred and twenty miles north of Bay Ridge, Brooklyn. Once clear of the metropolitan miasma, it became a carefree, relaxing drive—into the Hudson Valley, suddenly surrounded by trees and granite face, rather than concrete buildings and overpasses. Matthew had rented a car (a gutless four-banger—damn Kirsty to hell for taking the Altima, along with everything else). He drove with one hand on the wheel and the window open, singing along to his Bee Gees CD. Sunlight flashed off his prescription sunglasses, and he actually felt good, for the first time in weeks, despite the fact that he didn't know what Point Hollow had in store for him.

The good feeling didn't last. What should have been a calming three-hour drive turned into a five-hour clusterfuck. By the time Matthew arrived in Point Hollow, his head was thumping and he had blood on his hands.

The most frustrating thing was that he was so close to Point Hollow when it happened. Ten minutes away, at most. He had turned off NY 17 and was navigating the narrow roads leading deeper into the Catskills. Impressive trees towered on both sides, throwing broad shadows across the blacktop. He may have been singing too loud, or driving a touch too fast, but the deer leapt in front of his car with demented abandon, out of nowhere, and even if he had been paying absolute attention, and driving the speed limit, he would still have hit it.

It was impossible to read the expression in its eyes in the split second before impact. They were wide, black circles. Matthew slapped the brakes but they barely had time to engage before crunch-time, and he wondered if speed would benefit them both—if he might go *through* the unfortunate animal, applying similar physics used when whipping away a tablecloth and leaving the glasses and plates standing.

This was not the case.

Five seconds of noise and confusion. Terrific impact, as if a brick of C-4 had detonated under the hood. Matthew was thrown forward, shuddering under a thunderclap of sound, his prescription sunglasses flying off as the seatbelt lashed against his chest. The car slid into the opposite lane, brakes hissing. The hood buckled. The windshield cracked. Matthew glimpsed, in his peripheral vision, the deer pirouetting wildly along the passenger side, clobbering off various panels. The car rattled to a halt and for a long moment the only sound was the Bee Gees singing—with noted irony—about staying alive.

"Jesus *Christ!*" Matthew killed the engine, unclipped his seatbelt, and wobbled out of the car. He took his regular glasses from his breast pocket and slipped them on, then toured the front end to assess damage. Not good. Lots of shattered pieces and exposed parts. The passenger-side doors looked like they had been trampled by stampeding bulls. Matthew pushed his hands through his hair and gazed up and down the road. Quiet. No other vehicles. The deer lay in the middle of the eastbound lane. He saw one of its front legs twitching. Lots of blood.

"Oh, Jesus," he said. His hands were trembling again. He clenched them into fists. The deer snorted, pained and confused, lifting its head. It was trying to get up.

You know what you have to do, he thought, and shuddered. *Put it out of its misery.*

"I can't do that," he whispered to the empty road.

The deer looked at Matthew and he turned his back on it. The road was a silent grey ribbon, trees on either side, everything still. He remembered (and it came out of nowhere, like a piano falling from the sky) that his father always called this—the road leading into Point Hollow—the Dead Road.

Matthew glanced over his shoulder. The deer still looked at him. Huge eyes. Huge *hurting* eyes. It jerked and blinked. One of its rear legs was attached by a thin, furry strip of meat. It tried, once again, to get up, but could only paw pathetically at the air. It made a long mooing sound—possibly the cervine equivalent of a scream—that vibrated through Matthew, presenting thick chills that started in the vicinity of his anus and ascended promptly to his scalp.

"Don't *look* at me," he said.

It looked at him. Blood everywhere.

Kill it.

"I can't," Matthew said. "What am I going to do? Strangle it with my bare hands? Perform the Vulcan Death Grip?"

Just grab its head and give it a one-eighty, the darkness in his head grated. *Wait until you hear the crack.*

"Not going to happen." He shook his head firmly.

A car approached from the direction of Point Hollow and Matthew turned to face it with a desperate expression on his face. It slowed as it approached, pulling around the crippled rental and stopping alongside him. The passenger window buzzed down. The driver was old enough to outlive his children, sitting on a booster cushion to help him see over the steering wheel.

"Hit a deer, huh?" he asked, running his glasses up the bridge of his nose with one crinkly forefinger.

Matthew gawped at him, unable to reply. His trembling hands made puppet-like gestures toward the shattered front end of the rental, and then to the dying deer in the road.

"Yeah, you did," the old man said, as if Matthew needed it confirmed.

"It came out of nowhere," Matthew said.

"You can't help bad luck," the old man said. His rheumy eyes widened behind his glasses. "She's still kicking, huh?"

Matthew nodded. "Still alive, yes."

"Poor bitch," he said.

"Do you have any suggestions?" Matthew asked, looking hopefully at the old man "Do you know any farmers or hunters? Someone who might . . . you know, put it out of its misery?"

"I had a gun once," he replied. "In the sixties."

"Okay."

"She was a beaut. A twenty-two. Shot a raccoon once, nosing through the trash. Little bastard. Mary gave me three kinds of hell for that one."

"Okay," Matthew said again, nodding, frowning. *What the fuck?* "But do you know anyone who—?"

"Well, good luck," the old man said, and then the window buzzed up, ending their strange conversation. He drove away, steering between the rental and the deer, back onto his side of the road. Matthew watched his taillights disappear.

The deer bleated. Matthew covered his face and groaned. Silence descended. The sun danced behind a cloud and then broke again, beating red wings against his hands. After a few moments he gained a bead of composure and clung to it. He looked at the Dead Road. It hadn't changed. Shades of grey and green beneath the blue pall of sky. The rental oozed loose parts. The deer strained and worked for life.

He walked toward it. Its eyes snapped open and closed. He couldn't look into them. That was too much. Not that it was any easier looking at its body. A sack of broken bones. An L-shaped spine. It lifted one foreleg and stretched it toward him, as if it were reaching for help.

"I'm sorry," he said. "I can't."

But could he? How hard would it be to reach down, place one hand beneath its jaw, the other on the curve of its skull, and twist? Two seconds. Minimal effort. Like loosening the lugs on a wheel rim. His mind painted an easy picture, but he had always been able to spill blood in his mind (Kirsty's blood, specifically—God bless the pressure release). But in the real world . . . not so simple. Matthew turned away and closed his eyes. He took a moment to think this through, and resolved to call the police. Let them deal with it. Then he would call the rental company. They'd send a wrecker, provide him with a replacement vehicle, and he'd be rolling again. No problem. No sweat.

He shuffled back to the car, grabbed his BlackBerry, and dialed 911. The dispatcher told Matthew that an officer would be on the scene as soon as possible. Matthew hung up, thinking that "on the scene" sounded somewhat ominous, as if some terrible crime had occurred.

Still, that was one problem dealt with. Matthew hoped the police would arrive quickly, but didn't think they would—not because a dead (or not *quite* dead) deer would be considered low priority, but because this was the backwoods, where "quick" was not a way of life. He couldn't sweat it, though. It wasn't his problem anymore. The Podunk Police could take their sweet time, but Matthew was only prepared to hang around for as long as it took the wrecker to arrive.

He fished the rental agreement from the glovebox and dialed the appropriate number. After several minutes of automated frustration, he finally got to speak with a representative, and had just started to explain what had happened when a white police cruiser rolled toward him, sunlight bouncing off its windshield, HOLLOW COUNTY SHERIFF painted on the door. *Jesus, that was quick,* Matthew thought. He raised his hand to the sheriff as the cruiser slipped by, then gestured at the phone and flipped two fingers to indicate that he would be a couple of minutes. The sheriff nodded from behind the wheel, parked his cruiser in front of the deer, and flicked on his lightbar.

Slightly more than a couple of minutes, as it turned out. Matthew gave (and repeated) required information, wiping sweat from his brow, stealing glances at the sheriff to see what was going on. He couldn't see the deer because the cruiser was in the way, but the sheriff was standing with his hat cocked back on his head, hands on his hips, staring down at the unfortunate animal. *It must have died already*, Matthew thought. *He's waiting for me to finish on the phone so I can help drag it to the side of the road.* Finally he hung up, tossed the phone onto the passenger seat, and walked over to the sheriff.

"Sorry about that, Sheriff, you came a little quicker than—" Matthew's throat locked, allowing only broken sounds through. He had stepped around the hood of the cruiser, his eye drawn to the deer, seeing that it was still alive, after all. It blinked rapidly, foamy blood caked around its nostrils, one leg twitching.

"No problemo, amigo," the sheriff said. "I got all the time in the world."

Matthew took a step back. He needed the support of the cruiser's front fender to keep his legs from folding beneath him. "What—?" His throat jammed again and he shook his head. How long had he been on the phone? Six or seven minutes, at least, and all that time the sheriff had been standing here—hands on hips and gun in holster—watching the animal suffer.

"Jesus," he said. The word pounced out of him, breaking through his constricted windpipe. He looked at the sheriff with stricken eyes.

"Bitch of a day, huh?" the sheriff asked cheerfully.

Matthew blinked hard and gave his head another little shake. "You could say that."

"Well, you won't get much sympathy from her," the sheriff said, and—incredibly—kicked the deer. Not hard, but enough to make it jerk and look at him. Matthew felt a ripple of nausea roll through his stomach. He looked away—stared at the red and blue lights whirling on the cruiser's roof.

This isn't right, he thought. *I know they do things differently upstate, but holy God, this just isn't right.* He took a deep breath, counted slowly to three, and turned back to the sheriff.

"It happened about twenty minutes ago," he said, not able to look the sheriff in the eye. "Maybe thirty, I'm not sure. But it's been suffering for a long time, and I think—"

"You been drinking?" the sheriff asked. His voice had all the delicacy of a blunt axe.

"What?" Now Matthew *did* look him in the eye, to better express honesty, but also to gauge the earnestness of the sheriff's question. "Of course not. Jesus Christ."

"You sure?" the sheriff pressed. "You look a little glassy-eyed."

"I just hit a deer," Matthew said, his voice tight with tension. "Fucking thing came out of nowhere. I'm dazed . . . upset."

"Watch your tongue," the sheriff said. He took a step toward Matthew and leaned close (having to stoop, being a good six inches taller). He wrinkled his nose, testing Matthew's breath. The hairs in his nostrils trembled. Nodding, apparently satisfied, he retreated a step and directed his attention to the dying deer.

"It's a crying shame," he said, "that God made one of his most beautiful creatures so damn stupid. Look at her: pretty as they come, but a brain like a catch rag."

"She doesn't look pretty at the moment," Matthew said. "She looks in pain."

"Get dead deer on this road all the time," the sheriff went on. "Here and Boulder Pass, between Oak Creek and Wharton. It's like a goddamn horror movie some mornings. Blood and shit all over. You'd think they'd learn, huh?"

Matthew shrugged. His temples were throbbing.

"I'm not usually called out, of course." The sheriff looked at Matthew and smiled. "Country folk know how to take care of their own."

"I'm sure," Matthew said.

"I see the decals on that Jap rental you're driving," he said, nodding toward it with a distasteful expression on his face. "Brooklyn, huh? What brings you to our little slice of the pie?"

"I used to live here," Matthew replied. "A long time ago."

"Hollow County?"

"Yes. Point Hollow."

"That so?"

"Yes, sir."

The sheriff's stony eyes glittered in the shadow cast by his Stetson. He was broad as well as tall, with thick wrists and handfuls of flab spilling over his belt. There was a stain on the front of his shirt—blueberry jelly, or something—and rings of sweat beneath his arms. The name on the thin gold bar pinned to his chest read, TANSY. His nose was crooked, clouded with ruptured capillaries, and the cleft in his chin was deep enough to lodge a nickel in.

"What's your name?" he asked.

"Matthew Bridge."

"Bridge . . . ?" He looked at the dying deer while turning the name over in his head.

"My father was Peter Bridge," Matthew said. "He was an accountant at the mill."

Sheriff Tansy nodded and snapped his fingers. "I remember. Pete the Jew."

"We're not Jewish."

"I know that, but we called him Pete the Jew, anyway. Good with money. Went off to seek his fortune in the Big Apple, right?"

"That's right."

"Another flyaway. But then, he never did jig with the town."

The deer moaned, flicking its eyes from Matthew to the sheriff. Even its ears were trembling. Matthew looked at it, nervously rubbing his beard. How long were they going to stand here, making idle chat, while the deer bled and suffered?

"Do you think we could—?" he started, pointing at the deer, but the sheriff's voice bulldozed through the end of his sentence.

"Shit, you're the kid that got lost in the woods." He snapped his fingers again. His face wore the surprised, expectant expression of a man who has revealed three matching numbers on a scratch card.

Matthew nodded. "You remember that, huh?"

"I was part of the search party," Sheriff Tansy stated proudly. "That was what . . . eighty-three, eighty-four?"

"Eighty-four," Matthew said. "Listen, can we—?"

"We thought for sure you were dead as dogshit. We half expected to find you mauled by bears, or lying at the bottom of Abraham's Faith."

Matthew blinked, shook his head. He hadn't thought about Abraham's Faith since leaving Point Hollow, but now it towered in his mind again. And there was something else—a feeling, more than a memory, that he couldn't quite grasp. Frail images, possibly dream fragments, trailed across his consciousness. He shuddered, suddenly cold, despite the heat.

"—coming for you, then?" Matthew caught only the tail end of Sheriff Tansy's question.

"I'm sorry?" He hugged himself, feeling the ripple of gooseflesh on his forearms.

"I said, this is something of a homecoming for you, then?"

"Yes," Matthew replied. "Something like that."

The deer had fallen still, no longer bleating or pawing with its foreleg. Its wide black eyes continued to blink, though, reflecting the blank sky and the two men that stood watching it die.

"Not even across the town line and you're already making trouble." Sheriff Tansy grinned and booted the deer's rump once again. It made a hurt sound and showed its teeth. "Maybe you should have stayed away."

Matthew winced. "No maybe about it."

"Let's see if we can help you out, then."

Thank God, Matthew thought.

Sheriff Tansy sleeved sweat from his brow. "Boy, you surely knocked the beans out of her chili."

Matthew rolled his eyes. "Yeah, it's in a lot of pain."

"It's a *she*," Tansy said. "A doe. Beautiful, too."

"Okay. Sure. Whatever."

"A whitetail," Tansy continued. "About six years old."

"Maybe we can spare the life story," Matthew said, "and just get this over with."

"Sounds good to me," Sheriff Tansy agreed. He unclipped his holster and drew his gun. It was fat and black, too dull to catch even a bead of sunlight. The sheriff passed it from one hand to the other, as if measuring its weight.

"Right," Matthew said, and a trickle of sweat stung his left eye. "You're going to shoot it—*her*. Yes . . . I knew that. Okay."

"I'm not going to shoot her," the sheriff said. "You are."

Matthew knuckled the sweat from his eye and looked at the sheriff, trying to calculate, again, his level of earnestness.

The sheriff stared back with a serious expression.

"This is a joke, right?" Matthew said.

"No joke," Tansy said. "You ever fire a handgun before?"

"No," Matthew replied quickly. "And that's not about to change."

"Nothing to it." Tansy's eyes gleamed, small and bright. "Every God-fearing American should fire a gun at least once in their life. Now's your time to shine."

Matthew tried to smile. His lips twitched and trembled, presenting an expression closer to grief. "While I appreciate your wanting to expand my cultural vistas, I really don't think this is the best time for me to handle a lethal weapon."

"You'll be fine."

"Look at my hands," Matthew argued. "They're *trembling*. I could shoot my foot off."

"Uh-huh." Sheriff Tansy nodded, removed the magazine, checked it, and slid it back into the shaft. "This is a Glock 20. She's a 10mm, and more power than you need, so don't be holding her like a pussy."

"I'm not going to be holding her at all."

"Keep your arms straight, but relaxed, with your firing hand around the grip and your weak hand securing from beneath—not behind the slide."

"The slide?"

"Right." He tapped the top of the gun. "The slide. She'll rip back when you pull the trigger, and you'll lose a good part of your hand if it's in the way."

"Listen, I'm not—"

The deer interrupted him, piercing to the bone with another of those harrowing moos. Matthew shuddered and looked at it. Still broken. Still bleeding. Still suffering. Blood trickled around his sneakers and he stepped back with a little gasp.

"She's hurting," the sheriff said.

"Shoot her, then," Matthew said.

"You've been gone a long time. We take care of our own in Point Hollow."

"This is insane." Matthew uttered a cracked, nervous laugh. "You know, I left the city to get away from . . . *everything* for just a few lousy days. I'm not—"

"Listen carefully," Sheriff Tansy said, driving through Matthew's words the same way Matthew had driven through the deer. "When I hand her to you, she'll be live, which means there'll be a round in her chamber. Now, there's no conventional safety—no levers or buttons. The safety is built into her trigger. So keep your finger away from it until you are absolutely one hundred percent ready to shoot. Do you understand?"

"I understand, but—"

"Good." He yanked back the slide. Matthew imagined a slick 10mm round hopping out of the magazine and into the chamber.

"I'm not doing this."

Sheriff Tansy laid the gun flat on his palm and held it out.

Matthew shook his head.

"Take the gun."

He wiped sweat from his brow and, for some incredibly stupid reason, said, "I work in Internet marketing."

"Whoopee for you. Take the gun." Tansy nodded at the dying animal. "Take care of your own."

Matthew looked at the gun. Compact and black. He had a sudden vision of letting himself into the house he shared with Kirsty, creeping up the stairs, toward the sex opera booming in the bedroom—*his* bedroom. Opening the door to find Kirsty doing the reverse cowgirl on one of her young co-workers. Hips grinding. Pussy shaved clean. Too lost to notice him pulling the Glock 20 from inside his jacket. 10mm. Arms straight, but relaxed. Firing hand around the grip. Weak hand supporting from beneath. Bang. One shot. More power than he needed. Most of Kirsty's head sliding down the wall, only two shades brighter than the paint they had bought at Benjamin Moore.

He took the gun.

"There," Sheriff Tansy said. "How does that feel?"

"I'm scared," Matthew said.

"You're *pumped*," Tansy said. "That's seventy thousand amps of pure adrenaline bolting through your system. Now all you have to do is channel it, push it all into one bullet, and let yourself glow."

"Glow, huh?" Matthew curled his fingers around the grip, somewhat mesmerized by its cool, deadly feel. It was lighter than he thought it would be, and the fact that it could do so much damage—that it could end lives, whole *lives*—was staggering.

"Feels good, huh?" Sheriff Tansy said.

Matthew nodded.

The sheriff laughed. He removed his hat, ran one thick hand through his hair, then popped the hat back on, slightly askew.

The deer grunted. Its ruined body twitched.

"Now, remember what I told you." The sheriff made a pistol out of his fingers and pointed it at the deer, demonstrating arm and hand position. "Relaxed, but firm." He mimicked pulling the trigger. "One shot."

"Right," Matthew pointed the gun at the deer. "Head shot?"

"Head shot."

"What if I miss?"

"There are fifteen more rounds in the mag."

"Right. Okay." Matthew's skin prickled. He aimed at the deer's blinking eye, looped his finger around the trigger.

"Easy she goes," the sheriff said.

"I'm not sure about this."

"It's all you, city boy. You can do it."

Matthew held his breath. He took up the trigger slack—felt the biting point.

I can do this, he thought, and applied a little more pressure, waiting for the gun to snap in his hand. *I can—*

And all at once the world was spinning. A cowl of nausea wrapped around him and the gun became a block of lead, too heavy to keep steady. It pulled his arm down—dragged the sights away from the deer's blinking eye.

"No," he said, shaking his head.

"Jesus and Moses," the sheriff said. He took the pistol from Matthew, aimed it at the deer, and—as casually as lighting a

Zippo—pulled the trigger. The gun kicked in his hands as if electricity, rather than a bullet, had passed through the barrel. Half of the deer's head disappeared in a drizzle of red. Blood and pieces of bone peppered his pants.

It—*she*—wasn't in pain anymore.

Matthew stumbled to the side of the road and leaned over, hands on knees, sucking in huge breaths. The world revolved in a series of soft-edged shapes, and all he wanted was to lie down—to sleep and wake up in a different place, a different time. Long minutes passed, dragging their feet. He eventually stood and looked at the trees. The lights whirling atop the cruiser pulsed in his eyes like a visual headache. He heard the sheriff talking on his cell phone:

"—out here while she's still warm. On twenty-three, about five miles out of town. Not much left of her head, but her ass is still good for the grill."

I didn't just hear that, Matthew thought.

"I'll be over at nine-thirty, Gray. Pabst in hand. You just fire up the jets." The sheriff chuckled, hung up, and tossed his cell phone through the open window of his cruiser. He turned to Matthew, the mirthful expression falling from his face as if the elastic holding it in place had snapped.

"Okay," he said, pointing at the deer. "Let's haul her ass out of the road."

"Right," Matthew said distantly.

The sheriff hunkered down, grabbed the deer's forelegs, and nodded for Matthew to take the rear. Matthew flexed his fingers, tiptoeing through the blood, looking for a position to crouch and take hold.

"Bearded Christ, she's not going to bite you." Sheriff Tansy's eyes flickered impatiently. "Grab a handy-hold, city boy. I got places to be."

"But there's only one . . ." Matthew made qualmish motions toward the leg that was joined only by a thread of meat. "I can't . . ."

The sheriff shook his head and shuffled to the deer's rear end. He wrapped both hands around the one firm leg. Matthew stepped around him, leaned over, and sheepishly grabbed the forelegs. *My God, they're still warm,* he thought. *They still feel alive.* A streak of blood painted his palm and bubbled through the cracks of his fingers.

"On three," Sheriff Tansy growled. "One, two—"

They pulled. The animal's dead weight sickened Matthew, but worse was the sound—the *feel*—of it scraping across the blacktop, leaving a broad smear of blood. Matthew turned away, but not before seeing the mostly severed leg separate from the body.

"Almost there," the sheriff said. "One good heave."

After they had dragged the deer to the grass verge, the sheriff grabbed the severed leg and tossed it into the woods. He could have placed it with the rest of the body, but he decided to launch it, like a man throwing a stick for a dog to fetch. The leg flew end-over-end (not unlike a stick) and clattered among the branches, out of sight.

"Job done," the sheriff said, wiping his hands down the front of his shirt.

Matthew gasped. He felt sick and dirty. He wanted to step into a shower so hot that it would strip at least three layers of skin from his body.

"Thanks," he uttered.

"Just doing my job," the sheriff said. "I'd liked to have seen you pull the trigger, but . . ." He slapped Matthew on the back, a largely sympathetic gesture. *Okay, so you got nothing in your sack but a couple of dry old beans and some lint, but don't let it get you down.* Matthew opened his mouth, but had nothing to say.

"Adios, amigo," Tansy said, strutting back to his cruiser. "Maybe I'll see you in town, if you're staying a while."

Matthew nodded. Sweat trickled down his face. He wanted to wipe it away, but didn't want to touch himself.

The cruiser's lightbar whirled and throbbed and Tansy gave the siren an unnecessary three-second blast, perhaps in celebration of testosterone and good old country grit. He swept the cruiser around. Its rear tires splashed through the blood and dragged it across the blacktop, as if marking the occasion, like Zorro.

Matthew watched the cruiser disappear in the direction of Point Hollow, swallowed by a curve in the road.

Yeah, adios, amigo, he thought. *Let's hope that's the last I see of you.*

He trudged wearily to the rental and waited for the wrecker to arrive.

———

It was almost ten P.M. by the time Matthew arrived in Point Hollow. The town was dark and quiet. He drove directly to the Super 8 on Main Street, where he checked into a room, grabbed a much-needed shower, and slept for twelve hours.

CHAPTER
SIX

The lost memories were like
remnants inhumed by the
strata of time and repression,
and only a disturbance would
bring them to the surface. Same
for everyone, Matthew knew. No
person has total recollection. But he
wondered how many people had great
swathes of memory missing. It felt like his
childhood was a chalkboard that had been hurriedly
wiped, leaving pale smears and spectral half-words. His
aim, returning to Point Hollow, was to disinter—to disturb.
He knew there'd be ghosts, and that the weight of years would
shift with a dry sound, like old bones crumbling.

———————

He felt okay. Not great, perhaps, but positive. His sleep had been
disjointed, filled with dark rumbling and images of the deer. He
kept seeing the sheriff tossing the severed leg into the woods,
and the broad leaf of blood that had unfolded on the road. The
air conditioner in his room squeaked, and his sleep converted

this to the deer's constant, pained gasps (he eventually got out of bed, turned off the A/C, and slept, coated in sweat, on top of the covers). An unsettled night, certainly, but even so he felt . . . *okay*. Maybe it was because the sun was blazing and the air was impossibly fresh. Or maybe it was because he was away from the city—from Kirsty—and intent on lighting the darkness. A few days in Point Hollow, surrounded by ghosts and memories, and by the woods he had been lost in. When he returned to the city, and met with Kirsty to discuss their future, she would see a different man—perhaps one she didn't wholly recognize. It might not be enough to save their marriage, but Matthew thought it might save *him*.

He walked along Main Street, inhaling the clean air and feeling the morning sun on his shoulders. It hadn't changed much, from what he remembered. The Super 8 had replaced the flea market—a massive, barn-like structure that Matthew recalled walking around, handling curios that looked like they had fallen through portals in time, while his mother snapped at him to not break anything. *The Scratch*, Matthew thought, the name falling into place with a tiny click. *That's what it was called. How could I have forgotten that?* There were a couple of new franchise stores: a McDonald's (of course) and a Starbucks (of course), the latter having muscled out Cuppa Joe's. *Dad used to say they serve the best coffee in the country, and their chocolate chip muffins . . . made in heaven, I swear to God.* The water tower had been pulled down—a redundant, rusty structure, Matthew recalled. The fountain standing in its place was far more pleasing to the eye.

Another change brought a surprising pang of regret: walking past Buzzcut Billy's, Matthew had looked through the window, fully expecting to see old Buzzcut snipping away, but instead saw rows of footwear; the barbershop where he'd had the first forty-or-so haircuts of his life was now a shoe store. He figured that Buzzcut—who must have been eighty when he was cutting Matthew's hair—had passed away, joining the Scratch and the water tower in the pages of the town's history.

If there were other changes, Matthew didn't recognize them.

He walked around like a stranger, for the most part. Main Street was picture-perfect, lined with mom and pop stores that may or may not have been part of the commerce when Matthew left town. The post office, on the corner of Main and Sparrow, was a log cabin, quaint beyond measure, flying the Stars and Stripes, as large as a ship's sail. The library was on the opposite side of the road, a friendly looking building with a porch for reading on and a notice board out front. An elderly lady tended colourful flowers sprayed around the porch, occasionally swatting at a wasp or bee. He looked at the notice board, which was filled with small-town communiqué: a chili cook-off at Blueberry Bush Park on August 8; NASCAR Madness at the Rack—half-price pitchers and free wings during the races; Hollow County Idol, with celebrity judge Aretha Bell from Rise FM. The names and places were not immediately familiar to him. Neither were the Davy Crockett post office and the library. Matthew thought they *should* be, but there was nothing in his mind but a faint shimmer.

This is my hometown, he thought, over and over, as if trying to drill this unlikely truth into his mind. *I spent the first ten years of my life here.* Yet there remained a detachment, despite the things he could remember. It felt like an unrequited friendship—like speaking to an empty room.

The town's beauty was accented by its surrounding scenery: hills and ridges, carpeted with trees like green glaciers, and countless peaks splashed with austere colours. You didn't have to walk far before the sidewalk became woodland trail, and the asphalt became glistening river. Stroll for fifteen minutes in any direction, and you would leave the man-made world behind. No people, no cars, no bricks or streetlights. Simply nature, the sound of the trees and the rich tang of sap. It was breathtaking, and although outdoor groups had discovered Point Hollow's secret and spread the word, it hadn't lost its natural splendour.

And then there was the mountain.

Abraham's Faith, Matthew thought, turning toward it, his eyes squinted, as if it were a loathsome person. A living thing. *I could have gone the rest of my life without thinking about you.*

It had been twenty-six years since he'd looked at the mountain, and he wondered now if it was connected to the darkness inside him—to everything that had gone wrong. He remembered his parents warning him to stay away from it. *Stick to the trails,* they had insisted, because no trail came close to the mountain. He wondered if that was how he'd gotten lost all those years ago. Had he veered from the trails, drawn toward the mystery of Abraham's Faith, like some ill-fated character in a fairy tale?

Matthew shuddered and crossed the street, where the buildings blocked the mountain from view. An idea occurred to him—crazy, no doubt, but it *felt* plausible: that Abraham's Faith exuded a menace that spilled into the town proper; that Point Hollow had taken on its darkness. It was picturesque, certainly, with its quaint storefronts and patriotic bunting, yet there was something *untoward* about the town. Unfriendly, almost. He felt the locals staring at him, imagined their eyes narrowed to reptile-like slits. They glared from the opposite side of the street, from their cars, and from behind store windows, and when he turned to face them they looked quickly away. Maybe he was making something out of nothing—a shade over-sensitive, perhaps, due to him feeling like he didn't belong. They probably weren't staring at all, only curious. Still, his cheerful greetings and smiles were ignored.

And it wasn't just the people; his reflection in every window was distorted, as if there was a subtle ripple in the glass; the shadows were too deep, casting shaped impressions on the walls and sidewalks; and the sounds were *odd,* not all of them, but the traffic—what little there was—sounded the way it would in a tunnel, and Matthew winced when the town hall clock struck eleven, each peal punctuated with a static-like hiss.

My hometown, he thought again, and then shook his head. No, it didn't feel right. He wondered if Point Hollow—this mysterious iota of the world's geography—remembered that he had turned his back on it twenty-six years ago, and refused to forgive him. Had he somehow disturbed its energy pool by returning?

He crossed Jefferson Avenue, festooned with cherry blossoms and stars and stripes, and his gaze was drawn to the east, where

Abraham's Faith squatted beneath a curvature of sky that looked too small.

———

What better place to recapture that hometown feeling than the house you grew up in?

Matthew walked along streets with names like Pawpaw Avenue and Pussy Willow Road, past houses with pastel-coloured siding, comfortably placed on mature lots with white picket fences. Old folks in straw hats and sandals mowed their lawns, some of them scowling as he strolled by, others giving him barely a glance.

He took a few wrong turns, but eventually found his way, and the memories started to trickle through as soon as he turned onto Maple Road—a curved, green belt, basking in the shade of the plentiful trees it was named after.

Matthew had to stop for a moment. His mind flickered, like an old film reel with missing frames, excerpts from a childhood that blanched in the light. He saw himself tearing along the sidewalk on his BMX, believing that, if he went fast enough, he would take off and fly, like Eliott in *E.T.* He heard his sister crying after she had fallen down and grazed her knees. He saw a cluster of boys with tanned, bare backs, carrying patched inner tubes that they used to ride the rapids on Something River—*Gray Rock River,* Matthew thought, and there it was, catching sunlight in his mind. Other fragments: voices and faces that whirled like sand in the wind, and Matthew felt them on his skin, in his eyes.

He walked to one-thirty-eight, his old house. It hadn't changed. A fresh lick of paint, but that was all. It was like looking at a restored photograph. A silver tear curled from the corner of his eye. This was where he had spoken his first words, and taken his first steps. It was where he learned to use the potty, and read, and where the myriad examples set by his parents filtered into his grasping mind. But so what? No big deal. Everybody has to learn to drop their drawers and take a crap, after all.

Only it *was* a big deal, because his bruised soul, and the years he had spent with Kirsty, had left him empty. Standing in the sunlight looking at his old house, Matthew felt those places inside him begin to fill, and he realized—with an emergent feeling not dissimilar to waking—that his marriage was over. He didn't need Kirsty. He was more complete without her.

Matthew snapped his fingers and imagined a small flame, impossibly bright, popping from the tip of his thumb. *I'm lighting the darkness,* he thought. *I'm really doing it.*

He knuckled tears from his eyes and let the memories come. There wasn't a great flood of them, only drips, but frequent and rhythmic, filling the glass bowl of his past, hitherto empty enough to create an echo.

A dog barked in one of the houses across the street. The maples shimmered. Matthew shuffled his feet and his shadow wavered.

CHAPTER
SEVEN

Matthew walked a
different route back to Main
Street, passing the New Hope
Anglican Church on Clover Hill
Road, and turning left on Acorn
Street, where he passed the sheriff's
office. His cruiser was parked outside,
and Matthew got a dose of unwanted
recollection—the episode with the deer spilling through
his mind in its gruesome entirety. He walked a little faster,
imagining the sheriff sitting with his boots (still stained with
the deer's blood) propped on his desk, cramming a blueberry jelly
donut into his crooked mouth.

Acorn met Cicada Avenue, which intersected with Main beside
the shoe store that used to be Buzzcut Billy's. Matthew had planned
to go back to the Super 8, grab a cool shower and maybe a siesta,
but the sight of the neon beer signs fizzing in the windows of the
bar across the street got his mouth watering. His mind turned
into a beer commercial—rock music playing while a brunette in a
devastatingly tight T-shirt served him a fantasy smile and a glass
of ice-cold Budweiser. He crossed the road, blinking sweat from his

The brunette turned out to be a young bartender with tattoo sleeves, full-lobe ear plugs, and a soul patch that had been plaited and adorned with a single red bead that tapped against his chin when he spoke. The fantasy smile was anything but. The ice-cold beer, however, was exactly how Matthew had imagined it. He drained two thirds of the bottle with a purring sound, suppressed a gassy belch, then finished the beer and ordered another.

A song came on the jukebox that Matthew didn't recognize, but it set his foot tapping and was perfect for the bar's ambience. It was little more than spit and sawdust, but with a name like the Rack, Matthew hadn't expected anything more. The bartender flicked around on his cell phone between serving customers, and a waitress with fire-wild hair worked the tables and a small patio out back. It was cool and dark at the bar, away from the light slanting through the windows. A notice board filled with photographs rippled as a dusty fan turned its ponderous head that way.

The other customers were as somnolent as wildlife in the shade, occasionally raising their heads from their drinks, looking around with barely interested expressions. One old boy drew shapes in the spilled beer on the bar. A younger man with gunpowder-black eyes chewed his fingernails and spat the pieces on the floor. Matthew tended his own business, supping his beer, cooling down, and trying to get his thoughts in order. The song on the jukebox changed to something that skipped and ended in less than ten seconds. "That was my goddamn quarter," the man chewing his fingernails said, and the bartender took a quarter from the register and flipped it his way. It was snatched from the air without even time to flash. Lynyrd Skynyrd started singing "Comin' Home" and Matthew spied the waitress plucking her jean shorts from the cleft of her ass.

He had just started his third beer—it was going to be the last one before heading back to the hotel—when a tall man with a tiny Mets cap perched on his brick-like head strolled in, belly swinging, and sat at the bar three stools over.

"Hot as blazes," he wheezed, nodding at the bartender. "Get me a Pepsi, Jesse. Biggest glass you can find. Fill it with ice."

"Maybe I should just load a pitcher."

"Go for it."

Matthew raised his eyebrows. The man turned to him and he looked quickly away, suddenly interested in the photographs riffling on the notice board. He supped his beer, but felt the man still looking at him. Jesse returned with his pitcher of Pepsi, the ice popping and cracking with a sound like bubble wrap.

"There she is, Bobby."

Bobby curled his impressive hands around the pitcher.

"You want a straw?"

Bobby gave his head a little shake, lifted the pitcher, and took several noisy slurps. Foamy lines trickled into the folds of his chins. Matthew was reminded of Kirsty slurping from her massive Starbucks mug. He sneered and sipped his own beer quietly. Bobby set the pitcher down with a thump. Pepsi fizzed. Ice crackled. Bobby wiped his mouth and belched musically.

The old boy looked up from his beer shapes, smiled toothlessly, and then drew a shaky star.

"God and be damned," Bobby said. "Okay, get me a glass, Jesse."

Jesse fetched him a glass and went back to playing with his cell phone.

"I know you, don't I?" Bobby asked, pouring a tall glass that foamed and spilled over the top. He looked at Matthew, his brow creased.

"Me?" Matthew pointed at himself with the neck of the bottle.

"Yeah. Your face is familiar."

Matthew shook his head and smiled politely. "I doubt . . ." But the sentence melted in his mouth. *Bobby*, he thought, looking at his pink face and freckled nose. The band of his Mets cap was almost black with sweat. Still beads, like balls of candle wax, mottled the heavy pockets beneath his eyes. *Bobby . . . yeah, I think . . .* And it was the baseball cap, small and raggedy, that brought it home. Judging from the size of it on Bobby's head, it could have been the same one he was wearing when Matthew last saw him in 1984. He'd been a kid then, of course. Ten years old. Now he was an adult, but looking at him closely, Matthew still saw the little boy inside.

"Bobby Alexander," Matthew said. He hadn't spoken that name

out loud for many years, but there it was.

"You got it," Bobby said with a grin. Deep creases rippled his full cheeks.

"We were best friends." Matthew blinked like a man emerging from deep, confusing sleep.

Bobby snapped his fingers. "Matthew . . . Matthew Bridge."

Matthew nodded, smiling.

"I'll be damned."

Something strange happened then: both men slipped from their stools, met in the middle, and hugged. They did it simultaneously, neither prompted by the other, and although the hug was somewhat clumsy and uncomfortable, Matthew still felt warmed by it. The weirdness of the town, and the way it appeared to have turned its back on him, dissolved instantly. He found, in Bobby's arms, in the smell of his sweat and the firm bulge of his belly, confirmation that he had once belonged. A long time ago, but it was there, nonetheless.

They gave each other a couple of manly claps on the back and separated. The old boy and the man chewing his fingernails stared at them. Bobby grinned and scooted to the stool next to Matthew. The fan revolved, the photographs fluttered, and the jukebox played something else that skipped.

"I don't believe this," Bobby said. "How long has it been?"

"Twenty-six years," Matthew said.

"Too long."

"Well, life happens. Time races by."

"You got that right." Bobby slurped his soda, looking carefully at Matthew, as if expecting him to disappear any moment, and to be told that he had imagined the reunion—delusion brought on by the heat.

He pointed at Matthew's bottle. "You want a drink?"

"No, I'm—"

"Hey, Jesse. Get my old friend here another Bud."

Jesse grabbed a bottle and slid it across to Matthew, barely dragging his eyes from his cell phone.

Bobby topped up his Pepsi, ice tumbling from the pitcher into his glass, splashing, making foamy puddles on the bar.

"We've got a lot of catching up to do," he said.

Matthew nodded and smiled again.

"So what brings you to Point Hollow?"

Matthew looked at his left hand, twirling the ring on his finger. "I needed to get out of the city for a few days. Take some time for myself."

Bobby watched Matthew turning the ring. "Married, huh?"

"Well, I'm—"

"Divorced? Widowed?"

Matthew looked at Bobby, one eyebrow raised.

"Sorry," Bobby said, holding up both hands. "I have a tendency to poke my nose where it doesn't belong. Drives my mother nuts. My boss, too."

"It's fine," Matthew said.

"Take no notice of me."

"Really, it's fine." Matthew sipped his beer, then went back to twirling his ring. "I was *about* to say that I'm recently separated."

"I'm sorry to hear that," Bobby said. He reached over and gently squeezed Matthew's shoulder. "I hope things work out for you."

"We'll see," Matthew said, and shrugged. "One thing's for sure: feeling sorry for yourself doesn't help."

"Not a soul," Bobby agreed.

Matthew guzzled his beer, wiped his lips, and smiled. "I guess I'm looking for the silver lining. Every cloud has one, so they say."

"Yes they do," Bobby said. He lifted his own glass and kissed it against Matthew's. "I hope you find yours."

"Me, too," Matthew said.

They spent the next hour sharing drinks and conversation, touching on memories and trying to condense the last twenty-six years. For Matthew this was simple: high school, college, work, marriage, separation. In that order, as dull as you can get, despite the fact that he lived in one of the most vibrant cities in the world. Bobby's story, while unquestionably dour, had a dash more colour: his old man dropped dead of a heart attack at the age of thirty-nine. Bobby was fourteen at the time, and he told Matthew that it felt like all the sunlight had been kicked from his world. He quit school at fifteen and took a job at the mill to help his mother pay the bills, and continued to do so until summer of last year.

"That's when I got my wake-up call," he said, tapping his chest. "Heart attack, and nothing mild about it. That son of a bitch knocked me out of my boots. Lookit." He popped a couple of the buttons on his shirt and showed Matthew the long scar on his chest, directly between what Kirsty would have called his moobs. "Triple bypass. Thirty-five years old. Four years younger than my old man when he cashed in his chips. Scared the jippers out of me, Matty, I swear to God. But talk about your silver lining . . . I quit the mill and got a job at the post office. Less stress, right off the bat. Then I sold my F-150 and bought a bicycle. I also gave up the booze, started eating better food, and dropped a truckload of weight. I can't begin to tell you how much better I feel." Matthew nodded, wondering just how heavy Bobby had been when his ticker threw a rod, and further wondering if a sixty-ounce pitcher of Pepsi-Cola was part of the recommended diet.

He said as much, and Bobby only laughed. "My mom takes good care of me," he explained. "I get my five a day. No red meat, low sodium, low fat. I eat like a goddamn supermodel, so the occasional bucket of soda isn't going to hurt." It turned out that Bobby's mother was the only woman in his life. They lived in the same house that Bobby had been born in, thirty-six years ago. He still had the same bedroom, a fact that blew Matthew's mind and made him feel, paradoxically, both old and young.

They left the Rack together. It was cooler now, dipping toward evening. Main Street was a strip of peace and quiet. Most of the stores had closed, there were few cars on the road, and the sidewalks were all but empty. A soft breeze made the trees bristle and the sun offered mature light. It poured in from the western rim of God's Footprint, like gold.

"How long are you in town?" Bobby asked.

"I'm thinking four or five days," Matthew said. "I hope to have my head on straight by then."

They started walking, their long shadows tattooed on the sidewalk.

Ahead of them, Abraham's Faith reflected the falling sun: auburn shades, like something heated and beaten out of shape. Matthew was relieved when they turned left on Napanoch Avenue and the redbrick bulk of the town hall blocked it from view.

"So I'm going to see more of you?" Bobby asked.

"Yeah, absolutely."

"That'd be good. We can go fishing. Maybe walk a few trails, take a picnic."

Matthew nodded, thinking that picnicking in the forest (with a three-hundred-pound post office worker) was quite the stretch for his New York state of mind, but also that it sounded quite wonderful. "We can do that," he said, clapping Bobby on the back, and understanding, for the first time since he had been back, how they had been such solid friends when they were children.

They came, within a few moments, to a street that struck Matthew with memories as bright as constellations. He had walked this way hundreds of times, with his pack slung over one shoulder and his laces untied. Like the mountain, this neat strip of asphalt had folded into the crevasses of his mind, leaving behind a ghostly puff of dust.

"Our old school was on this street," Matthew said. "Rising Pine Elementary."

"Still *is* on this street," Bobby said. "Hasn't changed a jot."

Matthew smiled, quickened his step, and saw that Bobby was right. His old school, where he had pledged allegiance, plugged Bazooka bubblegum beneath the desks, and been the giver/recipient of countless awesome wedgies, looked hauntingly the same. It could have been air-lifted from a time when Reaganomics was in full swing. Matthew had to wonder how much it had changed inside. Were the walls the same drab shade of blue? Were the water fountains in the same places? Was his bubblegum still glued beneath the desks?

"Same, huh?" Bobby said.

"Scary," Matthew said.

"Principal Lawrence died . . . jeez, about ten years ago—"

"Principal Lawrence. *Jesus.*"

"Mr. Nordhagen is principal now."

"Nordhagen? Holy shit."

"All coming back to you, huh?"

"Yeah, it's . . ." Matthew shook his head. He made a vague gesture with his hand, as if trying to sum up what was happening in his mind. "It's like waking up."

He stood silently for a moment, letting the memories cascade, listening to the halyard tap against the flagpole out front. Rising Pine Elementary was a simple building of stone face and wide windows. There was a beautiful pine on its east side, with golden bark and broad, musical branches. A baseball diamond stretched to the west, and Matthew remembered how the clay looked so red under the field lights, and how the ball would sometimes lodge between the chain links in the backstop.

"Are you okay?" Bobby asked, touching Matthew's shoulder.

Matthew nodded, feeling his chest tighten with emotion, amazed at the power contained in such small things: the peeling school sign; the faculty parking lot with spaces enough for maybe a dozen cars. It was like looking through a keyhole and seeing the whole room. He strolled over to the pine and Bobby followed, kicking cones the way they used to when they were children.

"We used to sit here every lunch period," he said, touching the pine's golden trunk. "We'd trade food and comic books. I always got *Spider-Man* and *The Mighty Thor,* and you got *The Incredible Hulk* and—"

"*Justice League of America.*" They said it at the same time, and then started to laugh. Matthew felt warmth flow through him, as if one of his internal faucets had sprung a leak. He couldn't remember the last time he had genuinely laughed—when joy touched his soul and shook outward. *Too damn long,* he thought, looking at Bobby. Then he snapped his fingers and saw, again, a flame flickering at the tip of his thumb. *Light the darkness.*

They walked to the baseball diamond. Bobby, excited, assumed the catcher's position behind the plate. "Give me the number one, Matty. Straight down Main Street. Let's go."

Matthew grinned and jogged to the mound. He nodded, went

through his wind-up, and zipped Bobby an imaginary speedball.

"*Pop!*" Bobby exclaimed, jerking back his catching hand as the invisible baseball socked home. "You still got it, Matty."

"You know it," Matthew said, and then shivered; for a moment—the wink of an eye, no more—he fully expected to see the rest of his old friends standing around him: Candle Daniels on first base (his real name was Robin, but everyone called him Candle because he was waxy pale and his hair was orange as a flame). Lutz the Klutz in left field. Mark Kettle on third. Yo-yo Jones playing shortstop. Matthew wiped his eyes and stepped off the mound. The empty field spread like an open palm. Except it wasn't empty. Ghosts shimmered, caught in the drowsy light, like child-shaped haze.

"What happened to the rest of the guys?" he asked. "Are they still in town?"

"A few of them are," Bobby replied. He straightened with a groan and walked toward Matthew. "Most up and left, though, just like you. Yo-yo Jones moved to Pennsylvania . . . jeez, a long time ago. Twenty years, maybe. Robin Daniels married some European heiress—lots of money, but ugly as a slapped ass. Lutz the Klutz near-drowned in an ice fishing mishap, then moved to the Jersey shore with his boyfriend."

"His boyfriend?"

"Uh-huh. Turns out he was as gay as two dicks touching."

Matthew looked toward the outfield, rolling his gaze from left to right. The ghosts flickered, bright and dark, like afterimages. He could almost hear the crack of the bat, the cheers and shouts.

"Oliver Wray is still in town," Bobby said.

Oliver Wray. The name struck a chord. Something inside Matthew resounded coldly and he looked instinctively to the mountain. An image formed in his mind, too vague to discern—crumbled when he reached for it. He turned to Bobby and shook his head.

"You *must* remember Oliver."

"No," Matthew said.

"He was older than us. Four years, or so." Bobby flipped off his cap and wiped sweat from his brow. "A quiet kid. Didn't mix well. You'd see him sometimes with bruises on his face. No secret that his old man was keen with his fists."

"His name . . ." Matthew made a rotating gesture with his finger to indicate his mind was cranking. ". . . it's *sort* of familiar, but I guess some things are buried deeper than others."

"And some things are better left buried," Bobby added, then shrugged. His belly wobbled. "Anyway, Oliver is the town hotshot. He runs some million-dollar business that he started up himself, and does a whole bunch for the community. Not just Point Hollow, but Oak Creek and Indigo, too. Heck, he's the reason this school is still standing. He made a six-figure donation a few years ago—brought it in line with current education standards, and padded the teachers' pay envelopes, too. Mayor Woolens handed him the key for that one, and they're already talking about naming a street after him. As soon as they've laid down the blacktop, that is."

"Generous guy," Matthew said.

"Sure, a real golden heart." Bobby sneered and looked at the tops of his sneakers. "Everybody loves Oliver."

"But you don't?"

"No. I don't."

"You must have a good reason," Matthew said.

Bobby considered this, his lips pressed so firmly together that his chin dimpled like a golf ball. He removed his cap, scratched his head, swatted at a few mosquitoes, and for a long moment the only sound was the summer breeze. It skated across the infield and made the trees exhale. A swallow rippled across the sky, arrow-shaped, absorbed by the featureless silhouette of the peaks in the west.

"I don't trust him," Bobby said finally, sliding the cap back onto his head. "Everybody sees Oliver as this model citizen with a big smile and an even bigger cheque book. You'd think he could walk on water, the way they talk about him. But they don't remember the way he used to be. A moody, bitter kid who didn't like anybody, and who was always on his own."

"People change," Matthew said. "Maybe he just came out of his shell."

"I don't think so," Bobby said. "Think about it. He's handsome, successful, and incredibly wealthy. But he doesn't have a wife or girlfriend. No children. He lives on his own in a million-dollar house he built outside of town. Doesn't sound like someone who's come out of his shell."

"You've given this a lot of thought," Matthew said.

"Can't help it," Bobby said. "Naturally curious, I guess. Like I said . . . inclined to put my nose where it doesn't belong."

"You'll get the tip snipped off," Matthew said with a grin.

"That's what Mom says." Bobby's eyes gleamed beneath the peak of his cap. "But Oliver *makes* me curious. Take his old man, for instance. He's still alive—sick as hell, but still kicking. He lives in a tiny apartment on Blackbird Road. If Oliver is such a good Samaritan, why doesn't he move his sick father in with him? I'm sure he has the space."

Matthew shrugged.

"It doesn't make sense," Bobby said. He shook his head, and then tipped Matthew a wink. "I'm sometimes tempted to take a trip up to his house. Peek through the windows. Find out what he does up there on his own."

"Snip-snip," Matthew said.

Bobby smiled and let out a shaky breath, as if he'd just unburdened a wearisome load. Matthew wondered if he was overreacting. Maybe a touch envious, too. Oliver was clearly a success story: a self-made millionaire, but generous with it, loved by all. Bobby, on the other hand—from the same Podunk town—lived with his mom, shuffled mail for a living, and downed statins and nitrates to soothe his troubled ticker.

"I don't remember him," Matthew said, even though there was that dull glimmer, like an old injury on a cold day.

"Well, you're sure to see him while you're in town," Bobby said. "And he'll be super-friendly and grinning bigger than a kid in a Disney commercial. He'll probably invite you for Kobe beef steaks and a hot tub. You'll remember this conversation and think that I'm wrong—crazy, even. But I've known him all my life, Matty. And I'm telling you . . . something isn't right."

Both men stood in silence, Bobby lost in thought, Matthew gazing to the east, where Abraham's Faith cast its dark angles against the sky. A fingernail moon, as pale as spider web, touched that place in the heavens that was not quite night, not quite day. Stars gathered on one side. The sky looked like a flag.

"Anyway, forget about that," Bobby said, breaking the silence. His smile had returned, as big as the moon. He chugged to the plate and dropped into the catcher's position. "One more, Matty. For old time's sake. And put some steam on it."

Matthew stepped onto the mound, grinned, and threw a perfect four-seamer. Bobby caught it, then shook his hand as if it were on fire.

"Bringing the heat," Matthew said.

Bobby nodded. His boyish face was wide and gleeful. "*Pop!*" he said.

──────

They parted ways at Pawpaw Avenue, Matthew heading back to Main Street and the Super 8, Bobby heading home, where his mom was no doubt clucking because he was late for dinner.

"It's only rabbit food, anyway," he explained. "It's not like she spent the day cooking." Matthew declined the invitation to join Bobby for said rabbit food, saying that he was tired (which was true), and that he was going to get an early night (not entirely true; he simply needed to recalibrate after such an emotional day—*two* emotional days, if you factored in what had happened with the deer). Bobby nodded, as if to suggest that Matthew wasn't missing much, then gave him another hug and said, "Catch you later, alligator," getting the phrase slightly wrong, just like he used to when they were kids.

They went their own ways, drawing steadily away from each other, like two cowboys about to duel. Only Matthew turned around, though. The breeze lifted his hair, not as brown and wavy as it used to be—thinner on top, and dusty around the temples. Bobby had flipped his Mets cap backward and was stepping between the cracks in the sidewalk. Matthew's heart trembled. Tears prickled his eyes. In this geography, with the air so clear and the sunlight slanting just so, it was like the last twenty-six years had never happened. *I'm a child again,* he thought, and held the feeling close. It kicked inside him, unbroken.

With this nostalgia came a dim pulse of disquiet. Matthew found his gaze drawn, again, to the mountain. It ached in the burned light, one of earth's rheumatic joints, and Matthew fought to look away, down at his feet, and then back at Bobby, who was still just a child.

CHAPTER EIGHT

Oliver was with Tina Quinn when the mountain roared again. She had called earlier that afternoon. "Get your skinny ass out here right now and fuck me—*FUCK ME*." He had planned to take his MacBook onto the deck and finish a project for a customer in California, maybe sink a few mojitos while The Grooveyard played on iTunes radio. This plan was scratched before Tina uttered another sigh. His dick suggested that work (even work with mojitos and jazz) was a crazy idea, and that they'd have more fun partying with Tina. The rest of Oliver concurred, and by the time he arrived she had already gotten off twice—first with her fingers and again with the bedpost.

"You're some piece of work," he had said, unbuckling his belt, figuring he'd get her to tan his ass with it before the day was done.

She'd called him a dirty motherfucker and grabbed a box of Oreo cookies from a nightstand cluttered with all manner of erotica, and he'd dropped his slick on a half dozen of them (always good to get that first load out of the system) and watched as she chowed down.

He went to work on her then, and she on him, and for the next three (four?) hours everything was peaches. It all changed, though, and in a big way. He was wearing a latex zipper hood and chastity cock cage when Abraham's Faith boomed at him. He staggered across Tina's bedroom-cum-dungeon, his skin prickling, his soul turning cold. "Whafuckat?" he mumbled from behind the hood's zipper, even though he knew. His head snapped blindly left and right and Tina cackled and hoss-whipped his bare ass. The mountain roared again and he screamed, flailing his arms. This only encouraged Tina, and she worked the whip hard, drawing blood, until Oliver dropped to his knees and begged her to stop.

"Safe word," she snapped.

Oliver unzipped the hood, tore it from his head, and threw it at Tina. "Fucking dumbass skeeze," he said, and Tina was surprised to see tears in his eyes. He pointed at the cock cage. "Get this fucking thing off me."

The mountain didn't stop. It thundered at him as he drove home, vibrating through the plates of his skull. He jerked the wheel and the car zigzagged, mounting the sidewalk on Jefferson Avenue with a little flurry of sparks.

Not again, he thought, cranking the wheel left and bumping back onto the road. *I can't do this anymore. Leave me alone.*

It boomed. He glimpsed an image of a man wrapped in black flames. *LEAVE ME ALONE!*

But Abraham's Faith had other ideas and it clamoured as furiously as he had ever known. He wiped tears from his eyes and screamed at it, a torrent of blasphemy. Anybody watching would swear that Oliver had boarded the crazy train, but nobody was watching. He was alone, and always had been. Six and a half billion people on God's green earth and he was isolated from every last one of them.

The Corvette's headlights cut the darkness as he raced along Tall Pine Way—touching eighty, the engine howling—less than a mile from home. Another head-shattering slam from the mountain and Oliver took his hands from the wheel to cover his ears. The car veered into the oncoming lane and would have kept veering until it slammed into the trees, and for just a heartbeat Oliver considered letting it happen. He imagined the Corvette striking the bole of a pine, the headlights blowing out, the hood crumpling, and himself—having neglected, in his haste, to buckle up—meeting the steering wheel face first, caving in the front of his skull before slamming, raggedy-doll, through the windshield. There wouldn't be anything left of him but a torn bag of skin with some loose pieces inside. *No more of this,* he thought. *No more mountain.* Then—in the split second way such thoughts work—he saw himself not dead but wheelchair-bound, maybe cabbaged, listening to the mountain for the rest of his miserable days. He yanked the wheel and the car squealed into the right lane, laying twin arcs of rubber on the hardtop. The trees shook, even the stars shook, and Oliver wept and cussed, so sure that the world was breaking.

He fishtailed onto the unpaved road leading to his house. Sanctuary Road, he called it—a half-mile cat scratch among the trees. Dust ribboned from the tires as he sped toward the comforting glow of the one light he'd left burning. He ripped into his driveway and stomped on the brakes—had the door open before he'd even shut off the ignition.

"*What?*" he screamed. Abraham's Faith was drowned in darkness but he looked toward it anyway, sensing its unholy pressure. "I *fed* you, dammit. I've earned my keep."

Boom, and those black-fire hands grabbed his soul.

"I *can't* keep doing this."

In his house, he screamed from room to room, making chaos, toppling tables and chairs, throwing plates and pans, books and clothes. He unplugged the coffeemaker and hurled it across the kitchen. It hit the wall and separated in clunky pieces, except for the pot, which exploded, glass everywhere. He pulled open the fridge doors and spilled everything from the shelves. It broke and splashed, and Oliver screeched, hunching his shoulders every time the mountain retaliated. Struggling to breathe—to even *think*—he staggered onto the rear deck and dropped to his knees. Tears flashed down his face. He curled into a ball and the world trembled.

"Please . . . please stop."

His soul was wrapped in flames. The mountain was furious.

"Why me?" Oliver twisted his hands into fists. "What do you *want* from me?"

Another angry peal of thunder. Oliver imagined a child with water glistening on his thin chest, and more water trickling through the cracks of his fingers. He pushed the image away with a broken sound, his body shivering on the deck. Tears ran into his mouth, a taste that reminded him of childhood. The mountain's anger rolled into the distance and for a long time there was silence.

Oliver didn't move. One hour became two, and then three. He lay on the deck like a stone, afraid even to breathe lest the sound of his lungs wake the mountain. He drifted across the rim of the earth and reached for other planets. They dissolved when he touched them. He was naked and clean and painless. His mind was a perfect circle. Eventually he dared to move, shifting his body. It scraped across the wooden deck with a sound like a wave across shells. His muscles groaned like old piano strings. He flexed his toes and heard tiny bones pop.

Nothing from the mountain.

It was the dead of night—the *clear* of night, as Oliver called it, because he felt the earth, like everything else, was at its purest while sleeping. Perfection, without distraction. He sat up slowly, and with caution, held in a puddle of light thrown from the house. A curved moon rode high and Point Hollow shimmered low, but otherwise the world was a black sheet. He stood, shoulders sagged and scared, and turned child's eyes to the east. It was there, in the darkness, his Father and his God. Oliver chewed his lower lip until it hurt. He waited and prayed.

Silence.

Let me go, he thought.

But Abraham's Faith would not; like any god, it demanded of him. Oliver had taken only three steps toward the house when it boomed again. The most terrific crash by far. Were the trees uprooted and sent tumbling across the mountain? Had the other mountains crumbled to ash? Had the moon shattered, punched from the sky as if Child-God had thrown a stone at its pale glass face? Oliver had no idea. He swept rain-like through his house, into the master bedroom. *NO*

MORE, NO FUCKING MORE. The armoire. Bottom drawer. *I'M NOT DOING THIS ANY MORE.* Under the skin flicks and magazines. *THIS IS IT. THIS IS THE END.* A Plano pistol case. Hands trembling, slick with sweat. Oliver flipped it open and pulled out the pistol. *FIND SOMEONE ELSE IT'S OVER FOR ME.* A Colt .45. He thumbed off the safety. *IT'S ALL OVER NOW.* He put it in his mouth and pulled the trigger.

———

Sheriff Tansy had called the day before, inviting Oliver to Gray's backyard for some suds and a barbecue. "Doe fresh off the blacktop," he'd said, as if this would appeal to Oliver. "She's all bled-out and ready for the rub." Oliver had forced a smile (even over the phone it was important to maintain appearances) and declined.

"I got work coming out the wazoo," he said, which was true. What he failed to add was that the thought of hanging with the sheriff and his assclown buddies—and so soon after the last time—made him want to shit blood.

"I think you can afford one night off," Tansy said. Judging from the slur in his voice he'd already been at the suds. "It's Friday night, by Christ."

"True, but I had last night off. I took your money, remember?" He beamed across the line. "Sink a few for me, old friend. I'll try to make the next one."

"Well, if you finish early . . ."

"Sure." And Oliver was about to hang up when he heard the sheriff's diminutive voice cheep from the earpiece:

"*Oh shit, hold up, I meant to tell you—*"

He was *so* close to hanging up, anyway. Fuck the sheriff and whatever he had to say. But something—perhaps the thin thread of urgency in his voice—made Oliver lift the phone back to his ear.

"—still there?"

"Still here."

"Good. I'm not sure if you're all that interested, anyhoo," the sheriff started, "but the meat tonight is courtesy of an old Point

Hollow boy. One of those that flew the coop. He hit the deer earlier today while driving back into town. Yours truly was called to help him out."

Oliver wasn't particularly interested. Still, he said. "Yeah? Who?"

"Little goddamn pantywaist. I thought for sure he was going to piss his britches."

"Who?"

"Matthew Bridge. You remember that kid got lost in the woods?"

Oliver sat down hard and it was good fortune that the couch was behind him, otherwise he would have spilled to the floor. He felt his lower body filling with cold water and the room took a lazy spin. His mind drifted away. He saw Matthew's terrified face hanging in the darkness, illuminated by the flashlight, while small skeletons toppled with dry-stick sounds and bones crunched underfoot.

"Oliver? You still with me?"

"Still with you, Sheriff." But he wasn't. Not really. He was inside Abraham's Faith with Matthew, chasing him through the darkness.

"You went awful quiet there."

"Just trying to put a face to the name." His voice was as cool as dew, which hardly seemed possible given that everything inside him was clenched tight. The cold water had reached chest-level and his heart rattled, shriveled to a small stone.

The sheriff said something else but Oliver didn't catch it. He was lost in thought:

He remembered. That's why he's back. Maybe he's already led Sheriff Tansy to Abraham's Faith, taken him inside and shown him everything. That's why he's calling me now. The son of a bitch isn't inviting me to a barbecue at all; he's testing me, feeding me rope to see if I'll hang myself. I bet Matthew is with him now—the two of them together, looking to bring me down.

Still dew-drop cool, Oliver said, "I remember Matthew. What brings him to town?"

"Hell if I know," the sheriff replied. "He said something about wanting to get out of the city for a few days. I *think* that's what he said, at least. He's probably just here to see how much the place has changed."

"Hasn't changed much," Oliver said.

"Just the way we like it," Tansy said.

Oliver felt the cold water ebb. He could tell from the sheriff's dumbass tone that he didn't know anything. He relaxed his grip on the handset and breathed again, but was still far from comfortable. Matthew—back in town after twenty-some years—was the only person who had seen Oliver's dark side. Maybe he didn't remember. Maybe he *was* here simply to see how much his hometown had changed. But even so, Oliver felt decidedly vulnerable.

He had a stack of questions piled up for the sheriff and was burning to ask them, but he thought it best to keep them to himself. He had come a long way in this town—in this *life*—by simply smiling and being cool, and he intended to continue the trend. No sense in asking too many questions, rousing suspicion.

"Keep an eye on him," Oliver said through the biggest smile he could muster. "We don't want him getting lost in the woods again."

He hung up, then tried to work but couldn't. So he ended up going to Gray's backyard anyway, not because he wanted to, but because he *needed* to. He wore a big ol' shit-eating grin and drank beer and ate roadkill. Just one of the boys. He kept expecting Sheriff Tansy to approach him on the quiet and say, *Matthew Bridge told me something very interesting, Oliver. I think we need to have a serious talk.* Or worse: *I know what you did, you son of a bitch. I found the bodies—all of them— and I'm going to make damn sure you pay.* This didn't happen, of course. It was just another night with the assclowns, and by the time Oliver got home all the cold water had trickled from his body. He didn't feel quite as vulnerable anymore. In fact, he felt pretty good.

Untouchable.

―――――

Click.

Oliver had closed his eyes prior to pulling the trigger, but he opened them again now, his eyebrows knitted in a V of confusion that would have been comical if not for the .45 in his mouth. The *unloaded* .45. His eyes rolled around the master bedroom, as if to confirm that he was still alive—still here—while his ears analyzed the *click* and determined that it was indeed the sound of a firing pin dropping on an empty chamber.

"Hun uffa biff," he said, which is of course how you would say *son of a bitch* with a gun in your mouth.

He removed the gun. It left a coppery trail of grease on his tongue. He tossed it onto the bed, and then sagged to the floor. Abraham's Faith grumbled at him like a mean father in a neighbouring room. It thumped on the wall. Oliver rolled his eyes and tried to ignore it.

But couldn't.

His throat burned with all the tears he had swallowed.

***

August 1, 2010.
So much for silence. The light of a new morning—a new month—suggests hope, but I am not fooled. Abraham's Faith commands. I serve. It has always been this way.

I can still hear the children screaming in the darkness.

Who will be next, I wonder.

***

Some people use crystals to heal mind and spirit. Some will hop into sweat lodges or practise yoga, while others partake in asceticism or prayer. Whatever the device, all seek to purify the soul, to cleanse and attain guidance. Oliver's ritual was different, but no less effective—arguably *more* effective, in fact. What better way to purify than to become purity itself? Better yet, to do so in God's purest acre, away from people, from the stain of society and technology's deathless drone. Naked, he could stand among the trees and feel the breeze stir his glittering leaves. He could float in the lake and become a ripple. He could be a stone or a rock, or even a flower, unfolding in the sunlight. He had healing on his doorstep. It rolled for miles. He could fall into purity like a drop of rain into the ocean, and exist there—as a stone; ripple; tree—for as long as he needed to.

He cleaned his house thoroughly (getting the simple stuff in order was step one on the road to spiritual enlightenment; it was hard to find the Greater Meaning with a sink full of dirty dishes), moving from room to room, righting everything he'd wronged. He swept up all the broken glass and the debris scattered from the refrigerator, and then scrubbed the floors, the work surfaces—anything that *could* be scrubbed. He cleaned the blinds, vacuumed the couch, and plumped the cushions. He also removed anything from the refrigerator that could spoil in the time he'd be gone. The windows were washed, inside and out. He stripped naked, washed and dried the dirty laundry, and while it tumbled in the machines, he—still naked as a jaybird—dusted, scrubbed the bathrooms, and washed the cars. He folded the clean laundry, put it away, and then took care of the final details: an out-of-office e-mail reply for the business, and the audiobook version for voicemail. He switched off his iPhone, took one last look around, and was ready.

It was early afternoon by the time he set out, cutting through his back garden and across the land, walking with his shoulders square and his head high, like a buck-ass naked version of Caine from *Kung Fu*. Abraham's Faith boomed steadily at him, like a whip across his shoulders. Oliver didn't flinch. Nor did he weep. In the spring that he had crossed with Matthew in 1984—and many times since, sometimes carrying a small child—he lay down and let the natural water cleanse his filthy skin. It coursed over his recumbent body, cold and fresh, into his open eyes. Only his mouth emerged, occasionally, for air. Time passed. Oliver watched the sun—a quivering yellow orb from his perspective—drift westward. The sound of the spring filled his mind with wind chimes, tinkling excitedly when the mountain roared. Small fish suckled on the nutrients in his body hair.

He crawled, aching and hardened, from the water at a time that didn't matter. The sun had painted a flame across one edge of the world and the sound he thought to be birdsong turned out to be his mind, ringing with measured clarity, like a perfect bell. He stepped into the forest and sang with the trees, casting his pheromones, swaying as the breeze lifted his branches. He had no recollection of falling asleep, but awoke in a bed of ferns, a ribbon snake coiled around his arm and a cardinal on his thigh. He had no interest in the snake, but the cardinal was spectacular. He reached for it, hoping it would hop onto his finger. Its tiny black eyes regarded him curiously for a moment, then it flew away, red feathers burning.

New light. Oliver drank from the spring and sucked algae from pebbles. He went back into the forest and foraged among the fallen needles for roots and seeds. The mountain boomed and he let it, but knew—with a shim of human intuition—that he had to face it. As the sun climbed he made his way east. Rivers and lakes flickered in the distance but he didn't look at them—didn't want to see the specks of boats, or imagine the people inside them with their dirty lives.

Beneath shelves of rock and over matchstick trees, through brittle flora and across streams. The mountain was like the domed back of some Greek god. It spoke to him in furious tones and he went to it meekly, naked in body and prejudice. He tore the soles of his feet on the rocks and they bled, but he continued climbing, leaving red petals behind him. There was a deadfall close to the mouth of the cave and Oliver paused here to get the one man-made thing he couldn't do without. *If only I could see in the dark,* he thought, *like an owl or a cat.* He had stashed it here some time ago and used it often. He pulled aside sticks and small rocks and found it, as he had left it, in a Ziploc bag swaddled in sackcloth. An LED flashlight. He flicked it on, cupped his hand around the lens to test the batteries (there were spares in the Ziploc) and, satisfied, continued up the mountain. He soon came to the mouth of the cave, concealed with rocks and boulders, looking like a wound that wouldn't heal.

The sun pressed hard on his shoulders and sweat dripped from the tip of his nose as he dislodged nineteen rocks—always the same nineteen—and placed them to one side. He slipped through the opening and dropped down. The flashlight illuminated the cave's slick throat and he followed its familiar curves deep into the mountain. On it went, contorted, swallowing him. His breath was amplified in the narrow space, but the sound changed as it widened and he stepped into the cavern. The walls sloped away and the light splashed upon pale columns and stalactites, spars and bones. So many bones. He moved forward, slightly hunched, waiting for this great god to boom and spit him back into the outside world. The cavern stretched and echoed. A child's corpse regarded him with hollow eyes, rimmed with calcite.

"I'm here," Oliver said. His throat was dry. He hadn't spoken since removing the .45 from his mouth. "I come to you pure and naked. A vessel for you to fill. Tell me what you want from me. Once and for all, tell me what you want me to do."

He dropped to his knees and curled one arm over his head, but the mountain didn't rumble. Oliver wasn't sure that it even replied at all, although an incredibly clear image formed in his mind: a boy with curly brown hair playing in sprinkler spray that arced in the sunlight like a rainbow made up of dots. Oliver saw fine droplets of water on his chest. There was another flash, equally clear: more water spilling through small, cupped hands.

So cold.

Matthew Bridge. Was he linked to the mountain in some way? Or to the man in the grainy old photograph he'd copied from the Internet, with his wicked smile and terrified children? Was it simply coincidence that the mountain had resumed roaring—no, *booming*, the most strident peals that Oliver had ever known—upon Matthew's return to Point Hollow?

Matthew.

Water dripped in the vastness. And something else. Hitching breaths. Sobbing. Oliver unfurled like some strange, subterranean flower. He rolled the flashlight's beam from right to left, and that was when he heard Matthew say:

"Want . . . go home."

Except it *wasn't* Matthew. Oliver crawled toward the voice on his hands and knees, heart clashing, his teeth bared and clotted with dirt. And there, huddled among bones, were the children. They'd cut through their binds, using a rock or the points of one of the stalagmites.

"Please," the girl said.

They flinched from the flashlight's powerful glare, as if it would burn them. The boy's skin was stretched over his skull, almost translucent. His small hand clenched and opened, reaching for help.

The girl held him. Snow-pale, thin as a leaf. Oliver saw the tears on her face as she turned toward him, and wondered if she had been crying all this time.

"Please . . ." she croaked again. "Please let us go."

Her red hair burned like the cardinal's feathers.

FROM OLIVER WRAY'S JOURNAL (II)

Point Hollow, NY.
January 19, 2005.

The sign at the edge of town reads THE PEOPLE OF POINT HOLLOW WELCOME YOU. STAY A WHILE, which is somewhat misleading, given that the people of Point Hollow neither welcome you, nor want you to stay a while. The sign beyond this is less friendly, and more in keeping with the town spirit: DRIVE SLOWLY, SEE THE BEAUTY. DRIVE FAST, SEE THE JUDGE. A third sign proclaims Point Hollow's population to be 850. ("ALL GODS CHILDREN" is stenciled below the number—the missing apostrophe throwing the amount of gods into question.) This latter sign is faded and out of date. The population is actually closer to 1,100 now. The gods have been busy, I guess.

Point Hollow is the largest of six towns that make up Hollow County. The smallest is Shane (population: 16), although "town" is too glamourous a word for what amounts to a chicken farm and a tiny Presbyterian church. The remaining four towns fall somewhere between the two. Hollow County itself is a mere freckle on New York

State's schmekel. According to some maps I have seen, it doesn't even exist—the fifty-nine square miles of leaf-shaped land having been consumed by one of its bullish neighbours.

It all runs smoothly, with a sense of place and community. The county is united, but the towns are proudly individual (with the exception of Shane, which piggybacks neighbouring Indigo, not big enough to be much of anything). There are several churches and schools, two fire departments, two small hospitals, and three police departments, with state cops buzzing through every now and again. There's never much trouble, though—the occasional drunken dust-up or domestic dispute. Such incidents are always handled quickly and efficiently. Mayor Woolens credits the low crime rate and peace-loving way of life to pure American grit, and an unwavering faith in the good Lord Himself. I know for a fact (because he told me) that he personally appealed to every business in the county to hire only God-loving Republicans, and to politely dismiss any atheists, Democrats, or ethnic minorities (except he called them "spics and woggies"). When I pointed out that there are laws against employment discrimination, he made a shooing gesture with his hand, as if the mayor's office of Point Hollow was bigger and more powerful than the federal government of the United States.

The people in charge brandish their power colourfully and ostentatiously, mistaking ignorance for patriotism. Take Sheriff Tansy, an asshole of the very highest order, who rolls through Hollow County like General Patton. God knows what would happen if he were ever called upon to apprehend a felon. Get on the radio and call for backup, I suppose. He's not capable of much more. I rode with him a few times, for something to do. I knew it wouldn't be thrilling (I was right), but thought it might be interesting (I was wrong). We did a lot of driving the first time I went out with him. We drank a lot of coffee. We talked to the boys at Redline Auto in Oak Creek about whether or not it was time for Joe Torre to manage in pastures new. Then—wouldn't you know it?—we had the same conversation with a couple of the afternoon regulars at 100 Diner in Indigo. The most exciting thing that happened was issuing a ticket to an out-of-towner with an expired inspection sticker. At one point the radio squawked at Tansy and he made a dismissive gesture at it, similar to the shooing gesture Mayor Woolens had made. When it squawked a second time he picked it up, squeezed the button, and said (I *swear* this is true): "Breaker one-nine, we got some God-awful recep-*sheyonn*. We'll emulate at base. Over and out." Subsequent day trips have proved equally unexciting, but I have gone along to maintain pretense. Always smiling, right?

Sheriff Tansy looks like a cop. He's got the Stetson, the badge, and the gun. But at the end of the day he's only a scarecrow. Hollow County loves him because he's one of their own, and they'll continue to elect him until he either hangs up his hat, or drops dead of a heart attack. The law is enforced by the sheriff's deputies, and by the respective town and state cops. This arrangement suits everybody, including the sheriff. *Especially* the sheriff.

I rode with him again two days ago, not because I have any interest in Tansy or his joke of a day job, but because I thought it would give me an opportunity to ask him about Point Hollow's history.

"I'm thinking about writing a book," I said. "Non-fiction. *Point Hollow: From Past to Present.* That's a working title."

We were on Boulder Pass, one of the few straight roads in the county, and a favourite hidey-spot for police to snare speeders. We were running at a good clip and I felt the cruiser give a little wiggle as the sheriff's knuckles tightened on the wheel.

"Say that again." He tried to smile. "A book?"

I smiled wide enough for both of us. "Sure. We live in the most beautiful part of the world and I want to share it with people, let them know all about our wonderful town. I went on Amazon, I looked in bookstores and libraries, and do you know there's not one book—not even *one*—about Point Hollow?"

"That so?"

"I mean, it's never going to make the *New York Times* Best Seller list, but I figured I could vanity-publish and sell it in local bookstores. Tourists would snap it up, and I'm sure the library would stock it, maybe even Rising Pine—"

"I'm not sure that's such a good idea," Tansy cut in. The skin just above his collar had turned blotchy and the vein in his temple was ticking. "I mean, you'd be throwing away time and money, which is exactly why no one has done it before. Nah, you should forget that idea, Oliver. Not one of your better ones."

"I don't agree," I said colourfully. His expression was all rain and thunder. Mine was the middle of July. "The money doesn't bother me, and time . . . well you *make* time, don't you? It will be a project, like restoring a classic car or building a boat. And at the end of it, I hope to have a comprehensive reference book that will be enjoyed for many years to come. It's all about giving back to the community."

"You give plenty," Tansy grumbled.

We were going even faster now, and had to brake hard for the bend that swooped into Wharton. The tires moaned and I grabbed the door handle to keep from sliding into the sheriff's lap.

"Christ jumped up," he said, clearly ruffled.

"Of course, there'd be lots of research," I pressed, and wondered if the vein in Tansy's temple would explode if I didn't let up. "I'll have to dig real *deep* into Point Hollow's history—hunt through endless New York State books for any interesting town facts, talk to the old timers, and ride the Information Superhighway."

Sheriff Tansy isn't exactly *au fait* with the Internet, and I thought I could scare him by calling it the *Information Superhighway*. It worked.

"Get this damn idea out of your head, Oliver," he snapped. "You know how we are in Point Hollow. We're a small and private community—always have been, and that's exactly how we want to keep it. Bad enough we have to put up with the summer folk and the goddamn weekend warriors, kayaking down Gray Rock River and taking pictures of leaves."

"They bring good money into town," I said. "They don't think twice about spending six bucks on an ice cream, or twenty bucks on one of those stupid baseball caps with the moose antlers sticking from the sides. Jesus, Tommy Whipple's store would have—"

"That's why we tolerate them," Tansy interrupted. A line of sweat trickled out of his wiry sideburn and he turned down the heater (I saw how badly his hand trembled in the three seconds it was off the wheel), despite the fact that it was eighteen Fahrenheit outside. "It doesn't mean we have to *like* them. And we sure as hell don't want you publishing a book and throwing a goddamn spotlight on the town."

We stopped at an all-way and the sheriff looked at me. There was more sweat clustered amid the stubble on his upper lip. His grey eyes softened and he gave his head a little shake, as if pitying me. "We fly under the radar, Oliver. Mostly unnoticed. And that's just the way we like it."

Small-town horseshit, but everyone in Point Hollow feels the same way.

"What about me?" I asked.

"What about you?" Tansy jerked the cruiser forward and turned onto First Street, a strip of ramshackle businesses that make Point Hollow's Main Street look like Times Square.

"Forget the book for a moment," I said, not that there ever *had* been a book, of course. "What if I want to learn more about my hometown? What if I want to learn its history . . . find out where I came from . . . why I'm here?"

And why I do the things I do, I almost added.

Tansy nodded, waved to someone on the sidewalk, and said, "For an imaginative fellow, you've got one hell of a dull mind."

I clenched my teeth and felt the vein in my own temple ticking. "Hasn't my contribution to the community earned me a few answers?"

"You got questions, Oliver?" His eyes flicked my way, challenging me, and I came close to showing my hand. *Yeah, I want you to tell me about that mountain full of dead children.* I bit my tongue; the sheriff has never beaten me at poker, and that wasn't about to change.

"No questions," I said, shrugging, smiling. "Just curious, is all."

It's entirely possible, of course, that no one in Point Hollow, including Sheriff Tansy, knows anything about the mountain. Maybe the dead children are all out-of-towners, taken there by another out-of-towner: The Pied Piper of New York City, perhaps. It's a stellar hiding place, after all.

Possible, but it doesn't tango with me. I could tell from Tansy's expression that he knows something—that he's *protecting* something. It's the same with Kip Sawyer and all the other high muckety-mucks I've spoken to. Normally, I wouldn't give a shit. Let them get on with it. Only problem: whatever they're protecting, it's taken my soul. It's making me evil.

"It's not like we live in London or Rome," Tansy said, and I could tell he was fighting to keep his voice steady. He smiled, and it wasn't a bad effort, but the vein in his temple was still ticking. "It's *only* Point Hollow, Oliver. We came, we built, we stayed. There's your history lesson."

It was on the tip of my tongue to tell the sheriff that I'd already clocked some mileage on the *Information Superhighway*, and that I'd discovered some things about Point Hollow's history that he hadn't included in his lesson, and were likewise absent from the library's (sparse) local archives.

So you don't know anything about the shooting in 1953? Jack Braum, twenty-eight years old, grabs his Winchester and a fistful of double-ought, and goes for a walk down Main Street. He kills six people before finally being restrained, and is found dead in his holding cell that evening. You'd have been in short pants at the time, Sheriff, but incidents like this leave a huge hole—particularly in such a small town—and create an echo that would be heard for a long time afterward. I'm sure it was all neatly swept under the small-town rug and never spoken of again. But tongues wag, people move away, and things get written down, and fifty-some years later this incident creeps from under the rug and pastes itself on a blog called Gun Crimes of America. *And what do you know, Point Hollow is on the list. You have to scroll down a little way to get to us, but we're there. Fame at last.*

We pulled up outside Poppy's Coffee & Donut. Tansy let the engine run a while, looking straight ahead, his hands still gripping the wheel.

My lips trembled.

And maybe your police records don't go as far back as the hazy, crazy days of 1971. You were out of the country at the time, counting corpses in the Mekong Delta, perhaps, but there were plenty of corpses back at the homestead, too. Thirteen of them, in fact, discovered hanging in the woods just west of Rainy Creek. Mass suicide. One of the victims/ participants (whatever you call them) left a note that read: "It watches us. It remembers." *Again, swept under the rug. Forget it ever happened and move along. One of the blessings of living under the radar, right? But the graves are still there, Sheriff. I've seen them—checked the names on the markers against the stories I read on the Internet. Silent, flowerless graves. These are the victims of whatever secret you're trying to keep. And guess what . . . so am I.*

Sheriff Tansy sighed, then slapped me on the thigh all chummy-like, and said, "I don't know about you, Oliver, but I could use a sugar rush. Strong coffee, triple-dose the sweet stuff, with a Boston Cream on the side. Whaddya say?"

I smiled (of course) and returned the chummy thigh-slap. "Now we're talking the same language, Sheriff."

Poppy's is small and in need of a makeover, but the smell of fresh coffee and pastries is as close to heaven as you'll find in Wharton, especially on such a cold day. Tansy clapped warmth into his hands and grabbed his regular seat at the counter, and Poppy was right over with the coffee. A small TV was tuned to CNN, with Daryn Kagan telling *Live Today* viewers about the increased security for President Bush's upcoming second inauguration.

"Should give that man a third and fourth inauguration," Tansy said. His shoulders rolled as he chuckled. "He's a true patriot. I'll take one of those Boston Creams, Poppy. The one on the left. No, *my* left." He chuckled again. "Thank you, sweetheart."

"He's a hero," the man sitting two stools over from Tansy said. "He's all-guns blazin'. That's what this country needs."

"Amen," Tansy agreed.

"He oughta turn those guns on some of the sand niggers we got over here."

"Amen," Tansy said again—somewhat disconcerting from a man (an elected official, no less) with a Glock 20 strapped to his waist.

I drank my coffee and chatted idly to Poppy, but most of my attention was centred on Tansy. Less than five minutes ago he had been in a perturbed state, sweating hard, with that squiggly vein in his right temple thumping. Now—chatting to his new best friend and fellow fuckwit—he was happy as a pup with two tails. He had moved on from the conversation we'd had in the cruiser. That was history, done and dusted, forgotten about. He'd swept it under his own *très* convenient little rug. Microcosm of the way his precious town operates.

He fell on his ass tramping back to the cruiser—his boot sinking through unpacked snow and knocking him off balance.

"Jesus Chrysler," he said.

He'd landed in a snow bank so no damage done, although his ass was apt to be a little wet on the drive home. I held out my hand, smiling (always smiling) and he took it. With a grunt (from both of us), I helped him to his feet.

"What happened, Sheriff?" I asked. The question dropped from my lips the way Tansy had dropped into the snow—quickly, and with a little puff of surprise. I held on to his hand, feeling him try to pull back, but I squeezed hard. It put me in mind of how I'd held on to Kip Sawyer's pen and not let go.

His eyes flickered. "I just fell, is all. It happens."

"That's not what I mean."

"I don't know—"

"What are you hiding?"

My heart was running fast and my body felt hot. He was either going to tell me or put a bullet in my head, then sweep me under the rug. I heard his leather glove creaking as I squeezed his hand harder.

"Let it go, Oliver," he whispered, looking me in the eye with the intensity of a heavyweight boxer before a title bout. He jerked back his arm and his hand slipped out of mine, although I was left holding his glove.

"Let *what* go?"

He snatched his glove from my hand and slipped it on. "I have no idea what you're talking about." And he showed me that he could smile, too—a big ol' go-fuck-yourself grin. I saw threads of chocolate in the gaps between his teeth. "The people of Point Hollow pride themselves on their unity of spirit and singular way of life. We're the Small Town with a Big Heart. I admire your curiosity and tenacity, but while you're looking for clouds, you're missing the rainbow."

He got into the cruiser and started it, then gave the engine a couple of impatient rips while he waited for me to get in. I did, trembling noticeably, my heart paddle-balling off my ribcage, and we didn't share another word the whole ride home.

September 23, 2005.

Sometimes I wish I had someone to share my bed with. Someone I could curl up to and smell their hair and feel our nakedness pressed together like twins in the womb. Sometimes I just need to be held and loved. Amber used to kiss the corners of my eyes and I liked that. She told me I wept in my sleep, real thin tears, and that my top lip would pooch out like a baby's. I liked that she told me—that she felt she could.

I just woke from a horrible dream. It's already breaking apart in my mind. The cigarette smoke of my subconscious. Here's what I can remember:

I walk into Sheriff Tansy's office to tell him about the mountain and all the bodies inside because I know that's the only way I will get answers. There's music playing but it sounds like that crazy backward Beatles song, except for one word that punches through every now and again, different each time, and I realize it's the first names of the children I have taken . . . *DANIELLE* . . . *RYAN* . . . *WALTER* . . . over and over, running through them all. Tansy sits at his desk eating a jelly doughnut, and all the jelly is spattering out and dripping down his whiskery chin and the front of his shirt. His badge is made of paper, and instead of the word SHERIFF stamped in the middle there is a smiley face drawn in yellow crayon. All of a sudden I am carrying a heavy suitcase that I heave onto his desk. He says "Whoa" as the weight of it causes his desk to lift on one side and some of his important paperwork helter-skelters to the floor. I look down and see that the pages are blank. I snap open the suitcase and inside are hundreds of photographs. "What in Jesus?" he says, and I say to him, "Here's what's wrong with your town, you son of a gumball," and I empty that suitcase full of photographs all over his desk . . . *VICTORIA* . . . *CONNOR* . . . *DANIELLE* . . . and he kind of pushes back as if it's boiling water I've poured all over, even lifting his boots off the floor, and the jelly doughnut falls from his fingers and hits the floor with a sound like a bug hitting a windshield. They are photographs of the skeletons in the mountain, all of them, hundreds of them, but the first photograph the sheriff picks up in his sticky fingers is of *CONNOR* curled into a dry little ball. The sheriff's eyes grow huge. He picks up the photographs of *RYAN* and then *WALTER* and then *VICTORIA* and looks at me. "We got a nice little place for you downstate," he says. "Sing-Sing Correctional. You're going to be there for a long time, Oliver. And without anyone to feed it the mountain is going to boom and boom and you're going to hear it forevermore, night and day, driving you insane, and you're going to pray for death." I walk to the window and look out. Abraham's Faith is too big. It's closer. Coming for me . . . *DANIELLE* . . . *RYAN* . . . and I try to scream but no sound comes out. "Sing-Sing," Sheriff Tansy says. I look at him. He is holding a skull. A child's skull. His tongue flicks out and rolls around its eye socket and there is jelly inside . . . *WALTER* . . . *VICTORIA* . . . *CONNOR* . . . and I wake up and wish there was somebody beside me but know/no I am alone.

March 12, 2006.

I don't know how many hours I've spent trawling the Internet for information about Point Hollow. I almost always come up empty, but every now and then . . .

The following is cut and pasted from a site called American Memories:

> In the weeks before she passed away, my grandmother shared many memories with me, and I'm happy to say that most were happy indeed. However, one memory was so disturbing, and told with such emotion, that it saddened me to know that she had carried it with her for so long. I share it here to unburden myself, although I can't bring myself to write all the grisly details.

She grew up in a small town in upstate NY called Point Hollow. I recall the delightful glint in her eye when she told me how she used to stand in the river and try to catch fish in her under-drawers, and that she spent many a sunshiny afternoon chasing rabbits across the hillsides around her home. Her expression darkened, however, when she told me about the mountain that overlooked the town. She claimed it was haunted, and that it made people do terrible things. I would have thought nothing of it, except she said it with such conviction (and fear) that her belief was undoubted.

But why would she believe it, especially given the benefit of wisdom? (And Gran was extremely wise; she kept her marbles until the very end, I can assure you.) Well, a traumatic event can impact the way people think and feel for the rest of their lives. Some people find God, and I'm sure that some people can lose Him, too.

The traumatic event that Gran witnessed and shared with me so many years later would test anyone's faith. It was a regular Sunday in 1923 and my Gran, only five years old, was in the same place as just about everybody else that day: in church. She wore her prettiest dress and had a flower in her hair, and she told me she felt like the most beautiful little girl in the world. The minister had just started his sermon when one of the windows smashed and a bottle came crashing in . . . only the bottle was filled with gasoline and stoppered with a burning rag. It landed near the front pews and exploded into flame. The chaos was immediate, and at this point I'll censor my grandmother's account. Suffice it to say that the wood frame building burned quickly, and not everybody got out in time. The doors had, in fact, been barricaded, and it took several men - using one of the pews as a battering ram - to smash it open.

Eighteen people were burned alive.

They caught the man who committed this atrocity, but Gran didn't know what happened to him. She either forgot or never knew to begin with. She does remember seeing him, though. She said that he was raving mad, and that he'd deliberately burned off most of his skin—perhaps to punish himself. She also said that he kept screaming, over and over, something about being "touched by a bird."

Following Gran's passing, I tried to research this terrible incident, but was unable to find any information. I wrote to the library in Point Hollow, but never received a reply. I also searched online, of course, but without luck. To this day, I don't know if it really happened, or if it was something my grandmother dreamed, but *believed* happened. What I *do* know is how genuine her fear was when she told me about the mountain. I have never seen her so afraid. I also know that— because of this— Point Hollow isn't high on my list of places to visit.

Thanks for letting me share. Love the site, btw.
Elizabeth S., TN.

I had to take a long walk after I read this. Breathe the trees. Get my shit together. I walked with my back to Abraham's Faith and considered evil: a thing of the cosmos, untenable, but as real as rain, and looking—always looking—for harbour. I imagined the earth billions of years ago, new-formed and lifeless, with good and evil spinning around it like the rings of Saturn. I saw the knuckle of rock that would one day become Abraham's Faith, drawing on thunder and lightning, suckling evil from the cosmos and swelling to ruinous heights, dark and blind and hunched. A rook on Earth's gravestone.

I turned around and stared at its slick, hated face.

"You've always been evil, haven't you?"

It felt as though I had discovered something it didn't *want* me to discover. Elizabeth S. from Tennessee had confirmed that there had been others before me. But how many? Did the mountain tell Jack Braum to grab his Winchester and paint Main Street as red as the stripes in the American flag? Did it tell thirteen young townspeople to cut thirteen lengths of rope and take a necktie social in the woods beside Rainy Creek?

The pieces are starting to slide together but the picture is far from complete. Hoping for more information, I tried to get in touch with Elizabeth S. through the American Memories website. (The gist of my e-mail: *I'm from Point Hollow. Maybe we can help each other fill in the blanks.*) I received a reply this morning: *Mr. Wray, I forwarded your e-mail to Elizabeth. She thanks you for your interest, but insists that, with respect, this is not a matter she is comfortable discussing with Internet Strangers. She is sure you will understand. Thank you for visiting American Memories. Share with us again!* It was the reply I expected, but obviously not the one I wanted.

I'd ask around, but seriously . . . what good would it do?

March 14, 2006.

I saw my father today. I *tried* being nice to him. I fed him his goddamn tomato soup, didn't I? I spooned it into his gap-toothed mouth and listened to every hideous slurping sound. It was like a drain clogged with shit, gurgling and spitting, and I never said a word. Not once. He jutted out his chin when he'd finished, wanting me to wipe his face, but I put the brakes on the TLC at that point. I handed him a napkin and he looked at me with sad eyes, so I told him that wiping his face was only one step removed from wiping his ass, that I'd put a bullet in his head before that ever happened—that I'd put a bullet in mine.

I tried to be nice because I wanted to ask him about the town. I wondered if he knew anything about Jack Braum, the church fire, or the suicide pact in the woods. I took away his soup dish, wheeled him in front of the TV, put on *Days of Our Lives,* and sat through it with him. Then I flicked off the TV, angled his wheelchair toward me, and asked:

"What is this town hiding?"

I didn't expect to get much sense from a man who collects his boogers on a piece of five-ply chipboard he calls The Green Monster. He started to make a "Yuggh-yuggh-yuggh" sound and his glass eye sagged in its socket as if whatever supported it had partially collapsed. He's only sixty-three, my old man, but you would think him ninety-three. I guess he inhaled too much Agent Orange in 'Nam. "Yuggh-yuggh," he said, and there was a long runner of spit dangling from his lower lip. I called him a fucking disgrace. He stopped and looked at me—sucked that spit right into his mouth with the same sound he had made while eating the tomato soup—and then said with certain and chilling clarity:

"When you were three months old I put a pillow over your face. I wish to God I'd kept it there."

The mist was brief but velvety red and I grabbed my jacket from where I'd thrown it over the back of the armchair, balled it into a pillow, and pressed it against his face. He fought as hard as he was able, flailing weakly with his arms, jerking his legs so frantically that his wheelchair started to roll across the floor and I had to put my boot behind one wheel to keep it in place. I heard him trying to scream and watched the top of his bald head turn from freckled eggshell to . . . well, tomato red. It didn't take long for the fight to drain from him. His legs started to tremble and his left arm sagged like his glass eye. I took the jacket away at the last moment and he pulled a desperate rip of air into his lungs. He exhaled like a horse whinnying, spittle flying from his purple lips, boogers popping from his nostrils (the Green Monster will have to do without those particular trophies, but there will be many more, I'm sure). His hands clasped the wheelchair's armrests and his good eye rolled every which way, as if registering the minutia of a life he was still living.

"Son of a . . . *fuuugh . . . beeeeeesh.*"

I was disgusted with him. Myself, too. I told him I hated him. His prosthetic eye had rolled back in his skull so that only the bottom of the painted iris could be seen, but his good eye zeroed on me. I have seen pictures of my father as a younger man and we look alike, we really do, but I hope I never look like he did right then. An unloved doll. A wry portrait. He called me a hellbound cunt. I called him a vile, worthless cocksucker, then put on the jacket I had almost killed him with, and left.

So much for nice.

June 9, 2006.

More gold on the Internet. I found it by chance, panning through gigabytes of bullshit, my eyes trained to recognize the shape of the words "Point Hollow" and pick them off the page no matter how fast I scrolled. But I found something else: a photograph. I zipped past it to begin with but then my brain slammed on the brakes and I scrolled back.

The quality is not good (it's an old photograph) but I can see what I need to: the mouth of the cave. *My* cave. And in the foreground a man standing with three terrified children. He has a creepy, fishhook smile. Two of the children are clutching each other, but all three are crying.

I can't write anymore for now. This photograph has thrown me out of fix. The man unnerves me. It's his face. His *grin.* Tomorrow I'll copy and paste it into the journal, and see if I can find out more about him.

Mr. Fishhook.

Original me.

June 14, 2006.

One of the little girls in the photograph is wearing a white dress and dark socks. She is also wearing a bracelet on her left wrist. I went to the mountain and looked for her—spent seven hours sifting among the bones. So many bodies crumbled when I touched them. Their clothes, too. Like wet paper.

I searched the depths of the cavern—found damp culverts and recesses I had never seen before, filled with small bones. My throat was thick with the dust I inhaled and I have blisters on my fingertips from scrabbling along the slick stone.

I found her just when I was about to give up. Her ribcage had fallen inward. She had one sock on, clogged with grime, down around her ankle. The bracelet was looped over the fragile bones of her fingers, swollen with corrosion. But it was her, and I knew for certain that the photograph I had pulled from the Internet had been taken moments before she was led into the darkness of Abraham's Faith.

I was wrong about her dress. It was yellow, not white.

August 3, 2006.

I went out with Sheriff Tansy again today. The first time in eighteen months. It was actually okay. We started off talking about sports and work (briefly; I know nothing about sports, he knows nothing about work), and then our conversation turned to common ground: Point Hollow. He was as forthcoming on the subject as I've ever known him to be. He told me flat-out that certain incidents in the town's past had been kept from the outside world—that there were remarkably few such incidents, all things considered. There were no records, and the townspeople (those who remembered) held their silence.

"So you just forget it ever happened?" I asked.

Tansy winked. "We're in this together, my friend."

I wondered—without official records, and with the town locked in silence—how much the sheriff actually knew. How much *anybody* knew, given that these "incidents" were swept under the rug a long time ago. I decided that I probably knew more than him, and was almost certain that he had no idea about the children in the mountain.

"I should point out," Tansy added, puffing out his chest as if to accentuate the badge, "that these few *blights* were long before my time. I haven't had to cover anything up, and God pray I'm never put in that position. So far, Oliver my friend, I'm batting a thousand. Nothing has happened on my watch."

And I thought, *If only you knew.*

April 5, 2007.

I don't see much of Kip Sawyer these days; he's as fragile as the bones in the mountain. One hearty gust of wind and he's apt to separate like a handful of confetti. Which isn't surprising when you consider the town threw him a 100th birthday party three years ago (not knowing if it actually *was* his 100th birthday, but figuring it was ballpark-close). Poor old Kip is completely blind now. No more crosswords in the sun. He can't walk, has difficulty articulating, needs a hearing aid, and wears a nasal cannula plugged into an oxygen tank that he carries in a leatherette satchel, usually drooped over the push handles of his wheelchair. He's basically a heartbeat in a very old shell, and I wonder if his mind is as sharp as it used to be. I almost hope not, for his sake. That must be like trying to fly in a cage.

I see him occasionally, though. His helper will push him around town when the weather allows, and sometimes he'll sit on the corner of Pussy Willow Road, waving at passing cars. I have considered asking him about the town again (it's been ten years since our discussion in Blueberry Bush park) but have refrained; a man so advanced in life isn't likely to have a change of heart. Still, he was the first person I thought of asking when I found the photograph on the Internet. Kip would have been alive when it was taken—not much older than the three terrified children, depending on when it was taken, and how old Kip really is. He might recognize one or all of them. He might even recognize the man with the fishhook smile.

What can you tell me about this picture, Kip?

He might help me understand. Help me put an end to it.

Perhaps if Kip wasn't blind, I would have asked anyway, despite his frailty and stubbornness. It might have surprised him enough to get a reaction. It had to be worth trying. But I didn't see the point in showing him a photograph he couldn't see, so left it alone.

Until today.

I was at the doctor's office for my annual medical (Dr. Alex, not Ruzicka; it just isn't done to have your testes squeezed by one of the guys you play poker with). Everything checked out. Blood pressure a tad on the high side, but put that down to white coat hypertension.

Kip was in the waiting room when I came through, sitting in his wheelchair while his helper talked to the medical secretary. I glanced at him, nothing more, kept walking, and all of a sudden my legs decided to go left instead of straight ahead. Two seconds later, I was sitting in the empty seat next to his wheelchair.

"Hello, Mr. Sawyer. It's Oliver. Oliver Wray."

His cloudy eyes flicked my way. "Oh," he said, or maybe, "Hello."

I looked at his helper, who was deep in conversation with the secretary. I had some time before I was shooed away like the nuisance that I am.

"I'm holding a photograph," I said (the photograph was actually here, in a folder on this desk, but he didn't need to know that). "It's very old, probably taken at around the time Woodrow Wilson was in the White House and you were a young man. A long time ago."

"Mong bime," he agreed, and tried to smile.

"Perhaps you can tell me something about it," I continued, and leaned a little closer. "It's a local photograph. I'll describe the scene and maybe you can—"

"Mokul?"

"That's right, local."

His blind eyes flicked away from me. I saw the tiny water droplets in the cannula tubing tremble as he inhaled.

"It was taken on Abraham's Faith." I hesitated whether or not to tell him how I knew this, and decided it didn't really matter; old Kip was knock-knock-knockin' on heaven's door, and would take whatever I said with him. "I know this because I recognize the mouth of the cave. I've been there many times, Kip. I've been inside. I've seen the bodies."

His eyes drifted my way, as blank as bullet holes.

"There's a man standing in front of the cave. In his late twenties, early thirties, I'd say. He has thick, dark hair and a lopsided smile. There are children with him. Two girls and a boy, aged between—"

"Mo . . . I dun mo."

"Aged between four and eight years old. They're crying, Kip. They're terrified."

"Mo . . ."

"What happened?" I whispered. My heartbeat was louder than my voice, drumming so hard I thought my nose was going to start bleeding. "Why did he do it, Kip? And how did he make it stop?"

The old man shook his head. Tears trickled from his eyes, rolled as far as the cannula tubing, then ran across it like rain on a pipe. He mumbled something unintelligible and flapped his hand toward the exit in a gesture that was easier to discern: *Go pound sand, boy. Leave me the hell alone.* The helper came over at that point. She looked at me accusingly and I offered her a fetching smile in return.

"Just saying hello," I explained, getting to my feet. I squeezed Kip's shoulder as he knuckled the tears from his face, and then left. I whistled all the way to the door, but was clenched and burning inside.

Kip Sawyer is no help to me. A heartbeat in a shell. Even his soul is in chains.

He's taking his secrets to the grave.

September 10, 2007.
Abraham's Faith woke up today—pulled me screaming from my bed at four A.M. and I pissed myself like a little kid. It had been silent for more than ten years.

The thunder—booming in my head as I write this—reminds me how small I am.

September 12, 2007.
I don't know his name yet. I'll watch the news later and find out. I grabbed him from a playground in Kent, CT. He struggled all the way and now I *have* to sleep; I look in the mirror and see an extremely tired man.

Update: Felix Brodsky. Nine years old.
I look in the mirror and see a monster.

Chapter
Nine

Ninety-six by noon.

Dry, somnolent heat. Everything slower and brighter. The weekend had been a burner but now—Tuesday—it felt as if the ozone layer had been replaced by a sheet of Saran Wrap. It didn't look like cooling down anytime soon; the Weather Channel showed the same blazing sun icon deep into next week, and offered tips on how to stay cool and be safe, but to consider the environment and conserve energy when possible. The people of Point Hollow didn't feel the same rules applied to them when it came to ecological concerns. They lived in one of the greenist, *tree-eist* parts of the country. They *were* the environment, by God, and if they wanted to crank their aircons and sprinkler their lawns, then dammit, they would.

And they did. Walk anywhere in Point Hollow and you would hear the whir of air conditioners, all at maximum power, with intent to run until it either cooled down or the power blew out. Not that anybody was walking around. Too damn hot. If they had to leave the house, they drove their vehicles everywhere, even if it was just a two-minute trip to pick up the mail. There were a few foolhardy youths sunbathing or playing ball in Blueberry Bush Park, and a few more splashing around in Gray Rock River, but the older (sensible) folk stayed in their cool homes or places of work, or sat in the shade drinking chilled beverages with electric fans blowing at them like mini-cyclones.

Bobby Alexander went back to work after spending the previous two days with Matthew. They'd fished Sunday morning (while, at his million-dollar home on the eastern edge of town, Oliver Wray stripped naked and prepared to purify body and soul), but the smallmouth were too lazy to bite and stayed low, where it was cool. It didn't matter; Matthew and Bobby opened their shirts and slathered SPF 40 sunscreen on their thirty-something bellies, then cracked ice-cold sodas from the cooler and shot the breeze.

"I'm so glad you're here," Bobby had said, on more than one occasion.

"Me too," Matthew had replied, every time.

They laughed a lot, and their conversation had an easy, adolescent quality, allowing for conversation that was both unrestrained and unabashed. Grownups talked about mortgage rates, car repairs, and politics. Matthew and Bobby talked about *Lost* and *Survivor* and which superheroes hadn't been invented yet. They also talked about the past, of course, and Bobby eased a few more of Matthew's memories into the open. They were *good* memories, too (building a raft they'd taken down Gray Rock River, only to have it break apart in the rapids; the time they let the air out of Mr. Nordhagen's tires, using tiny pebbles to keep the valves open), and Matthew felt as if he'd removed a damp jacket that he'd been wearing for many years, its cold weight causing him to stoop. He stood and straightened his shoulders, laughing with Bobby and realizing, with no small relief, that his childhood hadn't been a playground of dark images, after all. His brain had locked something away, that was for sure, but perhaps it was one insignificant thing. A single cluster of nightshade in a pasture of orchids.

I don't need to concentrate on lighting the darkness, Matthew thought. *I need to concentrate on the light itself.* This concept burst from his ribcage like a hundred small birds, colourful wings beating fast, swirling into the blue dome of sky. He wondered how Dr. Meeker would assay such enlightened intellection. He further wondered, reaching into the cooler for another soda, if he'd even find out. Perhaps his sessions with Dr. Meeker were a thing of the past. Like his marriage.

One step at a time, he thought. *Let's see how you feel when you get back to the city. When you see Kirsty again and begin hunting for a ruthless-yet-affordable divorce attorney. When you're signing endless legal paperwork by day, and sleeping—alone—in a single bed by night.*

"Do you think you'll ever move back here?" Bobby had asked as they packed away the fishing gear, shooting their empty soda cans into the empty creel.

"Point Hollow?"

"Sure," Bobby said.

"I don't think so."

"Why not?"

Matthew frowned. Could he tell Bobby that he was enjoying himself, and *finding* himself, but that Point Hollow nonetheless gave off an eerie, *Twin Peaks* vibe? Would Bobby be insulted if he told him that he just didn't trust the town, that being here felt a little like keeping a wild animal as a pet? Would Bobby understand if he told him that, for all its natural beauty, and all the memories, it simply wasn't home anymore?

Bobby's eyes were big. Sad, almost.

"Work," Matthew said.

"We have jobs in Point Hollow," Bobby said. "It's not New York City pay, but it doesn't have to be. It's stress-free, and you'll live in a house, not a shoebox."

"I understand," Matthew said, tossing the last soda can into the creel. "But I work for a huge company, and there's potential for moving up the ladder."

Bobby shook his head.

"I'm just not ready to do the Grizzly Adams thing," Matthew said. "But I'll make you a deal. I'll visit two or a three times a year, but you have to come see me in the city, too. I'll show you around. We'll have fun."

Bobby smiled and patted his chest. "I'm not sure my ticker can handle the city."

"I'll take you to a Mets game," Matthew said.

"It *definitely* can't handle a Mets game," Bobby said, but he grinned and they shook on it.

Sunday afternoon had been spent at Bobby's house, being pampered by Mrs. Alexander while watching said Mets take on the Diamondbacks. Following a fine steak dinner (Bobby allowed to indulge—the rabbit-food diet put on hold for one night only), they walked to the Rack and shot a few games of pool. Matthew stiffened as soon as he walked through the door; Sheriff Tansy—the friggin' Deer Hunter himself—was sitting at the bar with his chums, dressed in his redneck civvies, but still managing to look self-important.

"Looky, fellers," he said, slapping one of his pals on the back. "It's Matthew Bridge, founder of Friday's feast."

Matthew nodded and forced a smile. "Good to see you, Sheriff. And thanks again for helping me out on Friday."

"That whitetail was hellish tasty, boy," he said, and licked his lips. His buddies guffawed and nodded in agreement. "Nicely tenderized, thanks to that Jap piece of shit you were driving."

The smile trembled on Matthew's face. "Well, I appreciate your help." Which was another way of saying, *Okay, Sheriff, you and your backwater buddies have had your fun, so how about you show a little professionalism and drop it now?*

"I thought you were going to piss your tighty-whities," the sheriff said.

"Or number two," one of his cohorts cracked.

"Number two," another one echoed, and they all laughed.

Matthew turned away from them. He looked at Bobby and the expression in his eyes said everything: *You see why I don't want to move back here?* Bobby squeezed his shoulder and asked if he still wanted to shoot pool, or maybe head back and watch the night game on ESPN. "Mom will bake cookies," he said.

"I'm fine," Matthew said. "Your mom's been in the kitchen all day. Give her the night off and we'll shoot a few frames. Rack 'em up, big guy."

Bobby did. Matthew took the first shot and potted off the break.

"He can shoot pool," Sheriff Tansy announced to the bar. "But he can't shoot deer."

They all howled at that one. Matthew smiled and raised his hand. Two and a half miles away, Oliver Wray emerged, cold and hardened, from the spring that he and Matthew had crossed as children. His head was clear. It chimed like a bell. He stood among the trees—in his mind he *became* a tree—as Matthew and Bobby played pool and Sheriff Tansy fired over the occasional bullying quip.

On Monday—hotter than Sunday, but not the scorcher it would be Tuesday—Bobby took Matthew to a place he said would help him feel better. "I think I'm the only person who knows about it," he said, leading Matthew off the trails and through the woods (Matthew wasn't entirely comfortable veering from the trails, but said nothing). Bobby stepped softly and pressed a finger to his lips as they approached the edge of a clearing, and peering through the branches they saw a gathering of whitetail. At least a dozen adults—the bucks adorned with splendid antlers—and twice as many fawns. They stepped among the goldenrod and hollyhocks, chewing the leaves and flicking their ears. The fawns trailed their mothers, big-eyed, their spotted coats looking almost wet in the sunlight. Matthew grinned, shallow breaths trapped high in his chest. *Thank you*, he mouthed to Bobby, who nodded and tried to shuffle a little closer, but stepped on a dry twig that broke the silence. The deer sprang from the clearing in shimmering bounds, tails flashing, gone in seconds, which in itself was marvelous to behold. "I thought you needed to see that," Bobby said, his face pink and sincere, his eyes shining. "Sort of an antidote to what you went through with the sheriff." And Matthew threw his arms around Bobby and hugged him tight. *Too* tight, perhaps, because Bobby wheezed and laughed a little bit, and a small tear trickled from the corner of his left eye.

"You know something?" Bobby said later in the day. They were sitting on the porch drinking Mrs. Alexander's lemonade, watching the sun turn the western peaks into copper. The air was scented with wild honeysuckle. Bumblebees purred on petals. Children's laughter tinkled from down the street, sounding divine.

"Tell me," Matthew said.

"While I was in hospital with my ribcage wired shut and my chest stitched together, I came to realize that I don't have any friends. It was the most frightening time of my life, yet the only person who visited me was my mother. That's sad, huh?"

Matthew nodded. He reached over and squeezed Bobby's arm.

"I've lived here all my life, and I know lots of people," Bobby continued. "The whole town, in fact. But friends? Not really. Nobody I can call and ask if they want to shoot some eight-ball or go fishing. Nobody who'll visit me after I've just had major surgery. And that's what friends do, right? They're there for each other."

Matthew nodded again. He sympathized because he felt the same way. Colleagues and associates, but no friends.

Only Bobby.

"I'm your friend," he said, and that made Bobby smile. He winked at him, squeezed his arm a little harder. "Next time you're in hospital, I'll visit you. Promise."

"There won't be a next time," Bobby said. "Anyway, you'll probably forget about me when you get back to New York."

"No, I won't," Matthew said, and he meant it. He looked Bobby in the eye and said it again. "I won't."

They sat on the porch for another three hours. They talked about *Dexter* and superhero movies and whether or not *Manimal* was a better TV show than *Automan*. When the sickle moon drifted above the treetops, Matthew gave Bobby a hug and said goodnight. Bobby stayed on the porch a little longer, watching the moths go crazy around the streetlamps, listening to the crickets sing.

He slept that night curled on his side, like always, but smiling as he dreamed.

Tuesday. The hottest day of the year so far. Matthew stayed in the cool hotel lobby and surfed the 'net, perusing potential divorce attorneys in the five boroughs. Oliver ran naked in the wild, his body painted with earth pigments, crow feathers in his hair. Bobby was at work at the post office, giving the smile he'd carried from his dreams to everyone who walked in.

———

"Good morning, Mrs. Anderson. Hot one today."

"It's the afternoon," Mrs. Anderson corrected him, mopping sweat from her wrinkled brow. "As in after twelve P.M. And it's not good, either. I'm as cranky as a kicked ass. Goddamn heat."

Bobby's smile became a grin as he watched Mrs. Anderson shuffle to her mailbox, dragging Dickens, her old bulldog, along behind her. Bobby took a Beggin' Strip from a stash he kept in his bottom drawer, came out from behind the counter, and gave it to Dickens.

"It's *bacon!*" Bobby said, and at this point Mrs. Anderson usually grinned and said, *Dogs don't know it's not bacon,* just like the commercial, but she only mumbled something under her breath and grabbed her mail. Dickens shared her suffering; he sniffed almost disdainfully at the treat, too hot to even open his mouth, and then collapsed on his side, tongue lolling.

"Okay," Bobby said, retrieving the Beggin' Strip. "Looks like I'll have to give this to Mr. Green's Labradoodle. You had your chance."

Dickens gave him a look to suggest he really couldn't care less. His owner, meanwhile, shuffled through her mail, then handed Bobby a card and grumbled, "Parcel."

Bobby smiled and flicked the card. "Be right back," he said.

Mrs. Anderson nodded drowsily and edged closer to the A/C.

Amid the incoming boxes and packages behind the counter (but out of the customers' sightline, so they couldn't see what a disorganized shitpile it was), Bobby found Mrs. Anderson's parcel, and noticed something else: three uncollected parcels addressed to Oliver Wray. Bobby frowned. Oliver was usually dead-on when it came to collecting his mail—had a lot of it, too, being a big-time businessman. They'd been delivered yesterday, while Bobby was playing hooky. *He must be on one of his business trips,* Bobby thought. He went out front and gave Mrs. Anderson her package. She thanked him and left, with Dickens slumping behind her, making a sound like a squeeze toy.

Bobby used his master key to open Oliver's PO Box. It was full of mail. Two thick bundles. One for yesterday. One for today.

"Where'd you go, Ollie?"

He checked the computer to see if Oliver had left a note. He usually did when he was going away for a few days. There was nothing.

"We got three parcels here for Oliver Wray," Bobby said to Vern Abbott, postmaster and friend-to-all. "His box is jammed, too. You know if he's on a business trip?"

"That's a big ten-four," Vern said. "Called his house yesterday. Voicemail says he's on a jaunt. Don't know when he's back."

"Probably on his yacht in the Caribbean," Bobby said, and couldn't keep the acerbity from his tone.

"That man works hard and gives harder," Vern said. He put a box of mail on Bobby's workstation. The front of his hairpiece lifted under the force of the A/C. Bobby saw the bonding on his scalp. "He's entitled to be wherever he chooses to be."

"One of God's faithful foot soldiers," Bobby said with a thread of sarcasm. Vern nodded in agreement (he was a sometime-sermonizer at New Hope as well as a friend-to-all; references to the Big Guy were certain to win approval) and sauntered away, whistling tunelessly, the sound quickly enveloped by the A/C's fierce drone.

He thinks I'm jealous, Bobby thought, and then remembered the look he saw in Matthew's eyes when they had talked about Oliver—how they crimped at the edges and danced fleetingly away. Matthew thought he was jealous, too. And what had Oliver said to him? *The only reason you don't like me is because I've got everything and you've got nothing.* But riches and success had nothing to do with it. The shark's grin, however, and the way his mask would sometimes slip . . .

Look at you, Oliver had snarled. *Fat as fuck and one heart attack closer to the grave.* Was that really the same person who wrote a six-figure cheque to keep the school open, and whose plaque adorned a bench in Blueberry Bush Park?

You're just an overweight prick seething with envy.

There was *more* to Oliver. A darkness that, apparently, nobody else could see. But Oliver had guile as well as money. A blinding combination. And besides, Point Hollow was guilty of its own disingenuous smile.

"Crooked as a barrel of fishhooks," Bobby muttered to himself, sorting through the box of mail, angling his broad back toward the A/C vents and feeling the delicate hair on his nape flutter. He'd give anything to see Oliver—*King* Oliver—fall on his ass just once, and hard enough to shatter that goddamn smile.

He had, on occasion (though he would never admit it, not even to his mom) opened Oliver's mail. Just a few letters, was all. Poking his nose in again, but eager to discover something—*anything*—less than perfect about the man that everybody loved. He came up empty, though (the most interesting thing he uncovered was an invitation to a party at former governor Spitzer's house). Bobby shredded the opened letters and swore to himself that he'd never do it again. But sometimes his curiosity got the better of him.

Even now his eyes flicked to Oliver's uncollected parcels. He wondered, if he were to open them, what he'd find inside. Black market firearms, perhaps, or the chemicals and fillers required to make dirty street drugs. Better yet, what would he find if he cycled up to that isolated house and peeked through the windows? A meth lab? A prostitution ring? Clothes made from human skin?

Ain't nobody home, he thought. *Why don't you find out?*

"Dumb idea," Bobby said to himself. Oliver could return at any time. What would he say—what would he *do*—if he found Bobby snooping around his house?

That won't happen. He'll be gone for days. He always is.

"Maybe," Bobby said, but it was still a crazy idea. Besides, it was in the high nineties out there. Too damn hot. No way was he cycling all the way to Oliver's house. Not going to happen, baby.

"So just forget it," Bobby said.

But he couldn't.

———

Oliver perched on a rock like a mountain lion, baring his teeth at the sky. The sun slammed him like a hammer and Abraham's Faith clanged in his soul. His mind had ceased operating like it used to. No longer a sequence of feelings and notions. More a collage of prescience, beta waves, and snap imagery. He was an animal, tuned to instinct. He hungered and howled.

A hawk circled above him, its shadow rippling over the rocks' grey skin. It saluted him with a cry and he responded, mimicking the sound, flapping his arms. In the ticks and beats of his mind his response could be translated as, *We fly together, hawk-brother*. The hawk drifted from view, pumping its wings just once, and Oliver watched it with shining eyes. He then turned back to his kingdom— spread below him, a breathtaking panorama—and puffed out his chest in pride. He roared, and with lithe movement clambered from his rock, scenting the air as he stalked on all fours. At the foot of the mountain he reverted to two legs—like a human—and ran amid the thickets and trees. Sweat coated his body, mingling with the mud, the blood, and the pigment he had used to paint his skin. He ran hard, until the breaths jerked from his lungs and his skin dripped. Abraham's Faith boomed at him, but he sensed that he was nearing the end. Not only of this contemplation, but of his communion with the mountain.

It would all be over.

Soon.

He came to a stream and drank deeply. He didn't use the water to clean his wounds or to soothe his sunburned shoulders. He simply drank until his stomach ached and moved on. Back on all fours. His mind flashed constructs that he would not have understood yesterday, and would not even conceive tomorrow, but in his present condition . . .

Rest. He needed rest.

Oliver's burned shoulders worked as his forelegs tracked across the forest floor. He soon arrived at a clearing, where a band of coyotes regarded him with suspicious yellow eyes. Oliver made a sound deep in his chest, then curled among them and slept.

———

The post office wasn't busy. A few languid customers staggered in to take care of correspondence that couldn't wait, but the little bell over the door barely chimed, and at one-forty—a whole hour and twenty minutes before his shift was supposed to end—Vern told Bobby to pack up and hit the road. "I can hold the fort, Bobby," he'd said. "Go home and jump into a bathtub full of ice cubes."

So Bobby had a little extra time on his hands. He'd arranged to meet Matthew at six P.M. They were going to Middletown for dinner at TGI Friday's (another night off the rabbit-food diet, but every now and then wouldn't hurt, even Dr. Ruzicka said so) and a movie. He figured he had at least three hours to kill. Maybe he'd sit on the porch with a jug of Mom's lemonade and read some of the new Lee Child book he'd borrowed from the library. Or he could sit in the living room with Mom and watch Dr. Phil and Oprah set the world to rights.

Or . . .

Oliver's uncollected parcels caught his eye.

Or I can cycle up to Oliver's house—take a quick peek through the windows.

"Too hot," he said, pulling his cap from his back pocket, slapping it on and stepping outside. The heat was like something solid and he retreated into the building for a moment to gather himself. He popped the top two buttons of his post office shirt and stepped outside again. His bicycle was propped against the wall, not secured to anything (there was no need for such measures in Point Hollow). He swung his leg over the crossbar, dropped his ample ass onto the seat, and wiped away the sweat that had instantly formed on his face. Sixty seconds later he was pedaling east on Main, imagining the blissful taste of his mother's homemade lemonade and the rattle of ice cubes against his teeth. He'd be home, guzzling that lemonade, in less than five minutes, and slumped on the porch, in the company of Jack Reacher, in less than ten. (Bobby's guilty pleasure, reading the Reacher novels, was to cast himself in the starring role—a little slimmer, of course, and the scar on his chest was made by a .38 rather than a surgeon's scalpel.) Then he could grab a cool shower and get ready for Matthew.

Happy days.

So Bobby surprised himself when he cycled past Grace Road, which would take him home, and stayed on Main, which led toward Tall Pine Way and Oliver Wray's house. *Just a quick look-see,* was how he answered this surprise. *Besides, I could use the extra exercise if I'm going to Friday's tonight.* He smiled at the thought. Maybe he could have a dessert, too. Vern had told him that the Chocolate Peanut Butter Pie was to die for.

———

Feverish.

Dreams? Hallucinations? Visions—yes, *visions.* In the first of them he faced a black bear named Ohkwari who stood on his hind legs and cut a shadow as broad as the river. Fire danced in Ohkwari's eyes and he spoke to Oliver in the language of Old Earth. Oliver listened carefully and responded in the same tongue.

"*M'kendu ra den karra d'ni,*" Ohkwari said.

"*Pashan fi tooc,*" Oliver said.

The black bear shook his head and roared. "*Shar mal lacca ke.*" His mighty teeth snapped, eyes blazing. "*Ra wak e ka'hai.*"

"*Keeshpa ra,*" Oliver said calmly. He pulled his shoulders square and looked at the mountain behind Ohkwari. "*Keeshpa ra mi. En t'al.*"

In another vision he ran with mountain lions. His muscles were firm liquid and the high grass smelled like a thousand summers. Everything breathed. The trees, the flowers, the rivers. His senses were heightened. The earth seemed young. He shared this with his catamount friends and they laughed good-naturedly at his unworldliness. One of them, a female named Kopa, purred and offered herself to him, and he took her as the mountain trembled, penetrating her tight but ready slit, eyes like drops of amber.

The third, and final, vision was the most powerful. Surrounded by coyotes, Oliver—the whelp of the band—whined and looked for his mother. An older male growled and snapped at him, while a grey-snouted female offered her withered teats. He snarled and turned away, then padded from the clearing to the foot of Abraham's Faith. A dark man stood amid a cluster of rocks. No, not a man, but fire in the shape of a man. Black fire. It licked and flickered.

"I'm looking for my mother," Oliver said to the black fire. "I need to feed."

"I am your mother," the fire said. "Your father, too."

"Can you feed me?"

"I'm the one who needs to feed." And the man-shaped fire stepped toward him on flickering legs, leaving a trail of smoke that soaked into the mountain and made it darker. Oliver dug his claws into the ground, his hackles spiked, teeth showing. The black fire crackled, and Oliver saw that his mouth was twisted. A fishhook smile.

"You're him," Oliver growled. "The darkness. The poison in the mountain."

"The heart of the mountain."

"You're darkness."

He came closer still and Oliver felt the black heat shimmering off him. He stomped his fire-foot. Smoke bloomed. The mountain shook and grew darker.

"Burn with me," he said, and his twisted smile glimmered.

Oliver snapped from this final vision with such a start that the coyotes leapt up and scattered, leaving petals of dust and their wild scent. He crawled to the nearby stream and took full, coppery mouthfuls—vomited powerfully, and then drank again, until his throat was lined with sediment. He shook the crow feathers from his hair and watched them flicker to the ground. *Like black flames,* he thought, and whirled to the foot of the mountain, expecting to see the man-shaped fire standing there. But there were only rocks, shadows, and broken trees.

Oliver got to his feet, held out his arms, and flew for a moment. A sweet, lazy circle over the treetops. Then he came back to earth—back to *body*—and started to trek through the untouched wilds.

Breathing deeply.

Cleansed. Pure. Ready.

It was time to go home.

———

Modern concept, split-level. Redwood siding and broad panes of glass. It effused a certain desperation, Bobby thought, like city wealth that was trying too hard to fit in. If he didn't know better, he'd think the owner was a Manhattan buckslinger without clue-one about country life, or a pretentious actor who needed to see trees in every direction. An Arcadian retreat from lights, cameras, and action.

Bobby stood astride his bicycle (he had pushed it the last quarter-mile), fanning himself with his cap and regarding Oliver's chichi residence with the same contempt with which he regarded the man himself. His heart drummed a tad too fast for comfort, making his chest ache and his breaths come in wheezy bursts. He didn't think he was in any danger of blowing a rod, but thought it prudent to take a moment to compose himself and try to bring down the BPM. Blame it on fatigue; the heat was a bitch and the ride out here had been tougher than expected. Tall Pine Way was uphill most of the way. Not a steep gradient, but long and gradual, and you damn well noticed it when you were pedaling a bicycle in plus-ninety-degree heat.

There was anxiety, too. A goodly heap of it. Strip away the heat and fatigue and his ticker would still be doing the funky chicken. Being on Oliver's private patch of land was unsettling, pure and simple. Also, he was that much closer to Abraham's Faith. Never a good thing.

Let's get this over with, he thought. There was nobody around so he took off his shirt, used it to wipe his face, and tied it to the bike's crossbar. He took a single step and paused, listening, wanting to make sure he couldn't hear Oliver's car tearing along Tall Pine Way before going any farther. Insects droned and birds whistled. Nothing but the calm of a summer's day. Bobby let out a trembling breath, counted to five, and continued across the driveway to Oliver's house.

I'm just going to take a quick peek through the windows, he thought. *Do the nosy neighbour thing, settle my curiosity, then make like horseshit and hit the trail.*

But he was nervous. Being Jack Reacher was all well and good when he could close the book, but in real life he wasn't designed for anything more exciting than a splash of hot sauce in his sandwich. Fat beads of sweat sizzled down his bare back and over the dome of his belly. He cast a wary glance at Abraham's Faith, looming behind Oliver's house. *Protecting* it, Bobby thought. He sensed it watching him, disapproving, and offered a paltry smile in return.

He clutched his chest and felt his heart bouncing against his palm. Coming out here had been a mistake, almost certainly, but it was too late to second-guess his decision. He leaned his bike against the garage door (if it had been open he would have seen all three vehicles inside, suggesting that Oliver had not gone far), and started to walk around the house, peering into windows along the way, careful not to leave hand or nose smears on the glass. The rooms appeared orderly, spotlessly clean. Bobby groaned. Had he really—deep down, where his weak heart beat hard and fast—expected to find evidence of criminality? Maybe not, but he *had* hoped to find proof of Oliver's imperfection. A collection of snuff DVDs, perhaps, or pornographic materials next to the bed. But there was nothing. Not even a box of Kleenex. His instincts were usually on the money, but maybe Oliver's smile was genuine, after all. Looking at his house, the only thing Bobby could pin on him was a possible case of OCD.

He made his way to the rear of the property, thinking he'd step into a lush garden. Copious, colourful blooms and a vibrant lawn, perhaps a topiary or a gold-plated bird bath upon which doves perched and cooed Oliver's praises. But there was no back garden, as such, only a large rear deck with steps leading down into . . . well, into the Catskills, as if to suggest it was *all* his garden. Bobby stepped around the deck (pausing to peer beneath it, looking for bones and burial mounds), then huffed and puffed up the steps.

There was a huge hot tub on one side (Bobby imagined Point Hollow's luminaries wallowing in there, drinking Champagne and smoking Camachos while getting hand jobs from high-class hookers) and a patio set on the other. But the view was the star of the show. Smoke-coloured ranges and a million trees, with Point Hollow gathered among them like stones clustered in an open palm. He could see Old Friend Pond and a flickering bend of Gray Rock River. And, of course, Abraham's Faith, rearing over the treetops in the east, like a cut face peering over a hedgerow.

Oliver's kingdom, Bobby thought, swatting bugs with his baseball cap and dropping into one of the recliners. His legs—his heart—rejoiced, and he sat there for a moment, taking in the view, imagining King Oliver sitting out here every morning, wearing a kimono or achkan, something like that, and sipping angostura bitters in hot water.

"Like an asshole," Bobby snapped. He was crotchety because he was hot, thirsty, and exhausted, but also because he hadn't found any dirt to dish on Oliver. It appeared the dude was as squeaky-clean as the house he lived in. Bobby sighed and stood up, then shuffled to the patio doors. They looked in on an open plan kitchen and living room, every surface polished to a high sheen. Bobby should have noted nothing out of the ordinary and carried on his way, but the sight of the refrigerator locked him to the spot and filled his volcanic mind with frosty fantasies: chilled cans of Sprite and Pepsi, polar bears skiing down glaciers, freeze pops and ice cream, Eskimos making snow angels. *Dear God*, Bobby thought, and a dusty sound escaped his throat. His eyes targeted the refrigerator's icemaker. He imagined hitting the button, catching a handful of crushed ice, and cramming it into his mouth. *Oh, dear God.*

"May as well be on the moon," Bobby croaked. The door was surely locked. His desperate thirst would have to wait. Unless, of course, he wanted to graduate to the more serious misdemeanour of breaking and entering.

Locked? You think? his volcanic mind queried. *I don't know many people in Point Hollow who lock their doors, for the same reason you never lock up your bike outside the post office. This is a safe, crime-free environment. Just saying.*

"It'll be locked," Bobby said. "He didn't go to the Rack for a beer. He's on a business trip. Europe, probably. He'll be away for weeks. Of course it'll be locked."

Sure. Okay. You're probably right.

Bobby licked his lips, slid aside the screen door, and—his gaze still fixed on the refrigerator—curled his hand around the patio door's handle.

Pepsi-Cola. Simply Orange. Poland Spring. I'm betting you'll find some Ben & Jerry's Chunky Monkey in the freezer, too. Again, just saying.

Bobby shook his head. Sweat streamed down his naked upper body. He took his hand from the handle, then put it back. *This decision is too big for me,* he thought. *Let's turn it over to the man upstairs.*

"Dear God in heaven," he began. "If this door is unlocked, I'll take it as a sign that I'm supposed to snaffle a drink of Pepsi and perhaps a mouthful of Chunky Monkey. If it's locked—as it should be—then I'll roll homeward, duly repentant, and with a promise to henceforth mind my own beeswax."

He pulled the handle. The door slid smoothly open.

"Thy will be done," Bobby said, and stepped inside.

———

Oliver Wray squatted in the shade of a yellow birch and ate wild blueberries and chicory and washed it down with spring water. Fragments of reality returned—points of light against a drapery of blackness, like watching stars appear. He became aware of the heat, the pain in his body, and who he was. *I am human . . . a man. A man. My name is . . . Oliver . . . Wray . . .* Not so long ago he had been something else. The radical centre. Take three circles: one each for man, animal, and bird. Intersect them. The point at which their axes meet is the radical centre, and this was as close as he could get to describing what he was—*where* he was. A thing between. A circular triangle.

I am vital. I am pure.

A falcon cried and swooped and came up with nothing in its talons but dead grass. Oliver wiped his mouth and moved on, out of the shade, into the bleached-hot day. He'd considered washing the mud and pigment from his body, but left it to give protection from the sun. As such he walked home, willingly assuming the man-circle, shedding the last of his feathers and fur and becoming Oliver Wray. He cut through a swatch of pine forest and joined Sanctuary Road close to his property.

He sensed that something was wrong before he even set foot on his driveway. Tapping into some residue of animal instinct, perhaps.

Somebody was in his house.

He snarled, crouched, shoulders hunched. *Sheriff Tansy,* he thought. *Matthew told him, after all, and now he's here, looking for evidence.* The animal-circle grew solid and he intersected it. *In my study. Reading my notes. My journal.*

Still bleeding, half-wild, he prowled onto his driveway.

READING MY JOUR—

No, not Sheriff Tansy.

There was a bicycle leaning against the garage door and Oliver knew immediately who it belonged to—had seen him pedalling around town countless times, with his baseball cap turned backward and his ridiculous belly sagging over the crossbar. Bobby Alexander, who, for whatever reason, didn't like Oliver. Didn't *trust* him. *That sack of shit,* Oliver thought. *That fat fuck.* Not the police, and that was a good thing, although any relief Oliver felt was drowned in a boiling sea of anger. His heart rushed in his chest, his body low to the ground, hackles raised. *I better find him sitting on the rear deck,* he thought. *And he better have a damn good reason for being on my property.*

Oliver growled deep in his chest and skulked to the rear of the house.

I am . . . am . . .

No one on the deck, but the patio door was open.

I am . . .

Oliver crept up the steps and into his house, naked of everything except the earth colours tattooed on his skin. No one in the living room or kitchen (an empty juice carton on the countertop—fucking slob), but a distinctive sound from his study.

Clickety-click went the mouse.

I AM . . . AM . . .

Everything inside Oliver raged. From purity to pure wrath. It burned inside him as he prowled toward his study.

Three circles again.

I am the radical centre.

CHAPTER
TEN

Bobby always said that his
biggest weakness was his
heart. Not that it was physically
weak (although it was, of course),
but that it was emotionally too large.
He would do anything for anyone,
and usually with a dumb, if slightly
heartbreaking smile on his face. This often
led to people taking advantage of him, and he rarely got
anything in return. His heart attack shook him up. It made
him see things—and people—in a different light. He came to
realize that, while it was important to help others, he had to live
for himself, too. Life was short, after all.

His mother insisted that having a big heart wasn't a weakness at
all—that it was, in fact, an honourable strength. She would further
insist that Bobby had no weaknesses, as such, merely a few (very
small) soft spots. One such spot would be his inclination to involve
himself in other people's business. *If it ain't your tail, don't wag it,*
she'd say. But sometimes Bobby couldn't help himself.

He knew that cycling to Oliver's house and peeking through his
windows was wrong. It was an invasion of his privacy, no different

than opening his mail. He reasoned that—as long as Oliver didn't find out—there was no harm done. It was therefore easy to blot out objections, or his mother's voice telling him—and Matthew had said the same—that he was apt to get the tip of his nose snipped off if he couldn't keep it from people's affairs. Events would have transpired differently if he had listened to his mother, or even if he had limited his curiosity to peeking through the windows. But he didn't. *Couldn't.* He pushed too far, pried too deeply, and in so doing found something unimaginable. The danger was bigger than anything he'd ever known, but by the time he realized, it was too late.

He would later think—while cycling for his life—that he should have stolen a quick drink and blown out of Dodge, leaving everything as he had found it. But he would think many things during those timorous moments (that he should never have cycled to Oliver's in the first place; how foolish he'd been to enter the house; that the unlocked patio door should have warned him that Oliver hadn't gone far). He *did* wonder why the air conditioner was running, but figured that Oliver—having more money than sense—would sooner return to a chilled house than save a few bucks on the utilities bill. Just one of many oversights, and imprudent actions, that could prove his undoing.

He'd found a half-full carton of orange juice in the refrigerator door, but that was all. No bottled water or soda, and no ice cream— Chunky Monkey, or otherwise—in the freezer. Bobby drained the juice in one hit, his lips forming a seal around the spout to minimize spillage. He drank with grateful grunts, his eyes screwed shut, as if this would enhance his drinking pleasure. When finished, he crammed the carton beneath the refrigerator's water dispenser and half-filled it again. Three drain-like swallows and it was gone. He placed the empty carton on the countertop, belched wonderfully, and dispensed a handful of crushed ice. This he smeared all over his chest and shoulders, gasping with satisfaction as his body temperature dropped to a more comfortable level.

"So good," he said, smiling as chilled water dripped from the broad lip of his belly. He took a deep breath and gazed around the kitchen and living room, thinking that he should quit pushing his luck and get out of there. But thinking never progressed to doing. The décor grabbed his attention, everything expensive and ultramodern. He was pretty sure he'd seen Gil Gerard strolling around something similar in an episode of *Buck Rogers,* only there had been a distant galaxy on the other side of the window, as opposed to the forestry of the Catskills.

Despite the state-of-the-art styling, and the precise placement of everything (*definitely* OCD, Bobby thought), there was something missing, and it didn't take Bobby long to figure out what it was.

No warmth, he thought, noting the irony. It was a furnace outside, but Oliver's house was cold and spiritless, and not because of the air conditioning. Bobby lived in a house that was adorned with photographs and pictures, plants and ornaments. They offered colour and character, and reflected the people who lived there. Oliver had *nothing,* and surely this reflected something, too. Bobby thought that a millionaire graphic designer would exhibit more imagination.

"You're a peculiar man, Oliver," he said, sweat trickling into the creases at the back of his neck. His curiosity piqued, he ventured deeper into the house . . . into the hallway, with doors closed on several rooms. This didn't stop him. He nosed in Oliver's bedroom (as bland and modern as the living room), and opened the door to the basement. *That's where the meth lab will be,* he thought. *Or the arms cache. Gotta remember to take a look before leaving.* And then he nosed in the bathroom, peeked in an empty spare room, and pushed open the door to Oliver's study. The window blind was pulled down, but thin enough to let the sunlight through, and Bobby saw everything clearly: an L-shaped mahogany desk, a bookcase crammed with textbooks and computer paraphernalia, a huge printer/copier, a filing cabinet. There were two computers on the desk—a MacBook and an iMac—along with a gooseneck lamp and various trays and folders. As Bobby stepped farther into the room, a voice at the back of his mind chirruped that he'd taken things too far, that entering someone's home was in a different league to opening their mail. Even police needed a warrant to—

"Yeah-yeah," he cut off his own thought process, even flapped a hand at the air: *Sure, I hear you. Now shuddup, already.* Something had caught his eye. The corner of it poked out from one of the folders on Oliver's desk. Clearly a photograph, black and white, but the only (possibly) interesting thing he had discovered thus far. He stepped toward it. Just a little look-see. Ten seconds—max—and he'd be on his way.

He opened the folder and looked down at an old photograph. Nothing remarkable, or even interesting, about it: a dark-haired man standing with three children. The quality wasn't great but Bobby thought the little ones were crying, while the man—their father, probably—wore a grin like a shard of glass. *Kinda creepy,* Bobby thought. *Probably Oliver's freaky great-grandfather.* He picked up the photograph and turned it over, thinking that people sometimes wrote names and dates on the back of prints. No date on this one, or name, but Oliver had scrawled "ORIGINAL ME" in one corner in angry uppercase.

"Freak," Bobby said. He slipped the photograph back into the folder, closed it, stepped toward the door, and then paused. He'd noticed a newspaper clipping in the folder, beneath the photograph. Ever curious, he went back to it and saw not just one clipping but a sheaf of them secured with a binder clip. The headline of the top one read: PSP WIDEN SEARCH FOR MISSING GIRL and there was a photograph of her, Courtney Bryce. Bobby's heart dropped in his chest, as it always did whenever he saw her face in the news. Only eleven years old, and missing for over a week. He flipped the clipping and saw that the one beneath was also about Courtney Bryce. Different newspaper, same photograph. The third clipping was from *USA Today*. The headline read: PARENTS' TEARFUL APPEAL TO FIND ETHAN. Another heartbreaking photograph, this time of Ethan Mitchell's anguished parents. Ethan was last seen outside his New Jersey home twelve days ago.

"What the hell?" Bobby said. He looked at the remaining clippings. There had to be thirty of them, at least, from various newspapers, and all concerning the disappearance of either Courtney Bryce or Ethan Mitchell.

Frickin' ghoulish, Bobby thought. He flipped back to the first clipping and looked into Courtney's eyes. A beautiful eleven-year-old girl, smiling as if the world were not a ruptured place, and no harm could ever come to her. He wiped a mist of sweat from his brow and looked at the old photograph again: the three children, all of them in tears, and the man with the twisted smile.

Original me.

A bell sounded inside Bobby's head. A dull peal that sickened him.

No way, he thought. He didn't like Oliver, and had never trusted him, but he couldn't believe he had anything to do with these missing children.

But why the clippings?

"Maybe he's researching something," he said to the empty study. He flicked through the articles again, the headlines flashing in his eyes. "Maybe he's starting a charity, or something."

Yes, maybe, but his eye was drawn, again, to the old photograph.

Original me.

Bobby shivered, as if he'd just emerged from warm water into cold air. He looked to see what else was in the folder: pages printed off the Internet. He glanced through them, catching underlined sentences: SIX DEAD; EIGHTEEN PEOPLE WERE BURNED ALIVE; IT WATCHES US. IT REMEMBERS. Random articles that made no sense, and Bobby couldn't link them to the missing children, or Oliver's possible involvement.

He tossed the folder back onto the desk. It hit the mouse pad. The mouse jigged and the iMac pulled itself from standby mode with little whirs and ticks. The monitor bloomed and showed Oliver's desktop. Like his house, it was bland and blank.

Bobby didn't pause to think about it. He sat in front of the computer, opened Safari, and checked Oliver's browsing history. It was empty. He went into preferences and saw that it was set up to delete every twenty-four hours.

"Okay," Bobby whispered. His heart thumped hard, not through heat or exhaustion, but with nervous energy. He closed out the

Internet, checked the hard drive, and found numerous Word documents. One of them was titled: *NOTES: JOURNAL 2010*.

Bobby opened it. The first thing he read filled him with dread and turned his world into a different place. A *broken* place:

January 1, 2010.

Last night I dreamed that one of the children clawed their way out of the mountain and came back to me. It may have been Victoria Guy. Or Connor Wright. Impossible to be sure. His/her fingertips were bleeding and he/she said in a cracked, small voice: "You don't even know what it wants." And then he/she turned into a horde of rats and attacked me. I felt them biting my flesh, eating my eyes. What a way to start the new year.

Bobby leapt back as if the monitor had sprouted arms and reached for him. He shook his head, feeling his peace of mind fray at the edges and unwind. His heart galloped uncomfortably in his chest. He looked at the old photograph. *Original me.* He looked at the newspaper clippings. Courtney Bryce smiled at him, her red hair draped over one shoulder.

Jesus Christ, what do I do? What . . .

"This isn't happening," he said. His voice was fractured, like sand falling through an hourglass. More sweat ran into his eyes and he palmed it away. The monitor stared at him with its pale, unblinking eye.

It's Oliver. Holy shit, Oliver took those kids, he TOOK them . . .

"No," Bobby breathed. It was too big for him to comprehend. He held his chest and whimpered. Oliver's face flickered in his mind. *What are you going to do about it, Bobby?* he asked. *I'm the King of Point Hollow. Everybody loves me. So what are you going to do to bring me down? How can—?*

Bobby scrolled to the next entry:

January 12, 2010.

Snowed all day. I drove into town and helped plow some of the smaller roads. I also plowed the Chase Bank parking lot, and a few of the longer driveways. Mrs. Stone gave me a plate of—

He shook his head, clicked on the little bar on the right of the screen, and dragged through a few months:

April 3, 2010.
Spent all day surfing the 'net for information about town's history. Nothing new. Now I feel nauseous and tired but I know I won't sleep. It's late. My eyes are aching. Think I'll take a bottle of bourbon out on the deck and see how long it takes me to get shitfaced.

What are you going to do, fatboy?
"I need proof," Bobby said. "*Real* proof." His heart rolled a little harder, responding to the panic lights flashing in his mind. He tried to control his breathing, but managed only shallow sips that felt like knuckles pressing against the inside of his ribcage. Courtney Bryce smiled at him from the newspaper clipping. *Courtney,* he thought, and placed his trembling fingers on the keyboard. He hit command + F. The "Find and Replace" dialog box bloomed on the screen.
He typed "Courtney" in the field.
I don't want to do this, he thought, gasping, shaking. *I don't want to know.*
Find All . . . click.
He read:

July 25, 2010.
Courtney Bryce. Eleven years old. Deer Grove, PA. I used the hands-full trick to grab her and she took the bait like I knew she would. It was a long drive home, with the little girl crying and struggling most of the way, and the mountain screaming at me. I carried her right into its belly and it fell silent almost at once. The silence—although it has only been a few hours—is as close to heaven as I can imagine.
I'm tired now. Going to bed. I think I could sleep for days. I pray the mountain doesn't wake me. I pray it's over.

Please let it be over.

If it's not . . . if it booms again . . . wants more . . .

No. Please God. No.

Bobby moaned and buried his face in his hands. His back hitched like an old machine rumbling into life. Heavy sobs rolled through his chest and tears crept from his eyes.

I can't do this, he thought, and with his face in his hands he didn't notice the man-shaped silhouette float across the blind. *I just can't. It's too big for me.* He wiped his eyes and the screen came into focus.

—*the little girl crying and struggling most of the way*—

She looked at him from the newspaper clipping. Her eyes shone.

—*carried her right into its belly*—

Anger touched him. Fear. Shock. He swayed in the chair and his eyes blurred with tears again. He blinked them away. His mouth was a trembling line.

He searched the document for Ethan Mitchell.

July 22, 2010.

The grab was reckless but I was desperate, on the verge of madness. The evening news is buzzing with the story of how seven-year-old Ethan Mitchell disappeared outside his New Jersey home. No one saw me grab him, but that was *too* close. Abraham's Faith must have been looking after me.

Perhaps now it will leave me in peace.

While his parents cry into news cameras, and the police search dumpsters and ditches in Lafayette, NJ, Ethan Mitchell sits alone inside the mountain, waiting to die. Correction: *not* alone; he has all those bones to keep him company. A schoolyard of skeletons.

I imagine him screaming in the darkness.

"Oh my God," Bobby whispered. The final sentence burned in his mind, and it occurred to him that Ethan Mitchell might still be alive. Courtney Bryce, too. They were inside the mountain. Abraham's Faith. If they found water, they could stay alive for a long time. Weeks, maybe.

—sits alone in the mountain, waiting to die—

Bobby's stomach turned in slow loops and he clenched his fists and screwed them into his eyes as if he could make this all go away. He had forgotten about the heat and the fact that he was trespassing. He had forgotten, almost, *who* he was. His world had become a thin skin of dust on an implausible surface. One good puff of wind and it would all blow away.

—imagine him screaming—

"Help me," he said, but his words had a distant quality. A fading radio signal. A voice behind a solid wall. "Please, God, help—"

His breath snagged in his throat. He thought he'd heard a sound from the kitchen. Something creaking. He turned in the chair and looked down the hallway.

Nothing.

He breathed again and turned back to the monitor. Enough of the real world returned for him to know that he had to take this information to the police. *I need a copy of this document,* he thought. *I can print it. No . . . e-mail it, and I'll print it at home. There'll be an IP address attached to the e-mail—proof that it was sent from Oliver's computer.*

Bobby knew that a printed Word document and an IP address couldn't be used as conclusive evidence, but it might be enough for the police to hammer a confession out of Oliver, and to find out where on Abraham's Faith he had taken the children.

And maybe—hopefully—save them.

Bobby wiped his eyes again, his heart sounding like a steel drum rolling downhill. He clicked on the Safari icon in the dock, so adrift in the moment—the terrible reality—that he had no sense of Oliver creeping into the hallway behind him. This detachment did not last; Oliver's reflection ghosted across the monitor. Bobby had time for realization to crash down like a burning, shrieking passenger plane, and for his heart to knock woefully against his ribcage, and then his world—already broken—blew apart, a thousand pieces, all hurting.

———

Oliver's mind was a white field where thoughts grew like pale flowers, all fragile, and all shaken to the roots by his fury. He considered nothing. No consequences or repercussions. His focus was raw and brutal, centred only on the intruder.

He leapt with a vicious hiss, springing from his heels and knocking Bobby's considerable bulk out of the chair. They went to ground, limbs entwined, Oliver naked, Bobby wearing only his post office shorts (his Mets cap had popped off his head like a bottle cap). Oily with mud and sweat, they tangled and clawed, kicked and rolled. Bobby got to one knee but Oliver pulled him down and they slammed into the edge of the desk so hard that the lamp toppled over. Its bulb shattered and made a glass puddle between the two computers. Oliver gnashed his teeth and tried to work Bobby into a headlock, break his fucking neck. Bobby lowed like a wounded cow, flailed his arms, and arched his back so that his belly rolled. He was not strong, nor was he vicious, but he had a weight advantage of one hundred and twenty pounds. His belly rippled and bucked Oliver off like a fearsome wave pitching an uncertain vessel. Oliver thumped down between the bookcase and desk, face to the floor and ass in the air. Several titles spilled from their shelves and a box of rewritable DVDs bounced off the small of his back.

Bobby scrambled to his feet, slipped to one knee, and crashed into the filing cabinet. He picked himself up as Oliver edged from between the case and desk. Bobby grabbed the chair and threw it at him. It wasn't a clean shot—didn't hurt Oliver—but it knocked him backward and Bobby was gone, lumbering out of the study, puffing down the hallway with his belly bouncing ahead of him. Oliver pushed away the chair, sprang to his feet, and followed, leaving bloody/muddy footprints on the study floor and across the pages of books that had fallen and lay open. He charged down the hallway and his mind was still a vast white field and all he wanted to do was catch the fat fucking animal that had invaded his territory. Catch it and tear it to pieces. Bathe in its blood like a warlord. His anger was so loud that he couldn't hear the mountain. He felt it, though. A burning hand on his soul.

Dark spots swarmed in front of Bobby's eyes. His heart lurched painfully. He pulled in a shuddering breath and for a terrible moment his interior lights shut down and there was only darkness. He gave his left tit a firm wallop and the pain subsided. He gasped and blinked—heard Oliver howling in the study behind him (mad, *naked* Oliver, his body painted with bright reds and yellows, and what the fuck was all *that* about?) and stumbled along the hallway. Thoughts crisscrossed his mind. *Need to get home. Need my meds. Need the police.* His heart throbbed and he felt himself sinking into darkness again. *NEED TO GET OUT OF HERE.* And that was *the* thought—the only thing that mattered. Get out of here, get to safety. Then, and only then, could he begin to worry about (*the children, oh my God the children*) everything else.

Bobby reached the entranceway and veered toward the kitchen and living room, simply because that was the way he had come in. He then remembered, in a moment of blessedly clear thought that he'd left his bicycle out front, leaning against the garage door. He bumbled left instead of right, threw open the front door, and dared a glance down the hallway. He saw Oliver burst from his study and start toward him, flapping his arms and cawing.

He's completely insane. Jesus.

Bobby threw himself outside as if the house were on fire. He careened across the driveway, toward his bicycle. Oliver was close behind. Bobby heard the front door crash open, followed by his birdlike calls:

"RAWWWR-RAWWWWWR!"

The bright day faded. It *sagged*, like his legs. Bobby moaned and held on, tears streaming from his eyes. His heart kicked like something in a cage and he thought he was going to lose it. The sight of Oliver—flapping his arms, streaking across the driveway— kept him moving. He reached his bike, grabbed the handlebars, and pushed. The world sagged again. Bobby wobbled but didn't go down. He threw his right leg over the crossbar and jumped on the seat, getting a moving start—a feat of athleticism he should never have been capable of. But fear impelled him. It was a whip.

"*RAWWWR-RAWWWR!*"

Right foot on the pedal . . . left foot, and he *pushed,* gasping hot air as everything swam between bright and grey and his poor heart screamed. Oliver chased hard. Bobby felt one hand claw at his shoulder. It grabbed nothing but sweat.

"*RAWWWWWR!*"

Bobby pushed harder and pulled away from him, his head over the handlebars, pedaling with everything in his soul, onto Sanctuary Road, not slowing.

Oliver stopped running. His rage gave way to fear. Bobby Alexander had been in his house, on his computer, had read his journal. He knew everything. *Everything.* The mask was off. Shattered. If Oliver didn't stop him, the whole town—the whole *world*—would see the monster beneath.

Stop him.

His head throbbed and his body ached. He cried out, watching Bobby's broad back get smaller as he pedaled away. *Think. Jesus Christ, THINK!* The mountain thundered and crowded his mind with images like thorns and saw blades. He *had* to stop Bobby before he reached town. It was the only way through this shitstorm. Silence him and reassemble the mask.

Oliver reeled and looked at the mountain. *THINK!* He could get in his truck and chase the fat son of a whore down, catch up to him in no time and smoke him like roadkill. But there would be enquiries, questions, damage to the truck. Not good.

THINK!

"His heart," Oliver whispered, and Bobby's scar flashed in his mind. That thick pink zipper between his man-tits. "Heart ain't up to much." It was already banging double-time, no doubt, and in this heat, under duress, it wouldn't take much to make it pop like a balloon.

Oliver's upper lip curled. Perfect. It would look like an accident. Stupid fat man has a heart attack while cycling in torrid conditions.

Oliver would hardly have to touch him. Simply scare him to death.

The mountain roared.

Oliver ran.

Sanctuary Road was half a mile long, intersecting Tall Pine Way, where Bobby would hang a left and roll for a couple of miles until he hit Main Street. He was no Lance Armstrong, but fear would make him pedal faster than the average bear, and Tall Pine Way was mostly downhill. Oliver figured that, even in this heat, Bobby would make it to Sheriff Tansy's office in less than twenty minutes. He also figured that, cutting a diagonal through the woods southwest of his land, he'd intercept Bobby on Tall Pine Way about a mile outside town.

He blistered through the woods, snapping aside branches and leaping fallen trees, assuming the circles once again, drawing on wild strength and speed. Birds started from his path in sprays of colour. He hooted and cawed at them, holding his line, over rocks and through a tangle of huckleberry. *Faster.* His body burning, arms pumping at his sides. He stepped on something hard and sharp and felt it pierce his foot, but didn't care, didn't stop. His mind was bruised with the image of Bobby invading his privacy—*reading his JOURNAL*—and he used this to fuel him. No pain. No fatigue. Nothing else mattered. Only Bobby. He *had* to stop him. Had to make him pay.

Faster.

Oliver approached Tall Pine Way, weaving between trees on a diagonal. He instinctively silenced his approach to the road, controlling his breathing and dodging branches to avoid snapping them and alerting Bobby to his presence. He scouted the road between the trees, and there—a glimpse of something heavy and pink. Oliver grinned. He had calculated to perfection. He would break from the woods directly in front of Bobby—would roar and rage. A feral, mannish thing. Bobby didn't stand a chance. His sad, blubbery heart was down to its last few beats.

Fifty feet away . . . forty . . . thirty . . . several long, animal-like paces, and Oliver leapt from the woods (in his mind he was part gazelle, part lion), onto the narrow shoulder and then into the road.

Bobby shrieked and jerked the handlebars. The bicycle went from under him and he hit the ground hard. Oliver heard his jaw shatter. He saw glistening flecks of spit and teeth burst from his mouth. The bicycle settled in the middle of the road, rear wheel spinning, front wheel turned sideways. Bobby rolled brokenly from his belly to his back. Broad leaves of skin had been scuffed from his body. His eyes whirled in mystified circles and then Oliver stepped toward him and his shadow was every cloud.

Bobby drifted through nothingness. Unknowing. Unfeeling. When he opened his eyes—however long later—the pain hit him, bringing everything else with it. His heart shuddered irregularly. He started to cry.

The children, who's going to—

The pain was everywhere but in his chest it was *deep*. A metallic, crippling pressure against his ribcage, as if the laws of gravity were applied differently there. He clutched and gasped, eyes blinking, willing his heart into sync with his body. Blood spattered from his mouth in tiny geysers. He felt two—maybe three—of his teeth floating in the well beneath his tongue.

"What were you thinking, Bobby?" Oliver asked. Except it *wasn't* Oliver. This *creature* was only partly human, dressed in wild paints, threads of saliva hanging from his jaw. Any shade of Oliver was hidden deep. The slipped mask had exposed a sick individual.

Tell . . . police, Bobby thought, unable to speak, even struggling to form words in his mind. He sank again. The bright day collapsed and greyness moved in. It droned and enveloped him.

"You're dying, Bobby." The voice drifted to him from the other side of the greyness. "You should have left me alone."

Dying.

Maybe. Probably. But he felt the tears running from his eyes and this was enough to make him hold on. He didn't want to die like this, whimpering in Oliver's shadow.

"No one can help you now."

Besides, he *couldn't* die. The children . . .

—*imagine him screaming*—

He *had* to help the children.

"Die," Oliver willed gently, but Bobby clawed at the greyness and opened his eyes. He saw trees, blue sky . . .

"*Gee . . . boo guy,*" he said, trying to articulate what he was seeing. A loose tooth spilled over his lower lip and landed in the road with a tiny click. "*Gee . . . boo guy.*" He blinked and tears made patterns on his round face.

Oliver stood over him, not touching him.

"Die," he said softly.

Bobby shook his head. His jaw throbbed and blood ran from his mouth.

"Die."

Children, Bobby thought, and tried to get up. His hurting body would not respond. He groaned and tried again—managed to sit halfway up, and then flopped heavily to the road. The pressure on his chest increased. His heart knocked, and every uncertain beat brought a fresh wave of pain.

No . . . Jesus no . . . please . . .

His left arm started to tingle.

"We're a mile outside town," Oliver said. His shadow was deep and it covered Bobby's fluttering eyes like a cold hand. "This is a quiet road. It sees maybe two or three cars an hour. There's no help for you here."

Bobby shuddered. His throat clicked and convulsed as he tried to breathe. He felt the fingertips of his left hand burning.

"Die, Bobby. Say night-night."

Bobby gasped and another broken tooth spilled from his mouth.

Oliver clapped his hands in front of Bobby's face. He roared. His breath smelled like wood and leaves. "*NIGHT-NIGHT!*"

Bobby went under again. The pain consumed him.

"Maybe I'll take you into the woods," Oliver said.

Please, God . . . please . . .

"Cut out your tongue, so you can't tell anybody what you've seen."

Bobby tried to breathe but there was no air.

175

"And maybe I'll cut out your eyes, so you won't be able to look into other people's business."

Bobby emerged from the greyness. He kicked his legs, and the pain—everything—was so terrible that he *wanted* to die. He thought of Ethan Mitchell and Courtney Bryce. Their faces flowered in his mind and he held on . . .

"Snip off the tip of that nose," Oliver said.

Please . . .

"Die."

Bobby's heart stopped.

Everything white. Only pain. Floating on pain.

"Say night-night."

And remarkably, with the children's faces still in his mind, he actually said it. His larynx throbbed. Blood oozed from his mouth.

"Nay-nay."

"Yes . . . night-night, Bobby Bear."

"Obby . . . air."

His body clenched, tightening from the middle out. A thunderous sound filled his head. He drifted in pain and his final thought, before he went under for the last time, was that he should have listened to his mother and minded his own affairs. *If it ain't your tail, don't wag it,* she'd say, and that he was apt to—

———

Oliver watched him shudder, watched him die, eyes filled with tears, reflecting blue sky. He stood for a moment, waiting for him to breathe again. But there was nothing. Blood—like his tears—ran. That was all.

Oliver stepped back, onto the shoulder, and then into the woods. He surveyed the scene. A terrible accident. Bobby had suffered a heart attack while cycling. Sheriff Tansy would have him zipped into a body bag and carted to the morgue, and the autopsy would reveal no sign of foul play. No investigation necessary. No questions. No forensic analysis (which would, undoubtedly, reveal traces of Oliver's blood and sweat on the corpse). Bobby would be in the ground by the end of the week, and Oliver—an upstanding member of the community—would attend the funeral. He'd wear his mask, and kiss Bobby's grieving mother.

He started toward home, adrenaline shaking through his body, the mountain rumbling ever on. He needed to clean and dress his wounds (he'd sliced his foot open while running through the woods—a wad of moss had stemmed the bleeding), and then sleep for as long as the mountain would let him.

He sensed, again, that he was nearing the end. Bobby coming out here was a sign that things were gathering momentum, falling into place. The mountain's energy was culminating. Something would have to give.

If I have to kill myself, Oliver thought, *I'm taking the whole town with me.*

He walked slowly, and eventually saw his house through the trees. Sunlight glinted on the windows.

It made him think of Bobby's eyes.

CHAPTER
ELEVEN

Matthew drove to Bobby's
house only to find no one
home. He was a little early, but
thought it strange that the house
was empty. Mrs. Alexander didn't
drive, and it was unlikely she had gone
for a walk in this heat (it was almost six
P.M. but the temperature was still in the high
eighties). Unlikely, but not impossible. Maybe she was
with a neighbour, but where the hell was Bobby?

Could be in the shower, Matthew thought. He took a seat on
the porch and waited. Ten minutes. Fifteen. He rang the doorbell
again. If Bobby had been in the shower, he'd be out by now.

No answer.

He took his BlackBerry from his pocket and checked the time.
18:08. He frowned, double-checking the arrangement in his head.
Six o'clock tonight. *Definitely* tonight. An hour's drive to Middletown,
TGI Friday's, and then the eight-fifteen showing of *Inception.* That
was the plan (devised, entirely, by Bobby, who was stoked about
going to Friday's, and almost wetting himself to see *Inception*). So
where was he?

Matthew scrolled to Bobby's home number on the BlackBerry, knowing it was useless but dialing anyway. He heard the phone ringing inside the house. No one to answer it.

"What the hell, Bobby?"

He hung up and stepped off the porch, thinking that Bobby had either forgotten (not likely, given how excited he was), or that something had upset the plan. An emergency, perhaps. As he pondered what to do, Bobby's neighbour shuffled to the edge of his garden and called over:

"Any idea what happened?"

Matthew looked at him, an old man dressed in a string vest, jockey shorts, and a fedora. Just another of Point Hollow's peculiar residents. Although, to be fair, it was too hot to wear much more.

"What do you mean?"

"The police were here," the neighbour said. "Deputy Sheriff Masefield. I don't know what for, but Moira left with him. About an hour ago."

"The police?" Matthew asked. Too many thoughts tumbled through his mind, and none of them had a happy ending. "Moira . . . is that Bobby's mother?"

The neighbour nodded.

"And Bobby wasn't with her?"

"Not that I saw."

"Doesn't sound good." Matthew muttered.

"Say again?"

Matthew shook his head. "Nothing."

"I guess you don't know what happened, huh?"

"No, I . . ."

The neighbour flapped a hand at Matthew and trudged back inside. His front door slammed behind him, and for long seconds the world was heavy and silent, until a bird called and a child laughed, and then Matthew heard his sneakers dragging along the path as he walked back to the rental. He got behind the wheel, but just sat there, with too many thoughts crowding his mind. All were bleak. He shook his head and told himself not to think the worst, then started the car and drove back to the hotel.

He was sure that something had happened to Bobby. In this heat, with his heart, it was the most likely explanation. He spent the next hour pacing his hotel room, wondering what he should do. At seven-thirty he called Bobby's house again. Still no reply.

What the hell is going on, Bobby?

News travels fast in a small town. Matthew went to the Rack because he thought the grapevine would be in full swing. He grabbed a seat at the bar, ordered a draft beer, and was able to piece together what had happened by the time it was served.

"—Ernie Fellows found him on Tall Pine Way, lying there like roadkill—"

"—just crazy to be bicycling in this heat, what with his ticker—"

"—heard it took four guys to lift him into the back of the ambulance. Even the sheriff had to break a sweat—"

Oh Jesus, Bobby. What were you thinking?

Matthew sat silently, sipping his beer but not really tasting it. He felt brittle, as if, with too sudden a movement, he would fall from the barstool in pieces, to be swept away at the end of the night with the dust, the peanut shells, and the beer labels peeled from their bottles. It wasn't grief, exactly—he didn't think he knew Bobby well enough to fully grieve—but a hole had opened inside him, and it was cold and wretched, spilling emotions he had no name for. So he sipped his tasteless beer and filled the cold place with memories: the chubby kid with the raggedy Mets cap on his head, swapping comic books, building rafts and dens. Fast forward twenty-six years: Bobby, still with the Mets cap, guzzling a pitcher of Pepsi, crouching behind the plate—*Pop!*—as Matthew threw an imaginary fastball, talking about TV shows and superheroes, taking him through the woods to see the whitetail gathered in the clearing. Hugging Bobby close, feeling the curve of his body and the thud of a heart that was no longer beating.

Tears glistened in his eyes and he wiped them away with the edge of his thumb. The locals talked. Someone laughed, and a woman with angry-red hair fed quarters to the juke and played the Eagles.

One beer was all he could manage. The Rack soon filled with uncomfortable sound. Not a fitting environment for whatever emotion he was feeling. He slipped from the stool and left quietly. The streets were touched by long shadows. The bruised sky reflected his mood.

Matthew crossed Main, thinking he'd go back to the hotel and catch an early night, maybe watch TV until he fell asleep. He had no enthusiasm for anything else. Tomorrow he'd decide whether to stay the remainder of the week—as planned—or return to the city, face Kirsty, and get the divorce ball rolling. Point Hollow wouldn't be the same without Bobby. It might even be unpleasant, with its spiny small-town attitude.

Bobby . . . Jesus.

And suddenly everything hit him. Not just Bobby, but a bombardment of the last two years. Even longer: the darkness inside him, the repressed memories, the nights he'd woken up screaming. And, of course, Kirsty. Her abuse. His sadness. It crashed against him and he wavered on the sidewalk, cold tears shining on his face in the bruised light.

He sat in the doorway of Hudson Holiday Homes (which used to be Norris Drug, back in the day) with his head in his hands, and didn't look up until he sensed red and blue light pulsing around him. There was a moment's disorientation before realization dawned. *Oh God, not now. Please, not now.* He lifted his head and peered into the swirling lights. Sure enough, Sheriff Tansy's cruiser rumbled at the side of the road.

"Unless you've got business in that doorway," the sheriff said, "I suggest you make like a bread truck and haul buns. You ain't in New York City now."

Matthew sighed and nodded. "Sorry, Sheriff."

"What were you doing in there?"

"I just . . ." Matthew stood up and stepped onto the sidewalk. The lights moved around him, as harsh and accusatory as pointing fingers. "I just needed to sit for a while. Get my head together."

"That so?" The sheriff flicked off the lightbar and stepped out of the cruiser. His boots made hollow sounds on the sidewalk. Matthew looked away from him—up at the sky. Dark blue, sprayed with starlight. The mountains in the west had a burned outline. He wondered how long he'd been sitting in the doorway with his head in his hands. He felt a little steadier now, but Sheriff Tansy was the last person he wanted to talk to.

"Tough day?" the sheriff asked.

"Something like that," Matthew said.

Sheriff Tansy nodded. He planted his hands on his hips and glared at Matthew, his eyebrows meeting, teeth showing. Matthew glanced away again, perhaps hoping the sheriff would simply nod, get into his cruiser, and drive away. But he didn't. He continued to stare, saying nothing. It felt as though his steely eyes were trained on pressure points, gradually weakening Matthew, like an android in a sci-fi movie.

"Again, I'm sorry for—"

"Why are you here?" the sheriff asked. Matthew wondered if he waited for people to begin talking, just so he could interrupt them.

"Here?"

"Point Hollow. Why did you come back?"

None of your business, Matthew thought. He felt himself trembling as the sheriff stared at him, and made an extra effort to pull his shoulders square and meet his stern gaze.

"Am I doing something wrong?"

"Not as far as I know." The sheriff opened his hands. His impressive chest swelled as he inhaled. "I'm just a curious old soul. Comes with the badge."

Matthew nodded, swallowed hard.

"I recall you saying that you needed to get out of the city for a few days." The sheriff breathed on Matthew. An old, unpleasant smell. "I don't know your reasons, and I don't care to know. None of my concern. But you could have gone anywhere. Why Point Hollow?"

"Because it called to me," Matthew said. The words spilled from his mouth as suddenly as they formed in his mind, giving him no time to ponder whether or not they were true, but as soon as he spoke them, he realized they were. Point Hollow *had* called to him, subtly, through his turmoil. A resonance accompanying every dark thought.

Sheriff Tansy took a step back. Matthew thought he would ridicule this response—too deep for him to understand. He didn't, though. He shuffled his feet and lowered his eyes, suddenly uncertain.

He knows what I mean, Matthew thought. *He feels it, too.*

"Called to you, huh?" Sheriff Tansy said. He looked at Matthew again. "Well, that may be so. But seems to me you brought a trunkload of bad luck with you."

"Bad luck?"

"Misfortune. Black clouds. Bad mojo." Sheriff Tansy shrugged. "Call it what you want, but you can't deny it. First the deer, and now Bobby Alexander."

"Bobby was my friend."

"That I don't doubt." Sheriff Tansy said. His nostrils flared, the map of burst capillaries almost glowing. "He was my friend, too. A friend to the town, by God, and we're all sorry as heck that he's gone."

Matthew doubted that was true, but said nothing.

"You see, we're used to blue skies here in Point Hollow," the sheriff continued. "By which I mean a simple, peaceful lifestyle. No black clouds. No bad mojo. I get a bad taste in my mouth whenever somebody comes along and upsets our little applecart."

"I didn't mean to upset any—"

"Makes me . . . uneasy." The sheriff sneered.

Matthew sighed and ran a hand down his face. So tired. So much emotion.

"Might just be best," the sheriff said, "for you to move along. Take your bad mojo back to the city, where it belongs, and don't come back any time soon."

You were reading my mind, Sheriff, Matthew thought. *I can't wait to blow this freaky little taco stand.*

"I'll even give you an escort as far as the seventeen," Sheriff Tansy continued. He grinned and crossed his arms over his broad chest. "We don't want you hitting any more deer, do we?"

"Very considerate of you," Matthew said wryly, and now it was his turn to sneer—a slight flare of the upper lip, but Tansy saw it and bristled, stepping toward Matthew and looming over him again.

"Go home," he said. Almost a growl.

"Actually, I . . ." Matthew stopped. He was about to say, *I plan on leaving first thing tomorrow morning, and you don't have to worry about me coming back*. But he remembered something Bobby had said last night (so surreal now—last night, when Bobby had been alive . . . breathing, thinking, smiling), sitting on the porch amid the scent of wild honeysuckle and the sound of children's laughter. Bobby had told him that he didn't have any friends, that only his mother had visited when he'd been recovering in hospital. Matthew had squeezed his arm, able to relate. *I'm your friend*, he had said, as much to comfort himself as Bobby.

Matthew blinked, sighed, and retreated a step. He smelled the sheriff's breath again, damp and bitter.

"He was my friend," Matthew said. He imagined Bobby lying in his hospital bed, a single Get Well Soon card on the nightstand, a single bunch of flowers. He imagined the empty chair in the corner, and Bobby's brave smile. Tears flooded his eyes and he wished, more than anything in the world, that he had known Bobby then, because that chair would *not* have been empty. He would have sat with Bobby and talked to him about the Mets and *Justice League* and whether or not the *Dawn of the Dead* remake was better than the original.

"Go home," Sheriff Tansy said again.

And if nobody had visited Bobby in hospital, how many would go to his funeral? How many would look in on Mrs. Alexander to see if she needed anything—to help her while she grieved? Matthew imagined the funeral: a scattering of flowers, with Mrs. Alexander standing beside her son's coffin, weeping while the Reverend's eulogy echoed in an empty church.

You'll probably forget about me when you get back to New York, Bobby had said.

No, I won't, Matthew had replied, looking him in the eye, meaning it. He wiped away his tears and looked at Sheriff Tansy.

"I won't," he said.

The sheriff's grey eyes burned. He inhaled, *expanded,* his brow a latticework of furrows. A car slipped by on Main, slowing as the driver rubbernecked. Crickets whirred in the long grass and the Rack's windows flashed, music pulsing like the vein in Sheriff Tansy's temple.

"I'm going to stay for Bobby's funeral," Matthew said. "Then I'll leave."

"That's not until the end of the week," Tansy said.

"Doesn't matter." Matthew looked at him and nodded. "I can help Mrs. Alexander with funeral arrangements, and with anything else she needs."

"She's got a whole townful of people to help her."

Matthew thought of the empty chair beside Bobby's hospital bed. The single Get Well Soon card. He opened his mouth. Closed it again.

"She doesn't need your help, city boy."

"Bobby was my friend," Matthew said again. His palms were slick with sweat, his heart beating fast. "I'm going to stay for his funeral, and I'm going to make sure his mother has all the support she needs."

Sheriff Tansy stared at him, boring into those pressure points. Matthew reached deep and held his gaze, despite wanting to turn away—run away forever. But he wouldn't turn his back on Bobby. And he wouldn't give Tansy the satisfaction of chasing him away. Matthew would leave in his own sweet time. He'd been bullied for too long.

The sheriff clapped one tough hand on Matthew's shoulder, then leaned close to him and whispered, "This isn't your town anymore."

Matthew said nothing. He swallowed hard and felt a cold sweat break on his legs.

"I'll be keeping my eye on you." Sheriff Tansy nodded once, then stepped back and grinned—a stained and unfriendly display of teeth—before turning and getting into his cruiser. He started it with an impressive roar, gunned the accelerator a couple of times, and pulled away.

Matthew watched the cruiser rip out of sight, then exhaled—a wheezy, jittery breath that left him feeling empty.

Looks like I'm staying the rest of the week. No doubt that he'd rather be blazing south toward the Big Apple, throwing a big fuck you at Point Hollow in his rearview mirror, but something more important had intervened.

Matthew stood in the streetlight with his head down, feeling the emptiness inside him fill with the woe of having to endure Point Hollow for a few more days. But he would do it. For Bobby. For himself.

I'm your friend.

He would be true to his word.

———

Something he had said to Sheriff Tansy followed him into sleep. *Because it called to me.* This reply, from nowhere, coloured his dream.

Come softly, Point Hollow said, quivering at the end of the Dead Road. He drove the rental, battered and clattering, splashed with the deer's blood. Abraham's Faith hulked beyond the town, covering the sky. *Come softly.* He put his foot down and trembled past the sign that read: THE PEOPLE OF POINT HOLLOW WELCOME YOU. STAY A WHILE. Sheriff Tansy was on the radio: *"That's seventy thousand amps of pure adrenaline bolting through your system. Now all you have to do is channel it, push it all into one bullet, and let yourself glow."* From somewhere else he heard laughter that sounded like Kirsty's. He looked over his right shoulder, expecting to see her, but the deer was sprawled along the backseat, broken and bleeding and blinking its terrified eye. *Come softly.* He looked at Point Hollow, at the mountain, and then saw Bobby standing beside a sign that read: POPULATION ???? Bobby smiled and waved at him, and Matthew saw, scratched beneath the row of question marks, the words: ALL DEAD CHILDREN.

Come softly.

The car hissed and rumbled toward town.

FROM OLIVER WRAY'S JOURNAL (III)

Point Hollow, NY.
August 4, 2010.

I slept well, my body waking to the softness of a real bed after three days in the wild. If I dreamed I don't remember. If the mountain called to me, I didn't hear. I went deep, and it was heaven.

Pain woke me: my sunburned body, the deep cut in my right foot. I moved tenderly from between the sheets and eased my wounds with a cool shower. My foot still bled, and following a delicate examination I decided to see Dr. Alex, who would clean and dress it properly, and ensure there was no infection.

But first . . .

Disarray. Evidence—reminders—of yesterday. My study in tatters. It forced fingers into my mind that pried and pulled. I couldn't face Dr. Alex, or anybody, with this chaos in my corner, so spent an hour putting everything right. The only thing I couldn't fix was the dent in the filing cabinet that Bobby made when he crashed into it. I removed the drawers and tried popping out the dent from inside, and although I improved it, there is still a deep crease in the panel (I can feel the same crease in my mind, and it *hurts*). Of course, I ordered another filing cabinet, to be delivered ASAP.

Unsettled, still in pain, I drove into Point Hollow to see Dr. Alex. I sat in the waiting room, closed my eyes, and imagined an icicle melting. My woes were the cold, steady drips. After a stretch of time that could have been as long as an hour, Dr. Alex called me in and took care of my injuries. He asked what I'd been doing (the gash in my right sole is bad, but both feet are raw, my palms, too—that's what comes of walking around on all fours). I told him that I'd been working around the house. An unsatisfactory reply, but he didn't question me further. He Steri-stripped and bandaged my foot, prescribed Vicodin for my pain, and Silvadene for the second-degree burns on my back and shoulders.

"You need to take it easy in this heat," he warned. "We've already had one fatality in town. We don't want any more."

"Fatality?" My eyes were wide. Baby-innocent.

"You didn't hear?"

"I've been busy."

"Bobby Alexander died yesterday."

"Bobby?" I imagined him lying on a slab with a shattered jaw and the skin scraped from his arms and belly, his heart motionless and refrigerator-cold. I shook my head and blinked my baby eyes. "That's . . . that's terrible."

"Heart attack."

"Terrible."

Dr. Alex said something else but I didn't catch it because I was imagining Bobby sitting at my computer, reading my journal, his pudgy hand folded over the mouse as he scrolled through pages. I muttered something and pushed the thought away. It wasn't important anymore. I'd dealt with it, although I still felt the crease in the filing cabinet, and so had to imagine the icicle again, slowly melting.

I picked up my mail and parcels from the post office (Vern Abbott told me about Bobby, looking suitably sombre, and I expressed my condolences and told him how shocked I was). Then I bought an ice cream—vanilla fudge ripple—and ate it like a child, grinning, licking drips off the cone. I drove home, slept until early afternoon, swallowed two Vicodin, and then opened my mail. Mostly business correspondence. There was, however, one letter, very few words, that touched something deep inside.

We need to talk. Call soon.

Regards,
Kip Sawyer.

I sat down and didn't move for a long time—not until my body started to hurt again and I needed another Vicodin. My mind buzzed with conjecture, but behind it was a certainty that things were culminating. First Matthew coming back to town, then Bobby, and now this. The mountain's energy was growing. It was reaching out.

I called Kip's house. His helper answered the phone and told me that Kip was very ill, and in no condition to speak to anybody.

"Tell him it's Oliver Wray."

"He's sleeping at the moment, Mr. Wray."

"Wake him up."

"I'll do no such thing. When he wakes up, on his own, and after he's eaten, I'll tell him you called."

"It's very important."

"I'll relay your message, Mr. Wray."

I hung up and wanted to pace but my foot was throbbing, so all I could do was sit and wait. Abraham's Faith trembled. I sensed, in every reverberation, a suggestion of closure. It was like riding a dying horse. A cracked vase, holding water for years, finally breaking.

The phone rang just after seven P.M. I leapt at it, forgetting my pain.

"You can visit Kip tomorrow morning, Mr. Wray. Ten o'clock."

"Very good."

"He's weak. I ask that you're not too demanding."

I've seen the helper around town. She has a pinched face, doughy eyes, and iron-grey bangs. She walks like a man and looks like her voice: severe and professional. I wished for a strong electrical current to travel down the phone line and zap her in the ear.

"*He* wrote to *me*," I said through gritted teeth. "I have no idea what this is about."

"I am fully aware of the correspondence, Mr. Wray. *I* typed and mailed the letter. All I ask is that you conduct business efficiently."

I snarled. She may have heard me. I didn't care.

"I'm sure you understand," she said.

"Ten o'clock." I hung up.

I sit here now, writing this, the mountain sounding like a constant bell—clanging, clanging—and my mind is littered with images, like the dead, clogging plague-torn streets, while the living cry and the bell tolls. I wonder why Kip Sawyer wants to see me. Will he finally spill his secrets? Is the mountain touching him, too?

I'm tired, but I can't sleep.

My eyes are drawn to the crease in the filing cabinet and I think of Bobby Alexander sitting in this chair, and it's not so much what he read, but *that* he read—that he invaded my home and my thoughts. I feel the same crease in my mind and know that changing the filing cabinet won't be enough. I need to change this chair, this computer, this study. Maybe I'll redecorate, or move to a new room. Maybe I'll bulldoze the house and rebuild. Whatever it takes to remove that crease from my mind.

Imagining him on the slab helps. Have they performed the autopsy yet? Has his brain been examined? Internal organs removed? Such thoughts, however macabre, are like the cream Dr. Alex gave me for my sunburned skin. Soothing.

It's almost midnight. Ten hours until I see Kip.

It's going to be a long night.

August 5, 2010.

It's late. My body is weary and hurting. Abraham's Faith is a constant sound. If I had time and energy I would return to the wild to cleanse and attain tranquility. I have neither.

I am not writing now; I am purging.

Imagine a plant deep in the forest, something fresh and green, but vulnerable, always seeking light. The trees surrounding this plant are broad and tall and their branches create a thick canopy, so that everything below is caught in darkness. But the plant doesn't wither, and it never gives up. It draws nutrients from the soil and stretches its green hand, and sometimes it is knocked down, but its roots are strong and it keeps growing, leaves springing from its body as it twists and spreads, determined to find light. And one day a huge storm blows through the forest and the larger trees are uprooted and cast aside. Suddenly the sky is open, and the little plant—kept in the dark, sheltered, for so many years—has all the light it will ever need. A gift of fate.

I am that plant. I see nothing but blue sky.

And I bloom.

The storm is Kip Sawyer. Thunder and lightning, rains of knowledge that sweep away all obstruction. Ironic that someone so feeble can harness such power. I arrived at his house at precisely ten A.M. and the helper scowled and led me to his room. It was a comfortable temperature and the blinds were drawn. A lamp on the nightstand offered pale light. Kip sat up in bed, propped against a pile of pillows. His ruined eyes followed my footsteps. There was an oxygen tank beside his bed, a mask looped over the headrest. He wore his nasal cannula, as he had when I last spoke to him at the doctor's office, more than three years ago. He had been frail then, dusty skin covering brittle bones and a heart that beat because it didn't know how to do anything else. But here he was, still alive. His chest hardly moved as he breathed.

"Hello, Mr. Sawyer," I said.

Our meeting lasted almost two hours—longer, I'm sure, than the helper would have wanted. But there was no way around it; Kip took a long time to say anything, and when he did it was all but unintelligible, so he would have to repeat it, or scribble the word/sentence blindly on a notepad, his brain recalling the shapes of letters, even if his eyes couldn't see them. Awkward, childlike uppercase slanting across the page.

I sat on the edge of his bed. His body appeared too small beneath the covers. I thought, if I pulled them back, that I would see something half-formed, barely human.

"Oliver," he said, a broken sound that I was able to decipher from the way his mouth moved, his tongue knocking off the roof of his mouth. He said something else. "Child," I think.

"It's good to see you again, Mr. Sawyer." I wondered if I should squeeze his forearm, thinking that's what you do with the infirm— squeeze them, gently, for some reason. My hand twitched but I kept it in my lap. "I called as soon as I got your letter."

He nodded.

"I assume you wanted to discuss—"

"The town," he said, pushing the words out. "The mountain." He started to write it: MOUN. I guessed the rest.

The room revolved. A single, slow circuit, and I had to close my eyes and imagine a level surface, concrete, bolted to the earth. My spine rippled and the air pressed moist hands against my skin. I sensed obstructive trees being blown away, all around me, branches tearing.

"You've done wicked things," he said. Words mumbled. Words half-scrawled. I filled in the blanks.

"Yes," I said.

"I don't know what, and have no desire to be enlightened. But I know Abraham's Faith is cruel, and that it has a will to reach out . . . to touch people. You feel it, don't you? You've been touched."

I started to cry. I don't know if Kip heard, or if he felt my tears splashing on the covers. He sat silently for a moment, perhaps waiting for me to stop, only the sound of the oxygen hissing through the tubing.

"The mountain speaks to me," I said, adjusting my weight on the bed. "It has since I was fourteen years old. Not in the same way that people speak. It *booms* . . . puts images in my head. Sometimes it's all I can hear. I thought, if I could find out what happened up there, that I could make it stop, but nobody wants to tell me anything. It's as if the truth is deliberately being kept from me."

"It is," Kip said. "But not just you. It's being kept from the whole town. The whole *world*."

"I need to know," I said.

He lifted his head, mouth open, a grey semicircle in the ashen rag of his face. I recalled our conversation in Blueberry Bush Park, how he had been so bright-eyed and articulate, ninety-plus years old (or so I thought then, but was about to learn differently), and positively robust compared to the withered mummy he had become. Again I felt the urge to reach out, clasp his hand, and squeeze.

Seconds passed. His mouth moved. The oxygen hissed. The air conditioner clicked on and maintained the room's cool temperature. I wiped my eyes and tried to breathe easy. The mountain rumbled in the east.

"I can still feel it," Kip said with great effort. "Can still feel *him*."

"Who?"

"Coming from the mountain . . . darkness." Every word was clumsy and brick-shaped. His papery hands trembled. "The whole town feels it. I don't have to tell you. We've had this conversation."

"Yes," I said, recalling, again, our exchange in Blueberry Bush Park. *What's wrong with this town?* I had asked, because I sensed— and always have—that the wind blows differently in Point Hollow. The beauty is cosmetic. Something lives beneath the surface. Something cruel.

"The town is cursed," Kip said.

I blinked fresh tears onto my cheeks, wiped them away. Kip rested his head against the pillows, eyes closed, mouth still open. I waited, and it occurred to me that he could die, right there and then, with all his secrets caught inside. What an unkind twist of fate, to be taken to the threshold of understanding, only to be denied at the last. I felt a surge of panic, as raw as white water, and spoke his name . . . twice, three times. No response. His eyelids didn't flicker. I studied his chest and couldn't be sure it was moving. His oxygen hissed, escaping from his open mouth like a broken valve, and now I did reach out and squeeze him—the thin pole of his left leg. His eyes opened.

"Bird," he said.

I exhaled heavily, unaware that I'd been holding my breath. Kip pointed across the room (unusual to see a blind man pointing, but there was nothing wrong with his coordination), either at a painting, or at the door to a walk-in closet.

"What?" I asked, and managed to decipher the words "closet" and "top" and he wrote down the word "SHELF." I limped across the room, opened the closet door, and looked on the top shelf. Folded clothes, shoe boxes, a leather briefcase.

"The briefcase?" I asked.

He nodded.

I lifted it down. My sore shoulders protested and I felt one of the blisters pop and trickle down my back. I carried the briefcase to the bed as Kip scrawled down the six-digit combination. I entered it with trembling fingers, opened the case. Inside was a sheaf of correspondence, mainly journals and letters. There were some newspapers and photographs. It smelled dry and old.

"It's all there," Kip said. "The answers to all of your questions. Every secret. Every sin."

"And you've held these secrets all along?" I whispered. "Only now, after all these years, all this suffering, do you decide to share them?"

He nodded. Such a simple response, yet everything inside me screamed. The room compressed with a grinding, crunching sound and suddenly I couldn't breathe. I shuffled to the window, ducking under the blind, throwing it open, my lungs snatching at the warm air. I stayed there until some trace of calm found me.

Kip's window, blessedly—certainly deliberately—faces west, where the peaks are greener, kinder. Not that I couldn't hear my old friend booming from the other side. A deranged inmate challenging the bars of his cell.

I closed the window, limped to Kip's bedside, and sat down. I wiped sweat from my brow, then looked from the caseful of secrets to the man who had kept them. I wanted to smother him with the pillow, but knew that, like me, he was a victim. The mountain had touched him, too. I reached into the briefcase, pushing aside journals and scraps of paper, and found what I was looking for— what I *knew* would be in there: a photograph of *him*. Mr. Fishhook. Original me.

It was a close-up of his face. An actual photograph, as opposed to a reprint. My heart dropped with a metallic sound and sweat moistened my upper lip. I looked at him. His eyes were light-coloured, too far apart, and the bridge of his nose was flattened. His cheeks were sprayed with tiny, cross-shaped scars and his mouth—as in my picture of him—was hooked to the left. It wasn't the way he smiled, but obviously some mild deformity. Bell's palsy, perhaps. His hair was the same colour as mine, but short at the sides, falling messily across his brow in front, where I could see more of those cross-shaped scars.

"It's all been collected, hidden away," Kip said/wrote. His eyelids fluttered and he appeared to be smiling, but it was simply the shape of his mouth, working to form words. "The letters, photographs, journals . . . anything that could defame our town and serve as a reminder. This is all that remains. I'm the last survivor from that time, and peace is overdue. Take these memories, Oliver. You've earned them."

I wept again and this time Kip heard. He tried to reach for me but I pulled away. My tears fell on Mr. Fishhook's face, as if we shared sorrows. I turned the photograph over and saw a name printed on the back in tight script:

Leander Bird.

His name. I spoke it and the mountain shook.

"He came to Point Hollow a preacher," Kip said. "With light in the palms of his hands. He left in flames, burning on the mountain, cursing us all."

I couldn't look at that twisted mouth, or into those burning eyes. I put the photograph back in the briefcase, facedown, and lifted out a journal bound in taupe leather. It cried when I cracked it open. A sound like wood stretching. The pages were creased, filled with faded type.

I read:

From Trey Moffatt's Journal.
April 25, 1917.
I ask you: is belief enough? Unto God, who sacrificed His only son, is the act of prayer, and adhering to the Holy Scripture, sufficient to walk alongside Him in the Kingdom of Heaven? Should our faith be tested, and to what degree? And more importantly, by whom?

There is a fragility to Point Hollow, a
harmlessness, like a child that seeks direction.
Should I, then, be watchful of this stranger
who has come among us? He offers salvation,
and his methods are alluring. He sermonizes
with striking character. I have witnessed him
heal pain.

Leander Bird. Even his name is exotic. The
Holy Trinity Anglican Church echoes with
emptiness. The Reverend Walter Geller prays
alone. His flock stands in the field behind Ade
Mooney's barn, because that's where Leander
Bird sermonizes. The townspeople come to him.
They fall to their knees in the mud, and they
pray. But not for long; the preacher has asked
that they construct a new house of worship.
"Bring tools and materials, and build in the
name of faith."

And so they build, desperately seeking
direction. This child of a town.

What else will he have them do, in time?

I am reminded (and perhaps it is unfair of me)
of Matthew 7:15: "Beware of false prophets, who
come to you in sheep's clothing, but inwardly
are ravening wolves."

And I ask again: is belief enough?

"We thought he was a man of God." Kip said. He looked at me with moist, sightless eyes. "We were wrong; Leander Bird was . . ." He stammered, and then wrote EVI in shaky letters, and I said "evil" and he nodded.

I wiped my eyes, seeing all too clearly the children in the mountain. The skulls. The bones. Piled high, leaning against one another, melded into new shapes, new creatures.

"One man," I said. "All those children. So *many* children."

"Therein lies our sin," Kip said, taking as deep a breath as he could manage and fixing his watery eyes on me. "It wasn't just one man . . ." He trailed off. Another deep breath, and then he said, "It was the whole town."

"*What?*" I shook my head. Numb. Dazed. Hurting.

"He possessed us," Kip said. "*We* killed our children. We killed them all."

A scrap of paper from the box:

And the preacher turned his orange eyes upon me, and laid his hand upon my brow. I felt, then, something pass from him into me, an inexplicable thing, but powerful, and although my body turned cold I thought it could only be the Lord . . . and so I grasped dear Daniels hand and led him into the mountain, both of us crying, and came into a vast stone chamber where the floor was slick and the faith visible. We crouched together, and prayed, and then I took my son and placed the knife to his throat, waiting to hear God's voice, for Him to intervene as He had with Abraham, but there was only silence. "It is God's will," I said, and drew the blade across Daniels throat, and felt him die in my arms.

Kip shuddered and wept with me, his tears trickling to the hollows of his temples.

"The whole town," I said. My voice was so small.

He nodded. "And now you know why we have kept this hidden away. Our sin continues, and our suffering is our own."

From Trey Moffatt's Journal.
June 18, 1917.
He recites from the Book of Genesis, and we listen in grief, in faith: "By myself have I sworn, saith Jehovah, because thou hast done this thing, and hast not withheld thy son, thine only son; that in blessing I will bless thee, and in multiplying I will multiply thy seed as the stars of the heavens, and as the sand which is upon the sea shore; and thy seed shall possess the gate of his enemies; and in thy seed shall all the nations of the earth be blessed; because thou hast obeyed my voice."

But Point Hollow seems, now, a broken place. A shattered place. We walk without air and look to

the mountain, where the children bled. And the
preacher smiles upon us, and tells us we are
saved, but all the time his face is bleeding.
  Saved? I think not. I fear for our souls.
  God help us all.

My tears gleamed in the pale light. My burned shoulders trembled.

"You say *we*," I said to Kip, and my soul was vast and open. "*We* killed our children.' That's what you said. But in 1917 you would have been young, a boy, twelve or thirteen years old. Why weren't you given to the mountain? Did your parents refuse? Did you . . .?"

I trailed off because Kip had raised his right hand, staring at me, his tear-filled eyes narrowed to ticks, as if he could see me.

"I was twenty-six years old in 1917," he said.

"That's impossible."

"I'm cursed, Oliver."

"But you had a brother. An older brother. He died in World War One."

Kip shook his head. "A fabrication. I needed to appear younger than I really was. The people of Point Hollow have no idea what happened in 1917. Well, some of the higher-ups, maybe, but they don't know everything. If people knew how old I really am, it would draw attention. And so I've been lying about my age for seventy-some years. It's not hard, and I have long outlived anybody who could contradict me."

It took almost ten minutes for Kip to write/mumble this revelation, during which I sensed the edge of the universe. I considered flinging myself into the void and falling forever, because nothing was real. It was all a stroke of imagination. Some bizarre god, with my face, building . . . destroying.

"All of your questions over the years," Kip said. "And you never once asked why I don't have any children."

"I don't understand this," I said.

"That picture you once described," he said. "The man—Bird—

standing on the mountain with three weeping children. Did you ever stop to think that somebody must have taken that picture? That there was more than one person involved?"

"I thought lots of things," I said.

"Yes, I'm sure."

"Did you take it?" I asked.

"I did."

"The children?"

"Percy, Margaret, and Bethany Sawyer. I took their lives in an act of faith. I thought . . ." He wheezed, struggling, his narrow shoulders trembling. Minutes passed and my heart hammered heavy hands against my chest. "I thought I'd see the glory of God, and that my faith—the town's faith—would be rewarded. But all I got was a shattered soul, and knew that we had been deceived by the devil."

I took a deep breath. The room was uncomfortably bright, despite the drawn blinds and the lamp's weak light. Kip wheezed, his fingers clasping the notepad and pen. There were ink marks on the sheets.

"So you're . . ." I calculated quickly—not easy with a whirling mind. "One hundred and nineteen years old?"

He nodded. "One hundred and twenty come November."

"You're cursed?"

"One hundred years of remembering. One hundred years of pain."

"Why you?"

He took a long moment to compose himself. I knew he was getting tired, and would be sleeping soon. My mind ached with questions that would never be asked. I looked at the briefcase of letters and journals, and hoped it contained all the answers.

"I saw Leander Bird for what he was," Kip rasped, his eyes fluttering. "Myself and my best friend, Trey Moffatt."

I looked at the journal in my hands.

"We were haunted, *wounded*, after what we'd done," Kip said. "Trey didn't have children, but he felt it, too, because he was a part of the town."

Another lengthy stretch of silence (although the mountain was anything but, clamouring in my head). Kip's lower lip trembled and the tears were running freely down his face.

"Leander was the devil," he uttered. "Or *a* devil. Some unspeakable thing. The town, without its children, was crippled and hurting. We were terrified, imprisoned by guilt, and by the guile of this . . . this *demon*. So Trey and I decided to do something about it."

"What did you do?"

"We bound him in chains," Kip said. "And we burned him on the mountain."

From Trey Moffatt's Journal.
June 23, 1917.
And so it is done. I am weary, and crushed inside. Point Hollow gathers in silence and prepares to heal. We pray for forgiveness, and that God will take us back. The healing will be long, but the evil is gone.
The evil is gone.
Everything I write here is true. I hope to ease my aching mind by committing it to paper, but moreover, I hope it serves as a lesson, that we may learn from our weakness, our eagerness to believe, and our abysmal lack of judgment.
We left at first light, laden with our supplies, moving heavily through Point Hollow's silent streets. Leander Bird's church—which we built, foolishly, with our trusting hearts— stood in morning shadow, lit from within. Kip levelled his pistol at the door as I pushed it open, and there stood our adversary.
"Gentlemen," he said. "It's a little early for prayer."
"We're not here to pray," Kip said. He was trying not to shake but I noticed the barrel of his pistol wavering, and hoped he would not have to shoot.
"Has your faith been tested?" Leander asked.
"Broken," I said. "We are bereft because of you."
Leander held out his arms. "Isaiah 53:11: ·He shall see of the travail of his soul, and shall

be satisfied: by the knowledge of himself shall
my righteous servant justify many; and he shall
bear their iniquities."

I shook my head, stepping toward him. "No,
Bird. This town has seen enough iniquity."

"You are exiling me?"

"No," Kip replied, close to my side. "You
slithered into our minds like a snake. You
bewitched us—had us sacrifice our children,
in the name of God. We're taking you to the
mountain, where our sin was born, and you will
be our burnt offering . . . this time, truly, in
the name of God."

Kip pressed the pistol to Leander's temple
and he did not struggle. I bound his upper
body in chains, heavy and thick, his arms
pinned to his sides. With the last lock snapped
into place, we walked him from the church and
through the streets of Point Hollow, which had
been silent only moments before, but were now
lined with townspeople. They hissed and wept,
venting their anger, their disappointment,
by shouting at the preacher—vile words—and
throwing items at him: children's shoes and
wooden toys. He walked passively, with his
head high, bearing the hatred with a smile.
The townspeople fell into step behind us, and
as one we walked the devil to the mountain,
traversing the cruel landscape, as we had less
than a week before, while holding the hands of
our scared, weeping children.

We were blind then, but not anymore. God
pray, not anymore.

Our plan was to lead Leander into the
mountain, and offer him among our sins, but
Kip stopped at the mouth of the cave. His eyes
were ghostly circles, his complexion as pale
as cloud.

"I can't go in there," he said.

I turned around to see the townspeople
gathered with similar expressions. They weren't

going to follow me in, and I certainly wasn't going in alone.

"Then we'll do it here," I said.

Amid a chorus of hatred, and with Kip's pistol aimed at Leander's skull, I pulled yet more chains from the bag I carried, wrapped them around his legs, and secured them with locks. Again, there was no struggle, but with a cold voice Leander looked at me and said: "You cannot stop me."

"We can," I said. "We will."

He smiled in reply and a freshet of blood trickled from one of the cross-shaped scars on his forehead. I wondered, pulling a bottle of kerosene from the bag, if it was an old wound, reopened, or new—if each scar represented an act of evil committed upon our world. I wonder this even now, and will for many years to come.

I pushed him backward and he fell heavily, trussed and helpless, and I drowned him in kerosene. Not one bottle but two.

"I doom your sorry life," Leander said calmly. "I pour my dark soul into this mountain, and your town shall forever suffer in my shadow."

I took a matchbook from my pocket.

"I give you," he said to Kip, "one hundred years of memory. Every day you will hear your children's cries."

Kip's finger tightened on the trigger. I think he would have shot if his eyes hadn't been so full of tears.

"And you," Leander said, looking at me. "Your children—your children's children—shall know my name."

I struck a match. I dropped it, and the devil burned. But the flames were as black as night, and the smoke flowed not into the wind, but into the pores of the rock face. He did not scream, and all the time I could see the small cross on his forehead bleeding.

The Reverend Walter Geller—who is old,

but had followed us all the way—stepped forward and recited from Matthew: "'Then shall he say also unto them on the left hand, Depart from me, ye cursed, into the eternal fire which is prepared for the devil and his angels.'"

And with these words Leander Bird began to laugh, and the sound echoed, and followed him into ashes. I prayed to see those ashes carried into the wind, and away, but, like the smoke, they were drawn into the mountain.

Again Reverend Geller stepped forward, to the mouth of the cave, and spoke a prayer that would echo over the bodies of our sleeping children. The stronger men then gathered rocks and concealed the opening. Our effort at burial, and the beginning of healing.

As one we walked to the mountain, and as one we returned. Although we were misguided, and beguiled, let it serve as a symbol of faith; the same faith that Abraham showed in taking Isaac to Mount Moriah.

And let God forgive us.

It is late now, and yes I am weary. Jane gives me comfort. Her arms find the cold places inside me, bringing warmth, and hope. The evil is gone, and the town can begin to rebuild. We are strong.

Dark outside, but for the glow of the fire: Leander Bird's church in flames, surrounded by townspeople, purging their grief. The glow is comforting, somehow. The flames are red and orange. Charred timbers crumble.

Built in innocence. Burned in faith.

From the Hollow County *Herald*.
September 10, 1920.
With God: Grace Alexandra, the baby daughter of Trey and Jane Moffatt of Point Hollow, died September 6, 1920, aged twenty-six

days. Laid to rest at Hope Springs Cemetery. "Suffer the little children to come unto me; forbid them not; for to such belongeth the Kingdom of God."

Kip appeared to be sleeping. His eyes were closed, but they rolled slowly beneath the membranous lids. His pinky finger twitched, the pen held between his forefinger and thumb. I covered my face with both hands and tried to take it all in—this sudden light, but it was blinding, and I could only glimpse it through the cracks of my fingers. I thought it would take me days, maybe even months, to come to terms with what I had learned.

"Kip?"

His eyes crept open. I had time for one, maybe two, more questions. Abraham's Faith shook its shoulders, stomped its feet, and I wondered what it had been like for Kip. So many years, haunted by memories, listening not to the mountain, but to his children's cries.

For all my sins, and all my suffering, I wouldn't want to be him.

"Did you ever think about taking your own life?" I asked.

The tiniest smile, but bitter. "Every day," he rasped. "For ninety-three years. Twice a day. More. Ten times a day, sometimes."

"Why didn't you?"

"And commit another sin?" He shook his head. "No, this is my period of atonement, and I'll bear the weight of my misjudgment. I *have* to. Only then will I be able to face God."

I nodded, feeling weighed down inside, but light all around. Kip sighed, his lips trembling. *Seven years to go,* I thought. *Seven years of hell, and then you can rest.* I closed the briefcase and gathered it to my chest. It seemed heavier now. The town's burden. I tried to stand but my legs were trembling too much and I sat down again. Kip's lower body shifted. His pale eyes found me.

"Sleep now," he said.

"Yes." I took a moment, then tried to stand again—managed to stay on my feet. I stepped toward the door. The case made my arms ache. The mountain roared.

"How do I stop it?" I asked.

No reply.

"Kip?" I turned and looked at him. His eyes were halfway open. "How do I stop it?"

"How do you think?" he replied weakly, and paused, licked his lips. "You have to give it—*him*—what he wants."

"Children," I said.

The word was like a bullet. His worn face turned aside, suffering. "But it's so hungry. It—*he*—keeps booming."

"Children," Kip said. "Or child? A specific child?"

I stood in silence, in a thousand pieces, but reaching toward the light. I blinked and saw water spilling through small, cupped hands. *So cold.*

"Think about it," Kip said, and closed his eyes again. "Most things can be solved with a little thought, Oliver."

I nodded and left.

Sunlight bathed me.

August 6, 2010.

They put Bobby Alexander in the ground today. The pallbearers couldn't carry the load, so they rolled him from place to place on a casket carriage. It lacked a certain dignity, I thought.

Light still surrounds me. I continue to bloom. I am exhausted but everything is happening. The mountain is thunder and I need to focus. I don't have much time. My study is chaos—the contents of Kip's briefcase arranged across my desk, across the floor. So much information, and I still haven't read it all.

I stopped taking the Vicodin because it makes me drowsy and lightheaded. My body hurts. Really, I'm in no condition to do what has to be done, but I have no choice.

It's time to end this.

From Trey Moffatt's Journal.
February 12, 1927.
Jane tells me to stop fretting. The twins
are two years old now, growing beautifully. But
I remember, all too clearly, Leander Bird's

```
final words: "Your children—your children's
children—shall know my name." Did he take
Grace from us? Did his black, burning hand
reach from the mountain and smother her where
she lay? I am cursed. My children are cursed.
And so I stand vigil over Annette and Lucy, my
heart twisted.
    I didn't want to have more children, but Jane
did. We have to rebuild Point Hollow, she said.
Fill it with young laughter and joyful faces.
We can't let the darkness win.
```

I knew about the fire that destroyed the church in 1923 (The Holy Trinity Anglican Church, confirmed by numerous letters, as well as the Hollow County *Herald*). I knew about the shooting on Main Street in 1953, and the mass suicide in 1971. Distraught correspondence propounds—in each case—ungodly forces at work. One letter, in regard to the shooting, suggests demonic influence: *Jack Braum's mind was not his own. Yes, I saw the shotgun, but I also saw a wolf's eyes and black wings.* Given how thoroughly the events of 1917 were concealed, and that by the fifties there would have been only a handful of people alive who could remember what happened, such detail is telling. It's impossible to deny a more sinister influence.

There are varied versions of what Dennis Shirley—our firestarter from 1923—was heard to scream as he was muscled away from the blazing church, but they all convey the same thing. In short: *Bird touched me. He's still here. He's still with us.*

Jack Braum, sitting in a holding cell, in the final moments of his life, said: *There's a black fire in my head, and it burns.*

The suicide note from 1971 (and I have the actual note) reads, simply: *It watches us. It remembers.*

There are other incidents: a mysterious house fire in 1960; a murder/suicide in 1964 (Eugene Gold poured sulfuric acid down his wife's throat before eating the barrel of his .38 Special. The suicide note—and I have that, too—reads: *From Bird, with love X.*); in 1968, a John Doe was found hanging upside down in the woods east of Old Friend Pond, drained of blood, his eyes gouged out, his hands cut off.

So much for our peaceful little town.

All of this has been covered up by the powers that be. To protect our idyllic reputation, of course, but more particularly to prevent the mass infanticide of 1917 being uncovered.

The people of Point Hollow live in ignorance. In bliss.

2:53 P.M. I'm running short of time. My body is crying out for rest, for healing. I have to deny it, because I need to end this. But first:

From the Hollow County *Herald*.
July 28, 1933.
COUNTY-WIDE SEARCH FOR MISSING GIRL. The search continues for eight-year-old Annette Moffatt, who was last seen playing in her neighbourhood on the morning of Tuesday, July 25. Annette (pictured) is the daughter of Trey and Jane Moffatt of Point Hollow.

Police have expanded their search to include the townships of Oak Creek and Wharton, and appeal for anybody with information to step forward. "Annette is one of our own," Sheriff Gordon Simms told the Herald. "A beautiful, intelligent girl. A loving daughter and sister. We urge the people of Hollow County to be vigilant, and to pray for her safe return."

Many townspeople have aided police in their search, spanning acres of dense woodland throughout Hollow County. On Thursday Reverend James Tarper held a special service at the New Hope Anglican Church, praying for Annette, and for Mr. and Mrs. Moffatt, who faced grief in 1920 when their first daughter, Grace Alexandra, died in her sleep aged only twenty-six days. The Moffatts have lived in Point Hollow ... cont. pg. 4.

```
From Trey Moffatt's Journal.
July 29, 1933.
Eight years old. An angel. So small
in my arms, her pale skin flickering in
the lamplight.
```

Your children—your children's children—
shall know my name.

Forever cursed.

I found her, as I knew I would, in the
mountain. Abraham's Faith. That's what the town
is calling it. A stupefying name for something so
unchristian, so close to hell. But it's a mask. A
falsehood. Just like the smiles the townspeople
wear. It helps them forget.

I don't think the mountain—Abraham's Faith—
will let us forget so easily.

The "search" (if that's what you can call
it; everybody knows where Annette was taken)
moved west, into Oak Creek, giving me the
opportunity I had been waiting for. I walked
to the mountain and removed the rocks from
the opening. With my heart crashing and my
soul in ruins, I ventured inside, following
a narrow tunnel until it opened into a damp
cavern (more like a charnel house), and there I
searched among the small bodies until I found
the one I sought.

So light in my arms. So fragile. No sign
of harm on her body. I wondered if one of the
townspeople had taken her there, possessed by
Leander Bird's evil spirit, as Dennis Shirley
had been when he burned down the church. Or
maybe Leander himself had swooped birdlike
from the mountain, his wings huge and black,
like the flames that had leapt from his burning
body, and grasped Annette in his wicked claw and
carried her to his underworld. I don't know. I
never will.

I could not leave her there, though, in the
mountain. With my grief as vast as the cavern I
stood in, I wept and whispered prayers and took
her from that terrible place. I lay her small
body aside while I covered the opening, and then
gathered her in my arms and carried her down
the mountain. I sensed Leander Bird behind me,

spitting black fire and laughing, but I never
turned around. I didn't want to give him the
satisfaction of seeing the tears in my eyes.

I buried Annette in a beautiful spot beside
Old Friend Pond, beneath the shade of a willow.
I dug the grave (mostly) with my bare hands,
using rocks and pieces of wood when they
started to bleed. I went deep, too. As deep as
my pain. I lay Annette in the grave and then
covered her, and I sat there and prayed and
watched the sun press a ragged red hand on
the water.

Kip said, *Most things can be solved with a little thought, Oliver.* And he's right about that. However, when you have the pieces in front of you, and you see how they are supposed to go together, it all gets much easier.

For years now—beginning with Danielle Dewberry in 1992—I have been settling Leander Bird's appetite for children, but never *satisfying* it. I have revelled in the mountain's silence, only to have it clamour again, demented and determined.

This past week it has been louder than ever.

Trey Moffatt died of prostate cancer in 1946, survived by his wife Jane (she died in '54) and his daughter Lucy. The proudest day of Trey's life—according to another journal entry—was when he walked his daughter down the aisle in the summer of '45. Lucy Moffatt married Point Hollow banker William Callum, and they had two children: Jonah Trey, born in 1948, and Sarah Marie, born in '51. I knew what I was looking for, and found it right away. A *Herald* article from June of 1958 with the headline: POINT HOLLOW BOY STILL MISSING, PARENTS DESPAIR. The boy was ten-year-old Jonah Callum, who'd set out early one morning for a spot of fishing on Gray Rock River, never to be seen again. A description of what he'd been wearing was printed: a white cotton T-shirt, blue jeans, and Converse All Stars.

My old friend, J.C.

I know exactly where Jonah is. Swallowed, not by a whale, but by a mountain.

I deduced the following from what I found in Kip's box, and from genealogy records found on the Internet. Again, when you have the pieces in front of you, it's easy to see how they all slide together:

The Callums—twisted with grief, I'm sure—decided to leave Point Hollow. They went to Utica, where Lucy and Will grew old and died, and Sarah blossomed into a beautiful young woman. She went to college at Syracuse, and met her future husband, an Accounting Major named Peter Bridge. They got married in 1972, and shortly thereafter left Utica for beautiful, small-town America: Point Hollow, NY. Why—of all places—did they choose Point Hollow? Maybe Sarah wanted to live in the town she was born in. Or maybe she was called back. A feeling . . . something she couldn't put her finger on.

Children? Kip had rasped. *Or child. A specific child?*

Peter and Sarah Bridge welcomed their first child, Matthew, into the world on April 2, 1974.

Your children—your children's children—shall know my name.

And the mountain booms.

3:44 P.M. I'm out of time. Perhaps I shouldn't have gone to Bobby's funeral, but I *had* to. Seeing his ornate casket, and imagining his lifeless body inside, helped ease the crease in my mind—not completely, but enough for me to focus. There were very few mourners. His mother, of course, dressed in black. Sheriff Tansy was there, looking solemn (although I'm sure his mind was filled with NASCAR results and winning poker hands). And Matthew Bridge, too. He stood beside Bobby's mother, eyes down and grey-faced. He has changed, of course, in the twenty-six years since I last saw him, but I recognized the little boy inside. In many ways, he hasn't changed at all.

So cold.

My soul roared and Abraham's Faith shuddered furiously. I sensed it crumbling, falling in on itself, tumbling into an abyss with the rest of the world being sucked in behind. Reverend Parfrey eulogized and I waited for him to finish. The few townspeople shuffled away, and I approached Matthew from behind. Dressed in grey, I wanted to appear as large as Abraham's Faith. I wanted to fill his vision and make him feel small. I pulled my shoulders square and loomed over him. The mountain reached through me—black, smoking hands—but I didn't touch him, and I didn't say his name. I just *loomed* and waited for him to turn around, and when he did his eyes clouded with confusion, vague recognition. My shadow consumed him.

"Hello, Matthew," I said.

CHAPTER
TWELVE

Matthew woke early on Friday—the day of Bobby's funeral, and his last day in Point Hollow. No doubt Sheriff Tansy would be rejoicing as Matthew's taillights disappeared into the sunset, but that didn't bother Matthew at all. He would be at his parents' home in Bay Ridge by the end of the day, listening to the sirens and trains, and to the skateboarders in Owl's Head Park. New York City had its problems—what big city didn't?—but it had never made him feel like an outcast.

He got out of bed, shuffled to the window, and pulled open the curtains. Most hotel rooms he'd stayed in offered a view of adjacent hotel rooms. Maybe the parking lot, if he was lucky, or the Interstate. But he couldn't fault this view: the open field behind the hotel grounds, climbing to an evergreen forest, and beyond this, Rising Pine—the peak that gave the elementary school its name. A breathtaking view at any time, but this morning it was particularly special. Mist shimmered on the field, reflecting light. It made the conifers appear *more* green, so full of life he could almost see them breathing. Rising Pine—the second-highest peak surrounding Point Hollow, and considerably more picturesque than the first—caught a belt of sunlight on its eastern face, as if the trees growing there were lit from within, like fibre optics, pink light pouring from every branch, every needle.

Matthew stood at the window for a long time, absorbing the view. Today would be tough—burying Bobby, drying Mrs. Alexander's tears. But at least he had this glorious mental snapshot. Something he could take with him.

In that one moment—in a world so beautiful—he felt that nothing could go wrong.

———

The sun pushed high, bringing weary heat and light that was too clean. Pollen drifted, and distant points shifted in the haze, as if viewed through an irregular lens. The handles and corner plates on Bobby's casket glimmered. His mother cried alone.

There had been a brief service at the church. The smell of wood and prayer. Sunlight lancing through the windows. Matthew had been asked to say something, which surprised him, given the twenty-six year gulf in his relationship with Bobby. He had agreed, partly because he couldn't say no to Mrs. Alexander, but mostly because he kept imagining that empty chair in Bobby's hospital room. *And that's what friends do, right?* Bobby had said the night before he died. *They're there for each other.* So Matthew had written a few words, and he stepped up to the lectern and spoke into the microphone:

"I moved away from Point Hollow twenty-six years ago. That's a long time. And I admit, there were things I left behind . . . people and memories."

He looked at the few townspeople scattered among the pews. Difficult to call them mourners, as only one of them—Bobby's mother—appeared to be mourning. Vern Abbott sat with his head down and his fingers steepled. Sheriff Tansy was using all his concentration to keep from inserting his finger into his nose. There were a few faces from the Rack, including Jesse, the bartender, with his full-lobe ear plugs and plaited soul patch. Matthew was unable to determine if his heavy metal T-shirt ("Lamb of God" emblazoned across the front) was inappropriate or not.

"Returning, after such a long absence," Matthew continued, and then stopped. He noticed another individual sitting in the back row. Dark hair, greying at the temples. Styled (not like Matthew's whirly bird nest). A clean, handsome face. He wore an immaculate suit (again, not like Matthew's) and his chest and shoulders were broad, swelling as he breathed.

I know you, Matthew thought. His heart was already drumming (he'd never been good at speaking in front of people), but now a mist of sweat formed on his brow. He felt a cold feather run from between his shoulder blades to the base of his spine. An old memory tried to stir but he forced it away, trying to concentrate on the words he had written.

"Returning to Point Hollow, I . . ."

The man's eyes were fixed on Matthew. Drilling into him.

"I was . . ." He gasped and the sound carried around the church. Sheriff Tansy rolled his eyes and this urged him on. "Delighted . . . I was delighted, and blessed, to meet Bobby again, and although the time I spent with him was too short, he taught me that some things, some memories, can never be buried. He taught me that friendship can't be broken by time, or by distance. It lives forever. The world has changed so much in twenty-six years, but I came back to Point Hollow and found something unchanged, and all the more beautiful because of it. I'm not talking about the picture-perfect streets or the breathtaking scenery. I'm talking about true friendship."

Matthew looked up from his hastily scrawled notes. His gaze flicked over the grey-faced townspeople, settled on Bobby's casket, and with a shaky breath he delivered his closing lines: "I know I hadn't seen Bobby in twenty-six years, but he was a true friend, and I'm going to miss him. Catch you later, alligator."

Stepping down from the lectern, he looked again at the man in the back row. He felt the same cold feather run the same cold course, and looked quickly away, toward the altar, where a huge crucifix watched over the congregation. Christ's eyes were pale, full of suffering, and fixed on Matthew, almost accusingly, much like the man in the back row. *Deus Misereatur* had been inscribed on a placard above Christ's head. Some mental archive informed Matthew that this meant, *May God have Mercy.*

The service moved from New Hope Anglican Church to Hope Springs Cemetery. As one of the pallbearers, Matthew helped wheel Bobby's casket to his grave and heave it onto the lowering device (there was an ominous creaking sound as the straps took the weight). He stood beside Bobby's mother as she wept and the sun blazed. Reverend Parfrey recited from the Book of Common Prayer. Matthew watched the haze shift, the pollen drift.

"In the midst of life we are in death; of whom may we seek for succour, but of thee, O Lord, who for our sins art justly displeased?"

Sheriff Tansy stood on the other side of Bobby's casket, in full uniform, and although he wore sunglasses, Matthew felt the uncomfortable weight of his eyes. His expression suggested he hadn't forgotten Matthew saying he'd leave after the funeral. Matthew hadn't forgotten, either. He'd already checked out of the hotel, his bag was packed and loaded in the rental's trunk. Mrs. Alexander had arranged a small gathering at her house. He planned to attend for thirty minutes or so, then say his goodbyes and hit the road. God willing, he'd be waving goodbye to Point Hollow by four P.M.

"Unto Almighty God we commend the soul of our brother departed, and we commit his body to the ground; earth to earth . . ."

Matthew looked away from Sheriff Tansy. His gaze drifted around the cemetery before settling on the wreath on Bobby's casket. Red and white flowers, painfully bright in a world blanched by heat. Mrs. Alexander sobbed and Matthew put his arm around her, supporting her, as he'd been doing all week. The sense of purpose had strengthened him, and in a way brought him closer to Bobby. He knew the big guy would be looking down, beaming with pride. It more than made up for Sheriff Tansy's cool expression, and the town's insipid energy.

"We humbly beseech thee, O Father, to raise us from the death of sin unto the life of righteousness; that, when we shall depart this life, we shall rest in him . . ."

Matthew was dressed in a too-large suit he'd bought at a consignment store in town. It was a coarse, heavy material that smelled of mothballs. The pants were itchy and his upper body was greased with sweat. Needless to say, he was somewhat relieved when Reverend Parfrey closed the service, and he wasn't alone; he watched men loosen their ties and women remove their hats, fanning themselves with the brims as they shuffled away at a pace they deemed respectful, but was still a touch too swift. He couldn't blame them. He wanted to be with them, throwing off his jacket and leaping into the nearest air-conditioned room. But he waited for Mrs. Alexander while she spoke with Reverend Parfrey.

A shadow fell over him. He thought a cloud had drifted from nowhere and covered the sun. He turned, looking up, and stared directly into the eyes of the man who had been sitting in the back row of the church. Despite the heat, Matthew felt the coldness again.

So cold

Not a feather this time, but something deep, like water inside . . .

"Hello, Matthew."

Like water inside a cave, Matthew thought. He shivered and took a step back, and the man pressed forward, as if he couldn't get close enough. He held out his hand and Matthew looked at it for a moment, his own hand moving forward slowly. A hazy memory scratched at the back of his mind, like something trapped behind a door: water—*so cold*—flowing around his knees; the sun on his bare back; his small hand reaching out and grasping . . .

The man grabbed Matthew's hand, shaking firmly, pulling him closer.

"I know you," Matthew said vaguely. He twisted his hand free and took another step back, looking carefully at the man. The feeling inside him was familiar; he'd felt it in his dreams . . . the ones from which he woke up screaming.

"Oliver," the man said. His eyes flashed. He inhaled and doubled in size. "Oliver Wray."

Matthew nodded. He felt the memories trying to emerge from that buried place in his mind. *Shine a light,* he thought, and tried, but Oliver's shadow consumed him, making everything dark.

"Do you remember me?" Oliver asked.

Sweat trickled into Matthew's eyes. He blinked and wiped them. The heavy jacket suffocated him.

"Do you remember anything?"

"I'm sorry, I don't," Matthew said. That cold feeling inside him spread. A waterfall now. Falling forever. "I've been gone a long time, I've forgotten—"

But there was *something*. It pressed against the shadowy places in his mind. A dull, icy pressure.

So cold.

"We should talk," Oliver said. "Catch up."

Matthew didn't know what to say. He tried to place Oliver—see how, or *if*, he was connected to his forgotten past. But the heat pressed against him like a slab, making thinking difficult. He *did* remember that Bobby didn't like Oliver, so whether he was linked to repressed memories or not, Matthew wasn't prepared to be buddy-buddy while his friend lay in a casket less than ten feet away.

"I have to go home," he said.

"When do you leave?" There was a hint of urgency in Oliver's voice.

Not soon enough, Matthew thought, and then Sheriff Tansy muscled between them, forcing Matthew back two or three steps. He leered and leaned close.

"Yes, Matthew," he said. "When *do* you leave?"

"Very soon," Matthew said, trying to pull his shoulders square. "I'll extend my respects at Mrs. Alexander's house, and be gone by four o'clock." He lifted his glasses, knuckled sweat from his eye, and looked at Sheriff Tansy. "Just a few more hours, Sheriff, and I'll be out of your hair for good."

Sheriff Tansy smirked. "Music to my ears."

"Now, if you'll excuse me." He nodded at both men, and stepped with relief from their shadows to join Mrs. Alexander, to whom Reverend Parfrey extolled God's undying love. She nodded, drawing comfort from his words, her tear-shot eyes flicking all too often to the casket poised above the grave. Then Matthew took her hand and led her away. They meandered between clusters of stone angels and markers, and Matthew turned back only once. His mind had warmed with the memory of the whitetail in the clearing, and he was suddenly sure he would see one of the deer—a fawn, perhaps—beside Bobby's casket. A whimsical thought, he soon realized; nothing there but the flowers, the trees beyond the cemetery, and Abraham's Faith, poised and scarred, marking the horizon like grief.

———

The gathering was mainly attended by Mrs. Alexander's elderly friends, who brought the general complaints of age along with their condolences. Vern Abbott showed up, as did Bobby's old boss from the mill, but it was—much to Matthew's disappointment—a poor showing. He wasn't surprised, given what Bobby had told him, but it was nonetheless disheartening to see so few people. He'd always thought that small towns were supposed to be close-knit, and most of them probably were, but Point Hollow was different. In so many ways.

Matthew checked his watch. 3:23 P.M. He'd be heading south in little over half an hour, Point Hollow fading to a distant memory (again) and the rest of his life ahead of him. He had promised Mrs. Alexander that he would visit whenever he could, and put some flowers on Bobby's grave. But those visits would be brief, three hours at the most, twice a year. He thought he could handle that. Just.

He spent the next fifteen minutes talking to Vern, who groaned about the weather between mouthfuls of potato chips. All he said of Bobby was, "He's riding in the chariot Glory." Matthew took this as his cue to exit. He started saying his goodbyes, which took longer than expected. Mrs. Alexander wept and thanked him for his support. She hugged him tighter than he thought her capable of, kissed his cheek, and told him to visit again soon.

"You have my word," he said.

He didn't take off his jacket or loosen his tie until he was out of the house and strolling toward the rental. He popped the locks, threw his jacket on the back seat, and was just getting behind the wheel when he heard footsteps behind him. He turned, and there was Oliver Wray, dressed in jeans and a T-shirt, a knapsack thrown over one shoulder.

"Matthew," he said. He stepped toward him, noticeably limping.

Matthew's eyes widened. The sight of Oliver standing in the sunlight with a knapsack on one shoulder hit something inside him. A memory broke, swirling through the strata of years: playing in the sprinkler spray as a boy, his upper body glistening, looking up and seeing. . .

"Oliver," Matthew said. He tried to develop the memory, but the edges were indistinct.

"Are you heading into town?" Oliver asked.

"I'm going home."

"But you'll be going through town, right?"

Matthew shrugged. "I guess."

"I'm in a hurry." Oliver pointed at the rental's passenger seat. "Could I grab a ride?"

"It's a ten-minute walk," Matthew said. "Not even."

Oliver smiled. "If I had ten minutes to spare, I wouldn't be asking."

Matthew looked at him. Oliver's smile was broad and his eyes flashed hopefully. He wasn't as oppressive as he had appeared at the cemetery, but Matthew had been uncomfortable then, too hot and emotional. Maybe his instinct—that icy feeling inside him, linking Oliver to some repressed memory—had been askew. Then again, Bobby hadn't liked him. Hadn't trusted him. *I've known him all my life, Matty,* he'd said. *And I'm telling you . . . something isn't right.*

Matthew only saw the smile. It didn't falter. It was, in fact, *warming.*

"What do you say?" Oliver asked. He pointed at his right foot. "I stood on a piece of glass earlier this week and cut myself badly. Hurts like hell to walk. You want to help an old friend out?"

"I don't remember you," Matthew said distantly. His heart rattled and his breathing was short, as if his lungs were filled with stones, but he could think of no good reason to deny Oliver. His mind offered only that single vague memory: playing in the sprinkler spray, his small body glimmering.

"Please?" Oliver said.

Matthew, who had never been good at saying no, shrugged and indicated the passenger seat with his eyes.

"Great, thanks." Oliver took off his pack and got in the car. Matthew closed his eyes for a moment, trying to shake the bad feeling. *Two minutes into town,* he thought. *I can do that.* He got behind the wheel and started the engine.

"Did you enjoy your stay in Point Hollow?" Oliver asked. "Other than Bobby's funeral, I mean. That couldn't have been easy."

"It's a beautiful town," Matthew replied, not really answering the question. He pulled away from Mrs. Alexander's house, then turned on the radio, hoping Oliver would take the hint; he wasn't in the mood for small talk.

"It's a wicked place," Oliver said.

"What?" Matthew looked at Oliver and frowned.

"I said, it's a wicked place."

"That's what I thought you said."

"It's a black cloud that covers sin. It's cursed." Oliver pointed out the window. "By the mountain. You remember the mountain, don't you?"

Matthew gripped the wheel and the bad feeling bloomed. It touched the tips of his fingers, the base of his spine.

"I'm not . . . I don't . . ." He turned onto Grace Road. Everything seemed far away and bleak. Except for Oliver, who swelled in the passenger seat, too big, too real.

"Must be nice to forget," he said. "Heavenly, even. But all I hear is the mountain." He thumped the side of his head. Hard. His knuckles popped. "Night and day. Constantly."

Matthew stood on the brake and pulled over. The tires locked, screeched, hit the curb.

"I think you should get out."

Oliver's smile dropped. His upper lip flared. His eyes, too. Wide and wild, like a cat about to pounce.

"Do you remember me, Matthew?"

"Get out of the car."

Oliver unzipped his knapsack and reached inside.

"You don't remember anything?"

"No," Matthew said, but it was coming back to him—drips of memory, all so cold, so dark. A strained breath escaped him. He

223

gripped the wheel with pale hands, thinking that, any moment now, he would wake up screaming.

"I didn't think so," Oliver said. His voice had changed, too. It was deeper, *creakier*. "If you remembered anything, you wouldn't have come back to Point Hollow, and you certainly wouldn't have given me a ride."

His eyes flashed cold colours as he pulled a pistol from his knapsack. Its fat barrel caught a bead of light. He pressed it to the centre of Matthew's forehead.

"I think you should keep driving."

Oh Jesus . . . oh Jesus Christ.

Matthew started to cry. He turned back to the road and felt the muzzle slide around to his temple.

Jesus please . . . Jesus . . .

"Drive."

Matthew took his foot—it felt like it weighed a hundred pounds—from the brake and the car crept forward. Onto the accelerator, pulling away from the curb, all so slowly. Tears streamed down his cheeks, dripped onto his shirt and tie.

"Turn left on Blue Jay," Oliver instructed. "Don't go down Main."

"Where are you taking me?"

"Treasure hunting," Oliver said, and laughed. A dry, breaking-wood sound.

Matthew turned onto Blue Jay Avenue, a residential street, quiet at any time of the day. He hoped he'd see someone walking their dog, or collecting their mail—someone who would notice him driving at gunpoint and run to call the police. But Blue Jay was sleepy-still. Lush trees and empty sidewalks. Not that he believed anybody in this freakshow town would offer help. They'd probably dash inside and draw the blinds. What had Oliver said? *It's a black cloud that covers sin.*

He was on his own.

A little faster now. The speedometer hovered at twenty miles per hour. Matthew considered flooring it and steering them both into the nearest tree.

His vision blurred. He blinked. Tears ran and dripped and ran again.

"Don't even think about doing anything stupid," Oliver said, as if he could read Matthew's mind. "This .45 is quicker than any decision you can make."

"I just want to go home." The pressure of the muzzle was like the world, balanced on a thimble.

"It wanted you all along, Matthew. All these years."

"What are you going to do?"

"What I should have done in 1984." Oliver used his free hand to wipe his eyes. Even he was crying. "No mistakes this time. I'm going to feed you to that goddamn mountain."

CHAPTER THIRTEEN

Oliver directed Matthew through backstreets, out of town, and down a narrow track north of Tall Pine Way. Branches scraped the paintwork, brushed across the windshield. The car juddered over uneven ground and Matthew held his breath, praying the gun wouldn't accidentally go off and paint the driver's side window with his brains.

"You can lower the gun," he said. "I'll do whatever you want."

"No mistakes," Oliver said. The gun stayed where it was.

A little farther down the track and Oliver told him to stop. Pine trees blocked the sunlight. Gloomy inside the car, but stifling hot. The radio still played. Three Dog Night singing "Joy to the World." A ridiculously happy song. Matthew wanted to snatch the pistol from Oliver's grasp and blow the goddamn radio out of the dashboard. The second bullet he'd use on his captor. He didn't think he'd have any trouble pulling the trigger.

"Shut off the ignition," Oliver said.

Matthew did. The retained power kept the radio playing. Oliver punched the button and there was silence.

"Now hand me the keys."

Matthew did.

"Do you have a cell phone?"

"No," Matthew lied.

"You're telling me you're the only person in North America who doesn't own a cell phone?"

"Left it at home," Matthew said. He felt the shape of it in his front pocket, and wondered if Oliver had noticed it, too. He had to play out the lie, though. "My entire office is on that phone. I wanted to get away from everything, so didn't bring it with me."

"Okay," Oliver said, pressing the muzzle even harder against Matthew's temple. "When we get out of the car, I'm going to check your pockets. If I find a cell phone, I'm going to shoot you in the shoulder. So I'll ask one more time . . . do you have a cell phone?"

Matthew looked at Oliver. The muzzle dragged around to his forehead, leaving a trail of grazed skin. He sobbed, his shoulders trembling. He reached into his pocket and handed Oliver his cell phone.

"You're not a very good liar," Oliver said.

"Please don't hurt me," Matthew said.

"It's not me, Matthew. It was *never* me."

"Please . . ."

"Listen carefully." Oliver put the keys and phone in the glovebox, then tapped the barrel against Matthew's forehead. "We're going to get out of the car at the same time. Move slowly, and remember that this gun is going to be aimed at you the whole time. Before closing the door, I want you to hit the lock button. Do you understand?"

Matthew nodded.

"Let's go."

But Matthew didn't move. He reached for air, his chest trembling. One hand remained locked to the steering wheel, as if it were the only thing of any substance in the world. The only thing worth holding on to. More tears tracked down his face.

"*Now*, Matthew."

"Please, don't do—"

More pressure with the gun and Oliver growled impatiently. Matthew moaned and opened the door. Branches pushed against it and he had to squeeze through a gap not much wider than his body. Oliver was getting out on his side, his free hand grabbing the knapsack, sliding it onto his shoulder. He bumped the door closed with his hip, sighting Matthew down the barrel of the gun. Matthew closed the door and looked at Oliver over the roof.

"The lock button," Oliver said.

"I forgot." Matthew opened the door, hit the button, closed the door. After a few seconds the locks engaged. The horn blipped, stirring something in the woods. It took flight urgently, and Matthew felt a wave of envy. What he'd give to be taking to the open sky, nothing but free. But that wasn't going to happen. Oliver would shoot him in the back if he tried to run, and now his keys and cell phone were locked in the car. He really *was* on his own now.

Oliver jerked the gun, indicating that Matthew move to the front of the car. He did, stumbling, having to duck the sprawled boughs of a pine, feeling the needles scrape along the back of his neck. Oliver stepped toward him and pointed the gun at his face.

"Empty your pockets. Front and back."

Matthew took his wallet from his back pocket and gave it to Oliver. He pulled out the lining of his other pockets to prove that they were empty.

"Nothing else?"

"Nothing."

"Okay." Oliver tossed the wallet into the woods behind him and used the pistol, again, to indicate direction. "Let's walk."

———

They walked east through the forest, Matthew three or four steps ahead of Oliver. He considered making a break for it. Oliver was limping, and there might be enough tree cover to keep him from getting off a clean shot. The possibility of escape was there, but it was *thin*. Could he risk it? This was Oliver's territory, after all. He knew the lay of the land, and no matter how badly he was limping, that didn't make the .45 any slower.

Matthew kept walking. It was the best way to stay alive. *I'm going to feed you to that goddamn mountain.* He had no idea what that meant, but Oliver's state of mind was clearly damaged. This was not the time for recklessness. He would wait it out, see what Oliver intended, and take his chances when he had no other choice.

The mountain's grey face appeared between the trees. Memories tumbled, colours bleeding. Matthew's anxiety kept them from being fully realized. If they got through he would have more to be terrified of. He could only deal with one thing at a time.

"What are you going to do to me, Oliver?"

"Just keep walking."

They emerged from the forest and started across a field where the grass grew wild and butterflies flickered between flowers. Matthew glanced over his shoulder. Oliver limped but held the gun steady. Behind him, clustered in a pocket of summer haze, Point Hollow shimmered blindly. Ahead, the mountain soared.

Matthew walked toward it, crying and small, like a child.

They came to the spring moments later.

As the water flowed from the mountain, cold and clear, so the memories flowed through Matthew's mind. Standing at the edge of the spring, looking across at the gloomy sprawl of spruce and fir, was like stepping into the past—a psychological jolt that brought everything back. The recollection was too powerful to contain.

He covered his eyes and fell to his knees.

"Get up," Oliver said.

He didn't move. His body wasn't his own. It had become a vessel, filling with memories, twisted into a new shape. The world blew away like a sheet of newspaper in the wind. Nothing *was.*

"I said get *up.*" But Oliver had faded. The gun, too. Only the memories had substance. Their bones clicked and clattered, and a fragment of Matthew's mind understood that the darkness inside him—the nights he had woken up screaming, the terrible things he had imagined doing to Kirsty—stemmed from what had happened with Oliver in the summer of 1984.

Abraham's Faith . . . the skeletons . . .

The mountain always gets what it wants.

The darkness had broken him. *Infected* him.

He wasn't going back.

Oliver fired the gun. A mad sound, echoing in Matthew's skull. He flipped onto his back and almost fell in the spring. Oliver stood with the gun pointed at the sky, but levelled it at Matthew. His finger flexed against the trigger.

"The next bullet will be between your eyes."

"Do it," Matthew said.

"Get up."

"I'm not following you. Not again."

"I'll kill you right here, right now."

"That's the only way you'll get me up to that mountain."

Oliver fired a second shot, then a third. Matthew flinched—felt the bullets tear past both sides of his face. An aching breath escaped him and he wondered if anybody in town had heard the shots. Would they come? Would they help? He imagined the echoes carrying through Main Street, making the windows tremble . . . and then the blinds being pulled, covering sin.

The ringing in his head faded. He screamed again.

"Don't make me do it." Oliver's finger tightened on the trigger.

Matthew closed his eyes. Skeletons filled his mind. He got ready to die.

"You son of a bitch." Oliver limped toward him. He raised his arm and brought it down in a hard arc, cracking the base of the pistol's grip against Matthew's head. His glasses were knocked crooked, hanging off one ear. Blood streamed from his hairline, down his forehead, into his wide eyes.

"No," Matthew said, and then everything went grey.

Chapter
Fourteen

With the mountain thundering, Oliver lifted Matthew onto his shoulders (still raw with sunburn) and limped across the spring. Slow going, and hard. Once on the other side, he dropped Matthew and had to rest, drawing grateful breaths, splashing his face with cold water.

There was still so far to go.

Abraham's Faith blared. A barrage of insane sound. Oliver howled in reply and collapsed next to Matthew, where he stayed until his breathing and heartbeat regulated. But the mountain didn't let up. A million drums. Ten thousand cannons. Leander Bird displayed his fishhook grin amid the shapes in his mind. *So close*, he said to Oliver. He beckoned with black-fire hands. *So close now.*

Oliver got to his feet and soaked his upper body with chilled water. He could have all the rest he wanted when the job was done. He could rest in perpetual silence.

Matthew groaned, spluttered, but didn't wake. His glasses had fallen off. His face was a red mask. Oliver put the .45 in the knapsack, strapped it to his back, and hoisted Matthew onto his shoulders. Bent double under the load, he limped through the forest. He had hoped to reach the other side before resting, but couldn't; his body was drained, his injured foot throbbing, sending a fierce ache all the way up his leg. He rested twice. The first time for twenty minutes, his hands clamped to his head, trying to suppress the mountain's voice. The second time he settled against a tree and fell asleep—not for long, but he woke with a start, cursing his stupidity. What if Matthew had woken and crawled away? What if he'd grabbed the .45 from the knapsack?

No mistakes.

His determination revitalized, Oliver got to his feet. Falling asleep had frightened him. Such a huge mistake, and so easy to do. The fear sent a wave of adrenaline crashing through him, which in turn brought strength and focus. He lifted Matthew onto his shoulders again and limped onward. The most difficult part of the journey was still ahead of him: climbing the mountain. He'd done it several times with a child in his arms, but this time, the *final* time—injured, exhausted, carrying not a child but an adult—would be the most demanding of all.

———

He staggered, then rested. He climbed, cursed, and bled. His right sneaker was soaked with blood. The skin on his shoulders chafed and frayed. One blessing was that the sun dropped westward and the air cooled, but everything else was stacked against him. Not just stacked but *pushing*—trying to make him fail. Even the mountain seemed to mock him: *You can't do it, Oliver. You have never been able to do it.* It boomed laughter and trembled beneath his feet. *All these years and still trying. Still failing.* He cried out and pressed on. One quivering step at a time. When it got too dark to see, he set Matthew down and grabbed a flashlight from the knapsack. A ten-minute rest, holding his head and weeping. *I'm so close,* he thought, trying to muster strength. *So close now.* He stooped to pick up Matthew. The flashlight passed over his bloodied face. His eyes were open.

Oliver staggered back, surprised, then grabbed the pistol from the knapsack and pointed it at him.

"Gzzzz," Matthew said. Something like that. Not a word. His eyes squinted in the flashlight's glare. He touched the bridge of his nose, perhaps feeling for his glasses.

"Can you walk?" Oliver asked.

"Gzzzz."

"Try to get up. Slowly."

Matthew lowered his hand. That was all.

"I said—"

"No," Matthew said, shaking his head to emphasize.

Oliver pressed the muzzle against Matthew's forehead, printing a white circle in the glaze of red.

Matthew said something unintelligible. His eyes rolled up, as if looking at the gun, then his mouth dropped open and he was gone again.

Oliver lifted him onto his shoulders and carried on.

———

He saw Leander Bird in the flashlight's beam, flickering on the mountainside. His eyes were tiny suns. His arms were like a crow's wings. Oliver drew a stuttering breath. The flashlight trembled. Leander laughed and disappeared, only to reappear moments later, poised on a boulder. His darkness meshed with the night and his fishhook mouth hung open, spewing black flames.

Are you real? Oliver asked.

I've always been real. Always been here.

I think you're a hallucination.

Leander reached for him. *I touch you.*

A chill wind stirred, moaning between the rocks and fissures. Leander vanished again. *Hallucinating,* Oliver thought. *Exhausted. Seeing things.* Everything thumped and ached but he limped on. The flashlight illuminated the mountain's upward path. Leander Bird came and went. Sometimes near. Sometimes far. Always burning.

———

Oliver collapsed a short time later. Matthew toppled from his shoulders and fell hard. He groaned, but didn't wake. More blood leaked from the gash in his head and half-painted a rock. Oliver curled up beside him and dragged in breaths that made his chest hurt. He didn't know how close he was to the cave—to the *end*—and was too tired to think about it. It was dark and he was disoriented. He needed rest.

The night sky was beautiful. Perfect starlight everywhere. Oliver bled beside Matthew, feeling the slight movement of his body. He flicked off the flashlight and drifted. Leander Bird's orange eyes blazed from atop a nearby boulder. His flaming body crackled.

You're so close, he said. His voice was as calm as the starlight, yet the mountain raged. Oliver wished it would split open and swallow him whole.

Give me a moment. I need to rest.

But you're nearly there.

Oliver closed his eyes and may have slept for a while but when he looked at the sky the starlight was the same. Leander Bird was nowhere to be seen or heard. Oliver got to his knees, flicked on the flashlight, and directed the beam along the mountain's crippled path. *You're so close,* Leander had said to him, but Oliver wasn't sure he could manage even a single step, and certainly not with Matthew slung across his shoulders. He considered the .45. Maybe he could shoot Matthew here and leave him to rot on the mountainside. Maybe that would suffice.

Orange eyes flared in the darkness. Oliver smelled smoke, and felt evil. An ash cloud of anger.

No. The mountain wanted him. *Inside.* It wanted to drink freshly spilled blood and add his skeleton to the collection. It wanted to feel him die.

Bring him to me, Leander said.

Oliver did.

———

He couldn't carry Matthew, though, so dragged him, the crooks of his elbows tucked beneath Matthew's armpits, hands linked across his chest. Slowly—*slowly*—up the mountain, moving backward, in the dark, without a free hand to hold the flashlight. He rested every twenty feet or so, dripping with sweat, ignoring the sharp pain in his lower back and the roaring in his head. He used the flashlight to illuminate the route ahead, then flicked it off, tucked it into his belt, grabbed hold of Matthew, and moved on, feeling his way around the rocks and dead trees. One inch at a time. Getting closer.

Closer, the hallucination echoed.

Until at last he was there. The opening, camouflaged with rocks, gleamed in the flashlight. A doorway to relief—to peace. Oliver shouted at the starlight, triumphantly, even though his work was far from complete. Infused with a sense of finality, he brushed aside the smaller rocks with ease, but struggled with the heavier ones and was forced to rest. He shone the flashlight on Matthew, who whimpered, his eyes fluttering but not opening.

The ghost flickered, moth-like, urging him on.

He worked, his hands ravaged and bleeding, his body screaming, removing the larger rocks one by one until the opening gaped, crooked, like Leander Bird's smile. Another triumphant scream at the stars. Another long rest, licking his wounds like a dog.

Matthew woke. He blinked in the flashlight, confused. His left hand trembled—all the movement he could manage, but enough to spur Oliver on. He dragged Matthew through the opening and into the cave, where children wept and silence waited.

CHAPTER
FIFTEEN

Here: a handful of
darkness, pulled from
between stars. Stained air,
broken sound, and dust as thick
as skin.

Now: the moment he falls.

"I brought him to you," he heard
Oliver say. His voice was as brittle as
the bones that littered the floor. "Now leave
me alone."

Matthew crawled, spitting dust, blinking cloud-coloured
tears. He knew where he was, despite the concussion, and even
before the flashlight shone upon small skulls and bones wrapped
in rags. Unconscious, he had sailed a blue sea. An infinite ocean.
There had been no pain, no fear. It was just him. Even now, crawling
through this nightmare, it was still just him. The world had closed
its eyes. He was helpless, and alone.

I escaped before, he thought. His hands scraped through bones
and splashed in shallow pools. *Maybe I can . . .* But he was too weak
to finish the thought. Blood ran into his eye. He faded. Came back.

"Please let this be the end."

Faded.

Now: the moment he dies.

The flashlight illuminated speleothems formed like protective hands. Matthew opened his eyes—came back—and saw, cupped within them, two children. A ghost-faced girl with red hair, who Matthew, even amid the hurt and confusion, recognized immediately, and, in her arms, a boy, barely moving.

The girl held out her hand.

No, he wasn't alone.

His wounded heart reached for the children.

Now: the moment he fights.

———

Courtney cradled the boy, listened to his rasping breaths, and wondered when they would stop. She had soaked her T-shirt in a pool and squeezed drops onto his dry lips, praying some small amount would go down his throat. His eyes flickered. He spoke her name every now and then, and asked if she was his friend. Courtney said yes of course and stroked his face. She felt the hollows of his cheeks, the tiny veins thumping in his eyelids.

She decided to show strength for as long as the boy (Ethan—his name was Ethan, but it kept slipping her mind, along with so many other things) was alive. Hope was nonexistent in this terrible place, but she wouldn't let him see that. Her touch was always caring, her words always soothing. Courage was an act that trembled and threatened to separate. She held the fragments together. As soon as Ethan died, she could stop pretending.

She had learned the cave's formation within the first few days. She knew where the freshest water was, and where she could climb to feel daylight on her face, even if it was out of reach. She knew the way out, also—had found the twisting tunnel and pushed fruitlessly against the heavy boulders that blocked the way. When Ethan had been stronger, they had pushed together. Courtney had even lifted him onto her shoulders so he could reach the smaller rocks higher up. But they were lodged in place and wouldn't move at all.

She knew the places where she could pray, and cry, crouched in alcoves, among bones, where Ethan couldn't hear her.

"We'll get out of here," she told him, so often, and he would smile and nod. She would hold him and touch his face, using her closeness to apologize for making promises she could never keep.

But now hope glimmered. It breathed. The man—the monster—who had brought them here had returned, and had brought a grownup with him. Courtney could see that he was hurt and bleeding, but she held her hand out anyway.

He looked at her. His eyes were wide and frightened.

Please, she said, speaking with her hand, fingers extended.

An imperceptible nod, and Courtney wept, clutched Ethan closer, dared to hope.

Everything hurt. His foot, his back, his eyes, his soul. Oliver would be a long time convalescing after this was over.

And still the mountain boomed.

"I brought him to you," he said. "Now leave me alone."

But *bringing* Matthew was not enough. Had he expected Leander Bird to swoop from the darkness and burn him where he lay? A brief and beautiful swirl of flame, and then . . . peace? He had hoped, certainly, but knew better.

The mountain had told him to bring the knife for a reason.

Just like 1984, Oliver thought, watching Matthew crawl through the bones. He removed the knapsack (his T-shirt was stiff with blood, plastered to his shoulders where the straps had been), and took out the knife. This would be . . . *different.* Oliver felt it in his soul, a stark and sickening pressure, like clamped nerve endings. He had brought eight children here to die. He was also responsible for Bobby Alexander's death. No use trying to candy-coat it, he'd done bad things for the mountain (although Bobby, the big chump, only had himself to blame). But he had never killed anybody. Not directly. Holding the knife and limping toward Matthew, that was about to change.

Do it quickly. Don't even think about it.

Oliver's fingers tightened around the handle. The flashlight trembled, its light covering Matthew as he crawled and cried, too big among such small skeletons.

"Please let this be the end," Oliver said, moving closer.

———

The girl tried to cry out but managed only a rush of broken air. Matthew—even without his glasses—saw the alarm in her eyes. He flipped onto his back and saw Oliver stumbling toward him, flashlight in one hand, knife in the other. The similarity to 1984 was absolute. He even remembered what had broken his paralysis and helped him escape: his mother's face, shimmering in his mind, a vision of love and safety. He thought of her now, twenty-six years older, still beautiful. Again, it gave him a burst of strength and he pushed himself to one knee.

"Mountain . . . always . . ." Oliver limped closer. His lame foot was tangled in an item of clothing and he tugged it along, spilling bones. "Always . . ."

Matthew was dazed. He had lost blood and his body felt like something that could be carried on the wind. But Oliver was weak, too. The knife trembled in his hand and his breathing was laboured. Matthew thought that if he attacked first, and surprised Oliver, he might gain the upper hand. It was his only hope—the *children's* only hope.

He steadied himself, still on one knee, waiting for Oliver to get closer. Dull pain in his head, in his heart.

Two shambling steps from Oliver. The knife flashed, too big.

"Always gets what it wants."

Matthew held his breath. He remembered the little girl's hand reaching . . . reaching.

Another step. Oliver's left foot came down on a small skull and cracked it into three pieces. His ankle rolled. He wobbled, momentarily off balance.

Matthew attacked.

———

Oliver saw Matthew spring toward him and tried to react but couldn't. Matthew came low and hard, his face a red blur in the flashlight. Oliver had time to raise the knife, meaning to plunge it between Matthew's shoulder blades, but was driven backward. He hit the floor with a crunch that sucked the air from his lungs. Matthew fell on top of him and the flashlight leapt from his hand. It spun in the darkness, throwing its glow, settling on two skeletons that had crumbled into one, their skulls conjoined by a patina of calcite.

Oliver still had the knife in his hand. He raised it, his arm trembling as Matthew's hands closed around his throat.

———

Matthew felt Oliver's body fold in half and crumple. Adrenaline rippled through him, bringing a flicker of hope, but he knew that any advantage was thin and wouldn't last. He reached for Oliver's throat and squeezed, his shoulders hunched, using his body weight. Blood dripped from his head and he imagined it splashing into Oliver's face. Maybe into his wide eyes or open mouth. One of many wild images to burn through his brain during that desperate moment. He considered the darkness, too. The darkness in his soul, which had infected him and stained his dreams. He channelled it now, replaying every terrible fantasy. It was surprisingly—ironically—bright, this darkness, and seductive.

He *squeezed*, feeling the tips of his thumbs sink into Oliver's throat, finding his windpipe and crushing it.

Oliver gasped . . . flailed. He still had energy and, judging from the way he struggled, disconcerting strength. He knocked Matthew off balance and struck with the knife—a clumsy attack, but Matthew felt the blade slice across his upper arm. He let go of Oliver's throat and rolled to one side. Confusion in the darkness. Blood and ragged breaths. Matthew scraped through bones and pushed himself to his feet. The flashlight was less than ten feet away and he wanted it. Light, in this dank and dreadful place, was too great an advantage.

Matthew heard the whoosh of the blade, too close to his throat. He stumbled backward and hit the floor with a thud, then flipped onto his hands and knees and lunged for the flashlight. His fingertips brushed over the barrel . . . about to close around it when Oliver surged forward and stumbled over him. They crashed into a cluster of skeletons that came apart like dry straw.

"It *wants* you," Oliver said. His breath smelled of dust and heat. "There's no getting away."

Matthew screamed and reached again for the flashlight, but it was too far away. Oliver pinned him to the floor, readying the knife to swipe downward, using his left hand to feel Matthew's body in the darkness, to pinpoint his heart.

––––––––

An idea flashed in Courtney's mind: the heavy rocks sealing the cave's opening would have been removed—had to have been for the men to get in here. She could run for it now, escape, and find help for Ethan. Her heart jumped with the possibility and she started to slide Ethan from her arms, but then stopped. Was it really the best idea? What if the bad man hurt Ethan—killed him—while she was gone? What if he came after her? She was weak and wouldn't be able to run very fast. He'd catch her easily. He had a flashlight. And a knife.

The flashlight. She could see it, spilling a puddle of light on the cave floor. She knew where the men were by the sound of their fighting, and was sure she could skirt around them and get to the flashlight quickly. Another idea formed, threaded with hope: turn off the flashlight so that the bad man couldn't see her, then move through the darkness she knew so well, to the opening, and then away. Once she had gone far enough, she could flick the light back on. The bad man, stumbling through the darkness, wouldn't be able to follow her.

Courtney's heart jumped again, and with an urgency that caused a wistful sound to escape her. She nodded, still not sure it was the right thing to do, but knowing it was more dangerous—more *hopeless*—to sit and pray for the other man to come to their rescue.

She remembered his face, covered in blood. His hurting eyes.

She had to do something.

Courtney detached herself from the boy and eased him to the ground. He curled into a ball, his lips making small sounds. She leaned close to him.

"We'll get out of here," she whispered, as she had so many times, still not knowing if they ever would.

She touched his face, made her move.

Matthew reached up and clasped Oliver's wrist, using what little strength he had to keep him from pushing downward. But Oliver had every advantage. He was stronger, heavier, crazier. Matthew cried into the darkness. *The mountain always gets what it wants,* he thought, and felt the point of the knife against his chest—felt his skin break and bleed.

The cave's geography formed in Courtney's mind and she stepped quickly. The flashlight shimmered, so close, but the men were close, too. She heard one of them cry out and the other laugh wildly. Both sounds were shocking, and she came close to losing her nerve and scuttling back to Ethan. Instead, she ghosted silently around them and retrieved the flashlight. It jigged and danced as soon as it was in her trembling hands and she felt along the barrel for the switch, aware that her position—and maybe her intention—was now evident. As if to emphasize this, the cave echoed with another cry. Courtney screamed and whipped the light in the direction of the sound. The bad man had the knife in his hands and was pressing it to the other man's chest. The glare caused him to flinch and turn away. He took one hand from the knife and held it in front of his face.

"*Me!*" the other man screamed, holding out his hand. "*Give it to me!*"

Courtney wanted to run but looked at the man's outstretched hand. She remembered the way she had reached for him in the darkness, and the fractional nod that told her he would help if he could.

She returned that gesture now. She gave him the light.

————

Matthew felt the pressure of the knife point decrease as the light hit them. Oliver had removed one hand to deflect the glare and his body weight shifted. Matthew, through squinted eyes, saw a corona of red hair. *The girl,* he thought. He reached out his hand and screamed at her to give him the flashlight. Not because he wanted its reassuring glow, but because he wanted something solid in his grasp. Something he could use to break Oliver's jaw.

As soon as the barrel slapped into his palm he brought his arm upward, twisting his shoulder, smashing the fat part of the flashlight against Oliver's face. His head rocked to the side. The light stuttered. Blood sprayed from his mouth and he raised both hands, drawing the knife away from Matthew's chest. Giving him no time to recover, Matthew lashed out again. The second blow was harder, more accurate, catching the hinge of Oliver's jaw. A resounding crack. More blood. Oliver groaned and rolled off Matthew. The knife spilled from his hand.

Matthew sat up. His eyes spiralled and the cave dipped, as if it were being lifted at one end by a giant hand, tilted forward. Oliver held his face and groaned. Matthew pushed himself to his knees but overbalanced, spilling across a small skeleton that cracked and separated. He dropped the flashlight and the beam rolled away from him, illuminating, for a moment, the girl's terrified face. He snatched it up again quickly, whirled, saw Oliver trying to get to his feet. Matthew gasped and looked for the knife but couldn't see it. Buried in dust, perhaps, or fallen into one of the many cracks in the cave floor.

Oliver rose unsteadily. He staggered toward Matthew.

"*Maah-fuggah,*" he mumbled. "*Goddamn maah-fuggah.*"

No knife, but there—not ten feet away—was a good-sized rock, hefty and jagged. Matthew imagined doing devastating, skull-crushing damage with it. The darkness inside him shifted heavily. He almost grinned.

"Goan fuggin keeeeel ooooh."

Matthew blinked blood from his eye and crawled toward the rock. His chest rattled. His arms shook. He collapsed, pushed himself up, clawed through the pain. Oliver screamed and spat out three teeth. His jaw hung at a broken angle and blood rolled over his lower lip. Matthew swept skulls and bones in his direction, knocking up a fan of white dust, and then threw himself forward, landing an arm's length from the rock. He reached for it. The light flickered.

"Maah-fuggin gogg-zuggah!"

Matthew's hand folded over the rock and he dragged it toward him. He heard the little girl cry out behind him—*"He's coming!"*—and pushed himself to one knee. He shone the light on Oliver, who reeled closer, wild-eyed and bleeding.

"Mowdun . . . orrway gedz . . . wooorrn."

Matthew teetered to his feet and faced him.

"Maah-fuggah."

"You ruined my life," Matthew said softly, almost disbelievingly. Oliver stumbled forward with another insane howl, and Matthew met him with the rock. It wasn't a hard blow—Matthew lacked the strength for that—but it didn't need to be. The rock carried its own velocity. It thumped like a hammer off the top of Oliver's head. Blood flowed from his hairline as if poured from a jug. A triangular flap of skin drooped across his forehead, revealing the wet bone beneath. Matthew stepped forward and delivered a second blow, then a third. He heard Oliver's skull crack—*felt* it crunch inward. Oliver slumped like a boxer one punch from hitting the canvas. He looked at Matthew, his eyes golden in the flashlight. Two more uncertain steps. More blood bubbled from his lips and a ghastly smile crossed his face, then he slumped to the floor and was still.

CHAPTER
SIXTEEN

The little girl threw herself around him so fiercely that he stumbled and almost fell. Her arms were thin, her hair matted and dry, and when she pressed her face against his chest and started to cry, he felt the points of her cheekbones, the ridge of her jaw. Matthew dropped the bloodied rock and held her. He stroked her hair and whispered her name and told her that everything was going to be okay. Her tears soaked into his shirt, and amid the spiralling darkness in his mind—the shock, the pain and mental fatigue— he tried to calculate how long she had been trapped here. Couldn't do it. Too much hurt running at him. The fact that she had been trapped here at all was terrible enough. One day would be too long. One second. Yet here she was, having survived, strong enough to hold him, and to cry. Matthew stooped and clasped her hand, his fingers folding evenly around it, so small and delicate, like some newborn thing. He held her like this not to give her reassurance, but to absorb her strength.

She led him to water and he drank, almost comically, like a dog in a river. The water was cold and invigorating. He removed his tie, balled it into a cloth pad, and used it to wipe the blood from his face and throat. Courtney shone the flashlight on the wound on his upper arm. It was deep, would almost certainly need sutures, but had started to coagulate, reducing blood flow to a few thin trickles. His sleeve was ruined, stained red. He tore it away, dipped it in the cold water, and used it for a bandage. Courtney helped tie it.

"We can go now?" she said.

"We can go now."

She shone the light on the cluster of stalagmites where Ethan lay, knees drawn to his chest, dust in his hair. Shadows fell across him in thick straps. They appeared to hold him down. His skin was so pale it was almost translucent. A small bundle of bones, barely breathing.

"His name is Ethan."

Matthew crouched and scooped the boy into his arms. So light, like a bird, something he could cradle forever without tiring. Ethan groaned. His eyes rolled behind his eyelids. His legs looped over the crook of Matthew's elbow, his head against Matthew's chest. Courtney led the way with the flashlight. She shuddered, seeing for the first time what she had hitherto only felt during her exploration. She stepped around drifts of bones, over fissures and between columns, moving wearily, and Matthew followed.

The tunnel, twisting a route to the surface, filled with light, its sick-coloured walls glistening, broad in places, narrow in others. Courtney and Matthew moved slowly but steadily, their breaths echoing off the rippled surfaces, their shadows ungainly. Matthew kept looking over his shoulder, remembering how Oliver had chased him along this tunnel all those years ago. Even though he'd felt Oliver's skull splinter inward, and had watched him fold lifelessly to the ground, he still expected to see him shambling along in pursuit—to *hear* him first. *Maah-fuggah . . . maah-fuggin gogg-zuggah.* And Matthew would whirl around to see Oliver close behind, bleeding from everywhere.

"Can you go quicker?" he said to Courtney.

She said she'd try, and she did, but fell twice on the slick floor, and the second time the flashlight flickered and Matthew thought for one long, terrible second that it would snap out and leave them in darkness. But it stayed on, hesitantly at first, and then more surely. Courtney wept and the tears flashed down her dusty face. Matthew bent at the knees, cradling Ethan in one arm so that he could help her up.

"It's okay," he said. "Go at your own pace." He looked over his shoulder again, thinking for one moment that he'd heard something shuffling through the darkness behind them. "We're okay now. Everything is going to be fine."

They moved on, Matthew stealing glances over his shoulder, where the light ended quickly and the darkness stretched forever. *Deeper than you can believe,* Matthew thought, knowing that it was still a part of him.

They came, eventually, to the opening. Courtney cried again when the flashlight showed that most of the rocks had been removed and they would be able to get out. She lowered her head, red hair spilling in tangles. Matthew saw the knobs of her spine, the severe curve of her ribcage, pressing through her wet T-shirt.

"Can you climb up?" he asked her.

"I don't know."

"I'll help you."

Courtney nodded and pushed the barrel of the flashlight into the front of her jeans so that the light shone upward, and suddenly the stars could be seen through the opening like broken glass on a patch of asphalt. They were so clear and real that their silence was a dubious thing, as if it were more likely they should be singing. Courtney wiped her eyes and started to climb, using the gaps between the rocks as rungs, as Matthew had all those years ago. Her weak arms strained, muscles like thin rope. Matthew set Ethan down, easing his head to the hard floor, and helped her. She stepped into his palms, like stirrups, and he hoisted her. A brief, brilliant pain flared in his body, ascending to his brain, where it jellyfished, trailing stingers. He saw Courtney's shape blot out the stars and thought, *good that's good,* and then everything faded, for just a moment, and when it came back Courtney was shining the flashlight through the opening. Ethan lay still, so thin and pale he appeared perfectly formed, like an ultrasound image.

"Let's go," Courtney said.

Matthew glanced over his shoulder again. No sign of Oliver, although the idea of him lurching through the darkness would not leave his mind. He drew a deep breath, picked up Ethan, and passed him carefully through the opening. Courtney helped, curling her arms beneath him. She lowered him to the ground, crouched, one hand cradling his head. The other still held the flashlight. She shone it on the opening as Matthew climbed out. Fresh blood dripped from his head and splashed on the rocks. *That's as much of me as you're getting,* he thought, smearing drips from his forehead, wiping it on his shirt. Then he was out, standing in the clear and empty night. The stars arced above him. Point Hollow glimmered distantly. Matthew wavered and his shoulders hitched but no tears came from his eyes. Courtney looked away. Her hair was brighter than the stars.

"Can we go?" she said after a moment.

Matthew wiped his eyes as if there had been tears. He nodded and told Courtney that they could go, but first he had to close the opening. "Bury everything," he said. He started to lift the rocks one by one, placing them across the opening, staggering them for structure. He couldn't lift the heavier rocks, so used the ones he could. At some point Ethan started to cough—a wheezy, dry sound, as if his throat had rusted and was full of holes that flaked and grew larger with every breath. His chest jumped like a muscle flexing. Courtney groaned and stroked his face and took off her T-shirt and wrung drops of water from it. They splashed against his lips, dripped into the dry purse of his mouth. She did it again and again, using different parts of the T-shirt, until he stopped coughing. He made a murmuring sound. His chest rattled.

Matthew selected a final rock—the largest he could manage in his weakened state—and dropped it into place. He stepped back, closed his eyes, and whispered a fragile prayer. Courtney tugged his pant leg. He touched her hand, then looked at the opening. It was not completely covered, but would have to do.

Blood trickled into his eye. He wiped it away, looked at the stars.

Courtney tugged at him again.

"We're going." Matthew said.

"Which way?" she asked.

Matthew pointed toward Point Hollow's lights. Courtney nodded and started to walk, wiping her eyes with one hand, finding a path with the flashlight. Matthew lifted Ethan into his arms and held him close. He felt the boy's heartbeat shaking through his small frame. The strongest thing about him. A cannon made of glass.

CHAPTER
SEVENTEEN

As it had for insufferable years, the mountain woke him.

One eye crept open, bleary with blood and tears. He blinked it clear, then rolled onto his side. The mountain roared, and with such ferocity that Oliver thought he should be rattled from wall to wall, tossed around with the bones. He dragged himself to his knees. The gap in his skull creaked and dripped fluids. His buckled jaw swung loose.

He let the mountain colour his mind. Furious reds and purples. One rumble led inexorably into the next. In its indelicate phrases and modulation he discerned his failure. Could he continue to live with this violence inside him? And even if he could, what life would he have? Prison and torment? Insanity and rage?

There's still time, a voice said. It spoke from *within*, but from within his mind, or the mountain, he couldn't be sure. *Matthew's weak. You can catch him.*

"Just leave me alone."

Get up.

"I'm dying. It's over."

Get UP!

And he did, crying out, struggling to his feet. He cringed when the voice spoke again, because it sounded so close, and with it came a burst of heat that managed to burn and chill at the same time.

I say when it's over.

Oliver turned and saw him. Dark on dark, wreathed in flames. Leander Bird's orange eyes blazed and the mountain trembled with his anger.

Are you really so weak?

"You're not even real."

Are you really so useless?

Oliver lifted the gory flap of skin from his forehead and pressed it back into place, feeling the depression in the bone beneath, like the fontanel in an infant's skull. He howled and shuffled away from Bird.

"It's over."

There's still time.

"Fuck yourself." He stumbled, dropped to one knee—

Get up!

—and got back up. And that was it: his innate doggedness, his refusal to stay down. It flickered inside him like the ghost in the mountain. *Are you really so weak?* the voice had asked, knowing that weakness was not an option. *Are you really so useless?* Knowing that Oliver had no grasp of failure. He was like the mountain in so many ways. Grey and unbreakable, and with a dark fire burning deep inside. It moved him—kept him running when others would fall. This was the reason he had been chosen.

Leander Bird stomped and smoked, his black arms reaching. Oliver's spirit strengthened with every remorseless boom. He stood upright, shoulders square, shaking pain like tired leaves from a branch. He closed his eyes and found his superhuman core. That rare and brilliant thing. His own flame.

"I am alive."

You are perfect.

"I am unstoppable."

The perfect flame.

Oliver roared and flickered. He went inside, called upon elemental energy, feeling the earth roll through his body, the fire in his veins. He held out his arms and embraced his animal- and bird-self. Their strength and instinct first healed, and then lifted him. He was a survivor in the wild. A bear. An eagle.

Now hunt them down.

Oliver snarled. He tore off his T-shirt, not feeling the skin on his shoulders peel away. He discarded the blood-soaked rags, unbuckled his belt, took off his jeans and underwear. His eyes opened to the sight of Leander Bird floating above him like strange, aquatic life, something darker than the ocean, but alight inside. A swirling, poisonous anemone.

Hunt them. Stop them.

Boom and shudder. An earthquake. A hydrogen bomb.

He felt no pain. His skin glowed and his heart drummed furiously. His penis was engorged, iron-hard, twice—three times—its usual size. It swayed impressively as he stalked forward. Fluid dribbled from the tip in a long, silver line.

He'd worked too hard, and for too many years, to fail now. He'd earned his peace, dammit. Oliver dropped to all fours and sniffed the cave floor. His heightened sense of smell detected clusters of bones and stagnant pools. He padded forward, sniffing among the skulls and ribcages, until he found what he was looking for: his knapsack. Oliver pulled it open and reached inside. His hand closed around the .45's grip. Standing again, he curled his finger around the trigger and fired twice into the air. In the brief bursts of light he saw the cave's dark throat, the only way out. He lowered the gun and moved toward it.

————————

Adrenaline barrelled through his body, producing prolonged hysterical strength that he believed, in his delicate mind, to be bestial force. He crawled through the tunnel, sometimes on all fours, with his erect penis bouncing and the .45 knocking on the cold rock floor. He saw only a window of purple light when he came to the exit. The human aspect of his mind registered that Matthew had attempted to cover the opening, but had used the smaller rocks and boulders and placed them inexactly. Oliver had little trouble dislodging them. They toppled with a satisfying sound. He licked his bruised knuckles and sprang onto the topmost boulder, into the opening, like a cat onto a window ledge.

At the foot of the mountain, less than a mile away, a flashlight blinked in the darkness, moving slowly, like a tired lightning bug, winking as it passed between the trees.

Oliver growled and followed.

The eastern sky was faded rose and a brushed, pale blue. An hour until full light. Oliver's eyes adjusted to the gloom. He saw the silhouettes of trees and rocks, asymmetric images printed on grey paper, which he moved among carefully, knowing he'd be quicker if he could see better. He grinned and drew on human memory, veered from the rudimentary path, and picked his way toward a monstrous, tangled shape: the deadfall where he stashed the flashlight, wrapped in a Ziploc bag and sackcloth. Oliver scratched among the dirt, found the light and flicked it on. Darkness separated. He scrambled back to the path and looked west.

Nothing. A breathless stretch of black between the foot of the mountain and Point Hollow's pretty lights. No sign of Matthew's flashlight bobbing hesitantly between the trees. Had he feared it would be seen and turned it off? Had he made it back to Point Hollow already?

Oliver's heart throbbed at the thought. Pain zigzagged from his damaged skull. He staggered, slipping from the radical centre and into his human circle. Behind, beneath, within him, the mountain roared. Oliver chased along the crooked path as fast as he was able, fighting to hold on to the place where the circles intersected.

"Please . . . *please* . . ." Hurting, human sounds. And then he screamed. A violent cry that didn't sound human at all. Frightened birds took flight, scattered against the mauve sky, but Oliver barely noticed them. His attention was drawn to a flicker of light between the trees. Matthew's flashlight. He'd obviously been startled by the scream, too.

Less than half a mile away.

Oliver was getting closer.

He grinned and eased back into the radical centre, where pain didn't exist.

———————

The gun. He clutched its grip—could almost smell the oil coating its tiny pins and springs. The mag held seven rounds, and he'd used five. Two remaining. Perfect. He'd shoot Matthew when they were back inside the mountain. In the stomach. Not as significant as the knife, but he would die slowly and the mountain would be satisfied. Oliver needed the other bullet to persuade Matthew to walk that twisted path one final time. If he refused, Oliver would shoot the little boy—or the girl, it really didn't matter—in the face. He would only refuse once.

Oliver grinned. He reached the foot of the mountain and veered southwest, moving as quickly as he was able toward his prey.

Chapter
Eighteen

"I've got you," Matthew said to the boy in his arms. "You're safe now."

But moments later Ethan started to tremble and wheeze. *I'm going to feel him die*, Matthew thought. A shocking possibility.

"Courtney," he said. "Your T-shirt."

"It's too dry," she said.

"Then we need to find water."

They were heading west, toward Point Hollow (they could just see the pink sky through the trees and used it to guide them, keeping their backs to it), but now Courtney ducked north, following her ears, and brought them to a coruscating brook.

"Good girl," he said. He lay Ethan down on the soft pine needles and indicated the water. "Have a drink, then rest. There's still a ways to go."

She nodded and took a drink. Matthew washed dry blood from his hands, scooped water into them, and formed a spout from which Ethan sipped—barely wetting his lips to begin with, but then his dull eyes crept open and he drew on the water with a weakly pulsing mouth. His throat clicked as it worked and before long the wheeze was gone from his chest.

"Am I going home?" he asked, only moments later.

"Yes." Matthew smiled and lifted the boy into his arms.

That was when they heard the scream. Terrible and piercing and much too close.

"What was that?" Courtney's eyes were wide and pale.

Matthew reeled toward the mountain. *Not possible,* he thought, recalling how Oliver's skull had cracked open, and how he'd folded to the ground like a wet sheet.

"Was it him?" Courtney jerked the flashlight every which way, even up, as if he would descend from above. A terrible bird.

Matthew shook his head. It *couldn't* be him. Yet he saw—between the silhouettes of trees and boulders—a narrow cone of light. Coming their way.

"Go," he said. "Don't stop."

"You said he was dead."

"Just *go.*"

Courtney shone the flashlight west and they moved on, but all too slowly—a limp, shambling pace that reminded Matthew of trying to run in a dream. His legs threatened to buckle every third or fourth step and the boy trembled in his arms. Courtney kept looking over her shoulder, her eyes magnified by tears.

"Keep going, honey."

"Is he coming?"

"Just keep going."

They pushed through branches and ferns, veered around boulders and between the trees. Matthew looked behind him again and saw the light almost immediately. A trembling, poisonous eye floating in the darkness. Closer now.

"A little faster, Courtney. Come on, sweetheart."

"I'm going as fast as I can."

They rounded a cluster of moss-covered rocks, then stuttered down a gradient bedded with roots and creepers. Slow going, having to choose their steps carefully, but they made it to the bottom without falling, then waded through a snarl of foliage that scratched their bare arms. The ground levelled, and then ascended, a long incline that Courtney scrambled up on her hands and knees.

"Faster, Courtney."

"I *can't*."

Matthew took the flashlight so she could use both hands. She grabbed thick roots and used them to hoist herself up. Her small back heaved and her hair hung in dirty red coils. She cried, slipped, pulled herself up again. Matthew cradled Ethan and teetered behind Courtney. The torn sleeve he had used as a bandage had come unravelled, hanging loose. A damp red streamer.

"You can do it." The flashlight trembled in his hand.

She mumbled something. Her small hands clawed and grabbed.

"Not far, Courtney. Almost there."

"Almost . . ."

"Yes."

The little girl nodded and dragged herself up the last few feet of the incline. She tried to stand but fell—crawled on her hands and knees for a moment, and then collapsed on her stomach. Matthew scrambled up behind her. He had hoped to see the lights of Point Hollow twinkling ahead, but saw only a dismaying sprawl of dark forest. He turned around, and there—flickering in the darkness less than a hundred yards away—the glaring eye of Oliver's flashlight.

"Courtney," Matthew gasped. "You need to get up."

She pushed herself to her knees . . . crawled . . . fell again.

"Please, sweetheart."

"Can't."

"You have to."

Matthew watched as Oliver turned the flashlight on himself. A ghost, naked and shimmering. He threw back his head and howled.

He had the .45 in his hand.

"Was that a wolf?" Courtney whimpered.

"No," Matthew uttered, thinking, *Worse than a wolf.*

"Was it him?" She pushed herself to one knee. "The bad man?"

"Yes."

"He sounds close."

"He is close."

Courtney nodded. She struggled to her feet and wiped her eyes. Matthew handed her the flashlight and she shone it into the woods ahead. Feet dragging, she carried on, shoulders hunched as the bad man howled again.

———

This was his heartland. All his life he had bathed in its cold waters and flown above the treetops. Little wonder he caught up to Matthew and the children so quickly, even with a fractured skull. As they shuffled around boulders and fallen trees, Oliver strode through clearings, crossed shallow streams, slithered through pockets of ferns and weeds. No hesitation. No pause to regain his line and make sure he was moving in the right direction. The land was his body and he swept through it as effortlessly as drawing breath.

Or so he believed. In his mind he was the radical centre—a between-creature drawing on primal energy and the secrets of the earth. In reality he was a shattered mortal infused with the endorphins of lunacy, not running like a wolf, but lurching . . . dying.

And—much like an injured animal—at his most dangerous.

He could see them. The cone of their flashlight, the little girl sprawled on the ground. Close enough that he could spread his wings and draw them in. Abraham's Faith made angry music and the ghost in his head danced. Oliver howled. A haunted wail that made the darkness tremble. For one beautiful moment he knew how it felt to be the mountain.

He scented the crisp morning air and howled again.

———

They needed to change their strategy.

Following Courtney, watching her dirty Crocs trudge across the forest floor, Matthew knew two things for certain. The first was that the flashlight—useful though it was—gave away their position. The second was that, even if they *could* outpace Oliver, they had no hope of outpacing a loaded .45.

He turned around and saw Oliver crawling down the gradient (disturbingly, on all fours, like an animal), edging from view. This meant that Oliver, for however long he was down there, couldn't see *them*.

"Courtney," he whispered. "Give me the flashlight."

She kept walking.

"Courtney?"

"What?"

"The flashlight."

She stopped and looked at him. Nothing in her face but pain and fear.

"Do you trust me?" he asked.

"I don't know."

"We have to find a place to hide."

"Like hide and seek?"

"Yes."

She dragged her eyes left and right, following the flashlight's beam. "Hide where?"

"Anywhere."

"I'll find a place," she said.

They veered south, cutting through a crop of spruce and around a pond with rags of mist drifting over it, caught in the light like lame swans. Matthew kept looking behind, trying to gauge how long it would take Oliver to clamber up the incline. They needed to be in their hiding place, with the flashlight switched off, before then.

"How about there?" Courtney asked, pointing at an old pine tree that had collapsed against a boulder, forming a natural lean-to. The trunk had sagged and there wasn't much room between it and the ground, but its dead branches covered the nook like a curtain. Matthew thought it might be too obvious a hiding place, but they were running out of time and he couldn't be sure they'd find anywhere better.

"It'll have to do," he said. "Quickly."

They lumbered toward it, gasping and dizzy with hurt. Courtney reached the pine first. She dropped to her knees, pushed aside the branches, and crawled into the space beneath. Matthew eased Ethan into the gap, then clambered in beside him. The branches drooped back into place and he pulled the children close.

"The flashlight," he said to Courtney. She flicked it off. The darkness was complete and terrible. They couldn't even see the dawn.

"How long do we have to stay here?" Courtney asked.

"Until the bad man has gone."

"He's like a monster."

"Yes, he is."

"I hope he dies."

"I hope so, too."

Matthew made a part in the branches with his fingertips and peered out, back the way they had come, his eyes slowly adjusting, seeing the shapes of trees. And there . . .

"Courtney?" he whispered.

"Yes?"

"You need to be really quiet now, okay?"

"Shhhhh . . . super quiet."

A flicker between the trees. Maybe fifty yards away. Darkness. Another flicker. And then a bold shaft of light and the partial silhouette of a man poised on all fours. Matthew lowered the branches and felt Courtney's thin body curl closer still.

"He's out there."

No sign of them.

Oliver growled deep in his throat. He swept the flashlight's beam from left to right, then dropped to all fours, searching for tracks, trampled plants, drips of blood, anything that indicated direction. He used his animal sense to hunt and his human intelligence to deduce. There were three possibilities: that Matthew and the children had quickened their pace and were out of sight; that they had switched off the flashlight and were fumbling forward in the dark; or that they were hiding. Oliver believed the latter most likely.

"Where are you, little boy?"

The mountain, for all its god-like force and wisdom, offered no suggestion, while its angel, Bird, flickered uncertainly at the edge of his mind. Oliver snarled and pawed forward. The flashlight's beam swayed in a cool semicircle, probing trees and bushes. He scurried right, his face close to the ground, but there was no hint that they had come this way. He paused and listened. Maybe he would hear the children crying. But no . . . only birdsong, and a breeze making the upper boughs creak. Oliver scowled and changed direction, moving south, covering ground quickly.

"Find you . . ." Mumbling through his broken jaw, pink frothing at the corners of his mouth. He was about to resume a westward track when he noticed something slick and S-shaped lying on the ground. *Snake,* he thought at first, crawling toward it, expecting it to slither away, and when it didn't he thought, *Dead snake,* and it was only when he got within touching distance that he saw it was Matthew's shirt sleeve. Torn from the white, sensible shirt he had worn to Bobby's funeral. Not so white and sensible now. Covered in blood, in fact. *Did you lose this while you were looking for a place to hide, Matthew?* Oliver grinned, setting down the .45 so that he could pick up the sleeve, lifting it to his face and inhaling the mixed odours. Blood, yes . . . but sweat, too, and a trace of aftershave. Monsieur Musk, perhaps. Or Brut.

"Find you," he growled.

Oliver sniffed the sleeve again, then tossed it away, grabbed the .45, and got to his feet. He shone the flashlight in the direction Matthew's sleeve had been pointing and limped along.

Ready or not . . . Oliver cracked a smile and the birds sang.

———

Courtney had curled so close to Matthew, with Ethan between them, that it felt like they were one body. They shared each other's heartbeat and breathed in hurting gasps. Sweat trickled from Courtney's hairline and Matthew felt it on his cheek. She tasted his tears, and cupped her hand over Ethan's mouth when he murmured in his semiconscious state.

One body, small and terrified.

Oliver's flashlight glimmered beyond the screen of branches. They watched it swell and grow brighter. He was coming their way.

"He's going to find us," Courtney said, a whisper, quieter than breathing.

Matthew touched her damp hair and said nothing.

"I'm so scared," she said.

He wanted to assure her that the bad man wouldn't find them and that everything would be okay, but the words weren't there. The *belief* wasn't there. He squeezed the bony knur of her shoulder. It was all he could manage.

Courtney started to pray, her lips moving silently, warm breath puffing against Matthew's cheek. He closed his eyes and tried a prayer of his own. It began "Jesus, please" and ended "Amen," but the words between were rushed, hollow. When he opened his eyes, he saw his hand on Courtney's face, her glistening eyes. It was lighter in their little hideaway, morning pushing slowly through the trees.

We won't need the flashlight, Matthew thought, *if we make a run for it. That'll make it harder for him to follow us.*

They heard him now, dragging his feet through the needles, wheezing like a dog on a tight leash. Courtney's breath hitched in her throat as if she were about to scream—to vent all her fear and anger, unable to restrain it any longer. Matthew covered her mouth, maybe a little too firmly, because she moaned, but breathed again, and he kept his hand there and felt her tears.

"Find you," they heard him say.

They waited, hearts trembling. A ragged, dismal trio clinging to prayer. Matthew peered through the branches. Rosy light filtered through the trees, enough for him to see Oliver stalking closer. He had the flashlight in his left hand, the .45 in his right.

"Here I come." Ugly words amid a backdrop of birdsong.

Matthew watched him limp closer. *He's going to find us,* Courtney had said, and she was right. Oliver wouldn't stop until he had what he wanted—until the mountain had what it wanted. Matthew's breathing became shallower. He felt Courtney's eyelash tickling his cheek. Her lips moved against his palm. She was trying to say something.

"Quietly," Matthew whispered.

She nodded.

He lowered his hand, cupped her face.

"We can't stay here," she hissed.

Matthew looked at Courtney, then beyond her, at the branches covering the other side of the hideaway. Thick, but brittle. They could push through easily. The fallen pine and boulder would obstruct Oliver's view.

They might even get away.

Jesus, please, he thought, the start of another prayer.

"We have to leave," Courtney said. Tears flashed down her face in the stained light. "Right now."

Matthew nodded. "Amen," he said.

———

Every so often the flashlight found a drop of blood on the forest floor, like a trail of polished copper pennies, easy to follow. Not that Oliver needed a trail. He knew every possible place to hide. The shirt sleeve had given him a starting point, and the rest was easy.

However, walking . . . *breathing* . . . not so easy. The circles had faded considerably; the radical centre had once been a booming heart, but was now a weakly flexing button. He tried to hold on to it, but in truth he didn't know what he was anymore. Not animal, bird, or human. The lines were indistinct—*floopy*, was the word that came to mind—and he knew that he was dying. A dying, floopy thing without structure, but still driven by the mountain. It occurred to him that all life existed thus, frail and brief, governed by intangibles—a way to look; to think; to act. Everybody has a mountain.

Morning light sifted through the canopy, vague, like the circles, and in the flashlight's glow he saw the old pine collapsed against the boulder with a trail of copper pennies leading toward it.

"Here I come," he said. A blunt throb in his skull. Pain, like a Mack truck, ran over him. First the front wheels, then a gap, then the rear wheels. There'd be another one along soon enough. A fucking convoy, by God. Nothing he could do about it. He tried to make an eagle sound but only gurgled and swallowed blood.

And as always, the mountain whip-cracked and spurred him on. He was a carthorse. A lone husky. A worker ant carrying fifty times his own body weight, trudging faithfully back to the anthill. One purpose. With everything stripped away, even his humanity, only one thing remained: to serve the mountain. He had been chosen because he was strong. He'd give it what it wanted, and when he died—which would be soon, no doubt about that—his soul would cut some serious rug with Leander Bird's. Together they would make the mountain rumble louder than ever before. They'd turn it into a volcano, and dance on the rim as it erupted.

His bloody lips cracked a smile and he staggered the last seven or eight feet to the fallen pine.

"I know you're in there, Matthew."

No sound. He had expected a whimper—had hoped for a scream. But nothing. He shone the flashlight on the curtain of branches.

"Matthew?"

Nothing.

Oliver frowned and used the barrel of the flashlight to part the branches, fully expecting to see Matthew and the children huddled like newborn pups, but the space between the pine and the boulder was empty.

"Nothing," Oliver said.

Not quite; he shone the flashlight on the boulder and saw a splodge of blood, still wet. Oliver touched it. Warm. So they *had* been here, and recently. He growled and shuffled around the boulder, looking for their careless tracks. And there, not too far ahead, a flash of white and red between the trees. He followed it with the flashlight and saw that it was the little girl. Matthew traipsed beside her, carrying the boy.

She sensed the light and turned around. Her face was like a crushed petal. She opened her mouth and *yes,* there was the scream.

It signalled another whip-crack, another Mack truck. Oliver let it roll over him, front wheels and rear. The pain knocked him to his knees, but he hoisted fifty times his own body weight and started to crawl.

The circles had faded. He was dying . . . floopy. But he wasn't going to stop now.

Couldn't, even if he wanted to.

CHAPTER
NINETEEN

Another beautiful summer morning in Point Hollow. Veils of mist were draped over the lower hillsides, blushing in the sunrise, and the peaks flashed bold colours, almost metallic. The sky appeared soft, like a huge comforter stretched over the town, pinks and baby blues, with a sprinkle of stars in the west. A breeze shared the fragrance of all that blossomed, while endless trees conversed in their secret language. The birds responded with sweet melodies that fell silent at the sound of the first shot.

Sheriff Tansy's cruiser rumbled down Clover Hill Road, turned left on Acorn, and pulled into its allotted space outside the office. The sheriff sat for a moment, making stiff morning sounds (not nearly as melodic as the birds) and blinking the sleep from his eyes. It was precisely 5:12 in the A.M and he felt, in his own parlance, like dry roasted dogshit. Too many brewskies at the Rack. He was supposed to run the nightshift but that didn't happen. Not even close. So whaddafuck . . . he'd come in early to make up for it. A few hours and then back to bed. Being the boss had its benefits.

He stepped out of the cruiser and entered the office. Empty. Ruby started work at six-thirty, and until then any calls were relayed to state. There was the batphone, in case of emergencies, but that motherfucker *never* rang. Tansy threw his hat on his desk and made a pot of coffee. While waiting for it to brew, he grabbed his favourite issue of *Finally Legal* from his bottom drawer and went to the restroom to jerk off.

He didn't hear the first gunshot, but he heard the second, by God.

The flags on Main Street rippled above empty sidewalks. Sparrows chirped on power lines. Squirrels played on lawns. On Pawpaw Avenue, two young coyotes strutted coolly down the sidewalk, like teenagers that had stayed out all night. One of them stopped to nose in a trashcan. The other waited, ears cocked curiously, but both took off with their tails between their legs when the first crack echoed in the still air.

Rex Mooney heard it, too—heard both shots, in fact. He was fishing on Old Friend Pond, as he did every Saturday morning from Memorial to Labour Day, and had just dropped-ass into his chair when the first shot rang out. He jumped and looked in the direction of the sound. Birds scattered from the treetops, wings shaking.

"Hell is that?" he muttered, but of course he knew. You'd have to be plumb stupid to think it was anything but a gunshot. He ignored it, though, because that was the way of things. Best not to think about it. Easier. But when he heard the second shot some moments later (this from the direction of town, and with a different sound—a *deader* sound, as he told folks in the Rack later that night), he decided he'd fished enough for one morning, so packed up and went home.

Others heard the shots (like Tina Quinn, who'd been up all night with a stomach bug, and Rupert Grayson, on his way to a little Saturday double-time at the Mill), and like Rex they turned a deaf ear. No need to get involved. Besides, it was probably just someone trying to scare a bear from their backyard. Those troublesome bears.

Most townspeople heard nothing, however; it was early morning, the weekend, and they were lost to the language of their dreams.

Blissful.

The mist on the hillsides sparkled tangerine. Rabbits hopped brightly in Gabe's Meadow, doves cooed from the eaves of New Hope, and the fountain on Main Street played softly to no one.

In the dense woodland to the southeast of town, Matthew Bridge clung to the last vestiges of his strength. He had a dying seven-year-old boy in his arms and an infinitely brave eleven-year-old girl by his side. They scraped through the trees and bushes, praying with all the passion in their souls.

And behind them, Point Hollow's favourite son, Oliver Wray, naked but for a pair of blood-soaked socks and sneakers, singing "God Bless America" and brandishing a loaded .45.

———

Close . . . they were *so* close now. Matthew saw the clock on the town hall through the trees. He didn't need to turn around to know that Oliver was right behind them—could hear him singing, each line punctuated by a shrill animal sound. It sometimes felt like he was breathing down their necks.

Branches whipped Matthew's face, drawing blood. He stumbled, lost one shoe, kept going. The clock blurred between the trees, seen one moment, gone the next. Matthew screamed and threw his legs one in front of the other. Ethan shuddered in his arms, thin legs swinging with the movement of Matthew's body. Courtney, incredibly, pushed ahead, her fathomless strength fuelling him, her bright hair rippling between the trees like a ribbon.

———

He was close enough to get off a shot. The gun was heavy, but Oliver lifted it and glared crookedly down the sights. The back of the little girl's head was fat and round, as red as the centre of a target. He curled his finger around the trigger. Time to end this. Time for Matthew to stop running. Dropping the girl, sending her brains flying through the front of her shattered skull, was a pretty effective way of doing that. Oliver sang about the land that he loved, then screeched like an eagle and exerted a touch more pressure on the trigger . . . and be damned if the itty-bitty bitch didn't weave behind a tree, momentarily out of sight. Oliver growled, lowered the .45, sang about the mountains and the prairies, and waited for that fat red target to shimmy back into view.

They broke through a tight band of hemlocks and stopped—just stopped. Dead. Matthew tried to breathe but his throat and chest constricted, allowing nothing in or out. Courtney threw her arms out in surprise. Ethan opened his eyes and said, "Deer."

There. They'd stopped. Rock-still. For some reason. Oliver lurched closer. He raised the .45, found his target. A perfectly motionless target, praise be to God, floating at the edge of a clearing like a fat red balloon waiting to be popped. He stepped on a twig that cracked like a bone in the still morning air, then hooked his finger around the trigger.

Held his breath and squeezed.

Matthew heard Bobby's voice in his mind, so clear, as if the big guy were standing right next to him: *I thought you needed to see that.*

They had stumbled into the clearing that Bobby had taken him to, bristling with whitetail. Three dozen, at least. The animals didn't spring in the opposite direction, tails flashing, as they had before. Instead they stood their ground and looked at Matthew and the children with their heavy, black eyes. Their expressions were passive, intelligent, beautiful. The bucks towered impressively, antlers spread like open wings, while the fawns were almost lost among the flowers. Matthew thought that, of all places to die, this really wasn't so bad. Cruel that they were so close to town—to safety—but he found solace in this outstanding beauty. *I thought you needed to see that.* Matthew found his breath and gasped, and then everything happened at once.

There was a crack from the woods as Oliver stumbled closer. The deer reacted, streaming like a slick, reddish river not away from, but toward them. At the same instant Matthew heard a gunshot. He felt warm fluid spatter against him. Blood, on his face and shirt. In Ethan's hair. He thought it was his own and waited to die. The ground trembled as the deer charged around him, their bodies close and hot. *This is death*, he thought. *The rush of death.* He smelled the hollyhocks and the full, woody odour of fur. Blood dripped from his ear. *Courtney*, he thought, and looked for her, couldn't see her. The deer snorted and bristled by, and Matthew saw Courtney's leg—just her leg—on the ground, glimpsed between the frenzied deer, her Croc standing out against the grass like a small purple toy.

Oliver had squeezed the trigger and the gun kicked in his hand as the round discharged, as if it were full of flexing muscle. In that same instant—from nowhere—a doe moved into the line of fire. The bullet struck its throat and it sagged to the ground, spurting a crazy wheel of blood, and before Oliver could comprehend what had happened, there was another deer—a buck, running at him, antlers low—and then another.

Another.

And another.

Charging toward him.

My forest brothers and sisters, Oliver thought, and closed his eyes.

The first buck hit him hard, gouging his stomach and chest, driving him backward. The second spun him on his feet and dropped him to one knee. The third, a doe, knocked him onto his back. The gory flap of skin drooped across his brow again. His broken jaw clanged and thunder exploded from the hole in his skull.

They ran over him, hooves trampling.

Nothing he could do but wait for it to end.

The last deer brushed by with a flurry of warm air and Matthew dropped to his knees beside Courtney. She lay facedown in the grass, blood on her T-shirt. He grabbed her hip and rolled her over, his heart rising in his chest like a thick red bubble breaking the surface of a pool.

"Courtney," he said.

"Courtney," Ethan said.

She opened her eyes, her lips quivering, and everything inside Matthew soared. For a moment there was no pain, no grief, no darkness. He even smiled, for just one second. Courtney sat up. A leaf of hair fell across her face. She curled her small, dirty hand into Matthew's and squeezed.

They walked through the clearing and through more woods, then joined a trail that was marked by coloured posts and this led them into town.

They trudged down the middle of Main Street, listening to the flags snap and sigh, looking at their harrowed reflections in dark storefront windows.

The town hall clock struck 5:30.

Eight minutes later. Main Street. Silent and ghost-townish. Everything peaceful, until a lone figure emerged from the trails and veered, scattering blood, from sidewalk to road and back again.

"*Gobless Amarr-huh,*" Oliver gurgled. "*Lamb darry lub.*"

His stomach had been ripped open by blade-like antlers. He used his shattered left hand to plug the ragged hole—felt his intestine pulsing, pressing against his palm, trying to eek though the cracks of his fingers. In his right hand he still held the .45. There was one bullet left, and you could bet your purdy neck he was going to put it to good use.

The birds on the rooftops sang and he sang with them.

"*Gobless Amarr-huh.*"

Another beautiful summer morning in Point Hollow.

CHAPTER
TWENTY

The sheriff poured coffee
he wouldn't get to finish.
Added three sugars and a
generous glug of half and half.
He sat at his desk and slurped
from the mug. Sweet and warm, just
how he liked it. Another slurp and he
put the mug down, pressed his thumb
against his brow. Good Jesus, his head was
thumping. Partly because of the night before, partly
because the fluorescent lighting in the office was hard on
the eye—and the light directly above his desk flickered every
now and again, like a goddamn nervous tic. Sometimes Tansy felt
like whipping out his Glock and firing a couple of rounds into the
son of a bitch. That would stop it from flickering, by Christ. It was
enough to drive a man crazy.

Paperwork littered his desk and he considered it for a moment,
then decided it could wait until later, even until Monday. None of
it was pressing. Nothing was ever pressing in Hollow County. A
report here, a signature there, check the payroll sheets, stick his
finger up his ass. If the people knew how little he actually did—or
needed to do, to be fair—there was no way they'd vote him in every

four years. It was the reason he went on his little patrols. Yes, it gave him something to do, but showing face, keeping *in* with the voters, was so important. Those monkeys paid his salary, after all.

Sheriff Tansy closed his eyes for a moment and massaged his temples with the heels of his hands. Perfect silence. It could stay like this all day and he'd be a happy sheriff, indeed. He took another slurp of coffee and grabbed the Tylenol from his top drawer. He fumbled with the cap and the bottle slipped from his fingers. It rolled across the floor and into the corner.

"Son of a whore."

He wheeled his chair backward and retrieved the bottle. As he was doing so, the door opened behind him. He thought it was Ruby, coming in early (ugly as a hatful of assholes, that girl, but keen—the best combo for the workplace, as far as Tansy was concerned), but when he turned around he saw that it wasn't Ruby at all. His breath snagged in his throat and he blinked hard. The bottle of Tylenol slipped from his fingers again, rolled into the same corner. Didn't matter. He'd forgotten about his headache.

"What in *the* Jesus?" Tansy gasped.

Matthew Bridge staggered toward his desk, covered in mud and blood, looking like he'd been ass-kicked through the devil's backyard. He carried a child in his arms. A boy. The *ghost* of a boy, really. Pale and bone-thin. There was another child behind him. She stepped into view, trembling, clasping Matthew's shirt tail. Her red hair was clotted with dirt and she looked at the sheriff with huge, grateful eyes.

It's the children, Tansy thought. *I'll be goddamnned.*

He stood up. Sat down again as his legs weakened. Something close to fear—hell, it *was* fear—gripped his barren soul.

Tears shone on all their faces.

"What did you do, Matthew?" the sheriff said.

Matthew shook his head and tried to speak but managed only hopeless sounds. The sheriff tried again to get to his feet, needing the support of the desk to keep himself up. His legs trembled. The fluorescent light flickered and sweat beaded his brow.

What are we going to do now? he thought. He'd never been so scared.

The little girl wiped her eyes and looked at him, full of trust. He was a policeman, after all. He had the uniform and a shiny badge and on the badge it said SHERIFF. She *trusted* him. He looked at her and she gave him a weak smile.

"Help us," Matthew said.

"Shut up," Tansy said. "Just shut the hell up."

Matthew shook his head again, his face crossed with confusion. There was a bench against a nearby wall and he shuffled over to it and lay the boy down. He crossed to the water cooler (the girl still clinging to his shirt tail) and poured a cone, gave it to the girl, who drank it quickly, then another. He handed her a third cone and she took it to the boy and cradled his head while he sipped. Sheriff Tansy watched all of this with his heart thudding and lines of sweat trickling down his face and between his shoulder blades. *What are we going to do now?* he thought again.

"I knew you were trouble," he said to Matthew.

Matthew took two uncertain steps toward him. "No . . . it wasn't me, Sheriff. I didn't do this."

"You've fucked everything up," Tansy told him. "Stick in my ass."

Matthew's mouth hung open, stupidly.

"Stick in my goddamn ass," Tansy said again.

"No," Matthew said.

"It was the bad man," the girl said, and then her face crumpled and she said, "I want to go home."

"The bad man," Matthew said. He looked from the girl to Tansy and nodded pathetically. His expression was desperate—somewhere between hopeful and hopeless. "The bad man . . . Oliver . . . Oliver Wray did this. He took them, Sheriff. He took the children."

Sheriff Tansy sighed. "You think I don't know that?" He wiped his face and his palm came away wet, as if he'd dipped it in warm, briny water. "You think I don't know what Oliver has been doing all this time? Jesus Christ, boy."

Matthew gave his head a little shake, as if he hadn't heard clearly. He had, though. He *must* have, because the room rolled slowly and—like Tansy—he needed the support of the desk to keep from falling.

"As soon as those kiddies went missing," Sheriff Tansy continued. "When I saw their pictures in the newspapers and on TV, I knew that Oliver had taken them. And I knew exactly where they were."

"I don't understand," Matthew said. He looked so weak and small and this made the sheriff feel a little better. He puffed out his chest and sneered.

"Of course you don't understand," he said, "because you left town twenty-some years ago. You forgot how we do things in Point Hollow. Like I told you before . . . country folk take care of their own."

"No," Matthew uttered.

"Yes," the sheriff said. "And the mountain . . . Abraham's Faith . . . it's demanding, Matthew. It's *hungry*."

"No," Matthew said again.

"Oliver has been keeping it settled for the best part of twenty years. And when the mountain is settled, the town runs smooth. It's a happy place."

Matthew blinked and swayed. Sheriff Tansy took a step toward him.

"But now you've come along and fucked everything up." He held one finger up to Matthew's face and breathed all over him, a foul odour of beer and coffee. "So now we're going to have to throw you—and those goddamn children—back in the mountain, otherwise there's going to be hell to pay."

The light flickered again.

"Hell," Matthew said weakly.

———

Matthew took three steps backward. He needed to get his thoughts together and that was hard to do with the sheriff's finger in his face. Not that it was any easier having retreated a few steps. His mind struggled. It reached for anything that was solid, but everything broke apart. He was a drowning man, grabbing onto ropes that crumbled like sand. Nothing was real and he was going down, swallowed by waves. Endless waves. From the shore, a thousand miles away, he saw Courtney and Ethan looking at him expectantly. He remembered the way she had moved ahead of him in the woods, her hair like a ribbon. And that memory was *real*. The only real thing in the world. Her hair like a ribbon. Matthew *reached* for it. Bright red and streaming. He felt it in his palm. And it didn't crumble, and he pulled himself free.

The fluorescent light sparked like a moth flying into a bug zapper. The sheriff looked at it, scowling, and that little snap—that flash— brought Matthew closer to reality. *I'm in Point Hollow. This soulless place. No hope for us here.* He looked at the sheriff and saw malice: a voluminous cloud the colour of everything bad; a diseased aura. His eyes then dropped to the pistol on his hip. *A Glock 20,* he thought. *10mm, and more power than I need.* He knew this because the sheriff had told him—had taught him, in fact, how to hold it . . . fire it. The darkness that had lived inside Matthew for so many years surged again. It *rushed* violently from him, and it wasn't Kirsty feeling his wrath this time, but Sheriff Tansy. Matthew imagined grabbing the Glock, pointing it at Tansy, and pulling the trigger. He *felt* the pistol jerk in his hand and saw—all too colourfully—the top of Tansy's head peel away, blood peppering the walls and ceiling, pieces of skull pinging off the coffee pot, little chunks of brain speckling the Charlie Chipmunk poster for a Safer Community.

Imagining had always been easy.

Matthew couldn't move, save for little winks and flinches from his exhausted muscles. He didn't even have the will to pray. *I'm in Point Hollow. This soulless place.* He looked at the children and shook his head. *No hope for us here.* And just when he thought the situation couldn't get any worse, the door crashed open and Oliver Wray stumbled in.

———

Matthew looked bad—a cracked, bleeding eggshell—but he was a picture of vim and vigour compared to Oliver Wray. Barely recognizable, broken out of shape, Oliver reeled across the floor, bopped against the water cooler (left a splat of blood on the bottle), and settled against Deputy Sheriff's Masefield's desk. He bled all over it, and all over the floor, from multiple traumas, most notably a hole in his stomach large enough the slot the business end of a baseball bat into. He tried to seal the wound with his left hand, to little effect.

"Glurb," he said.

His body was sticky red, with just a few pale flashes on his chest and throat. It disguised his nakedness, but made his eyes gleam. Wild pinpricked circles. The gun in his right hand gleamed, too. Blue steel and blood. His jaw was swollen and kinked, as if it had been kicked by a horse.

"Look at the goddamn state of you," Sheriff Tansy said. His heart drummed with sick rhythm while his mind assessed the situation. One hell of a mess to sweep under the rug.

"Glurb."

He had hoped, initially, that Oliver could take care of his own mess. Looking at him now, he realized that wasn't going to happen. The dumb son of a bitch was hammering at death's door—had minutes left, at most. Which meant that the sheriff was on clean up duty. Not how he wanted to spend his Saturday.

Matthew, meanwhile, had shifted protectively in front of the children. His final stand, for all the good it would do. Oliver grinned and lifted the gun. He pointed it at Matthew, and those pinpricked eyes flicked in Sheriff Tansy's direction.

"Don't stand in my way, Sheriff," he warned. Broken sounds: *Dome tan im my yay, Shurf.* Blood leaked from his mouth and something pink and ropy oozed from between the fingers of his left hand.

The sheriff deciphered what Oliver said. "Stand in your way?" He barked laughter, false and dry. "I've watched you serve the mountain for Christ knows how many years. Why would I stand in your way now?"

Oliver narrowed his eyes. His broken mouth hung open.

"You think I didn't know?" the sheriff asked.

The fluorescent light winked again and Oliver sagged, as if several ribs were removed from his chest. He shook his head and looked at the sheriff. The exposed portion of his skull flashed like a cracked mirror.

"You . . . you *knew?*" The gun dipped, aimed at Matthew's feet, blood dripping from the barrel. "All this time?"

"The mountain speaks to me too, Oliver." Tansy's upper lip flared, showing stained teeth. "It speaks to everybody, even if they're not aware of it. You've seen their faces, their fragile smiles. The mountain demands reverence. It makes people scared, fills them with darkness. And sometimes it makes them do evil deeds. Like Jack Braum, shooting up Main Street in '53, or Eugene Gold funnelling acid down his wife's throat."

Oliver shuddered, spilling blood. It spattered Masefield's desk, his computer keyboard, the photograph of his twin boys.

"I don't know why this town is cursed," Tansy said. "I've never known—never *cared* to know. I'm guessing some ungodly shit hit the fan back in the day . . ."

Oliver nodded and said, "Burr," but it might have been *Burn* or even *Bird*.

"But I *do* know that the mountain has touched you, Oliver, and that you serve it, like a good little doggy. You've been taking kiddies up there for Christ knows how many years, and I've been watching you, making sure nobody gets in your way. And I assume you're doing exactly what it wants because we haven't had an incident in Point Hollow for a long time. That's just the way we like it, of course. Blue skies and happy days."

It was impossible to read Oliver's expression. His mouth was out of shape and his eyes were wide and mad. But he *keened*—a crushed sound. More animal than human, Tansy thought. Or the way some animals can sound human when they're hurting.

"Who else?" he asked.

"Who else what?"

He lowered the .45 to steady himself on Masefield's desk. "Who else knows what I've done?"

"Jesus Christ, *nobody* knows." Tansy said. "Everybody thinks you're the cat's balls, Oliver. Thanks to *me*. I've been protecting you all this time . . . protecting the town."

The little girl spoke again, saying—oh so sweetly—that she wanted her mommy and daddy. The sheriff looked at her. Oliver looked at her. Matthew didn't; his eyes were fixed, not on the crazy motherhumper pointing the gun, but on the sheriff. He'd even taken a step toward him.

"All the pain I went through," Oliver said, looking away from the little girl, back to the sheriff. "For years . . . *years*. And you knew. You let it happen."

"You're damn right," Tansy said. "You were keeping the mountain settled. I didn't want another church fire. Another Main Street massacre. I did what was best for the town."

"What about me?"

"What about you? Nobody cares, Oliver. You're a servant. A fucking dog."

"I was chosen."

"Yes."

"Because I'm strong."

"No, Oliver, because you're weak. Easily led." Tansy grinned again. "You have no foundation. Your mother was an emotional cripple and your old man has always been a waste of goddamn space. You needed something powerful in your life and the mountain was there. It knew you couldn't resist, that you would do whatever it wanted. That's not strength, Oliver. That's subservience. Weakness. Subjection."

"No—"

"You stupid son of a bitch."

"You don't know what happened on that mountain." Oliver swayed and spat blood. "You don't even know what it wants, yet you watched me all these years and never tried to stop me. What does that make you?"

"Smart," the sheriff said.

"Weaker than me," Oliver said.

"Is that what you think?" the sheriff said. "Well, maybe. But I'm still going to be drawing breath in five minutes, and you'll be deader than yesterday's turds."

The clock ticked. Not even six o'clock, and the sheriff felt like he'd already lived through a full day of hell. He was definitely going back to bed after this. His head whirled and his heart continued to boom hard. He was angry, but more than anything he was scared.

"You've left me one hell of a mess to sweep under the rug," he said to Oliver.

Oliver swayed again. His legs buckled but he stayed on his feet.

"All for a peaceful life," Tansy said.

And Oliver said, "That's all I ever wanted."

———————

Matthew knew what he had to do and waited for his chance. It came just after Oliver said, "That's all I ever wanted." The fluorescent light buzzed and flickered and the sheriff growled—actually growled—and turned his stony eyes up to it.

Less than a second: the window in which Matthew had to act. And in that time his heart must have drummed fifty times. Every dark thought he'd ever had stormed through his mind. Several happy thoughts, too: fishing with his old man on Lake Ronkonkoma; when Kirsty first said that she loved him; Bobby taking him to the clearing in the woods, his glowing, chubby face. *I thought you needed to—*

Less than a second.

"Motherfuck—" Sheriff Tansy said. That was all.

Matthew leapt at him, one hand in his face, the other reaching for the gun on his hip. He came from the side and was able to release the retention strap quickly, but struggled with the gun, fumbled the grip. Tansy realized what was happening and put up a fight. Matthew's window closed and there followed a struggle that lasted no more than three seconds but felt, for both men, like three hours. But Matthew's determination (not to mention the fact that he jammed his thumb in Tansy's eye) prevailed. He snatched the gun and pointed it at the sheriff's face.

"You sick son of a bitch," Matthew said.

Sheriff Tansy backed up, his shoulders rolling with fury, the eye that Matthew had poked squeezed shut.

"You all-out ballsy dicksucker," he said. "And *still* a stick in my ass."

"Here's what's going to happen," Matthew said. "I'm going to lock you two in a holding cell while we blow the fuck out of this shithole town."

"I don't think so," the sheriff said. Fluid oozed from his eye.

"I do. So let's go, fat boy. The keys."

The sheriff threw back his head and brayed moronic laughter. His good eye rolled toward Oliver. "How about you shoot this asshole, Oliver? Or one of the children?"

Matthew stepped forward and pressed the Glock's muzzle into Tansy's cheekbone, directly beneath his squinted eye. "There's no conventional safety on this gun. No levers or buttons. Am I right, Sheriff Tansy?"

"You pint-sized prick."

"I should keep my finger away from the trigger until I am absolutely one hundred percent ready to shoot. Am I right?"

The sheriff tried to pull away but Matthew kept the gun locked in place.

"And would you look at that—my finger is right on the trigger." It was Matthew's turn to grin. "How do you like that?"

"You couldn't even shoot a dying deer," Tansy said, spittle flying from his lips. "You expect me to believe you're going to shoot the High Sheriff of Hollow fucking County?"

"That was a long time ago," Matthew said. "Things have changed."

"I'll take my chances." The sheriff opened his eye, bloodshot and crazy. "Look at you: five-foot-nothing and trembling like a dog shitting razor blades."

"That's adrenaline," Matthew said, still grinning. "Seventy thousand amps of pure adrenaline bolting through my system. I'm *pumped*."

"Shoot this son of a bitch, Oliver. *NOW!*"

"A loud noise could cause my finger to twitch."

"*OLIVER!*"

"He might miss. I know damn well I won't."

"*NOW!*"

Perfect calm fell over Matthew, from out of nowhere. A dusky, easy blanket of calm. He took a step backward, keeping the gun levelled at Tansy's face, noticing how the tip of the barrel—his arm, his whole *body*—had stopped trembling. He felt extremely cool. Not cool like Bootsy Collins, but like a bird of prey in an arctic aerie, so high he could see the earth's curvature, feel the wind in his icy feathers. He'd gained an intense awareness of his surroundings, as if he had eased from his body and was ghosting around the room. Morning light reached through the blinds and touched the floor. He saw the imperfections in the walls, the stains on the ceiling. A frayed flag stood in one corner. Off-white stars and faded stripes. The children were balled like two sheets of newspaper, pine needles in Courtney's hair, a drop of blood on the strap of her right Croc. Oliver sagged to one side and pumped blood, a blazing red devil-man with a part of his stomach slipping between the cracks of his fingers, but swinging the .45 upward, his finger looped around the trigger.

This is the end for someone, Matthew thought, knowing that Sheriff Tansy would sooner take a bullet than concede. *This is how it feels.*

He exhaled with bird-of-prey coolness and looked at the sheriff through the gun's steady sights.

Perfect calm.

"What are you waiting for, Oliver?" the sheriff said, wheezing and sweating. "Do as you're told, boy. Pull the goddamn trigger."

This is the end.

Oliver did as he was told. He pulled the trigger.

CHAPTER
TWENTY-ONE

The bullet hit Sheriff Tansy
in the middle of his chest
and pushed him backward so
hard and fast that he left one
of his boots standing empty by
his desk. He slammed into the wall,
bounced off it, then jigged sideways,
three shaky steps, before falling. He was
dead before he hit the floor. The American
flag toppled from the corner and draped over him,
covering his face and chest. Blood flowed among the stars.

Oliver dropped the gun. It was empty now, and useless. The
final bullet had been used. And in a most satisfactory manner,
he thought.

"I never liked that asshole," he said.

"Me, either," Matthew said. The calm had dispersed. Not so cool
anymore. He lowered the Glock, taking his finger off the trigger,
struggling to process what had happened. He looked at the sheriff's
empty boot, the laces untied, one eyelet missing. It didn't seem real.
Nothing seemed real. He looked at the children, wrapped together,
their faces turned away from everything.

"Let us go, Oliver," he said.

Oliver shook his head. "It won't let you go, Matthew."

"Abraham's Faith?"

"It wants you. It *will* find you."

"Maybe one day."

"One day." Oliver rolled his eyes to the ceiling, then slumped to his knees with a red splash. His hands dropped to his sides and a figure-eight of intestine slithered from the hole in his stomach.

Matthew went to the children. He lay his palm on Courtney's trembling back, feeling her heart run, the knotted rope of her spine.

"All I wanted was to be left alone," Oliver said. Hard, ragged words. He coughed blood. His chest rattled. "When I was . . . three months old, my father . . . put a pillow over my face." His gaze dropped to Matthew and his mouth twitched. "I wish to God he'd kept it there."

Matthew lowered his head. A tear rolled from his eye, fell, and splashed on Ethan's leg. The boy opened his eyes.

Sunlight moved deeper into the room. Oliver turned toward it, looking out the window, to the east. He managed one final, rattling breath. "Boom," he said. "I'm a hellbound cunt."

He closed his eyes and said nothing more.

Matthew considered using Sheriff Tansy's phone to call the New York State Police, but that would mean waiting for them. They would arrive promptly, no doubt, but he didn't want to stay in Point Hollow any longer than he had to, and he certainly didn't want to risk another crooked townsperson showing up at the station.

"We're going," he said to Courtney and Ethan. "Right now."

He unclipped Tansy's keys from his belt (expecting, for one terrible moment, Tansy's hand to spring to life and clamp around his wrist) and they left the office, locking the door behind them because it felt safer, somehow. Matthew put Ethan in the back of the cruiser. Courtney wanted to sit up front with him, but he told her to sit with Ethan and hold his hand, and she did. Matthew got behind the wheel, backed out of the space marked: RESERVED: SHERIFF, and drove away.

He looked in the rearview mirror as they took the Dead Road out of town.

The mountain looked back, fierce and grey.

It wants you. It will find you.

He kept driving, and didn't stop until they reached the State Police Department in Liberty thirty-three minutes later. He opened Courtney's door, and then went around the other side and scooped Ethan into his arms.

"Go on," he said to Courtney. "It's okay."

She nodded, managed the slightest of smiles, and walked toward the building.

Matthew followed the red ribbon of her hair.

CHAPTER
TWENTY-TWO
2011

Their divorce was uncontested and finalized within eight months. To celebrate, with measured irony and a brazen humour that Matthew had long admired, Kirsty suggested they go on a date. "The tryst of the final decree," she called it. "In the interest of amity." Matthew asked if Scalini Fedeli's in Tribeca—where he'd taken her on their first date— was a suitable venue for so significant an occasion. "It's a date thing, baby," Kirsty had replied.

Matthew had agreed to the date because he still cared about Kirsty, and valued amity in a world where fractures ran deep. He also wanted to see if she looked as good as he remembered. And she did. Better, in fact. She arrived fashionably late, dressed in a satin one-shoulder number that accentuated her toned figure. Her hair was shorter, darker, and the heels she wore insisted Matthew get on tiptoes to kiss her cheek.

He seated her at the table and told her that she looked fantastic, that he knew she would. She indicated his leaner physique, his shorter haircut, and said he looked quite charming.

"Charming?" he said.

"Different," she said.

"Good different, or bad different?" He took his seat and smiled at her over the candlelight.

"Good," she said. "Considering."

Matthew smiled. He had known there was more to this meeting than the furtherance of amity. To the chagrin of numerous news and entertainment companies, he had remained tight-lipped to everybody but the police and Dr. Meeker about the events of last summer, and Kirsty wanted her inside scoop—the pound of flesh owed for six years of marriage, two of which were utterly miserable. That one word, *Considering*, casually affixed to the compliment, was a blatant invitation for disclosure.

"Should we get the Ca' del Bosco?" Matthew asked.

Kirsty's lips twitched. "Very good."

His reticence could only last so long. He didn't need Dr. Meeker to tell him that he couldn't keep the darkness inside, that one day he would have to release . . . to purge. When the time was right, he would accept one of the publishers' offers and write a book. But he wasn't ready yet. The wounds were too tender and the nightmares hadn't stopped. Most nights he woke with his heart pounding wildly, positive that Oliver wasn't really dead—that he was looming in the darkness, bleeding on the carpet. *Boom,* he would say. *It wants you, Matthew. It will find you.* Matthew sometimes slept with the light on, like a five-year-old, and often checked outside his bedroom window, wanting to make sure Oliver wasn't standing beneath the streetlight, gazing up at his room.

No, he wasn't ready yet.

His priority, he told Dr. Meeker, was to resume as normal a lifestyle as possible. Dr. Meeker said that his ambition was admirable, but would take time, and wouldn't be easy. Determined to prove him wrong, Matthew stayed with his parents in Bay Ridge, went back to his job in Internet marketing, hit the gym three times a week, and streamed movies on Netflix. He soon came to realize that such normalcy was a charade. It was, much like Point Hollow's smiling faces, a veneer, concealing the truth. Life *wasn't* the same. People looked at him differently—*treated* him differently. His colleagues invited him to social functions where they never had before. Even the company president invited him to dinner (a nice, albeit somewhat diluted affair, after having had dinner with the *actual* President). Jon Stewart and Conan O'Brian had cracked funnies about him. *Family Guy*, too. He had his own Wikipedia page and several people were pretending to be him on Twitter.

Life was a long way from normal.

"The soft egg yolk raviolo, to start," he said to the waiter. "Followed by the wild striped bass."

Kirsty ordered foie gras and venison.

"How's work?" Matthew asked.

Her eyes fluttered. "Busy," she replied. "After the promotion."

"The promotion? Congratulations." He raised his glass.

She clinked. "Thank you. How are your parents?"

"Oh, they're—"

"Enjoying your new-found fame?" Her lips were red from the wine, accenting the acerbic quality of her voice. "Proud of their little boy?"

Matthew took a sip from his glass and set it down. "Firstly, I wouldn't call it fame. Secondly, whatever it is, we rarely talk about it."

This was true. Matthew's ordeal, and the ensuing fallout, had proved demanding on Matthew's parents, particularly his mother. Of the human remains recovered from the mountain, forensic anthropologists confirmed—consistent with written documents gathered at Oliver Wray's house—those belonging to ten-year-old Jonah Trey Callum, missing since 1958. Jonah was Sarah Bridge née Callum's older brother: Matthew's uncle. Sarah, who was seven years old when Jonah went missing, claimed to have no memory of him, or of the incident. Her parents never spoke about him, she said, which was why she had never mentioned it to either Matthew or her husband. It sounded plausible, but Matthew secretly questioned his mother's reasoning, and shuddered at the idea of her being part of Point Hollow's enduring secrecy.

They buried Jonah next to his parents (Grandma and Grandpa Callum) in a cemetery in Utica. His was one of many bodies removed from the mountain, and finally laid to rest.

The FBI searched Oliver Wray's house. Information taken from his computer, as well as handwritten notes and documents found on floppy and compact discs, incriminated Oliver in the disappearance of eight children over an eighteen-year period. A matter of formality, subsequent evidence—consistent with statements from Matthew, Courtney Bryce, and Ethan Mitchell—found Oliver guilty of the three survivors' kidnap, incarceration, and attempted murder. In all instances, Sheriff Edgar Tansy was named an accomplice.

Both men were cremated at a private service in Point Hollow. Sheriff Tansy's ashes were given to his widow, who scattered them in Gabe's Meadow. Oliver's were given to his father, who, according to rumour, poured them down the toilet and shit on them.

"How's the foie gras?" Matthew asked.

"Delectable," Kirsty replied. "The raviolo?"

"Wonderful." He showed her an entirely false smile. "More wine?"

"Please."

Matthew poured, still exhibiting the fake smile, which he had come to master over the preceding months. So much of his soul was in pieces that a mask was entirely necessary, at least until said pieces were retrieved and slotted—*forced*, if need be—back into place. Otherwise he would be walking around with the stricken expression of a plane crash survivor. Memories of the ordeal, the nightmares, were bad enough, but documents recovered at Oliver's house revealed the reason Matthew had been targeted.

FBI Special Agent Nicola Blount showed him these documents to ensure he had "appropriate information" in the event of him selling his story.

"It is prudent of us to clarify and advise," she said. An older woman with a firm chin and no upper lip. "And to remind you that Oliver Wray was highly delusional."

"And Sheriff Tansy?"

"Highly delusional."

"Convenient," Matthew said. "I smell chicanery."

"On the contrary," Special Agent Blount said. "You're a smart man, Mr. Bridge. I wanted to show you these letters and journals so you can see how ludicrous they are."

"But I *am* related to Trey Moffatt," Matthew said. "He would be my great-grandfather, right? And my Uncle Jonah's remains *were* found in the mountain. That doesn't sound ludicrous to me."

"Certain aspects are true, but not nearly all. You want to believe in curses, Mr. Bridge? Haunted mountains? Fine by me."

Matthew flipped through the aged letters, reading snippets here and there.

"Or you can believe," Special Agent Blount continued, "that the people of Point Hollow did an unspeakable thing in 1917, and invented this story to cover their guilt. You can believe that this fabrication influenced certain weak-minded individuals to commit terrible crimes, Oliver Wray among them."

Matthew closed his eyes and pushed the letters aside.

"Oh, and by the way," she went on, tapping her chin with one finger. "Kip Sawyer isn't really one hundred and twenty years old. He's a senile old man. Also, we looked into this Leander Bird character and found nothing conclusive. That's because he didn't exist, Mr. Bridge."

"There's a photograph of him here."

"That could be anyone."

"True, but all those children," Matthew said. "Why did the people of Point Hollow do it, if Leander Bird didn't exist?"

To which she replied, "Why did they do it, if he *did?*"

She went on to explain that there would be a "minor adjustment of facts" when presenting this story to the public, in order to protect the people still living in Point Hollow. The official line was that Old Bear Mountain, known colloquially as Abraham's Faith, was an ancient Mahican burial ground. Oliver Wray (a paranoid schizophrenic) discovered the site and believed the human remains to be offerings to a demonic spirit that lived in the mountain. Actual quotes were taken from his journal: *I felt its voice . . . It coerced and commanded . . . I look in the mirror and see a monster.* Oliver, in cahoots with the sheriff of Hollow County (who also had mental health concerns), took his victims to the mountain to offer as a sacrifice. The press called it The Mountain-God Murders.

Matthew understood this "minor adjustment of facts" was necessary, and Special Agent Blount's reasoning made sense, but his uneasy feeling ran cold and deep. He'd read the old newspaper articles and townspeople's letters—he *knew* the truth—and saw how he was linked to the mountain. Furthermore, he'd been to Point Hollow. He'd walked the streets, seen the fragile smiles, and sensed the bad energy. The mountain was evil. Of that he had no doubt.

It wants you. It will find you.

And so—like the people of Point Hollow—he had mastered the spurious smile.

"You used to have the venison," Kirsty said, dabbing the corners of her mouth with her napkin. "Change of heart tonight?"

"A change of heart in general," Matthew said.

"Yes, you're quite different."

"Good different, or bad different?"

"Didn't we already cover this?"

Matthew grinned and it was, at least in part, genuine. Kirsty was digging furiously for information and it felt good to be in control. He looked at her. An attractive woman in her mid-thirties, with endless ambition, a wonderful sense of humour, and emotions she could detach like a lizard's tail. He had loved her once, and cared about her still. Always would. But she wasn't a part of him anymore. He tried to imagine seducing her, drawing her stony nipples into his mouth and slipping into her cool body. But he couldn't. He tried to imagine reaching across the table and driving his knife into her left eye. But he couldn't. She was out of his soul. He had neither love nor darkness for her.

"Dessert?" he asked.

"A moment on the lips . . ." She wavered in the candle's haze, red crescents in her eyes. "But what the hell? It's a celebration."

"I'm having the banana tart."

She nodded. "What did you have at the White House?"

"We ordered pizza and then shot some hoops."

"You're impossible."

Matthew smiled. "One of those things is true."

Earlier in the year the President had invited Matthew, Courtney Bryce, Ethan Mitchell, and their respective parents to dinner at the White House. It was, thankfully, a non-press affair, and the first time that Matthew had seen Courtney and Ethan since the ordeal. Meeting the President was an honour, but seeing the children again meant so much more. Ethan was six inches taller, and probably twice as heavy as he had been when Matthew carried him from the mountain. He had a contagious smile and liked to laugh, but the hurt in his eyes was all too familiar. For all the laughter, the boy would be a long time healing.

It was the same with Courtney. She looked strong yet delicate, and stood with her shoulders straight and her chin held high. Her skin was the colour of winter mornings and her hair was full, rich, burning. Her eyes, though, however bright, were stained with hurt.

"I remember you," she said, and smiled beautifully. "The guy who saved my life."

Matthew grinned and pulled her close, hugged her so tight that he felt—familiar again, but welcome this time—the forceful peal of her heart.

"I remember you," he said. A tear slipped from his eye and fell into the flames of her hair. "The girl who saved mine."

Now he stood with Kirsty in his arms, holding her tight but not feeling her heart. He was reminded of the time they hugged on the morning of their separation, how she had leaned into him, sparing a moment of her loveless body before leaving for work. *You're hurting me,* she had said, but he didn't hurt her this time, and she didn't hurt him.

"Thank you for dinner," she said.

They separated, hesitantly, as if knowing this was the last time they would touch, and were not sure how to feel about it. Matthew trailed his hand down Kirsty's arm, gave her wrist a gentle squeeze, and then stepped to the edge of the sidewalk to hail her a cab.

"So what are you going to do now?" she asked.

"Go home," he said. "Probably watch the end of the Mets game."

"Silly," she said. "I mean with your life."

A cab pulled over and Matthew opened the rear door.

"I was thinking of moving away," he said. "A fresh start. Maybe Florida."

"Really?"

"Really."

"Why Florida?"

No mountains, he thought, but said, "They have beautiful beaches."

Kirsty nodded and got into the cab, but held the door open a moment longer. "You'll be all right," she said. "Won't you?"

Matthew thought about the things he had seen, the scars on his body and in his mind. He thought about the nights he had woken up with his heart hurting, drenched in sweat, with no one beside him, no one to hold him. Endless pain. Endless darkness. Too thick to breathe and constantly booming. He thought about Oliver, a red ghost floating at the foot of his bed, his pinpricked eyes flaring in the dark. And the mountain, filled with ash and misery, reaching for him with its infinite arms . . .

It wants you. It will *find you.*

"Goodbye, Kirsty," he said.

The door closed. Matthew caught the suggestion of a smile, the suggestion of a wave, then the cab pulled away and she was gone.

He knew he would never see her again.

It's a fate thing, baby, he thought, and hailed another cab.

CHAPTER
TWENTY-THREE

Matthew moved to Florida in early June. He bought a beachfront property with floor-to-ceiling windows overlooking the Atlantic. The rooms were spacious and light, filled with the sound of the ocean. It was the perfect place to heal.

Dr. Meeker recommended a colleague in Daytona Beach, whose methods were different, but effective, and with her help it didn't take Matthew long to settle. He started a small business designing websites, and made several new friends. Florida was good for him. White sand between his toes. Sunshine on his face. Chess with the old folks in Marlin Park, and starlight over the ocean.

But best of all, Angela Vega.

He met her at a coffee shop in St. Augustine. They were reading books by the same author, which served as an introduction, and within moments were engaged in comfortable conversation. Angela was pretty, a little younger than Matthew, with a Bob Marley tattoo on her shoulder and a ring through her eyebrow. She laughed immediate. He asked for her telephone number before the foam had faded from his latte macchiato.

"Are you going to ask me out on a date?" She raised one eyebrow. The one with the ring through it.

"Yes," he said. "I am."

"Why?"

Because you're healing, he thought, but said, "Because you like Ian McEwan and Bob Marley."

"This is true." She smiled. "You'd be the first person I dated who doesn't have a tongue stud and/or dreadlocks."

Matthew's turn to smile. "Yet," he said.

They dated, they danced, walked along the beach . . . kissed. Angela settled into his soul like it was shaped just for her. Over the weeks they talked, listened, and laughed often. She called him baby, and always looked him in the eye.

He shared his darkness, and she took it.

———

August 3rd was the first anniversary of Bobby Alexander's death. Matthew sent flowers and phoned Bobby's mother. Even talking to someone in Point Hollow—knowing that his voice was being heard there—made him shudder. Mrs. Alexander sounded delighted to hear from him. She asked how he was doing, and reminded him of his promise to visit.

"I'm not quite ready for that, Mrs. Alexander," he said, knowing full well he would *never* be ready. That was one promise he wouldn't be keeping.

"I understand," she said.

Two weeks later, she sent Matthew a card thanking him for the phone call and the lovely flowers. In the card were two recent clippings from the Hollow County *Herald*. The first of them was an article about three Catholic priests who had arrived in Point Hollow, intent on "driving the evil from Abraham's Faith." The article made no mention of who had sent them, or what was meant by "evil." It did say that the priests had spent four days on the mountain, and had returned adamant that the "cleansing" had been successful. "This is God's town again," one of them stated before leaving. Reverend Parfrey added that Point Hollow had *always* been God's town—God's Footprint, in fact—and that they didn't need the Catholic Church to remind them of that.

The other clipping—from the following week's *Herald*—was more an extended obituary than an article: Kipling Sawyer, Hollow County's oldest resident, had passed peacefully in his sleep.

Age unknown.

———

Matthew sat on his balcony in perfect darkness, listening to the ocean boom. It was seductive, that sound, like a voice, calling to him alone. He closed his eyes and imagined himself a bird, taking wing and arcing above the crashing waves. He felt the spray in his little black eyes, the cool night in his feathers.

Light crossed the balcony as Angela pulled the blinds behind him. She stood for a moment, naked, always healing, before stepping outside and putting her hand on his shoulder.

"Are you coming to bed?"

It was the first night they would spend together. Matthew had put it off, wanting the nightmares to subside, afraid that he would wake up screaming, crying, and she would see him, like a child, and leave him.

He squeezed her fingers.

"You okay?" Her eyes shone softly in the light. "You want to do this, right?"

"More than anything," he said. "But . . ."

"But?"

"I have dreams," he said. His chest trembled as he breathed. "Terrible dreams, and sometimes I wake up . . . don't know where I am. And scared . . . *so* scared."

Angela kissed his eyes. First the left, then the right. She placed her hand on his chest and the trembling stopped.

He followed her into the bedroom, where it was light and kind,

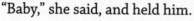

and where their bodies were mirrored, like colour on a butterfly's wing. They didn't hear the ocean, and there was no need for healing. Afterward, they blinked the world back into their eyes, and Matthew drifted into sleep. The darkness waited for him, an inescapable thing, constantly booming. It reached with hands like black fire and Matthew woke up with a scream rising in his chest. Sweat rolled down his body, thick as blood. He thought he was lost . . . and then Angela was there, her hair on his shoulder, her lips close to his face.

"Baby," she said, and held him.

ACKNOWLEDGEMENTS

This is my second novel with ChiZine Publications, and I'm just as thrilled and honoured as I was the first time around. My thanks, then, to my publishers, Brett Savory and Sandra Kasturi, for the faith and support they have shown me over the years, and for the light they have shone on speculative fiction not just in Canada but throughout the world. They are giants in reputation, and it is richly deserved.

I extend my thanks to the entire ChiZine team, in particular my editor Samantha Beiko, whose pen is as just as it is red, and Erik Mohr, who makes every book a more cherished thing.

Huge thanks to my beta readers: Christopher Golden, Tim Lebbon, and Joel Sutherland. Wonderful friends and writers, all. I feel blessed to have had their direction and advice. I've always said that showing raw work to someone feels a little like standing in front of them without any clothes on. Well, these guys have seen me naked; they have seen my imperfections, my scars, and my wobbly bits. For this alone, they deserve a standing O.

And of course, thanks in shameless abundance to my family—to my wife Emily, who is a mountain of strength, love, and support. I could climb forever and never reach the top. And to my amazing children, Lily and Charlie. They are new to this world but already wise to the crazy ways of Dad. Hey, kids . . . if you think I'm crazy now, just wait until you're old enough to read these stories.

ABOUT THE AUTHOR

Rio Youers is the British Fantasy Award–nominated author of *End Times* and *Old Man Scratch*. His short fiction has appeared in many notable anthologies, and his previous novel, *Westlake Soul,* was nominated for Canada's prestigious Sunburst Award. Rio lives in southwestern Ontario with his wife, Emily, and their children, Lily and Charlie.

EMB
RACE
THE
ODD

WESTLAKE SOUL
RIO YOUERS

"All superheroes get their powers from somewhere. A radioactive spider bite. A science experiment gone awry. I got mine from a surfing accident in Tofino. The ultimate wipeout. I woke up with the most powerful mind on the planet, but a body like a wet paper bag . . ."

Meet Westlake Soul, a twenty-three-year-old former surfing champion. A loving son and brother. But if you think he's just a regular dude, think again; Westlake is in a permanent vegetative state. He can't move, has no response to stimuli, and can only communicate with Hub, the faithful family dog. And like all superheroes, Westlake has an archenemy: Dr. Quietus—a nightmarish embodiment of Death itself. Westlake dreams of a normal life—of surfing and loving again. But time is running out; Dr. Quietus is getting closer, and stronger. Can Westlake use his superbrain to recover . . . to slip his enemy's cold embrace before it's too late?

AVAILABLE NOW
ISBN 978-1-926851-55-6

CHIZINEPUB.COM

THE ACOLYTE
NICK CUTTER

Jonah Murtag is an Acolyte on the New Bethlehem police force. His job: eradicate all heretical religious faiths, their practitioners, and artefacts. Murtag's got problems—one of his partners is a zealot, and he's in love with the other one. Trouble at work, trouble at home. Murtag realizes that you can rob a citizenry of almost anything, but you can't take away its faith. When a string of bombings paralyzes the city, religious fanatics are initially suspected, but startling clues point to a far more ominous perpetrator. If Murtag doesn't get things sorted out, the Divine Council will dispatch The Quints, aka: Heaven's Own Bagmen. The clock is ticking towards doomsday for the Chosen of New Bethlehem. And Jonah Murtag's got another problem. The biggest and most worrisome . . . Jonah isn't a believer anymore.

AVAILABLE NOW
ISBN 978-1-77148-328-5